NOT A GHOST OF A CHANCE

The dwarf Raspnex used his powers to survey the big house in the trees.

"What can you make out?" Rap asked.

"An old woman," the dwarf said. "Huge place, all run down—" Raspnex twitched. "She's expecting visitors."

"Impossible!"

"Here—look." The warlock opened his mind so that Rap could see the ramshackle mansion, the fire crackling in the great hall, and the housekeeper bent over a boiling pot. Dust covers had been dragged off chairs and piled behind a sofa, and candles had been lighted.

But the long driveway was cloaked in untrodden snow. No one could have warned her they were coming . . .

Then Rap felt something else . . . a sense of awareness so faint it was barely detectable. Amusement? Expectancy? In the *rafters?* Rap gasped. "Ghosts!"

By Dave Duncan
Published by Ballantine Books:

A ROSE-RED CITY

The Seventh Sword
THE RELUCTANT SWORDSMAN
THE COMING OF WISDOM
THE DESTINY OF THE SWORD

WEST OF JANUARY

SHADOW

STRINGS

HERO!

THE REAVER ROAD
THE HUNTERS' HAUNT*

A Man of His Word
MAGIC CASEMENT
FAERY LANDS FORLORN
PERILOUS SEAS
EMPEROR AND CLOWN

A Handful of Men
THE CUTTING EDGE
UPLAND OUTLAWS
THE STRICKEN FIELD
THE LIVING GOD*

*Forthcoming

UPLAND
OUTLAWS

Part Two of
A Handful of Men

Dave Duncan

A Del Rey Book
BALLANTINE BOOKS • NEW YORK

A Del Rey Book
Published by Ballantine Books

Grateful acknowledgment is made to John Murray (Publishers) Ltd., for permission to reprint an excerpt from "The Highwayman" by Alfred Noyes.

Library of Congress Catalog Card Number: 92-54990

ISBN 0-345-38477-6

Manufactured in the United States of America

First Hardcover Edition: May 1993
First Mass Market Edition: October 1993

❦ CONTENTS ❧

❮ PROLOGUE ❯

"Ghosts?" said the old woman. She raised her lantern and peered up into the dark. "Something bothering you tonight, Ghosts?"

Wind wailed in the high rafters and stirred the hems of the dust sheets shrouding the furniture. Casements rattled far off. The hall was very high, rising clear to the roof of the house. The faint glow of the lantern did not reach up there, but she needed no light to know of the staircases and balconies, the great fieldstone chimney at one end, the minstrels' gallery at the other, and all the grimy windows. She sensed something fretting, something intangible up there in the dark, listening amid the cobwebs and the beams.

"What ails you tonight, Ghosts?" She cackled.

Casements tapped in the darkness. Wind howled around a gable. Underfoot, little gray balls of dust rolled away out of sight.

The woman shivered, as the cold sank into her old bones. She tugged her shawls tighter with knotted fingers and began to hobble along the hall. The golden glow of her lantern reflected back from high windows and threw her shadow on the dust sheets. Often in ages past this hall had rung with the laughter of joyous parties, with music, and dancing, and feasting. No one but she had trodden these boards in many years.

Again she sensed the watchers, the listeners. She felt their hatred, their anger.

"No one coming tonight, Ghosts!" she cried. Her thin voice

1

could barely raise an echo over the wind. "Snowing outside, Ghosts. Heavier than ever. Rare to see such snow, and three weeks yet till Winterfest! But he won't come tonight!"

Shrill wails . . .

Only the wind, others would have said, but she knew better. Then she paused, head cocked, straining dull ears.

"Ah!" she said. "Bells?" She waited. Yes, again she heard that heavy note, carried on the wind. "So that's it? That's what disturbs your sleep, is it?" She cackled once more, reassured. "He's gone! The Evil has his black soul tonight, then? Small wonder you stir tonight, Ghosts!"

She paused, listening to the darkness. "The other one won't come tonight, Ghosts. Too snowy tonight." She felt resignation for an answer, overlying the triumph. Reassured, chortling to herself, she turned and hobbled away, back to her own nook in the basement.

Casements rattled, and the wind moaned.

❲ ONE ❳

Burning deck

1

Winter and grief lay heavy as conquerors' boots on the great city. No lights showed in the deserted streets as the solitary coach rumbled slowly through the ever-deepening snow.

The continuous tolling of the temple bells was a jarring torment. For fifty-one years Emshandar IV had ruled the Impire. His passing had left a gaping wound in the lives of his subjects, a sorrow that only the imps themselves could comprehend.

The unseasonable snowstorm added to the misery of the bitter night. The wheels and the horses' hooves sounded strangely muffled. The carriage was traveling unaccompanied, although Ionfeu, being both a count and a proconsul, would normally rank an escort of Praetorian Hussars within the capital. But tonight secrecy was more important than protection against footpads and sorcery a much greater danger than any mundane violence.

From time to time Rap would rise from his seat and call directions through the hatch to the driver on his box, for darkness and whirling snow had reduced visibility to almost nothing. He could have managed without a coachman had he wished, controlling the horses directly, but any such blatant display of sorcery on this ill-omened night would be dangerous in the extreme. Even the farsight he was using to guide the carriage was perhaps a risk, although farsight was a very inconspicuous use of power, not easily detected.

The brief outbreak of sorcery he had sensed after the emperor's death had died away. The occult plane of the ambience had fallen silent again, just as mysteriously silent as it had been all through his bone-breaking forty-day ride in from Kinvale. Now he could perceive no magical activity except faint tremors from the minor sorcerous gadgetry so common in the capital—magic locks, trained dice, cloaks of invisibility, and other such fanciful devices. Those would mostly belong to mundanes. Of course occult shields had always been popular in Hub, and many buildings were wholly or partly shielded; he could not tell what sorcery might be in use within those. But the silence was ominous, in a city that normally seethed with sorcery.

He was exhausted by a long day on the back of too many other long days. He felt old and weary. Thirty-five was not *old*, he told himself sternly. It wasn't *young*, either, he retorted snappily. It was twice the age he'd been the last time he'd visited Hub.

Furthermore, his companions must be close to twice as old again, and they had both had a trying day also. Count Ionfeu was hiding his worry and weariness under a gracious concern for his royal guest's comfort, although his twisted back was tormenting him sorely in the jiggling carriage.

Even in darkness, Rap knew of the old aristocrat's pain. To ease that affliction, or even cure it, would be a fitting gratitude for hospitality so eagerly extended to an unexpected visitor. Still, he dared not use power that would reveal his presence to the inexplicable evil overhanging the world.

Countess Eigaze's efforts to appear cheerful would have fooled anyone but a sorcerer. She was a credit to the long-ago training she had received from Inos' Aunt Kade. To describe Eigaze as plump would be more charitable than realistic, but her bulk contained a large heart; she was motherly and vivacious, loving and widely loved. Having packed the remains of a snack back in the hamper, she had produced a large box of chocolate candies and was munching them with genuine enjoyment.

Conversation had dwindled as the carriage lumbered past one of the nerve-hammering temples. There was much to discuss, and yet little of it seemed worthy of discussion when the fate of the Impire was so shadowed. Rap had listened politely to news of his hosts' vast family, including not only children and grandchildren but also cousins to the farthest degree, as was the imps' wont. He had responded with tidings of Krasnegar, reporting that Inos was in excellent health, or had been six weeks before. He had answered innumerable questions about Kadie, Gath, Evi, and Holi.

Tomorrow was the twins' fourteenth birthday, and he would not be there.

"Not long now," he said, as the immediate clamor of bells began to fade mercifully into the background. "The one with the golden spires was the Temple of Prosperity, was it not?"

He knew it was, and the count confirmed it. Rap rose and directed the driver around a corner. He wished he could use a little calming magic on the poor man, who was almost out of his mind with the strain of driving through the dark and snow— not to mention the entirely normal terror of having a sorcerer on board. Under the circumstances, he was doing a magnificent job of controlling the horses, but then he was a faun, like Rap himself. Fauns and livestock went together like rolls and butter.

The journey was taking too long. The imperor did not know Rap was coming. If he left Sagorn's house before Rap arrived, then all kinds of disaster became possible. Patience!

"Tell me once more, my lord," Rap said, "what you saw in the Rotunda, if you can bear to. Perhaps another telling may spring some detail that has been missed so far." He had heard the story secondhand once and firsthand once. It still made no sense.

Despite his weariness, the old count nodded graciously. "Gladly. Just as if you were hearing it for the first time?"

"Please."

"Very well. The imperor's failing health had persuaded Shandie that a regency would be necessary. We were rehearsing the enthronement ceremony. Shandie—his Majesty now, of course— was sitting on the Opal Throne and becoming very impatient at the time it was all taking. The princess . . . impress . . . was on the chair of state at his side. The Rotunda was almost dark, because of the snow collecting on the dome."

"It was also exceedingly chilly," Eigaze remarked between chocolates.

"Yes, it was. Then word arrived of the imperor's death."

"Who brought that word?" Rap inquired.

"A soldier."

"Centurion Hardgraa," Eigaze added. "Shandie's chief of security."

"A trusted man, then," Rap said. He decided the point was irrelevant. Sorcerers need not rely on spies to learn secrets. The Four had probably known that Emshandar's heart had stopped beating before even the doctors at the old man's bedside.

"Trusted, certainly," Ionfeu agreed. "He spoke to young Ylo. A bit of a rascal, that one, but Shandie's personal signifer, so of course he must be completely trustworthy, also. I can't see why that . . . Well, never mind. Ylo went up to the throne and told the new imperor. Of course everyone in the whole place had guessed what the news must be."

"You can always tell, can't you?" Eigaze murmured vaguely.

"I suppose there was about a minute," Ionfeu said. "The impress embraced her husband . . . He said something to the lord herald . . . Then the warlock appeared. A minute at the most."

"The Opal Throne was facing which way?"

"North. It was a north day. The four thrones of the wardens are arranged around the perimeter . . . but of course you are familiar with the Rotunda."

Rap shivered. "Very! I almost died there once."

So Raspnex had been temporarily senior warden of the Four. It had been his right to invoke the council. Was that significant, or would he have intruded anyway? What in the name of Evil were the Four up to? What was really happening in the occult politics of the Impire? Rap ground his teeth in frustration. Midnight had passed, so technically the senior warden was now East—Warlock Olybino, pompous idiot. Did that matter?

"Everyone turned to see," the count said. "I told you how dark it had been getting, and the White Throne sort of blazed . . . well, glowed, maybe. Like a lantern. All the jewels sparkled. And the warlock was standing in front of it, on the dais."

"I know Raspnex, too," Rap said. "Surly as any dwarf, but not a conspicuously evil person." How much could eighteen years change a man? "Just a year since he became warden?"

"A little less."

"He's a middling-powerful sorcerer, is all." When Bright Water had died, why had the remaining three wardens not found a stronger replacement to be warlock, or witch, of the north?

The count described Raspnex's dramatic demand that the new

imperor have himself proclaimed immediately. He smiled as he described the ancient chief herald's paralysis and the fast action by Signifer Ylo, reciting the proclamation from memory.

"He sounds like a very quick-thinking man," Rap remarked, but the Shandie he had known had been a sharp, zealous boy. He would never have grown up to become the sort of ineffectual leader who surrounded himself with dullards.

"Ylo was always a scallywag." Eigaze sighed. "His mother was a close friend. He still calls me Aunt. Er . . . He is an Yllipo, you know." In the dark, her face displayed a sorrow that she would have masked by day.

"The last of the Yllipos," her husband agreed.

"What is an Yllipo?" Rap inquired, puzzled by their sudden discomfort.

"They were a very rich family," Ionfeu said cautiously, "a large, long-established clan. Three or four years ago there was a scandal. Accusations of treason . . ." Even more warily he added, "Emshandar probably overreacted. He was very old, of course."

Imps did not lightly speak ill of their imperors, especially a newly dead one. Only one man left, out of a whole clan? Rap drew his own conclusions—and then wondered how that solitary survivor had turned up as close confidant of Emshandar's grandson and heir. Curious!

"So Shandie was proclaimed imperor by his signifer . . . Emshandar V, of course?"

"Of course."

Eigaze chuckled. "The whole Impire calls him Shandie, though!"

"Long may it do so," her husband said.

With a muttered excuse, Rap rose to direct the coachman around the corner into Acacia Street. Sagorn's house had several entrances, but there was no reason not to go to the public one tonight.

"Almost there," he said as he sat down.

"Well, you know the rest," the count said. "Shandie took up the sword and buckler and tried to summon the other wardens. Only Witch Grunth answered the call."

"And very briefly!" Eigaze remarked disapprovingly.

"But her mere appearance was enough to show that the wardens acquiesce in his accession. Two wardens are enough. He's legally imperor now, until his dying day.''

Rap knew Grunth, also, if only from afar. She was reasonably powerful, but indolent, like most trolls. With a painful sense of time passing, he realized that the big woman had reigned for eighteen years now. She had replaced the odious Zinixo.

And always he felt that nagging hunch that Zinixo was in some way responsible for the incorporate evil now looming over the world. Sorcerers' hunches tended to have sharp edges.

Neither Raspnex nor Grunth seemed the type of person to overthrow the Protocol and plunge the world into chaos. Olybino, now, was a dimwitted, posturing idiot. The warlock of the east might get himself involved in almost anything. And Lith'rian of the south was an elf and therefore totally unpredictable by any normal logic. Why had those two not appeared in the Rotunda to hail the new imperor?

Peering along Acacia Street, Rap detected a group of three carriages standing in the snow, guarded by a score or so of Hussars. The horses whinnied greetings to one another. The coachman could probably make out the light of the lanterns now. What would the neighbors be thinking of this invasion? Sagorn and his associates would be furious at having their privacy disturbed.

"I wish I could remember the dwarf's final words exactly," Ionfeu said. "I may not have heard them correctly, even. The Rotunda echoes so much when it isn't crowded, and he has a very low-pitched voice."

"As I recall Raspnex," Rap said, "he sounds like a major rock slide at close quarters. Would you permit me to jog your memory?"

He saw the horrified expression that darkness was supposed to hide, but the old count's voice was quite steady as he said, "By all means do so, Sire."

The amount of power needed was infinitesimal, little more than the charm dispensed by a fairground hypnotist. Minds were easy to influence.

"Good Gods!" the count said. "I . . . Bless my soul! Er . . . Would you consider quoting me a price on reviving the rest of my memories, also, your Majesty?"

"I'm not sure you'd thank me. Everything might be a little too much."

"Yes . . . I see the danger." Still blinking, Ionfeu chuckled uneasily and again tried to make himself more comfortable on the bench. "What Warlock Raspnex said before he vanished was, 'Now flee, Emshandar! Take your wife and your child and begone, for the city is no longer safe for you. The Protocol is overthrown, and Chaos rules the world!' That's it exactly!"

His wife smiled uncertainly at him and fumbled for his hand to squeeze. "And then the four thrones all exploded as if they'd been hit by thunderbolts," she said, "simultaneously! Whatever message that was supposed to convey, I do feel it was expressed with rather vulgar intensity."

"Thank you," Rap said grimly, although he had learned little new. Without the Protocol to control the political use of sorcery, the world would become a place of nightmare and horror.

The carriage rumbled to a halt alongside the others. A bronze-clad arm reached up to open the door.

2

The willowy Hussars in their dandified uniforms stood smartly at attention, but a sorcerer could sense their aura of sulky disapproval. Even more than the foul weather and slummy neighborhood, they resented being under the command of a non-Praetorian. Centurion Hardgraa's shiny bronze breastplate bore the lion insignia of the XIIth Legion. That had been old Emshandar's outfit and young Shandie's, also.

The centurion was a gnarled hulk of a man, who glared with dark suspicion at the stranger. His nose had been broken at least once, and the thick torso under his armor bore many old scars. When Rap was introduced, however, his ugly face at once broke into a wide grin. He saluted sharply. Apparently he had brains to go with his bulk, as was to be expected of a prince's body-guard.

"The imperor will be delighted to learn of your arrival, your Majesty," he rumbled.

"And I shall be happy to renew our acquaintance, Centurion. No, forget the pomp; just lead the way."

Radiating approval of this practical approach, Hardgraa offered the countess an arm to steady her on the snow-laden steps. The newcomers climbed to the front door. Rap could sense the occupants of all the adjoining houses and even those across the street—most of them now abed, some still sitting around, mourning—but the Sagorn residence was masked from him by its shielding.

The narrow street was cramped into a gorge by continuous façades of buildings, whose regularly spaced doors and windows implied that the interiors were more or less identical. This was far from the case, however. Sagorn's dwelling had been extended in all directions at some remote time in the past, stealing rooms and corridors from all its neighbors, so that now it was a complex labyrinth on many levels, a maze of stairways and corridors and oddly shaped rooms. It had entrances on other roads, also.

Halfway up the steps, Rap risked a brief glance at the future. The impact was so intense that he doubled over and almost fell. He slammed his defenses shut again, appalled at the scale of the looming disaster. The distant evil he had sensed for weeks had now infested the city. It was everywhere—perhaps that had been the rumbling of sorcery he had detected earlier. Despair screamed at him that there was no way to resist the tides of history. Every nerve twitched with the need to flee, although he knew of nowhere safe to hide. For a moment he shivered in near panic.

He thought of Inos, and the children, and Krasnegar, calling up their likenesses in his mind's eye. He thought of the God's censure, and warnings. If he was somehow responsible for this impending catastrophe, then he had a duty to fight it, however hopeless the struggle might seem.

He squared his shoulders and continued on up to the door.

Still shaky, he passed through the shielding. The outside world vanished from his farsight, and he saw only the convoluted interior of the warren itself. The present occupants were all huddled into a room on the floor above, and the rest was deserted.

As he followed his companions up a narrow, creaking staircase, he noted that the place was in no better shape than it had been eighteen years before. If anything, it was even shabbier and more untidy. Each of the five bachelors who inhabited it in turn seemed content to leave housework to the others.

Still, the security of occult shielding gave him a great feeling of relief and safety. For the first time in weeks he could relax the rigid control he had been holding over his powers. Just for starters, he banished his own physical weariness, and then he unobtrusively eased the painful inflammation in the backbone of the old count climbing slowly ahead of him. Sorcery brought ethical burdens, but it could also be a blessing.

He heard himself being announced as he followed the others into the crowded room. It was a pigsty of a place, stuffy and dimly lit by wavering candles, and there were only three chairs for, now, eleven occupants. The window was tightly shuttered, the grate heaped with litter.

He had no trouble recognizing the imperor, although he was merely a young man in doublet and cloak, with nothing remarkable about his appearance. Physically, the puny little boy had grown into a nondescript adult, cursed with unsightly acne like so many male imps. Royal responsibilities had expanded his psyche, though. A sorcerer could pick him out immediately as a man worthy of notice, one who burned brighter. He was staring at Rap with his mind racing, weighing risks and probabilities and possible deceptions.

"Rap!" he whispered. "Really Rap?"

Rap said, "My, Shandie, but you've grown! I'll bet you can't wriggle through that transom into the Imperial Library anymore."

"Ah, Rap!" The imperor strode forward and enveloped his old friend in an embrace of welcome.

Yes, this was a worthy young ruler and trained warrior—he was cautious, yet he could make fast decisions. Even as a child, he had possessed charm. Rap was reassured. If he could like the new imperor as a person, that would make cooperation easier in whatever trouble was brewing.

On the other hand, by remaining in his capital, Shandie was ignoring the warnings of a warlock, and that was plain pigheadedness, whatever Raspnex's motives had been. Rap would have to pound some common sense into the imperial skull, and quickly. He had no mundane authority to wield. He detested the thought of using sorcery to impose his will on other people, although in this case the stakes might be high enough to justify even that obscenity.

Little Princess Uomaya was asleep in her mother's lap. Impress Eshiala did not attempt to rise; regarding the newcomer gravely, she held up fingers to be kissed. She was very young, breathtakingly beautiful, and terrified out of her wits. She was concealing that fact totally from everyone else.

Rap bowed, kissed, murmured polite greetings. Did Shandie not realize that his lovely wife was teetering on the edge of a nervous breakdown? Gods! Who would want to be a sorcerer? Whatever evil was rending her was more than the handiwork of a single stressful day, though, and it would have to wait.

There was something oddly familiar about her face. Perhaps it was just the perfection of classical beauty, and yet Rap had a strange hunch that he had seen her before somewhere. She had certainly never visited Krasnegar. Kinvale, perhaps? She was not the sort of woman a man would forget meeting.

He turned to greet Sagorn. In a room full of imps, the old jotunn towered like a spruce tree in a bramble patch, a head taller than anyone else. His rugged face was winter pale and twisted in a familiar sardonic sneer, ice-blue eyes glinting below an incongruous dusty skullcap that sat awry on his thin silver hair. The deep clefts framing his mouth were as marked as ever. His robe was shabby and in need of a wash; he wore nothing under it. He seemed no older than Rap remembered, but that would be because Rap's own sorcery had put much of the last eighteen years out of his reach.

Shandie's associates were waiting. The strengths and weaknesses of the new imperor's most trusted confidants would reveal much about his judgment and ability. The first was a well-dressed fat man, beaming nervously at the renowned sorcerer. Instead of presenting him, Shandie began to pontificate about returning to the palace.

Not likely! Not only might that move be suicidally dangerous, but it would envelop them all in a swamp of courtly pomp and protocol, and Rap had no intention of enduring any of that rigmarole. Granted, Shandie had been born to the purple, and the king of Krasnegar was only an erstwhile stableboy with a knack for magic, but even with his sorcerous abilities pruned to a stump of what they once had been, in the present circumstances he must still be the senior partner. He would have to convince Shandie of that as soon as possible.

"This is an excellent place for a confidential meeting," Rap said firmly. "The building is shielded against sorcery. It is one of the most private locales in the city, and I vouch for Doctor Sagorn's discretion." He noticed the old jotunn's frosty eyebrows shoot upward at that remark. "No, let us discuss the problem here before we go anywhere else."

The imperor glowered. "Very well. However, we may not need quite so large an audience."

The fat man's face sagged like warm butter. Rap was amused at that telltale reaction—and still determined to have his own way. He thrust out a hand. "My name's Rap."

Shandie capitulated. "I have the honor," he said icily, "to present Lord Umpily, our chief of protocol."

Umpily beamed, agog with excitement at these untoward events. Imps were notoriously inquisitive people, but he clearly had the trait in excess. Whatever his official title, he was more likely Shandie's chief of intelligence, the imperial gossip-monger.

"Sir Acopulo, political advisor . . ." The next aide was a diminutive, wizened man with a priestly air to him. His eyes were as bright as a bird's. Sensing a sharp mind there, Rap tentatively assessed him as the strategist of the group.

Then came a strikingly handsome youngster in armor, bedecked with a signifer's wolfskin cape. His grip was firm, his manner confident, his smile faultless. Rap chided himself for being prejudiced—good looks were not necessarily a drawback in a man, and Signifer Ylo was entitled to his self-esteem if he was at once a military hero, the sole survivor of his clan, and a trusted confidant of the new imperor. Face and physique had not won him all that.

As he turned away, idly wondering how the unscrupulously handsome Andor was wearing his years now, Rap detected a sudden wash of fright. The youngster's cheerful smirk hardly wavered, yet something close to guilt had flared up in Signifer Ylo, some remembered secret he did not want to reveal to a sorcerer. His heart was thumping at twice its former beat.

For a moment Rap was sorely tempted to pry . . . *Ethics!* he reminded himself. To dig into another man's thoughts was a despicable abuse of power.

And that, evidently, had completed the introductions, for he had reached Centurion Hardgraa, picketing the door like a granite monolith. Hardgraa he had already met.

Eight men, two women, and a sleeping child.

Time to get down to business.

Time to deliver the useless warning he had brought too late.

The doughty Countess Eigaze was still standing, and that would not do. "Do be seated, my lady," Rap said. Ignoring more imperial frowns from Shandie, he arranged the company, with the women and old Sagorn on the seats.

The imperor settled on the arm of his wife's chair. His manner was chilly, but he was tolerating the upstart, although he must know that Rap was baiting him a little. Would he be willing to listen to reason, or would he flare into an autocratic rage? He had already flouted a warlock's warnings, so what argument would convince an accomplished warrior that he must flee from his city immediately? How could anyone persuade a newly succeeded monarch to give up his throne and run?

Rap leaned back against the fireplace and surveyed the room. They were wary, all of them. Now what?

"I bring no good tidings," he said. But that was not quite true, for things could be worse. "The only cheerful news I can give you is that I detect no magic on any of you—no loyalty spells or occult glamours or any abominations like that. I can't be quite certain, because a better sorcerer could deceive me."

"You are modest, your Majesty," Sagorn said acidly.

"No, Doctor. I admit that I had great powers once, but not now. I'm not going to try to explain that at the moment. Perhaps never." Seeing that the old jotunn did not believe him, Rap turned back to the imperor. "I shall do what little I can, Shandie, but magically it will be very small. If you are expecting me to solve things, then you will be disappointed."

"I see," the imperor said. He was not convinced either, although he was trying to hide his doubts. He did indeed expect Rap to solve things.

Well, Rap was not going to use sorcery to persuade them. "I do not even know the name or nature of the enemy. Does anyone?"

"Sir Acopulo?" Shandie said. "You are our advisor in such matters."

"Speculation upon insufficient data is invariably hazardous. As a working hypothesis . . ." The little man looked like a priest, but he sounded more like a schoolmaster. His ideas of warden behavior seemed improbable even to Rap, whose experience of the Four would let him believe almost anything of them. Sagorn was making no attempt to conceal his mounting skepticism, and eventually his disdainful sneer registered on Acopulo.

"It fits the facts!" he snapped, glaring.

Shandie asked for a second opinion, and the jotunn went on the offensive.

"It fits a judicious selection of the facts, Sire. As a student, Acopulo was always selective in his use of evidence, and I see he has not changed. The last news we had of the wardens, Lith'rian was hurling his dragons at Olybino's legions. They were at each other's throats! Now we are to regard them as allies?"

Scholarship was an uncommon calling for jotnar. Sagorn was an unusual jotunn, but not so unusual that he lacked belligerence, and now he was obviously intent on exterminating the unfortunate imp with traditional ruthlessness. The tongue was mightier than the ax, that was all.

Little Acopulo bristled. "That is your only objection?"

"It is the least of them." Sagorn sneered. "Granted that the Four often squabble, you have failed to explain why this disagreement is so much more virulent than all others in three thousand years—so dire that it required desecration of the Rotunda. You did not explain the dwarf's prophecies and warnings. You did not explain why King Rap has come from Krasnegar. And you have most certainly failed to explain why, after a thousand years of extinction, a pixie should reappear now, and to his Majesty."

"*Pixie?*" Rap exclaimed. Shandie had met a *pixie*?

"A possible pixie," the imperor said, smiling at a sorcerer's surprise. "On my way back to Hub, I broke my journey at a post inn in the Wold Hills. An ancient crone appeared to me, but not to my companions. From my description, Doctor Sagorn believes that she may have been a pixie."

Rap shot a glance at the old rascal and saw glitters of satisfaction in the faded blue eyes. Sagorn would not have admitted how much he had been guessing. His knowledge of pixies was probably limited to what Kadolan had told him in a conversation on board *Unvanquished*, beating up the coast of Zark one blustery morning eighteen years ago—Rap himself had been down in the hold with the ship's gnome, but eavesdropping nonetheless. Inos and her aunt had narrowly escaped being murdered in Thume, and it was odd that . . . *Holy Balance!*

Relying on the shielding to keep out the overweening world disaster, Rap risked a peek with premonition—yes, he was on to something. Inos had mentioned her adventures in Thume a few times, but he had never paid much attention. How odd! He had never visited Thume on his solitary sorcerous travels.

He had never really thought about Thume at all!

Perhaps he could only keep it in mind now because he was inside a shielded building. Obviously the defenses were enormously powerful, and perhaps even selectively aimed at sorcerers. Remembering the amount of power he had needed to renew the inattention spell on tiny Krasnegar, he was appalled at what would be required to cover a land as large as Thume.

No inattention spell would endure a thousand years without renewal!

Shandie was still relating how he had gone to Wold Hall and consulted the preflecting pool. Rap had heard most of the story from Ionfeu and Eigaze: Lord Umpily had seen a dwarf sitting on the Opal Throne itself; Acopulo had seen Sagorn, which was why the emperor was here now; young Ylo . . .

Young Ylo was starting to sweat again, his face locked in a meaningless smile. Obviously Signifer Ylo knew some curious secrets, although this might be the same one that had upset him earlier. Young Ylo had seen a vision of a beautiful woman.

Impress Eshiala was clenching mental teeth, also . . . Oh?

Who would ever be a sorcerer?

They were both young. She was a beautiful princess, he was a handsome hero—there was only one secret they might share. Rap sighed and put the matter out of his mind. He couldn't solve all the problems of the world, and he certainly was not going to pry into this one with Shandie present.

The imperor had ended his tale. "So I think I saw your son," he added. "I feel that I should apologize, somehow, but of course it was by no choice of mine."

"You did see Gath," Rap admitted, "and he saw you! It may even have been the same night, but it doesn't matter whether it was or not. He had a brief vision of a soldier; we didn't realize it was you until about a month ago, or I would have come sooner. I fear I should have come a year ago, for I was warned then that the end of the millennium was brewing trouble."

"Warned by whom?" Sagorn demanded, white eyebrows perking up like a dog's ears.

"A God." Rap spoke offhandedly, just to annoy him. "I'm not sure which God They were—one doesn't think to shoot questions when Gods appear. I thought that the end of the millennium was awhile off, but I seem to have interpreted the date too literally. A year or two either way . . . When did the War of the Five Warlocks begin?''

"Around 2000.'' Acopulo was not certain, though, and he had left himself open to another thrust from the old jotunn.

"The Festival of Healing, 2003, was when Ulien'quith fled the capital,'' Sagorn snapped. He was excited, and that was encouraging. The old sage was not easily persuaded, and if he accepted that the coming year 3000 was important, then something in his endless studies of ancient lore had led him to that belief. "You are right, your Majesty. A year or two either way does not matter.''

"But the millennium itself does!'' Rap agreed. "The pixies disappeared in the War of the Five Warlocks. Now his Majesty has seen a pixie. That seems to fit, somehow, doesn't it? Every sorcerer from the wardens on down seems to have disappeared— I detect almost no occult power in use anywhere. I sense a terrible evil overhanging the world. Warlock Raspnex's warnings of chaos and the fall of the Protocol—those may fit, also, although I am far from ready to trust the dwarf. Any dwarf.''

The great pending evil was rooted in Dwanish, and therefore dwarvish in origin. Not knowing that, the mundanes frowned disbelievingly and began to argue. Rap started to explain and was distracted by farsight. Downstairs in the kitchen, a dirty rag hanging on a nail had started to move in a breeze that had not been blowing until now.

He felt the hair on his scalp prickle. The shutters had been forced, and two massive hands were gripping one of the bars that blocked the window. The owner of those hands was still outside, and hence shielded from him, but their size and their gray color were unmistakably dwarvish.

The bar bent like a rope and was removed. Its neighbor followed, a moment later. The hands grabbed the stiles of the opening; a large head appeared, and massive shoulders. Raspnex squirmed into the room, and the ambience shivered as he used power to complete his acrobatic entrance and land on his feet.

He found Rap at once, and recoiled in shock. For a moment the ambience was shadowed by images of thick stone walls. *"I come in peace, your Majesty!"*

Raspnex believed that Rap was still his better at sorcery, but there were no secrets in the ambience.

Trapped!

"Then you are welcome," Rap said. *"You are in no danger from me, Warlock."*

The warden of the north was squat and broad, in the manner of dwarves. However he might look to a mundane, in the ambience his age was obvious. His hair and beard were still a normal iron-gray, but the turf on his chest was silver. The years had softened his rocky muscles like cooled lava, and his skin hung limp on him. He was still a powerful man, though, as his treatment of the window bars had shown. Now his agate eyes slitted in astonishment as he appraised Rap's image in the shadow world.

"So I see!" He grinned, showing quartz-pebble teeth.

He turned and thrust an arm out through the blank of the window embrasure. With a shiver of power, he hauled another man inside bodily, and then there were two dwarves down there in the kitchen.

Two sorcerers—no bets on that.

The second dwarf was an adolescent, but age had nothing to do with prowess in sorcery. He inspected Rap warily. Apparently reassured, he closed the shutters without raising a hand, while Raspnex started for the kitchen door.

"What the Evil happened to your powers?" he demanded angrily. *"Or is this some sort of trickery?"*

"No trickery," Rap said. *"They're long gone. I can't pull a rabbit out of a hutch now."*

"That's impossible!"

"No, but it's a long story. Who's the enemy?"

"My nephew."

"Zinixo!" Just what Rap had feared—but it was a great relief to know that Raspnex himself was *not* on Zinixo's side. If he were, Rap would be a devoted slave already.

"Thank the Gods I have only one!" the dwarf said sarcastically.

In the ambience, the two of them were face to face. In the slower mundane world, Rap's companions had barely registered his sudden silence, and Raspnex was trudging across the kitchen, closely followed by his young companion. They wore the drab, shabby work clothes that dwarves preferred, and they were both wet with melted snow.

So even a warlock dared not use sorcery in the open now? God of Horrors!

"I thought I had nailed that blackguard into a box he'd never get out of!" Rap said bitterly. He had used every scrap of his enormous demigod's power when he sealed his enemy in an occult shielding. How had the former warlock escaped?

"Thank Bright Water," Raspnex growled. He paused to scan the house. *"Name of Evil, this place is a labyrinth, isn't it?"* Approving images of mine tunnels . . . *"She gave him Kraza."*

Kraza? The name was familiar. Raspnex threw up a brief image of a female dwarf, quite pretty by dwarvish standards, and then Rap remembered. The wardens had sent her as their emissary, the third time they had begged him to take Zinixo's place on the Red Throne.

Raspnex had located the correct staircase. He scowled at its ramshackle condition and chose to levitate up it, perhaps not trusting its treads to withstand his great boots.

His young companion grinned and followed suit. He jangled the ambience less than Raspnex did, which meant he was intrinsically more powerful. His occult image was more solid, too, which was usually a good indication of occult potency.

And that was the key to the whole mystery! That was how Zinixo had escaped from his cocoon to threaten the world . . .

Rap's mundane companions were all regarding him with apprehension. As far as they were concerned, he had been leaning against the fireplace and staring glassily at the floor for the last couple of minutes.

"Stand back from the doorway, Centurion," he said. "Don't go for your sword. It will do no good."

Hardgraa reached for the hilt automatically, then reluctantly released it. He stepped a pace sideways.

"Cousin!" Shandie said, jumping to his feet. "Rap? What's wrong?"

Even as Rap named the visitor, the warlock hurled the door open and stamped into the room. "You're a fool, imp!" he growled, glaring across at the imperor.

Fury flickered over Shandie, but he bowed respectfully. "You honor us with your presence, your Omnipotence."

"You can forget that rot! No more omnipotences. It's over!"

Dwarves were not known for tact, or delicacy of phrase. "No more wardens, no more warlocks, no more witches. Why in the name of Evil didn't you get out of town while you had the chance?" Raspnex stalked forward to the center of the room, dominating it completely, although everyone else was much taller. "Flee, I told you! But oh, no! You had to come into this warren, on the one night in centuries when you would leave a trail through Hub that a blind toad could follow! Idiot!"

The imperor flushed darkly in the flickering candlelight.

The second dwarf followed the warlock in, slamming the door. There was a shimmer of sorcery on him, probably a loyalty spell. He was very young, with a hint of down like gray moss on his sandstone cheeks. His hair dangled in elaborate curls like iron turnings. Typical dwarf, though—his pants and boots had been patched repeatedly.

"Tell us why you came, Sorcerer," Shandie said coolly.

"I'll be buried if I know!" Raspnex pointed at Rap. "Well, I suppose I came to appeal to him, but I see now that I wasted my time. I'd hoped he could help, but he can't."

"Who's your companion?" Rap asked.

"Grimrix. He's a votary. Don't laugh at his hairstyle or he may turn you into a woolly caterpillar."

The youngster scowled; blue fire flickered ominously in the ambience.

"*Steady!*" the older dwarf snapped. "Well, imp," he said aloud. "So you didn't listen to me! Who outside this room knows where you are?"

"No one," the imperor said, "except Legate Ugoatho."

"Who's he?"

"Head of the Praetorian Guard."

Raspnex snorted. "They'll have gotten him already, then. One of the first they'd go for. In fact, it's amazing they're not here yet."

"The legate is utterly loyal!" Shandie protested.

The warlock showed his big teeth. "Not anymore."

"Tell them the problem," Rap said sadly.

"You tell them. I already tried, and seems they don't heed me."

"I'll have to be quick, though." Time was precious, Rap realized. Whether or not Zinixo had brought in his main occult strength yet, if he had perverted the head of the Praetorian Guard, then a thousand men might be on their way already. Four carriages stood outside in the snow, there were tracks. "The problem is Zinixo. I'm sure you remember him."

"Former warlock of the west."

"Right. He tried to destroy me, and I won . . ." Then Rap recalled something else, and looked to Raspnex. "A year ago a God told me that this mess was all my fault. That must be because I didn't kill Zinixo when I had the chance, and the excuse."

"You did worse than that," Raspnex said grimly. "Much worse. But carry on. Can you explain to these mundanes what you did to my nephew?"

As he described how he had rendered the sorcerer impotent by enveloping him in a magic-proof shielding, Rap wondered what error could possibly have been worse than sparing Zinixo, that vindictive, lecherous, sadistic . . .

"So what happened?" the imperor demanded.

Raspnex shrugged his bull shoulders. "Oh, he went totally insane. He'd always been unstable, even as a kid. He'd always been suspicious and timid, and the greater his power grew, the more timorous he became. You believe that, imp?"

"I've met people like that," Shandie said. "They think the world is out to get them."

A lot of dwarves thought that way—both Raspnex and Grimrix were notably jumpy now—but Zinixo had carried distrust to the point of obsession.

"So he can't use his magic," the imperor said, frowning. "Why is he dangerous?"

"Because of Bright Water," Rap said. "She couldn't break my spell, either, but she must have taken pity on him. She gave him a sorcerer."

"*Gave* him?"

Raspnex snorted and snapped his fingers. Young Grimrix stepped forward obediently at the summons, but occult fire flickered faintly again. "Sir?"

"Tell them how you feel about me, sonny."

The boy blushed and looked down at his boots. "I love you."

"There! See? He's a votary. I've laid a loyalty spell on him. He'll do anything to help me." Raspnex glanced at the kid, showing his pebble teeth again. "He'd die for me! Actually, his power's greater than mine. It took three of us to hobble him—me and two of my other votaries. Now do you understand?''

The mundanes were radiating horror and fright as they realized the possibilities.

Raspnex thumped a massive hand on Grimrix's shoulder. "Go and scout. See if anything's happening outside."

The boy nodded and transported himself down to the front door. He opened it, peered out cautiously, then vanished from Rap's ken.

It was all so confoundedly obvious now! Zinixo had collected at least a dozen votaries in his brief tenure in the Red Palace. Because he saw danger everywhere, he had also made it his business to identify as many of the other wardens' votaries as he could. With a sorceress eager to do his bidding, all he had needed to do was set Kraza on the weakest. Then the two of them would have sought out another and jointly imprinted that one. Not just votaries—they must have hunted down every sorcerer they could. And so on . . . Rap explained to the audience.

"He's been at it for almost twenty years," Raspnex added. "He's got an army of them now, all loyal to the death. We call it the Covin."

Shandie sank down again on the arm of his wife's chair. His face was taut. "Why did nobody stop him?"

"Because nobody knew!" the dwarf rumbled in his sepulchral voice. "Except maybe Bright Water, and she was too crazy to care. I think he was extra careful with her brood, anyway—he made his compulsion secondary to hers, to take effect after she died. So she didn't mind. *Now he's cornered all of the sorcery in Pandemia!*"

The crowded room fell silent as the mundanes struggled to comprehend the disaster. Sagorn sat down again, also, muttering and shaking his head.

"So although he has no real sorcery of his own," Shandie said, "he controls an army of sorcerers? How many?"

"Scores, maybe hundreds. All eager to help. And the little snit may have his own sorcery back too now, if the Covin's been able to break Rap's spell."

"Surely it was the wardens' duty to prevent such an abomination?"

"It was, but they didn't know it was happening until Bright Water died." Raspnex's eyes were hard as flint. "They brought me in as the new North in the hope I could stop him, because I knew him and how he thinks. But it was too late."

The imperor looked around the group, but no one had any comments. "What does he want?"

The dwarf snorted. "Everything! I told you—the greater his power, the more fearful he is! He knew he'd become a threat to the Four, so he feared the Four, because they were the only power that could threaten him. That's how he thinks."

"That was why you came to the Rotunda today?"

Thunder rumbled in the ambience. "Of course it was! Why are you so stupid? We expected him to strike when we answered your summons at the enthronement, so he could swat all four of us at the same time. Probably he'd have blasted us as he blasted Ag-an, years ago. Grunth and I got the jump on him. We made you imperor, sonny, but it isn't going to do you any good."

Shandie frowned. "And why destroy the thrones? Zinixo did that?"

"No! I did!"

"The four thrones were occult," Rap said. This conversation was a stupid waste of time! Nevertheless, the imperor had a right to know, and Rap himself had no idea what was going to happen next. If Zinixo's Covin had already infested the city, then the situation was as close to hopeless as he could imagine. "They were portals into the wardens' palaces. He could have forced entry through them."

"I thought you didn't know all this?" the imperor said.

"I didn't, earlier. Partly I'm working it out as I go along, from what Raspnex told me as he came in—you weren't privy to that conversation, is all. He hasn't used sorcery on me yet, although he could. And you'll have to take our word on that. You can't trust anyone now, your Majesty. Once Zinixo's votaries pin a man down, he's theirs. As Raspnex says, Legate Ugoatho would be a logical first choice. He'll serve Zinixo from now on, to the death. They all will."

"To what purpose?" Shandie demanded grimly.

Rap shrugged. "He's mad, he sees danger everywhere. The imperor is powerful, so he must be loyal to Zinixo—everyone must, who has any sort of power at all. He'd make everyone in the world love him, if he could."

"Where are the Four?"

Rap looked to Raspnex. *"Good question!"*

"Gone," the dwarf said. "Most of their votaries have been stolen from them. Lith'rian panicked first and fled to Ilrane. Olybino was next. He's just vanished. Can you imagine what Zinixo will do to those two when he gets his hands on them? No, you can't possibly imagine. Even I can't. But it will be long and nasty—that I do know." He pulled a face. "And I'm not on his friendship list either."

"And Grunth?"

The dwarf shrugged, rolling his eyes.

"So Zinixo will imprint *me* with a loyalty spell?" Shandie demanded, glaring.

"Slow, isn't he?" the warlock said, in an aside to Rap. "Of course. It will be easier than proclaiming himself imperor. The Impire is just too big for him to ensorcel everyone, and a dwarf imperor would not be acceptable—he would always be frightened of revolution, see? But you will reign for his benefit. You will serve him loyally to the end of your days." He jabbed a finger like a crowbar toward the child asleep in Eshiala's lap. "And so will she, and her children after her! You know how long sorcerers live."

"No!" Shandie bellowed. "I won't have it!"

The dwarf curled his big mouth into a sardonic smile. "And your so-beautiful wife? My nephew is oddly partial to female imps . . . Now don't you wish you'd taken my advice?"

Shandie put an arm around Eshiala. "What is your advice now?"

Again the dwarf shrugged his barrel shoulders. "I may be able to get us out of here. *May*, I said. He's so suspicious that he tends to be too cautious. He may not commit his real strength quickly enough to block me."

That sounded like a very leaky lifeboat to Rap. As soon as the fugitives emerged from the shielding, they would be visible in the ambience. There was no hiding place in that featureless void, no way to outrun a superior force. Only power mattered.

"If I can escape . . . ." Shandie said. "If we can . . . If you can get us out of here, what then?"

"Retire. Hide. You can't hope to win your impire back, you know. Just go into hiding and maybe, in a couple of centuries, your descendants can come forward and claim their inheritance."

The mundanes stared at one another in dismay, while Raspnex

curled his lip contemptuously at them; but in the ambience he was scowling up at Rap with a worried expression. *"The kid's taking a long time, isn't he?"*

"Let's hope he's still yours when he comes back," Rap said pointedly. "Zinixo's here, in Hub?" he added aloud.

"Maybe. More likely not, not yet. But he's sent his minions. I could smell 'em."

"So could I. And I'm not exactly his best friend, either, am I?"

Raspnex chortled, a noise of ice floes in a polar storm. "Not much, you're not! You and your kingdom. Your wife and children. I bet the little turd has dreamed of you every night for twenty years, *your Majesty!*"

"Why did none of you warn me?" Rap said angrily.

"Because we thought you knew! Because we thought you were laying low—and because we thought you could handle the matter when you got around to it!"

"You mean you were all relying on me? Waiting on me to do something? Fools!" Rap had always assumed that the Four knew how he had lost his paramount power years ago. Probably such an absurdity had never occurred to them, and they had been frightened to spy on a demigod. Fortunately Zinixo must have made the same error.

"That's obvious now, but we didn't know that, did we?" the dwarf snarled.

"I'm surprised he hasn't come after me already."

"He didn't know, either! But it won't be long now. And he couldn't try to settle with you earlier without alerting the wardens." The warlock's sneer was almost an offer of sympathy by dwarvish standards.

Rap thought of the battles in which he had defeated Zinixo— the brutal one-on-one struggle when the dwarf had attacked him in the Rotunda, and then the greater battle when Rap had single-handedly stormed the Red Palace, an avenging demigod blasting aside guards and defenses in fiery cataclysms, rending walls in pursuit of his fleeing prey. Zinixo would have forgotten none of that, especially his own screams for mercy at the end.

He thought also of Krasnegar, and Inos, and the children, hopelessly vulnerable. *Gods!*

"Suppose he does seize the throne," Sagorn asked hoarsely,

"the Imperial throne, I mean, not Krasnegar—either in his own name or through a puppet—then what?"

"He will wipe out any threat, any threat at all. Any hint of disloyalty, any loose talk." Raspnex threw contempt at the old jotunn, but Sagorn had already analyzed the logic to its absurd conclusions.

"But it will be his Impire then, won't it? So any threat to the Impire will be a threat to the Living God? The caliph, for example."

Surprised, the dwarf nodded. "Exactly. The caliph is a threat to the Impire, so the caliph will have to go. The goblins are about ready to launch their big attack—Zinixo will smash them. Of course he'll go after Lith'rian and the elves first."

Sagorn snapped his teeth shut with a click. "He will rule the world," he muttered.

"In a year or two, yes."

"Is there nothing we can do to prevent this obscenity?" Count Ionfeu said. Old and frail he might be, but generations of imperial pride showed on his weathered features. Thousands of men like him had built the Impire, and he would sooner die than let it all fall into the hands of a dwarf.

Silence fell.

Was there nothing to be done?

"Surely he can't have cornered every word of power in Pandemia?" Rap asked Raspnex privately.

"Near enough. He has people out hunting down every sorcerer—Evil!—every adept and genius, even. If you go looking for allies, you can't expect to collect them faster than his Covin can."

There was the awful truth, then! *"Faerie's the problem, isn't it? That's where I made my great mistake?"*

Raspnex's shadow image bared its teeth. *"That's it!"*

The mundanes were all waiting for an answer to the count's question. Was there an answer?

Rap said, "There might be. It's an Evilish long shot, but we could try, if Zinixo hasn't beaten us to it."

"Dross!" the dwarf snarled, disbelieving.

"There's a lot of magic lying around in the Nogids!"

Raspnex gasped aloud. "You'll get yourself eaten if you try that!"

"I'd rather have my flesh eaten than my mind, I think," Rap said. "And it *was* all my fault."

"Yes, it was."

"Why was it?" the impress asked. All through the discussions, she had been sitting as still as a statue, holding her sleeping child. Why was her face so familiar? "What did you do, your Majesty?"

"I cut off the supply of magic. I can't tell you all the details now, but I went back to Faerie—" A stab of pain reminded him that sorcery did not like to be discussed. "Never mind. I did it, and it's done." Each word of power represented a dead fairy, but almost no one except the wardens had ever known that simple fact. It was the ultimate secret behind the workings of sorcery, and the Protocol.

Faerie . . . Raspnex projected a whiff of nostalgia and a fleeting image of the riotous party in Milflor when Zinixo's votaries had celebrated their release. They hadn't noticed Rap arrive on the island, or what he was up to—not that they could have stopped him, anyway. By the time he had joined in the festivities, the fairies had vanished, from jail and jungle both. He had stamped out forever that ghastly farming of people, or so he hoped.

"And you can't undo it now, can you?" the dwarf said angrily. "Your stupid, blundering good intentions! Where *did* you put the fairies?"

"I can't even tell you. And no, I can't ever undo it. I used every scrap of power I possessed." Power he possessed no longer! "It's done now. Forever. Unless the Gods take pity on us."

He turned away from all the shocked faces. Good intentions? Only now did he see that the fairies' suffering throughout the ages had at least helped to stabilize life for everyone else, by buttressing the Protocol. The arrangement had been grossly unfair, but it had held some good as well as much evil. By ending it, he had upset the balance of the world.

The one time he had tried to be a God, and he had blundered!

"I don't understand!" Acopulo bleated.

"He cut off the supply of magic!" Raspnex growled. "The Protocol was set up to prevent exactly this sort of happening! The supply of magic was the prerogative of the warlock of the west. If any one sorcerer ever tried to build a sorcerous army and make himself paramount, West could create an opposing army! As a last resort. That's why it's never been done before,

although Ulien' came close in the War of the Five Warlocks.''
He scowled, as if in pain.

Sagorn made a choking noise. ''A safety net!''

''And your faunish friend cut it down!''

Ulien'? Again Rap felt a nudge of premonition.

Zinixo was the disaster at the end of the third millennium, but
there had been trouble at the end of the first and the second,
also, and it had been overcome both times. A thousand years
since Thume had become the Accursed Land, since the whole
race of pixies had vanished, and now . . .

''*The imperor met a pixie!*'' he told Raspnex excitedly.
''Ulien', you said? War of Five Warlocks? Thume! There's another hope, then! *The War of the Five Warlocks? Maybe there
is an answer—in Thume!*''

''You're crazy!'' Raspnex mumbled, staring.

''Maybe! But craziness is all we've got left, isn't it?''

The door downstairs opened briefly, and young Grimrix shot
through it like a rabbit. Even before it had slammed shut again,
he had translated himself back upstairs. He was flushed, and
panting, and so excited that he shouted aloud. Rap and Raspnex
both stiffened defensively, but he did not notice—and he did not
seem to have been warped from his loyalty.

''They're here, sir! Hussars, all around the house. All
three streets.'' Images of several hundred soldiers and their
mounts . . .

''Any occults?'' Raspnex demanded.

''Didn't stay around to look, but if you'll let me go down
there again and thump ass, I can find out!'' He was twitching
with battle lust. Drums and trumpets . . .

''Can't we leave the same way as Master Jalon did?'' Signifer
Ylo inquired in a shaky voice.

''Quite impossible!'' Sagorn snapped, and Rap resisted a desire to laugh.

''You seem very certain of that,'' Hardgraa growled.

This was no time to start explaining the workings of a sequential spell. ''He's right, though!'' Rap said. ''And we'd leave
tracks in this snow, wouldn't we? Raspnex, got any ideas?''

''I can try. I'll try to move us all to my palace.''

''But the house is shielded.''

The warlock leered. ''It won't be in a minute. Grimmy, can
you lift this shield by yourself?''

The ambience shimmered as young Grimrix flexed his power. His very-solid image spat on its hands, and he grinned. "Easy, sir!"

"Don't be too sure—some of these old spells have been renewed a lot of times. Watch out for underlying layers. When I push, rip it. Then slam it back fast! You've got to stay and cover for us."

The young votary paled, shocked. "But if they catch me—" The ambience rang with grief louder than the bells of the city.

"Then you'll be just as happy serving him as you are serving me," Raspnex said. "Hold them off as long as you can. Don't try to follow me, understand?"

"Not even—"

"Not at all! You arguing?"

"Of course not!"

"Good . . . Listen!"

One of the back doors shuddered noisily.

"Axes!" Rap said. "They're trying the courtyard door. That one's a poor choice. It's got some occult tricks to it."

"Nevertheless, the time to go has arrived," Raspnex growled. "Get up, woman!"

"This'll never work!" Rap said. *"Soon as the kid opens a window, they'll fry us!"*

"They want us alive—you especially!"

Being fried might be the better alternative, Rap thought. Quite apart from a lingering revenge on his person, Zinixo would want to interrogate him on the whereabouts of the fairies.

The mundanes were all on their feet, the imperor holding the still-sleeping child.

"This may be rough," the warlock told them. "But I've got some friends standing by to shield us as soon as we arrive—I hope. If the enemy got there first, then . . . well, it's worth a try."

"Wait!" Shandie said. "What happens after?"

"I told you. You go into hiding, and stay there."

"No!" The imperor set his jaw stubbornly. "Maybe my realm has been stolen from me, but I will not have my mind stolen, also! I will not give up. I will fight!"

Good for him, Rap thought.

A fusillade of blows rocked the courtyard door. Now the other

doors were under attack, also, and that meant a sorcerer had
identified them for the legionaries.

"I will never rest," Shandie repeated, "until I have won back
my impire!"

"Indeed?" The dwarf sneered. "You and what army?"

The imperor glanced around. "These good friends will do
for a start. Maybe there aren't very many of them, just a handful,
but they're loyal and they're good. Are you with me?"

"Gods save the imperor!" the signifer said.

"Gods save the imperor!" the others echoed, some louder
than the rest. The room was so jangled with mixed emotions
that Rap could not locate them all—fear and doubt and
defiance—but he detected a blaze of anger from the beautiful
Eshiala, and that was surprising.

Shandie was looking at Rap. "And you?"

"I have no choice," Rap said with an approving smile. "Zinixo won't rest, either—not until he has my guts in a pot and
Krasnegar is gravel. Down with the tyrant!"

"Well said! Victory or death!" Shandie shouted.

It was fortunate in a way that he didn't realize how hopeless
his cause was.

"No!" The impress tried to wrestle the child away from her
husband. "You must not!"

"My dear!" Shandie turned his back on her, and little Maya
awoke with a cry of bewilderment.

"You must not risk our baby!" She grabbed again, and again
he turned. This time she clung to him in an absurd dance.

"Eshiala! Be silent!"

"She is more important than your precious throne!"

They were yelling at each other, struggling together, the baby
howling between them.

"God of Fools!" the dwarf muttered.

The front door collapsed in screams of rending wood and
ruptured hinges. The temple bells were suddenly louder. A torrent of bronze-clad men burst into the house.

"I'll take them!" Rap said quickly, anxious to avert serious
violence. He was still capable of throwing sleep spells. Bronze
clashed on chain mail, swords clattered. In a moment the entrance was plugged by heaps of snoring legionaries, so that no
more could enter. Mundanes were easy. Grimrix was probing

gently at the shielding, seeking the thinnest spot. The courtyard door was about to fail.

Then the shielding shuddered as if it had been kicked by a giant. That was more than mundane assault.

"Move us, Warlock!" Rap said. "Now!"

"Grimrix?"

"Ready!"

The ambience exploded in lightning and thunder.

3

Countess Eigaze sat down abruptly on the grass, Lord Umpily sprawling headlong beside her. Shandie almost dropped his daughter. The impress staggered backward into Sagorn, and an eruption of military obscenities announced that Signifer Ylo had landed in shrubbery. The ambience rang with echoes of the brute-force power the warlock had used to move them all.

Rap had a brief vision of the whole city spread out below him, wrapped in night and snow. In the distance, the ambience rumbled and flashed as Zinixo's votaries stormed Sagorn's house. There seemed to be plenty of them, but Grimrix was holding them off. The strength of the kid! He should have been the warlock, not Raspnex.

This secluded little rooftop garden was not located in the White Palace, as Raspnex had promised. That was typical of dwarves, though. Knowing he would have to sacrifice Grimrix to the other side, he had automatically left a false trail to divert pursuit. It probably wouldn't work.

High among the turrets of the Red Palace, the courtyard was dense with tropical trees and bushes, occultly preserved from the Hubban climate. The air was hot and muggy and pleasantly earth-scented after the mustiness of Sagorn's room. At least four sorcerers had been standing by, and now they were pouring power into the shield, patching the hole through which the fugitives had come. None of them was a troll, so the witch of the west was not present to welcome her unsuspecting guests.

Making shields was noisy work. Knowing his feeble powers would make little difference, Rap did not try to assist, but he felt as if his head were being hammered inside a white-hot furnace. He helped Eigaze to her feet. Ylo emerged from the bushes, cursing and rubbing scrapes on his arms. Everyone seemed to have arrived safely—a superb demonstration of precision sorcery. Most of the mundanes were whimpering, bewildered by darkness and the sudden change of location.

The occult clamor continued. The main shield of the warden's palace was centuries old and thick enough to deter the Gods Themselves. To cut a hole in it must have taken much time and power, as well as being a highly unlikely thing to do. To plug the gap adequately would take just as much time and power, even if the evildoers let the operation proceed undisturbed—which they wouldn't. Busy as he was, Raspnex was also talking to a gangling jotunn at the far side of the lawn, and yet he managed to flash a pebbly grin at Rap in the ambience. *"So far so good!"*

"Very nice work. Now what? We'll be under siege in no time."

"Now we move on!"

Even as Rap caught the thought, the makeshift shield shuddered and buckled. It held, though. The escape had been detected, naturally, and the battle was now joined, builders versus destroyers.

"So we are refugees within the White Palace?" Shandie demanded. He was still holding little Maya, shouting over her cries and peering through the darkness.

"The Red Palace," Rap said.

"And how safe are we here?"

"Not very."

Of course neither the emperor nor any of his mundane companions could sense the test of strength going on overhead, or the ominous tremors in the shield. Beyond it, city and impire slept on, unaware of the war that had begun—a war that might end very shortly.

A moment later, though, the tops of the trees exploded into flame, illuminating the night and the falling snow. They must have long ago grown right through the shielding, although obviously not out of their occult local climate. An eerie golden glow played over faces and flowers and shrubbery and reflected off the thickly drifted roofs behind them. The mundanes cried out at the spectacle.

"This way!" the dwarf boomed, scurrying off on busy legs. The fugitives surged obediently after him, some faster than others. Shandie was burdened by a struggling, hysterical two-year-old, and Rap threw a hasty sleep spell over the child. He checked on the older folk, and they seemed to be coping. Ionfeu had an arm around his wife. Umpily and Sagorn were both beaming at this opportunity to snoop inside the Red Palace.

The air was rank with eye-nipping smoke from the burning trees. The shielding sagged abruptly, then ballooned upward as the defenders threw power into it. Then it buckled again.

Raspnex had stopped at a low, circular parapet. The refugees gathered around and stared down into what seemed to be a bottomless dry well. The warlock cackled. "What sort of a back door would you expect from a dwarf?"

"I don't believe I can see the ladder," Lady Eigaze said.

"Ladder? You mean imps need ladders? You, faun—you want to throw or catch?"

"I'd rather catch," Rap said. Throwing might require compulsion, and that would give him an attack of scruples. He sat on the stonework and swung his legs over. He could detect shielding a few stories below his boots, but not the bottom of the shaft.

The warlock's occult image was leering at him. *"It's twice as deep as you can see. Two layers of shielding. You can drop free until you're through the second."*

"You're dropping some free advice, are you?" There was a proverb about gifts from dwarves. Rap pushed off and let himself go. He wouldn't give Raspnex the satisfaction of seeing him use sorcery to slow his fall. He hurtled into the dark. Masonry flashed by his nose at breathtaking speed. His doublet pulled up and tried to choke him, and his cloak cracked to and fro like a whip overhead. The shielding seemed to rush up at him and he was through it and there was the next layer and that was gone and there was *rock* right below—

He hauled on the reins and slammed to a halt with his feet only fingerlengths above the floor. Ugh!—he had almost lost his insides. He let himself down until his boots were on the floor, somewhat surprised that it was not paved with flattened predecessors. Then he reeled through the doorway, clearing a landing place for the next fugitive. He gave himself a large jolt of calming spell, bringing his heart out of its hysterics and buttressing his quivering knees. He was standing at the start of a very long, very narrow tunnel. Extremely long—he could barely detect an end to it, and he had no idea how far away that end was.

He flashed a light to tell Raspnex he was ready.

He hoped his reflexes would prove fast enough. He could barely see the glimmer of fire at the top of the shaft, and the shielding blocked his farsight.

Seconds passed, then something blocked the light overhead and Ylo was there. Rap caught him in time, but he impacted harder than Rap intended, grunting as the weight of the breast-plate descended on his shoulders. He toppled forward, enveloped in a flurry of wolfskin. Rap steadied him and pulled him out of the shaft.

Grinning, the signifer fumbled to adjust his cloak and hood. "That was invigorating!" he said with approval. Obviously the warlock had applied a calming spell. "Where in the Name of Evil am I?" Eerie echoes crawled away into the distance.

"Sorry!" Rap said, and created light. "Now get out of the way!"

Ylo squeezed past him, leaving him ready for the next arrival. The tunnel would be single file, barely wide enough for a dwarf's shoulders and a tight fit for a troll—and Rap snatched old Count Ionfeu out of the air. This game required strict attention.

One by one the mundanes appeared, only seconds apart. Soon Ylo had vanished into the distance at the head of the line. They were all quite relaxed, chattering about the interesting experience. Little Maya was awake and laughing, demanding that her father do that again. Lord Umpily was not quite as heavy as he looked, Countess Eigaze even heavier. Sagorn made a very un-dignified arrival in his voluminous robe, but he was too engrossed in events to care.

And then came Raspnex, smirking evilly. *"You didn't miss any, I see."*

Flashes at the top of the shaft showed that the battle was raging more fiercely than ever, so obviously the four votaries were being left behind to cover the warlock's departure. Dwarves hated to part with anything, and Raspnex's ruthless sacrifice of his forces showed how desperate the situation was.

The mundanes' voices were becoming louder and shriller as the calming spells wore off.

"Quiet!" the warlock roared, and the deep bellow rolled away along the tunnel, leaving a twittering silence. "I'll shift you in fours. Move out of the way as soon as you arrive!"

Ylo, Ionfeu, Eigaze, and Eshiala all vanished from the head

of the line. The tunnel curved, Rap noted, and was heavily shielded. It must lie far belowground.

"Is this new?" he asked quietly. "Dwarf work?"

"Dwarf work, certainly, but not new."

"Then Zinixo—"

"But it doesn't end where he thinks it does," Raspnex chortled. "It changed course recently."

Shandie and his daughter disappeared, Umpily and Hardgraa, also.

The witch of the west must have approved this alteration to her palace. It could have been done any time in the years since Zinixo had been driven out, but the devious thinking was not trollish. Dwarves made good accomplices in a jailbreak, Rap decided.

Then power enveloped him. With Sagorn, Acopulo, and Raspnex himself, he was translated to the far end of the tunnel, and a rocky, underground chamber.

Here was troll work—massive stone walls and a high corbeled ceiling. Under a ghostly blue light of no visible source, the fugitives were standing around the walls, shocked now into silence. A flight of stone stairs spiraled up to the roof in the center of the chamber. It seemed to have no purpose whatsoever, but Rap detected a break in the shielding there and guessed that the next move was going to be tricky. The paving was wet, the air chill. Water was dripping somewhere.

A woman in dark, heavy work clothes had joined the group. She was taller than anyone present except Sagorn, and the white-gold hair bound on the crown of her head made her seem even taller. As impish women tended to stoutness in middle age, jotunn women were inclined to become scraggy. This one was neither old nor young. Her bare shins and feet showed that she was a sailor; her rawboned form was powerful, almost masculine, and yet she was still handsome enough to catch a man's eye. She would be capable of blacking it, too.

She had identified him, the royal faun. She nodded respectfully. He returned the nod, noting the shimmer of the loyalty spell on her. He wondered if she knew how her fellow votaries were being so callously squandered this night.

"Jarga," Raspnex said, half to her and half as an introduction to Rap. *"Everything well?"*

Her grim features softened in affection. *"Well, master."*

"Test it once more."

Without a word, Jarga elbowed Hardgraa aside like a cotton drape and marched over to the stairs. Her head vanished before it reached the roof. The rest of her followed, with her big, horny feet being the last to go. Several of the mundanes moaned.

Rap was impressed, though. *"Beautiful work, again!"* he said to Raspnex. There had been hardly a shimmer in the ambience. *"Yours?"*

The dwarf shook his big head. *"Grunth herself."* He sighed. *"Grimrix would have done it even better. I'm going to miss that kid."*

Faint tremors of power were filtering down through the gap in the shielding, so at least one of the struggles was still in progress. Almost certainly Grimrix would have been overcome by now, so he would be fighting on the other side, as fanatically loyal to Zinixo as he had been to Raspnex. Perhaps he was already using his might against the defenders at the palace. And when that fell, the Covin would gain four sorcerers more.

A moment later, Jarga reappeared down the magic staircase. "All clear," she said aloud. There was a sprinkle of fresh snow on her broad shoulders.

"Come on then, all of you," the dwarf rumbled. He looked weary. They all did.

Jarga ascended again, with the dwarf rolling after her. Rap waved the others on. Again Ylo led the mundanes, so perhaps he regarded himself as the most expendable. He vanished systematically, from wolf's head to sandals. Hardgraa followed him.

Sagorn stepped closer to Rap. "Have you any idea where we are, your Majesty?" he inquired. His pale face bore a livid hue in the spooky light.

"Under Cenmere, I think."

The jotunn gulped.

"After you, Doctor," Rap said, and brought up the rear.

At the top of the stairs, he emerged on the snow-covered deck of a barge—anchored, but rolling slightly under his boots. Waves slapped, ropes creaked. Although his eyes could see nothing at all, he sensed that he was a long way offshore. The two sorcerers were helping the mundanes climb overboard. Even as Rap arrived, the imperor clambered over the rail and then turned around to accept his daughter. Beyond him, Ylo, Hardgraa, Lady Eigaze, and Ionfeu were similarly suspended on nothing but a layer of snow. A couple of buckets hung near them, and farsight also detected some recently replaced ropes and snowy furled sails overhead. As his eyes adjusted to the dark, Rap began to make out the fabric of the shielded vessel tied alongside.

Very clever! Who would ever suspect a dwarf of escaping by boat? And once it was cast off, it could drift away unseen over the great freshwater sea. When the fugitives went belowdecks, even they would be undetectable to sorcery. Unless the use of the magic stairs had been noted, Raspnex had achieved the impossible.

Rap headed for the rail, but he declined Jarga's offer of assistance. "I'm not all faun," he said. "Count me as crew."

Despite the knee-deep snow, she was still barefoot. "Not much need for crew, King, but thanks."

Rap paused, taking a last scan before guiding his companions to the companionway. His farsight was too weak to inspect the city in detail, although he could tell where it was. The ambience was another matter. Once he had been able to sense power in use at the ends of the world. His range was pitifully limited now, yet there was enough power still crackling around the roof of the Red Palace to illuminate some detail for him. The roof-garden fire had spread to two of the towers. Badly outmatched, the defenders had retreated to some inner layer of shielding. Under the attackers' blows, the ambience shook like a tablecloth in the hands of a spring-cleaning housewife.

Nothing to the south . . .

Then, as he started to walk across the deck, the south erupted. Fury blazed in the ambience. He staggered at the mental din, the pain. He sensed buildings collapsing like soap bubbles—several blocks of buildings, men crushed, burning, terror, death . . .

Much death!

Raspnex swung around with a cry. *"Grimrix!"*

There could be no doubt what that conflagration had signified. The young votary had refused to let himself be turned. He had stayed loyal to the death.

Burning deck:

> The boy stood on the burning deck,
>   Whence all but him had fled;
> The flame that lit the battle's wreck
>   Shone round him o'er the dead . . .
>
> There came a burst of thunder sound;
>   The boy,—Oh! where was he?
> *Ask of the winds, that far around,*
>   *With fragments strewed the sea.*

Felicia Hemans, Casabianca

❰ TWO ❱

Newer world

1

In Krasnegar, in midwinter, daylight was a brief something that happened sometimes. When it did appear, it came at noon, long after the day's work had begun, but often it was so muffled by the weather that no one noticed it at all. Jotunn faces grew as pale as the ash-blond hair around them—or on them—and the imps pined. Jotnar and imps alike bore lanterns everywhere they went, mingling whale oil reek with the peat smoke of the fires. Shadows jumped and danced, but no one who took fright at shadows had any business living in Krasnegar.

The great hall of the castle was normally a very shadowy place, lit mainly by one or more of the huge hearths along the kitchen end, but it could shine brightly enough on special occasions, such as royal birthdays. Now the darkness had been driven away. Pages were lighting candles and lamps; crystal and silverware sparkled on the high table. A whole sheep sizzled on a spit. In an hour or so, Prince Gath and Princess Kadie would be entertaining their friends at a formal dinner. "To celebrate the beginning of their fifteenth year" was how Kadie had described the event on the invitations. That had sounded more grown-up than "fourteenth birthday."

She had confessed to her mother that a grand ball would have been more appropriate, but her men friends were mostly poor dancers. Inos could have told her that boys of that age were strongly resistant to dancing with girls taller than themselves, but she had merely agreed that a dinner was probably better. The boys would be in favor of a dance next year—Kadie probably had it planned already.

All morning she had been organizing, ordering, rearranging. Mostly the servants had ignored her and gone about their business with practiced efficiency. Now Inos had come to inspect the table.

Rotund Master Ylinyli loomed discreetly in the background, smiling quietly through a coal-black mustache that would have impressed a walrus. The major-domo would be recalling a similar fourteenth birthday dinner held here some twenty years ago—recalling how thrilled the guests had been to be treated like gentry, served by footmen, and how he had eaten too much and so made a terrible fool of himself.

"Very nice," Inos said, "but what are those for?"

"They're wineglasses, Mama."

"I think I knew that, actually. You plan to drink lime punch out of my best crystal?"

"But, Mama!"

"No wine, Kadie."

Kadie's face was stricken with intimations of disaster. "But I promised them!"

"That was not wise."

Two sets of green eyes locked, in rebellion and tyranny respectively. Tyranny won.

"Beer?" Kadie asked disconsolately.

"No beer, either."

"Not even to drink my . . . our . . . health? A toast . . ."

"Fruit punch." If her daughter only knew it, Inos thought, a punch made from the carefully preserved supply of fruit that kept Krasnegarians healthy during the winter would cost considerably more than wine.

Kadie flounced around to hide her annoyance, swirling the train on her gown and almost overbalancing. The gown was the day's gift from her parents, but the royal jewel box had been looted without permission. Again. Ylinyli caught the queen's eyes and smirked knowingly into his mustache—the wineglasses would be removed.

"That is your present to Gath?" Inos said, pointing to a baggy parcel. "Shouldn't you hide it until later?"

Kadie squirmed slightly. "It's no use hiding it from *him*! No use even wrapping it, even. He probably knows already. I thought I'd give it to him before the guests arrive."

"As you please, dear." Of course Gath would know what a parcel contained an hour or two before he unwrapped it, but that was not what was bothering Kadie.

"Well, it *was* expensive," she explained, "and I wouldn't want any of them to feel that their offerings were, er, inferior by comparison."

"Very tactful of you," Inos said.

The gift in question was a tattered copy of *The Kidnapped Princess of Kerith*, a torrid romance of great age, illustrated with faded hand-tinted woodcuts. Kadie had discovered it in a shabby little junk shop near the harbor, and coveted it greatly. Only by proclaiming it her birthday gift to Gath had she managed to wheedle enough money out of her mother to buy it.

She had undoubtedly read it from cover to cover several times already, and Gath would be fortunate if he managed to hang on to it for the rest of the week. He had very little interest in books anyway. This one was obviously a present from Kadie to Kadie. Her friends would know that, which was why she wanted it safely out of sight before they arrived.

And at some private time, later, their mother might—or might not—explain how enormously valuable that antique volume would be back in the Impire, and how Gath could trade it to some impish ship's captain for many times what it had cost his sister. Kadie would be aghast. Sometimes Inos let her sense of humor overrule her better judgment, and that was the only reason she had agreed to the charade in the first place.

She wished Rap was around to share the joke. She wished Rap was around for many, many reasons. She wished she was not so worried about him.

"Do you know what Gath's giving me?" her daughter asked offhandedly.

"No, dear."

"He's very secretive!" Kadie complained, failing to hide her disappointment. If her mother did not know, then Gath must have financed the gift out of his allowance. Gath was invariably broke, proverbially hopeless with money. "Well, this is very nice," she remarked cheerfully, admiring the table. "Real flowers would be even better, of course. If only Papa were here! . . ."

"Whatever do you mean?" Inos said icily. Gath's premonition was common knowledge, but official doctrine in Krasnegar was that the king was *not* a sorcerer, and Ylinyli had notoriously sharp ears.

"Oh . . . nothing. I must go and redo my fingernails. Do you think the ruby earrings would be better?"

"Those are lovely, dear, and here's your chance to give Gath his present."

Winter pale, gangly as a tent pole, Gath was advancing along the hall, keeping his hands behind him. Inos looked him over approvingly. He had inherited, or copied, his father's dislike of formal dress, but today he had donned his best blue doublet and beige hose without even arguing—her babies were growing up! He had also inherited his father's unruly hair, although it was jotunnish fair instead of faunish brown. His efforts to tame it had produced something that resembled a lodged barley field. He was wearing his usual contented smile.

Kadie registered that he was holding something behind his back. She stiffened like a bird dog.

"I have a present for you, Gath," she said brightly, and hastened to fetch the misshapen bundle.

"That's very kind of you! Thank you!" He sniggered. "Funny old pictures, aren't they?"

Kadie shot her mother a what-did-I-tell-you look and waited expectantly, holding out the parcel.

"You really didn't need to wrap it up." Gath was making no move to take it.

"It is customary!" his sister snapped.

"Aren't you going to accept it, dear?" Inos prompted.

He beamed, obviously very pleased with himself and much more interested in whatever he was planning than in the book. "Don't want to drop it. I'd need both hands. But it's very nice. Kadie, I decided that since you were giving me my present now, I'd give you yours."

His sister hastily laid the parcel back on the table, unable to conceal her impatience. "Well, I'm not a seer, so you'll have to let me look at it before I can thank you."

"I just wanted to explain," Gath said slowly, "how I *couldn't* wrap it, because I couldn't think of a way to hide its shape. You'd guess what it was right away." His grin was pure torture now.

Kadie glared. "At least that would make two of us!"

He nodded. Unable to think up any more delays, he dramatically produced a slim, shiny sword, laying the blade across his forearm, proffering the hilt to her. "Happy birthday!"

Kadie somehow managed to squeal and gasp at the same time. "Oh, *Gath*! It's gorgeous!"

A flourish of steel flashed in the candlelight, and it was Inos' turn to squeal. "Careful!"

"It's all right, Mother!" Kadie said scornfully. "A real rapier! Oh, Gath! Where did you get it?" She threw her spare arm around him and kissed him—to everyone's astonishment.

"Yes, indeed!" Inos said. "Where did you get that dangerous-looking thing, young man?" Not only dangerous but valuable—there was shinier metal than steel there.

"It's beautifully balanced!" Kadie said and struck a fencing pose, blissfully absurd in her voluminous gown. "And light!"

Gath was smirking. "Tush found it for me. I told him what I wanted, and the next night he brought it to my room. It's almost as long as he is!"

"Tush?" said Inos. "The gnome?"

"Course. It was down in the cellars somewhere. It doesn't matter that I didn't spend any money on her present, does it? I didn't have any. I did spend a lot of time cleaning it up. I mean, it was *black*!"

"It's the thought that counts," Inos said, wondering how many times a parent had to repeat that catechism per child reared. "Obviously you have made her very happy, which is what matters."

"I don't care what it didn't cost!" Kadie said ecstatically. "It's splendoupolous!" She paused in her phantom fencing to examine the hilt. Inos and even Ylinyli moved in cautiously to see.

Gath was chuckling, pleased with himself. "Know something, Mom? She came bouncing into my room a couple of nights ago to tell me that—"

"I do not bounce!" Kadie's glare was as pointed as the sword.

"Whatever it was, then. But I'd been working on it, and it was lying right there on my dresser—" He chortled. *"And she didn't even notice!"*

His sister was not interested in her own shortcomings. "Mother! Are these rubies?"

"Garnets, I think," Inos said. Dwarvish steel, certainly. The guard bore three leaping narwhals in silver filigree. Originally each had possessed a garnet eye, but now one was blind, the stone missing. Leaping narwhals? She had seen that insignia before somewhere. "I hope it was one of our cellars this came out of, not someone else's?" Gnome thinking tended to be misty on the subjects of property and territorial boundaries.

"I think so," Gath said. "Tush told me it was in among a lot of junk, so no one knew it was there—but I think it was in the castle. It was very dirty!" he added defensively. "No one knew about it, wherever it was."

"Narwhals?" Kadie squealed. "We . . . I mean *you*, of course. You have a brooch like that, Mama!"

"So *I*, I mean *I*, do," Inos agreed. "It belonged to Ollialo, Inisso's wife!"

"That's why this is short—it's a lady's weapon! Will you give me the brooch, to match my sword?"

"No, I won't!"

The rapier must be a long-forgotten family heirloom. It would rank as part of the Krasnegarian crown jewels, if Krasnegar had any crown jewels. It must be far older than Gath's book. Even without a historical provenance, a weapon that old was worth a fortune. The joke had rebounded.

"Mm!" Inos said, watching her daughter's renewed capering, as she massacred invisible hordes. Kadie's curious fascination with fencing was showing no signs of diminishing, although most of her friends had tired of the sport long since. Innumerable romances like *The Kidnapped Princess* were her main motivation, but a juvenile crush on Corporal Isyrano was part of it. Fortunately he was an honorable man and happily married.

Meanwhile, Kadie with foils was bad enough, and Kadie with a real rapier was an unnerving thought. Armed children? Oh, the joys of motherhood!

"No, you can't wear it at dinner," she said, and Gath sniggered as he at last began unwrapping his book.

"Mother!" Kadie said with infinite scorn, although she must have been considering the idea. Even Kadie would not be able to reconcile a sword with a ball gown.

"Well, lay it down before you kill someone. Last inspection—what else do you need?"

All eyes went to the table.

"Pity about the wine," Gath remarked wistfully.

Kadie shrugged. "I tried."

"No luck at all, huh?"

"Stubborn as a mule."

"I am not deaf," Inos said coldly. "And I resent being called a mule. Now, let's go over the seating, shall we?"

Kadie reluctantly switched back from deadly swordswoman to royal hostess, but she used the rapier to point. "Me here. Gath, there. Nia . . . Kev . . . Brak . . ."

"Brak won't be coming." Gath was staring off to the other end of the hall, suddenly tense. His face had lost its merriment and gone very wooden. Inos felt a twinge of alarm.

"Why not?"

"He just won't."

"Why not?"

"Concussion." Gath dropped his book on the table. "Thanks, Kadie. No, I can't!" Then he spun around and ran.

"Gath, wait!" Inos cried, but she had already been answered. Her son vanished out the side door.

Mother and daughter exchanged worried looks.

"Go and find him," Inos said quickly. "Tell him to come straight back here at once! No, leave the sword."

She bit her lip as Kadie went scurrying off, holding up the hem of her gown. When she left the hall she took four or five young pages along. The palace cubs would have a much better chance of finding Gath than Inos would.

Ylinyli was still there, a look of concern on his chubby impish face.

"Concussion?" Inos said. "He did say 'concussion'?"

"I fear so, ma'am."

Rap, Rap! I need you!

She pulled out a chair and sat down.

It made no sense. If Gath had foreseen an accident, then he could have warned Brak, surely? Gath's strange prescience didn't work for other people, or so Rap had thought. Gath could only know ahead of time what he was going to know anyway. That was Rap's theory. But if Brak was about to have an accident, Gath would learn of an accident eventually.

She smiled uneasily at Ylinyli. "I expect it's some sort of prank."

He bit his mustache. "I shouldn't say this, ma'am . . ."

"Sit down and say it."

Frowning, he leaned on a chair back and dropped his servant voice. "Inos, they've been picking on him. Didn't you know?"

She shook her head. But Gath had been rather morose lately. She'd blamed Rap's absence. Concussion? Brak was the son of Kratharkran the smith, older than Gath and about twice the size. A red-haired jotunn lout! Oh, my baby!

"Why?" she whispered, horrified.

The major-domo squirmed. "Because . . . I don't know, ma'am."

"Sit down!" Inos spoke quietly, but she still wore the occult royal glamour Rap had laid on her years ago. Moving like a flash of lightning, Ylinyli sat.

"Now tell me," she said.

"Because of his Majesty."

"That is ridiculous!" Still she did not raise her voice, but Ylinyli quailed.

"Of course it is, ma'am! But you know children!"

Inos forced calm on herself and reassured the major-domo with the best smile she could muster. "Oh, Lin! I don't need secret police to be a queen, but I do need friends to be a mother! Now, please, tell me?"

Typical imp, Lin brightened and said hopefully, "First dance at the Winterfest Ball?"

"Granted! Now, what do they say?"

"That he's run away, Inos."

Rap had been gone for six weeks, in the dead of winter. As far as his loyal subjects knew, there was no way he could return before summer. Inos had never announced why he had gone, or where. How could she? What could she say? That he was a sorcerer and had had a premonition? That he'd gone rushing off to save the world? Rap would never forgive her.

She tried to see the situation as they must see it, the humble folk of Krasnegar. The stableboy king had run away—deserted his wife, the true queen. Another woman, perhaps?

The adults would just gossip, but children were sadistic monsters.

"They bait him?"

The imp's fat jowls wobbled as he nodded.

Of course they would. She could imagine what the boys would

say, and Gath would have to defend his father's name. This was Krasnegar. Even the peaceable Gath would have to fight. *Oh, my poor baby!*

Lin was the nosiest, most gossipy man she had ever known. He was quivering now with the urge to ask impertinent questions.

"Do you know the ringleaders?" she asked. "I could call in their fathers and talk to them."

Lin shook his head regretfully. "There would be just as many the next day, Inos. Maybe if you made a general proclamation . . ." But his face said it wouldn't work.

"Why haven't I heard?" she demanded angrily.

"Far as I know, he's been doing very well. He thrashed Nev, and Oshi."

She'd seen young Oshi. "That was Gath did that? Gods!"

" 'Stremely well. But you know jotnar—it's always one-on-one with them."

Not *always*, just *usually*. And he hadn't added the obvious—when imps resorted to violence, they fought in packs. If the imp boys started in on Gath, also, then sheer numbers would overcome his occult ability to dodge.

Oh, Rap! I need you!

"Inos . . ." Lin chewed his mustache again. "Gath has second sight, doesn't he?"

Whatever Lin knew, everyone would know, but the secret was obviously out now. "He has a slight prescience, yes."

Lin tried vainly to hide his satisfaction at this confirmation. "Well, then! He didn't say he wouldn't be at the dinner. Only that Brak wouldn't."

Inos felt a huge relief. "That's right! And he knew there wasn't going to be any wine! He came in after I told Kadie that, didn't he?" Today, at least, Gath was going to win again.

But tomorrow, and the day after?

She needed her husband, but Gath needed his father much more.

How long until Rap came home? Where was he, and what was he doing?

2

"Wake up *NOW*!" Hardgraa said, slamming the cabin door.

Ylo grunted. He had been fast asleep, but he had always had the knack of going into or out of sleep quickly. That did not mean he wished to leave his warm bunk.

"You are wanted on deck in five minutes," the centurion said. "You will be there. I think you will find it chilly with no clothes on, but please yourself."

Ylo stretched and rubbed his eyes. "Your mother plied her trade in ditches and paid her customers. What clothes? Where are we? What time is it?"

"Those clothes. Somewhere on Cenmere. About an hour after breakfast."

Ylo sat up and scratched. A century or so ago, this rotten hulk had been a fancy craft, plying the luxury trade on Cenmere, bearing aristocrats to and from their grand lakeside mansions. Now she leaked and creaked and swilled putrid fluids around in her bilges—just the sort of ship a dwarf would choose! The cabin was shabby and stale-smelling. Nevertheless, he had slept extremely well, and he did not feel in the least bit seasick, which was remarkable.

He had left his mail surcoat and his wolfskin draped over the chair. A heap of other garments had been laid on top of them.

"I'm a civilian now?" he demanded, noting that Hardgraa was garbed in doublet and hose and a warm-looking cloak.

"We all are, stupid."

"Who made those—the dwarf?"

"Ha! We'd all look like mine workers if he had. No, the faun did. They're plain, but they're good stuff."

Ylo reluctantly threw off the covers and swung his feet down to a cold and dirty floor. "Shaving?"

Hardgraa whipped out a dagger and offered it hilt first. "Lots of water outside. Bucket and rope on deck." He had obviously shaved recently, and without nicking himself. Ylo had never understood how he ever managed to do that, even with hot water and soap, because his face had the texture of tree bark. It might be as tough. Perhaps he used sandstone.

"I'll think about it." Ylo began dressing. If Shandie really had ordered him on deck in five minutes, then the centurion would not be bluffing about delivering him there ready or not.

Hardgraa leaned back against the door. "You'll miss that wolfskin, won't you? Girls will take longer?"

"At least another ten minutes." Ylo shivered into the shirt. "You do realize that the imperor is now deposed? Legally he can't give us orders anymore."

Hardgraa grinned menacingly. "He can give me orders!"

"Somehow I thought you would see it that way."

The centurion tested the edge of his dagger with a horny thumb. "Are you telling me that you don't recognize Shandie as imperor?" The grin was still there, and the menace more obvious.

Ylo pulled on hose. What was his relationship to Shandie now? An imperor could reward his associates with vast riches. A deposed ruler had nothing to offer but danger and hardship. On the other hand, if he ever did win back his throne, then his gratitude to those who had stood by him in his time of troubles ought to be infinite. Obviously a cautious man would assess the odds with great care. Last night the situation had seemed utterly hopeless, but perhaps by daylight there might be some rays of encouragement.

He met the centurion's steely eye. Hardgraa would not be thinking that way. His loyalty to Shandie was personal and absolute; he would serve Shandie if he had to hide out in a cave until his dying day. He and Ylo were longtime comrades now, but the old legionary would not hesitate to slit Ylo's throat if he suspected he was a threat to the imperor, and obviously anyone on this ship who was not totally loyal would be a threat. The rule of law did not apply here, as Ylo himself had just pointed out.

"I think I'll discuss my allegiance when Shandie himself asks me."

The centurion put his dagger away, but his face alone was still an open threat. "Should have taken that dukedom while you had the chance, shouldn't you?"

Ylo bent to buckle a shoe. It was a perfect fit. "Rivermead? That was just a rumor, just court gossip. Why would he have offered to make me a duke? Would I have turned it down if he had?"

"He told me he had, and you had."

Ylo did not look up. He had been very stupid to refuse that offer. The preflecting pool had promised him Eshiala, but even if he still put any faith in that vision, what was a seduction compared to a dukedom? He had hoped to win both—tumble first and Rivermead second.

"I expect you'll believe him and not me, then."

"Every time," Hardgraa said.

Shoes fastened, Ylo rose to his feet, balancing against the gentle roll of the ship. "Any idea where we're going or what we're doing?"

Hardgraa's face was unreadable now. "Not much. The most urgent business is to find a safe retreat for the impress and her daughter."

Ylo picked up the cloak and adjusted it on his shoulders. "Sounds logical."

"Of course she'll need protection—someone will have to stay and guard her."

Their eyes met.

"Old Ionfeu and his wife, I expect?" Ylo said, but his heart had started to beat a little faster.

Hardgraa nodded. "Plus a fighting man."

"Then we'll see who he really trusts, won't we?"

"Yes, we will, won't we?" the centurion said darkly.

Ylo felt quite hurt by his obvious suspicion.

The deckhouse was bright and reasonably warm. Everyone was sitting around on shabby chairs and well-worn sofas, and the prevailing mood seemed to be one of dark brooding. There was no talking. There was no sign of food, either, so Hardgraa had not been lying when he said that Ylo had missed breakfast. His arrival seemed to go unnoticed.

Shandie was sitting by himself, staring into space, thinking. His face gave nothing away, but then it never did. He was the most impassive of men. Whether he was deciding what to have for lunch or how many thousand men to send to certain death, he always looked like that when he was thinking.

Ylo walked over and bowed. He needed practice in bowing.

He had the imperor's full attention instantly—Shandie never thought about more than one thing at a time. The midnight eyes appraised him with a hint of amusement. "Ylo! Morning! I almost didn't recognize you without your wolfskin."

"Nor I, sir. The back of my neck feels very chilly."

"It will feel worse, I'm afraid. I've appointed you high admiral for the next half hour. The helmsman needs a break."

"Aye, sir," Ylo said in a growly Nordland accent. Resignedly he headed for the door. When he glanced back, Shandie was lost in thought again. The general glum silence in the room suggested that no one had found a solution to the problem yet.

Ylo went out on deck and crunched across the snowy planks to where the big jotunn heifer was holding the wheel. The wind blowing over Cenmere was colder than a snake's smile. An inland sea more than a hundred leagues long could raise fair waves when it wanted to. It wasn't trying very hard at the moment, but imps were never good sailors and Ylo was astonished at his feeling of well-being. Sorcery, likely.

The water was the exact color of lead coffins; the clouds hung low overhead like lids. Snow had stopped falling, but there was enough still up there to bury this unpropitious ferryboat. The horizon all around was hazy, and blank—not a sail, not a trace of land. Ylo's landlubber impish soul cringed in horror at the sight of so much water.

The big woman did not look as weary as she should if she had been driving this hulk all night. He hated women bigger than himself, and he wanted nothing to do with sorceresses.

"I was sent to relieve you," he said.

"May the Gods preserve us, then. Do you know how a compass works?"

"Yes."

"Wonderful. Hold the wheel steady and try to keep that red bit exactly where it is now."

"Sounds easy."

"But you won't find it so." She crinkled the weatherbeaten wrinkles around her ugly pale eyes, and walked away.

The wood was cold. In a few minutes his fingers were frozen and he was chilled to the bone. The compass needle refused to stay where he wanted; when he looked back he saw the wake was about as curly as his hair. He found that evidence of his own incompetence very irritating, and knowing he could do no better even more so.

How could Shandie fight an army of sorcerers? How could a deposed imperor ever regain his throne against those odds? If anyone in that deckhouse had found a convincing answer, they would not all have been looking so black. Always Shandie had been an inspiring leader, and a generous one, but a sensible man did not stay with a doomed cause. Contrariwise, a band of outlaws did not tolerate potential traitors. Common sense whispered that Ylo's best course of action was to swear eternal loyalty until he reached shore—and then just vanish. He would never be Duke of Rivermead now. A wealthy, buxom widow was his only hope.

But there was one interesting advantage to the sudden change in his fortunes. The preflecting pool's prophecy seemed a lot more believable since yesterday. He had never quite believed that he would ever find means to seduce an impress. Royal ladies were always very carefully guarded. His chances were much better now.

Boots crunched on the snow, and the king of Krasnegar arrived with a rush. He grabbed the wheel, began turning it. "Easy, there!" he said, laughing as if he were calming a horse. "You almost had her in irons, Admiral!" He had remarkably callused hands for a king.

"I did what she said!" Ylo protested, stepping back and letting the faun do as he pleased with the wheel, as he obviously knew what he was about.

"The wind shifted on you! And we need to make a course change, anyway." He was taller than Ylo, this so-unlikely faun, and he had very penetrating gray eyes. "Stick around a minute. I need to ask you something."

"Me, your Majesty?"

"We've been establishing motives," the king said. He had the hulk's sharp end pointed the way he wanted it now, but he didn't give the wheel back to Ylo. Apparently he was enjoying himself. "In effect we're outlaws, you know. Even the imperor is! So the question everyone must answer is: Do you want to stay with the team, or do you want out?"

Ylo inspected his surroundings. "And walk?" A couple of sails had appeared on the western skyline.

The faun chuckled contentedly. His doublet and hose looked no warmer than Ylo's, he wore no cloak or hat. Jotunn blood in him, obviously. "No, we can hail a boat and put you on. We'd pick one going north, probably, and you'd have to make your own way home. But that shouldn't be hard."

Ylo pulled his skimpy cloak tight and studied the faun's innocent expression, remembering that this blunt, seemingly open man was actually a sorcerer. "And what happens when I get home?"

"That I do not prophesy."

And where was home? Ylo had no home, no family, no real friends, even. "What's the alternative? Where are we going?" He steadied himself with a hand on the rail. The ship had a new motion that he did not approve of, although it had not started to affect his insides yet.

"I won't tell you that," the faun said, eyes narrowing. "Not until you declare. But we need a hiding place where the impress and her daughter can remain—a sanctuary, and headquarters. Countess Eigaze had suggested a spot that sounds promising. We're going to see."

If he would answer questions so willingly, then Ylo had a bushel of them ready. "Shandie still wants to get his impire back?" That one got a nod. "How?"

The king smiled, but suddenly there was threat in that smile, or at least a hint that walking on lakes was unhealthy. "That also I won't tell you yet. Are you with us or against us, Signifer?"

"With you, your Majesty. Of course."

"Of course?" the faun mused. " 'Of course,' you say? Why 'Of course,' though? What ties you to Shandie now? He's lost his throne. He can't shower wealth and power on you. What holds you to his cause? A sense of justice? Loyalty to the Impire? Friendship?"

"Hadn't thought about it. Gratitude?" That felt safest.

The king did not look very convinced. He pursed his lips. "If this proposed refuge is satisfactory, then the impress will remain there while the rest of us go off to reconquer the world. Someone will have to stay and guard her."

"I suppose so."

"The imperor mentioned you for that job." The iron-gray eyes stabbed straight into Ylo's heart.

Or it felt as if they did.

"Face the other way, Signifer," King Rap said harshly. "If Shandie looks out and sees that blush, he's going to wonder what provoked it."

"Are you suggesting that I am not a man of honor?"

"You're blushing, not me. She's incredibly beautiful. I don't blame you at all. If I weren't happily married and she wasn't, I might dream myself.''

"What are you hinting?" Ylo demanded. "There is nothing between the impress and me!''

"No?'' The faun chewed his stubbled lip for a moment. "But that's not quite true, is it? Not yet, you mean?''

"You're rooting around in my mind!''

"No, I'm not! I don't do that! But I can read your face like a dog's tail, and you're guilty of *something*. The preflecting pool, was it?''

Ylo nodded angrily.

"Doing what?''

A hot retort died stillborn before that metallic stare. "Lying on a blanket, on grass. Smiling at me.''

Unexpectedly the faun grinned. "An intriguing prophecy! It would certainly inspire a man. But you haven't . . .''

"Not yet. There were daffodils.''

"What're daffodils?''

"They're a spring flower.''

"I see.''

"They bloom about third or fourth moon. So four or five months from now.''

The faun nodded thoughtfully. "Forgive my prying, Signifer. Shandie saw my son in that pool. I wanted to know all about it. You've told her?''

"No one else, though.''

"Wise of you.'' The sorcerer fell silent, either studying the distant sails, or just lost in thought. Ylo waited, shivering.

"Tell me something,'' King Rap said eventually. "What do you think of Shandie himself?''

"He'd make a great imperor.''

"As a man?''

"Courageous. Dedicated. Honorable.''

"You're evading the question. I swear that this is just between the two of us.''

Oddly, Ylo decided he trusted this rustic king, although he couldn't imagine why. "He's decent. I admire him.''

"You'd like to be like him, you mean?''

"No.'' Shandie took life much too seriously.

The gray eyes drilled into Ylo again. "He's not your imperor at the moment. Would you say he was your friend? No—would you say you were his friend?''

''I suppose so. I'd like to help him.''

A shadow of a grin curled the big faun mouth. ''Then how can you plan to seduce his wife?''

What use to lie to a sorcerer? ''I said I'd like to help him. I can't give him lessons. I can teach his wife, though.''

The king looked startled, then he laughed. ''So you all benefit?''

''Exactly.''

''Well, that's the finest rationalization I've ever heard!''

''It's true, though,'' Ylo protested. ''I'd gamble my life that they were both virgins when they were married. With women he's blind, and deaf. I've heard them practically ask him outright, and I'd swear he hadn't a notion what they wanted. Not just in bed. He has no idea how to treat his wife as a human being. He never talks to her as if she had a brain at all. He thinks she loves him because he gives her presents. In the Imperial Library—''

The king snapped his fingers. ''That's it! Ever since I saw her, I've been trying to remember. The middle statue!''

Astonished, Ylo could only nod.

The faun shook his head sadly. ''He pointed it out to me when he was ten years old!'' He fell silent again, frowning. After a moment he added, ''His mother was a bitch, you know. He had a wretched childhood.''

What had that to do with anything? What had any of this to do with Zinixo, or the Protocol? Furthermore, why need Ylo stay out on this snowy, freezing deck when the king was obviously so much better qualified to handle the wheel? The sorcerer might be occultly sensitive to the emotions on people's faces, but he was strangely blind to Ylo's convulsive shivering.

''So you'll do them both a favor?'' the faun said, showing his wry grin again.

''Certainly! I'll show her. Then she can show him. What harm in that?''

The faun chuckled. ''What harm indeed? So if Shandie leaves his wife in your care, you'll seduce her?''

''Yes.''

''Think you can?''

''Know I can.''

"What happens if she conceives your child?"

Ylo shrugged. "Women have ways of dealing with that problem."

King Rap studied him thoughtfully for a moment. "You enjoy life, Signifer."

"I try to. That's what it's for, isn't it?"

"Yes, I suppose it is," the king said sadly.

3

The big Jotunn sailor emerged as Ylo reached the door, wiping her mouth on her sleeve. He felt her eyes on him as they passed, but he ignored her. Too tall, not young enough.

The deckhouse felt warm after the windy deck. He stripped off the stinking cloak to let himself thaw out. Shivering, he chose the best-looking vacant chair, then sat and blew through his fists while he summed up the mood of the room. No one paid any attention to him except the dwarf, who was standing by a window, peering over the sill. He turned round to stare at Ylo with an aggressive glower on his rocky, rough-hewn face.

There seemed to be no deliberate pattern to the group, and yet the imperor's chair was nearest the center. Impress Eshiala was down on the floor at his feet, helping her daughter pile a set of red and green wooden blocks. Where had those come from? Shandie was still engrossed in thought. How could he ignore such a beauty? In civilian clothes, he seemed very unremarkable for an imperor. Of course that was not inappropriate for an imperor with no impire.

Seated in a very irregular halo around him, everyone else brooded in silence—or perhaps they were listening to the little voices of the ship itself, the wood and water noises, the rhythm of creaking and swishing. The only exception was Countess Eigaze, chattering cheerfully to Centurion Hardgraa as if unaware of the misery all around her.

Fat Lord Umpily seemed to be in a deep sulk. Old Count Ionfeu was slumped on a sofa, nodding. Stretched out in a soft chair, the ancient scholar Sagorn stared at the roof and sucked his knuckles, lost in thought. Sir Acopulo was scowling at nothing in particular or everything in general, frustrated by his inability to frame a brilliant solution to the problem.

So far as Ylo could see, there was no solution; the case was hopeless. He was very glad that strategy was not his responsibility. No one expected him to come up with answers.

Cold air swirled around when the door opened again to admit the faun, and closed. A shimmer ran through the company, as if a pebble had dropped in a still pond.

Shandie looked up expectantly. "Now can we have that council of war?"

"Was just going to suggest it," King Rap said cheerfully. He leaned back against the wall and folded his arms. "The signifer says he is with us, also."

All eyes flickered briefly to Ylo.

"I never doubted him for a minute," Shandie said.

Startled, Ylo glanced around. He met the faun's eye and looked away quickly.

"I don't doubt anyone here," the imperor added. "I notice that the one person you did not ask was my wife." He smiled at her.

Now the attention went to Eshiala, down on the rug with Maya. She glanced up, cold and beautiful as the Qoble Mountains. "What exactly is the question, your Majesty?"

Shandie blinked, which was about as close to showing surprise as he ever came.

The faun studied her intently for a moment, then said, "The dwarf Zinixo has stolen the Impire, and we are going to overthrow him and steal it back. Are you with us?"

"You are questioning my loyalty to my husband and the Impire?"

"I am asking where your first loyalty lies."

She frowned, then suddenly colored. "To my child."

"Eshiala!" the imperor exclaimed, his normal impassivity cracking.

"Steady!" the faun said softly. "She's absolutely correct."

Eshiala lifted Maya and hugged her. The marble calm seemed to crack for a moment, showing fires of panic within. "My only concern is her welfare! I don't want to see her serving a dwarf all her days. If we fight, then we'll be discovered and captured. I just want to hide! Some safe retreat where Maya can grow up in peace and freedom—that's what I want."

The king nodded. "But she would be healthier and safer in the palace than in poverty and hiding."

"I don't agree at all!" the impress said sharply. "I despise the court!"

"Eshiala!" Shandie exclaimed again. Had he never realized that? How could a man so perceptive be so blind to his own wife's feelings?

The faun raised a hand to silence him. "Now you see why I didn't ask her! She has no choice, and we have no choice in her case. The princess would be almost as valuable to Zinixo as yourself. Ma'am, we are unanimous in seeking only safe refuge for you and your child. To have the two of you fall into the dwarf's hands would be disaster." He scratched his tangled hair ruefully. "Not that we aren't in a disaster already, of course! But if the enemy were offering prizes, that little beauty might have a higher price on her head than even Warlock Raspnex or myself."

"We are agreed, then," Shandie said testily. "My wife and child must go into hiding. But she will require companions. Proconsul, would you and your wife be willing to accept such an exile?"

"We should be honored, sire," the old man said, flushing, and his wife nodded vigorously, her chins flexing.

"I am grateful! I wish I could say that the term will be short, but obviously I cannot. And you will need a trusty guard—Ylo, or perhaps Centurion Hardgraa. Possibly Doctor Sagorn would like to join you, also?"

Ylo carefully kept his eyes on the scruffy rug in front of him. Let them all go off and fight an army of sorcerers! Looking after the impress was certainly the job he could handle best!

The old jotunn cleared his throat. "I think not, Sire."

Ylo glanced up in surprise, and everyone was staring at the old man's grim smile.

"I should think that a safe sanctuary would be your choice!" Shandie said, frowning suspiciously.

"A jotunn is never too old for battle, Sire!" The sinister old man exchanged smirks with the faun and then addressed the imperor again.

"I have near as much to fear as you do, your Majesty. I have never admitted this in public before. I know a word of power." He glanced around sardonically, assessing the reaction. "One word only. I am, in the occult sense, a genius. My native talent is intelligence. That is why run-of-the-mill scholars, like Acopulo there, always seem so *slow* to me. As I understand the situation, Zinixo has been hunting down all the words he can find. If he catches me, my lot will be torture and death. Have I stated the case fairly?''

"Very," Raspnex rumbled, with a hideous leer.

Sagorn sighed. "My motives are as strong as your own, therefore. And I think my friends will agree, when they have had time to think on it.''

What friends? Frowning faces told Ylo that others were wondering the same as he was. King Rap was smiling, however, in his wry way. There was something very odd about the old sage—the way he had appeared so quickly the previous evening, and the way the minstrel Jalon had disappeared. Perhaps there was more than one word involved, for one word did not produce miracles. Sagorn was hinting at more than he had admitted.

"I do not question your motives or loyalty," the imperor said tactfully. "I was merely thinking of physical stamina and endurance."

"His help and counsel will be very helpful," King Rap said innocently. "And he does have much to lose.''

"Such protestations are unnecessary!" Sir Acopulo snapped. The little man had been glaring with loathing at Sagorn. "As I understand the situation—in my *slow* way—Legate Ugoatho is presumed to have been enthralled by the usurper. Therefore anyone who was present in the Throne Room last night is on his proscription list, and that means all of us.''

"Then you do not comprehend the situation at all," the jotunn retorted sharply. He curled his long lip. "We are not talking of any normal rebellion, or *proscriptions*." He sneered the word.

Acopulo colored furiously. "Perhaps you will explain for the benefit of us run-of-the-mill mundanes?''

"Gladly. Listen carefully. You are in no physical danger, and to fall into Zinixo's hands might even be to your advantage. Let us take Signifer Ylo as an example. By supporting the imperor in his bid to overthrow the dwarf, he becomes a hunted outlaw—cold and hungry, friendless, and perpetually risking his life. On the other hand, if he merely grabs the first opportunity to betray Emshandar to the Covin, then they will both be turned into loyal supporters.'' The old man's water-blue eyes seemed to burn brighter as he threw the awful words across at Ylo. "As a vassal, the imperor's primary duty and desire will be to protect the dwarf, which will mean keeping his hegemony secret. His Majesty will therefore proceed to rule as much as possible as he would have done anyway. Do you follow? As far as his overriding loyalty to Zinixo permits, that is. And obviously that will include rewarding his own supporters. His former signifer will certainly be granted advancement.''

Everyone was staring at Ylo. Why had he been picked out to endure this? "Slanders!" he shouted, fighting a rising panic. Advancement? Duke of Rivermead? "If you were younger, sir, and a gentleman, I would call you out for those words!" He thought he might even mean that, although he had never fought a duel in his life.

The old jotunn granted him a sinister smile. "Of course the same is true of the others. I merely use you as an example, Signifer—why do you take this so personally? Indeed, it goes further. Once Emshandar is bound in fealty to the dwarf, he will feel enormous gratitude to whoever has led him to see the error of his former recalcitrance, and—"

"That's enough!" the faun barked. "We know that we are fighting a dreadful evil. You need not labor the point, Sagorn. I had rather face a horde of goblins than what threatens us now."

Easy for him to say, but could any of them trust Ylo from now on? Could he trust any of them? Worse—could he even trust himself? What exactly could he hope to gain by supporting this ludicrous revolution? Eshiala, of course, but what after that? Now he saw why the faun was so interested in people's motives. Zinixo had all the imperor's powers plus his own sorcery. Perhaps he would reward Ylo with a dukedom if he betrayed Shandie? Or handed over the faun, even?

God of Horrors!

"Let us progress to business!" Shandie said impatiently. "If this were any normal rebellion, I would hasten at once to the nearest legion."

"The army would rally to you, of course, Sire," Count Ionfeu said softly. "No imperor has ever been more popular with the army."

"Thank you. But that won't help in this case, will it?"

"No." The faun sighed.

"So what can we *do*?"

"Sorcery can only be fought with sorcery. We must gather an opposing covin."

Shandie's dark eyes narrowed. "Last night I was told that was impossible."

"It may well be," Rap admitted. "The first question is, where can we even begin to look? The warlock said last night that his nephew had gathered up every sorcerer in Pandemia. He now admits that he may have been exaggerating."

As he had the previous night, Ylo sensed that the two sorcerers were speaking to each other by some occult means that he could not detect. It was irritating, and Lord Umpily's scowl of frustration had deepened. The faun was now suggesting the dwarf repeat some of that private conversation aloud.

The dwarf scowled also, and tugged his rough beard. "Maybe. Something very odd began to happen about a year ago. The news got around. Magic sort of disappeared."

King Rap nodded. "I rode in from northwest Julgistro, and detected almost none, the whole way."

"It happened all over," Raspnex agreed in his rough voice, "and suddenly. Of course the Four have always pounced on free sorcerers when they found them, and set loyalty spells on them. Usually, though, it was a fairly benign rule—with a few exceptions, like my nephew, when he was a warlock. Old Bright Water had dozens of votaries, but for the most part she left them alone as soon as she had made sure they wouldn't misbehave. It was a way of keeping the peace, really. Once in a while they would be required to perform a service, and of course they reported any news of importance. What Zinixo has been doing is a lot more active. He conscripts them, to aid him."

"And the lesser talents?" the faun prompted.

"The same with them. A sorcerer is normally aware who in his area has power—mages, adepts, even one-word geniuses. Whether or not he interferes with them, he will know them. About the time North died, the free sorcerers sensed the problem, or told one another, and they all just spread the word to the juniors. Everyone went to ground."

"Nobody told us, er, me," Sagorn muttered.

"You were fortunate to escape detection," the faun said solemnly. "The fact that your house was shielded undoubtedly helped. But we conclude that there probably are a great many sorcerers still around, lying low. And lesser talents, also, of course."

"If you can find them?" Acopulo said.

"Exactly."

"And, as the warlock pointed out," Sagorn said, "Zinixo has a whole army of searchers, and there are only two of you. Or do you have some votaries left, your Omnipotence?"

The dwarf shot him a stony glare, like a mountain lining up a killer avalanche. "I do, but I have no way of reaching them. Except one."

That confirmed Ylo's suspicions about the Jarga woman.

The old jotunn smiled grimly. "The other wardens must still have some, surely, but the same problem arises?"

Raspnex grunted agreement.

"Warlock Lith'rian is in Ilrane?"

The dwarf sneered at this mention of elves. "All the yellow pretties are back in Ilrane, and I'm sure they have the border sealed as tight as . . . as . . ."

"As a dwarf's pockets," the faun said.

"So where do we start?" Shandie demanded irritably.

The king pursed his lips and glanced at the warlock as if seeking agreement. "With respect, Majesty, I prefer to side-track that question at the moment."

Lord Umpily made a noise like a boiling pot. "Come, Sire! Either you trust us or you don't!"

"Oh, I do trust you! I trust all of you—today. But tomorrow you may think differently. The same is true of everyone, including myself. So we shall not discuss tactics, not yet."

Shandie was displeased. "Then the council of war is completed?"

"By no means!" The faun smiled and strode over to a chair. "No tactics, but we can discuss strategy." He settled himself and stretched out at ease. The dwarf left the window, waddling to a bench, and some of the tension and anger seemed to seep out of the meeting.

"Our first requirement," Rap said, "is information. We need a set of ears and eyes in Hub."

He was calling for a volunteer. The room stilled, and there was no sound except the quiet creaking of the ship and the drip of melting snow on the roof.

Shandie frowned. "How could such a person report?"

"There is a way," the faun said. "This ship is shielded, you understand, which is why we have escaped detection. We can't escape any farther in it—I am sure the mouth of the Ambly is being well watched. But we can use sorcery on board. The warlock made breakfast, for example, and arranged for you all to keep it where it belongs. He has also crafted a device called a magic scroll. It is a very minor sorcery, and will enable our spy to send reports with very little risk of detection, and no chance of betraying our whereabouts."

Shandie turned and looked at Lord Umpily. Everyone looked at Lord Umpily.

The fat man shied like a startled horse. "Wh-what's involved?"

"Just go home," the king said. "Listen, and observe. And report. At worst, you will be converted to a Zinixo supporter, but that will not upset you, once it has happened. There is no physical danger that I can see."

"B-b-but then they will ask me where you are!" The chief of protocol was understandably pale.

"There will be no torture," the faun said. "You will willingly tell them all you know. So you must not know where we are, obviously. Nothing personal."

"I will not order any man to do this!" Shandie snapped.

"No," the king said, "it must be voluntary. If you agree, though, my lord, then we shall put you aboard one of those fishing boats. You will make your own way back to Hub, and discover as much as you can about the present state of affairs in the capital. That is all."

Umpily licked his lips and nodded to Shandie. "If that is how I may best serve you, your Majesty."

"It may be." The imperor sounded doubtful.

"Good!" the king said cheerfully, as if everything was decided. "There is another matter we must discuss, and it is no secret. Indeed, we must strive to advertise our purpose as widely as possible! Warlock Raspnex and Sailor Jarga and myself . . . Doctor Sagorn. You have three sorcerers and one genius, Sire. Zinixo has hundreds! Possibly Lith'rian and the other wardens can be inspired to come out of hiding and aid us, or perhaps not. If those were mundane odds, how would you rate your chances?"

"Hopeless!" Shandie said sharply.

"And if force will not work, what else remains?" The faun was making a guessing game out of the problem. Frowning, the imperor looked to his advisors.

Ylo's stomach rumbled loudly. No one paid any attention.

"Diplomacy is out of the question?" Umpily muttered.

"Completely." King Rap sighed. "You cannot negotiate with a craven despot. You could never trust him and he would never trust you. He does not even trust himself!"

Acopulo shot a suspicious glance at Sagorn and said, "Subversion, then?"

The dwarf rumbled impatiently. "A votary cannot be bribed—occult loyalty is absolute! If we can catch one alone and can bring greater power to bear, then yes, we can turn him, but that is the same as using force, isn't it?"

"The same odds," Shandie agreed, staring impassively at the faun's quiet amusement. "Hunt down the noncombatant sorcerers, then? The free ones you mentioned?"

"But Zinixo has been doing that for years and has vastly greater resources to continue doing so," the faun said blandly. "Do you see? Our cause is hopeless *unless we can find another weapon*! We need something that Zinixo does not have!"

Sprawled in the big chair, Sagorn had bared yellow teeth in his gruesome smile. "Bribery?"

"You can't bribe a votary!" Acopulo protested.

"No," the jotunn said complacently. "But you can bribe civilians to enlist." His pale eyes gleamed with satisfaction.

"He has it!" The faun chuckled. "Listen! In straight contest we cannot outdo Zinixo's press gang, because we are hopelessly outnumbered. The Covin will catch a dozen for every one we catch. But we may be able to *coax* the free sorcerers out of hiding and *persuade* them to aid your cause voluntarily."

Shandie leaned back and stared at him for a while, and no one else interrupted. "How?" he asked eventually. "What do I have that I can offer?"

Nothing, Ylo thought. No mundane could ever offer anything a sorcerer could need. But obviously there must be something. He was annoyed that the big rustic faun had seen something he could not. Acopulo was scarlet with frustration and Umpily almost as bad.

"Freedom," Rap said. "And security."

"Safety from Zinixo? Restore the Protocol, you mean?"

The faun shook his head. He glanced briefly at the dwarf, as if seeking consent to continue. "That's not good enough, Shandie. We're not going to restore the Protocol! Raspnex and I have talked it over, and we've decided that Emine's Protocol has failed. It served the world and the Impire well for three thousand years, but now it's dead. So we're going to make a new one, a better one. Emshandar's Protocol, we'll call it. We'll write it, and if you want your impire back, you'll sign it."

It took time to assess the idea. It was big! Ylo felt a sense of history stirring. *The Conference of* . . . of whatever this stinking hulk was called. Umpily was rubbing his pudgy hands in delight.

Ropes and spars creaked, waves rushed along the hull, and no one spoke for quite a while. Young Maya methodically hammered a wooden block on the floor, unaware that her entire future was being planned over her head.

"What new protocol?" Shandie demanded eventually.

The faun had been waiting for the invitation. "First," he said, holding up a thumb, "we'll outlaw votarism! No more loyalty spells! Not even the wardens will be allowed to enslave other sorcerers."

The imperor smiled for the first time. "Carried. That one was easy!"

Forefinger. "Second, sorcery will be declared a weapon. We'll outlaw not only the political use of magic, but any harmful use of it."

"Won't that be hard to define?"

"Is an ax hard to define?" Rap demanded, starting to sound excited. "In Krasnegar the queen's subjects may use axes to chop wood, but not to chop one another."

The imperor nodded. "Fair enough. Third?"

"We'll still need the wardens, to supervise all this. We also need a Court of Sorcery! When I cut off the supply of magic, I left West without a prerogative, so maybe West can be authorized to keep the peace and discipline transgressors. Or something."

"And fourth?"

"Well . . . That's about as far as we got." The king flashed a sheepish and oddly appealing smile, as if ashamed of his enthusiasm.

Shandie looked to the dwarf, who was swinging his little legs on the bench, his pebbly teeth showing.

"It's got promise," the little man growled. "Grunth will like it. Don't know about East, 'cause he needs his votaries to tie shoelaces for him. Hate to say this, but I think even Old Yellow-belly may support the idea."

Sagorn had been rubbing his chin, displaying little of his usual scorn. "Can you do something about the wardens themselves? I wish there were some way of keeping them honest!"

The dwarf bristled menacingly.

"They won't have votaries to back them up," King Rap said. "If they breach the peace, they'll be vulnerable to prosecution like other sorcerers."

Ylo thought that sounded like the wildest sort of hare-brained optimism he had ever heard. He could imagine his father's contempt. Consul Ylopingo had been a crafty, cynical politician, and he would have dismissed such wishful dreaming out of hand.

And yet . . . There were crafty politicians here in this stuffy, shabby deckhouse, and they were not laughing. Shandie was being his usual inscrutable self, but Acopulo looked impressed, and so did Umpily. The old count was beaming.

Abruptly the imperor rose and stalked over to a pile of discarded cloaks on a chair near the door. All eyes followed him. He rummaged for a moment, then pulled out a roll of vellum. "Lucky I brought this along, then, isn't it?"

Old Sagorn straightened in his chair with remarkable agility. "That's it?" he barked.

"This is it," Shandie agreed, holding up the roll. "The Protocol itself."

"An authentic copy?"

"I think it's the original. It has Emine's seal on it."

King Rap was squinting. "There's sorcery on it, certainly."

"Preservation spell," the dwarf rumbled. "There's one like it in the White Palace."

Shandie smiled. He walked over to Sagorn and passed him the scroll. The old man grabbed it, began unrolling hastily. Acopulo jumped up and hurried across to read over his shoulder.

"Ylo?"

"Sire?"

"Remember some of the dreadful things Warlock Lith'rian said last year? About the Protocol?"

Ylo thought back to that rainy night in the forest of Nefer Moor and shivered at the memory. "Vaguely."

The emperor frowned. "He was quite right! The Protocol *has* been perverted. It doesn't give East a free hand with the legions. It says that only East may use sorcery on them, but the context is that he must use it to restrain the legions. That is his duty!"

"Then the dragons . . ." Ylo said.

"Yes! South is supposed to restrain the dragons. Lith'rian was equally at fault. And North is supposed to restrain the jotnar—you don't see much of that in history!"

The two scholars were engrossed in reading the Protocol. Umpily was on his way to join them, but everyone else automatically looked at Raspnex. He scratched his beard, then shrugged like a boy caught in mischief. "They haven't been misbehaving too badly lately, have they?" Inasmuch as dwarves ever smiled though, he was smiling.

"Did you ever read that copy in your palace, your Omnipotence?" Shandie asked, and his eyes had found their old brilliance.

"No . . . your Majesty."

"Obviously the wording needs to be made more explicit," the faun said, and chuckled. "The wardens' responsibilities will have to be defined more strictly. Well, your Imperial Majesty? What do you think of our proposal?"

"Your New Order?" Shandie said dryly. "Your plan to reform the world?" He glanced around. "Lord Ionfeu?"

"It is a staggering concept, Sire," the old man said. He exchanged smiles with his wife. "But a worthy one!"

"Do I understand correctly, though?" Eigaze said. "This new protocol would prohibit only evil use of power? Well-meaning sorcerers could practice healing, or build bridges, or banish famine? Sorcerers need no longer hide? Sorcery could become a source of positive good in the world?" Her plump face bulged in an excited smile.

The imperor turned to the king of Krasnegar, who shrugged and nodded at the same time. "Why not?"

Shandie smiled. "Doctor Sagorn?"

The jotunn did not take his gaze from the ancient scroll he was studying. "Brilliant!"

"I agree, Sire," Acopulo said without waiting to be asked. He pointed at some wording on the vellum, and his two companions nodded excitedly.

"Ylo?"

Ylo nodded—what choice was there?

"It appears to be unanimous!" the imperor said.

"Ma'am?" the faun asked, rising to his feet.

Eshiala had apparently been engrossed in entertaining Maya, but she looked up at the king. "A just cause is a nobler purpose than mere survival," she said hesitantly, and blushed.

Shandie drew a long breath. "Well put, my dear. So, my sorcerous friend! My own view is that it's a mirage of absurd idealism. It's the most impractical, visionary, utopian dream I ever heard of. But, as my wife says, it is worth fighting for!"

"It's also the only chance we've got!" Rap said.

"That, too!" Smiling, the imperor walked across to him and shook his hand.

4

"Certainly!" Inos said. "Of course there are some things worth fighting for."

Could a thirty-five-year-old mother and a fourteen-year-old son ever agree on what those things were?

Gath was in his bed, and she was seated on the edge of it. Despite her thick fur robe, she was chilled. Her breath hung in the air like steam. Ice coated the leading between the black little casement panes. Yet many bedchambers in Krasnegar were colder. Peat glowed brightly in the hearth here, but few citizens could afford that princely luxury, especially this winter, when peat was scarce.

Only the tip of Gath's nose protruded between his woolly nightcap and a huge drift of downy quilts. Even in the tiny candlelight, the tip of it was visibly pink, but at least it was undamaged. Hostile and suspicious, one gray eye peered up at her out of nests of many-colored swellings. The other was covered with a slab of steak. The broken tooth annoyed her most, though, and he was keeping that out of sight.

"Like Dad," he said stubbornly. "Dad's worth fighting for!"

She sighed, searching for reasons that would make sense to him.

Downstairs, the dinner party continued. It was turning out to be very subdued for an affair attended by twenty-five adolescents, lacking its host and one guest. The medics said Brak would be all right, but no one could mend a boy's broken tooth except a sorcerer, and the one sorcerer she knew almost certainly wouldn't. Most likely it would abscess and have to come out. All her life, she was going to recall this day every time her son opened his mouth.

"Your father is worth fighting for, of course. But you weren't fighting for him, Gath! He wasn't there. If he was in danger from a bear, or goblins, or a gang of raiders, then you would be right to go to his aid and fight for him. That wasn't what happened. You were fighting because someone called him names, and that's not the same thing at all."

He stared at her stubbornly, saying nothing. This lecture was a father's duty, not a mother's. He probably knew exactly how long it was going to continue, and every word she was going to say. He was hurting, inside and out, his doubts worse than his wounds. Doubts about himself, doubts about her, doubts about his father.

"What exactly did Brak say?"

"He said . . . He said my dad had run away to live with the goblins. He said he had goblin wives."

"Do you believe that?"

"Course not!" But the pain in his solitary eye increased. Doubt.

"Did Brak say he was a sorcerer?"

Gath thought for a moment. "Not today."

"What do you answer if the boys say that about your father?"

"I say, 'What if he is? That's his business.' "

"That's a good answer, a very good answer, because it's true. But your father's a king, and if his royal duties require him to go away for a while, then that's his business, too! Can't you just say that?"

Silence. Hurt, angry silence.

"You could say that, Gath, and you know it! You weren't fighting for your father. You were fighting in case they thought you were afraid to fight. And usually that's very silly."

Except that this was Krasnegar, not the Impire. Gath looked like a jotunn so his peers judged him as they judged jotnar. And so did he. An imp they wouldn't bother with, but he was blond and big for his age, like a jotunn. He must think of himself as a jotunn, although he was normally the least quarrelsome boy she had ever known. Everyone knew that jotnar would accept any odds.

She tried another tack. "You must have known what was going to happen when you went to meet Brak and the others."

Pause, then a grudging whisper: "Yes. I knew."

"Then why did you go?"

"Because I knew I would go."

No hope there!

"You won't go anymore!" she said sharply. "From now on, you stay in the castle. Is that clear?"

Even with so little of his face visible, the sullen, rebellious expression was obvious.

"Is that clear?" she repeated.

"Yes."

But the fight with Brak had happened within the castle, so house arrest wouldn't do much to solve the problem. There were dozens of adolescent jotnar living in the palace, and townsfolk could stream in and out as they pleased. She couldn't declare a state of siege just to stop kids brawling. Not in Krasnegar. And if word got around that the queen was protecting her son, then he would be fair game for everyone, even imps.

"So your father is away on business? There's nothing odd about that! Other boys' fathers go out of town—trappers, whalers, fishermen—"

"He didn't tell anyone."

Ah! "Since when has your father had to ask Brak's permission to go on a trip?"

The humor didn't work; she hadn't expected it to. *Gath's* permission was what they were discussing now, even if Gath himself didn't know it.

"He didn't have time to say good-bye to you, dear. I told you—he had to leave on very short notice. He didn't know he was going when you went to bed." She thought back to that tragic evening. "Did you? Did you know?"

Gath blinked. "I can't see tomorrows."

"No, but I recall you looked sort of surprised at one point. Did you suspect?"

"Maybe. I'm not sure. Wasn't sure. Maybe a little, I did."

A big disappointment might throw a longer shadow than little things, and a father's disappearance was a very big disappointment to a fourteen-year-old. Rap had promised the whole of the following day to the children and been gone when they awoke.

She sighed. "Listen, you big lummox! Maybe one day you'll

be king of Krasnegar. Kings have to keep their private lives separate from their royal duties, and you're going to have to learn that. Your father doesn't go around fighting everybody!''

''If someone said bad things about you, he would!''

He probably would. It was much easier to imagine Rap throwing a punch than it was to think of him calling out the guard and laying charges of lese majesty. That was certainly not an option for Gath when his friends jeered. No hope there, either.

She tried another tack. ''I know he broke a promise to you. Do you think he would do that, or stay away this long, or miss your birthday—except for something really important?''

''No.''

''Well, it is important! Terribly important! I can't tell you what it is. I don't even know all the details myself, but I trust your father, and so should you! I told you he'd gone away for a couple of days. Then I told you that it was going to be longer. I couldn't tell anyone else that, just you and Kadie, because he sent me word by sorcery! Now do you understand?''

He nodded, almost imperceptibly under the covers. She shivered as the cold worked deeper through her furs; she wriggled icy toes in her boots.

''Gath, you know he's a sorcerer! You know things that Brak and those louts don't know! You know that your father went away by sorcery—or you can guess he did. He'll come back by sorcery, too, as soon as he can. Stupid Brak and the others can only think that the harbor was frozen, so therefore he must have run off to the goblins. That isn't true, and you know it.''

''Can I say so?''

''You can tell them they don't know what they're talking about.''

''I did.'' Gath closed his eye.

Oh, my poor unhappy baby!

She lifted the second piece of steak from the plate by the bed and placed it over the swollen lid. She kissed his forehead.

''It isn't easy being fourteen, Gath. I was fourteen once, and I remember. I think it may be even harder for boys than it is for girls. It's worse than being fifteen, even. You're big and strong already, and you have prescience. You can hurt people, even bigger people like Brak. Strength and power bring responsibility.'' She was about to demand a promise that he wouldn't fight anymore, and then common sense told her not to be crazy.

Manhood was the problem, the manhood he looked for whenever he saw himself in a mirror, the manhood that was much farther off than he could believe . . . the manhood that would never be the universal answer he thought it would be. And boyhood betrayed.

She stood up. "Gath, I've known your father a lot longer than you have. He's a fine man, Gath, a noble man. He's a father to be proud of, in every way. I'm sure he doesn't want you getting hurt just because a young jotunn thug filthy-mouths him."

She got no answer, because the remark was irrelevant. Gath had been fighting for Gath, not for Rap.

"I know he wouldn't have missed your birthday unless he had to. I know he wouldn't have gone away unless he believed that what he was doing was very, very important."

She took the candle, shielding it with her hand as she walked across the room.

"Good night, my darling. I still love you. You were wrong to fight Brak. I'm sorry you were foolish, but I'm proud that you are brave."

She heard a quiet sniff as she closed the door. She bit her lip. *Rap, whatever you are up to had better be worth this!*

Newer world:
       . . . but something ere the end,
    Some work of noble note, may yet be done,
    Not unbecoming men that strove with Gods.

       Come, my friends,
    'Tis not too late to seek a newer world.

                                   Tennyson, *Ulysses*

❮ THREE ❯

Parts to play

1

Nobody seemed to be thinking about lunch, except Ylo. *White Impress* rolled gently on the slate-gray waters, heading from nowhere to nowhere, and he sat alone and neglected in a corner.

At the far end of the deckhouse the politicians were at work—the imperor, the king of Krasnegar, Sagorn, Acopulo, and Ionfeu—all clamoring like a verbal smith's shop as they heatedly shaped a new protocol to rule Pandemia for the next few thousand years. When the scholars' bickering became too personal, then king or imperor would crack a joke. The others would laugh respectfully and calm down. Old Ionfeu spoke less than anyone, but the others always seemed to agree with him when he did. It was an exercise in dreaming, but perhaps dreams were all that remained now.

Hardgraa had gone below and was undoubtedly catnapping, being a veteran campaigner who knew how to take sleep when it was available. Off by themselves, impress and countess chatted quietly, watching over the child dozing on a nearby sofa, under a blanket. The Jarga woman was still steering the ship, her iron endurance more confirmation that she had occult power to sustain her. The dwarf stood outside in the cold, resting his forearms on the rail and staring stonily underneath it at the horizon.

He might be taking a last occult look at the fishermen's smack now fading into the skyline mist. Lord Umpily had departed an

73

hour or so ago, borne off in that cockleshell at the price of a gold crown. With him he had carried a magic scroll and many false good wishes. As soon as he had been out of earshot, Shandie had said, "How long do you suppose he's got?"

King Rap had shrugged. "A week if we're lucky."

So everyone was busy except Ylo, who had nothing to entertain him except the realization that it was almost twenty-four hours since he last ate. Of course he could ask one of the sorcerers to magic up a meal for him, but he wasn't going to. He would get himself laughed at for oversleeping and missing breakfast.

The best way to take his mind off his stomach was just to study Eshiala. Guard her? Oh yes, he would guard her most jealously! That would be his role in the war! She was listening intently to Countess Eigaze, her profile showing the perfect classic beauty of the statue in the Imperial Library, with an expression as inscrutable. He remembered her happy smile in the pool's preflection. He would make her smile like that, often. All the time! The pool had promised her with daffodils, but that did not mean he could not have her now, at midwinter, and still be her lover at daffodil time. He'd never tried a really long relationship like that before. It would be an interesting experience, and she was certainly worth it.

The door slammed as Warlock Raspnex came in. Countess and impress looked up briefly; no one else seemed to notice.

The little man clumped across to a table near Ylo and then glowered at him. "Come here, lad." He laid his elbows on the table, and had no need to stoop to do so.

Ylo felt shaky as he rose to obey the order—not from the motion of the ship, just from lack of food. But he was certainly not going to beg from a dwarf, not even a warlock dwarf.

"Your Omnipotence?"

"Bah! I told you that rigmarole's defunct! You know my name; use it."

"Of course, Raspnex," Ylo said. "Do please call me Ylo." He rested fingertips on the table and smiled down at unfriendly gray eyes colder than pebbles on a shingle beach.

"I'll call you anything I want. Now, I need your help."

In return for a snack, perhaps? "Help?" Ylo inquired uneasily. "What help can I give to a great sorcerer?"

"Well, not much." Raspnex ran fingers like chisels through

his iron-gray hair. "And I'm not a great sorcerer, I'm a middling-good sorcerer. What I meant is I need to use your memory. I'd rather you agreed to let me do it than make me use force on you, but I will if I must. We need a conferral."

"Huh?"

"A deed, a charter. Something imposing-looking with the imperial seal on it, transferring land. Shandie said you'd handled a thousand of them recently."

"Er, yes. But I'm no scribe! And it takes days to do all that lettering and illumination and—"

"No, it doesn't. Can you remember one where a sizable estate was gifted directly from imperial domain?"

Feeling very uneasy, Ylo said, "Emshandar deeded the Honor of Mosrace to the Marquis of—"

The dwarf slapped an oversize hand on the table. "Look there!" He removed his hand. "Now, think of that document. Pretend it's lying there and you're reading it."

"I haven't got that kind of memory!" Ylo felt panic rising.

"Yes, you do, you just don't know how to use it. Keep looking. Think about the deed. Don't think about anything else."

Ylo was shaking and sweating. He didn't want this ill-shaped little monster prying around in his mind, seeing things he shouldn't, secrets like the preflecting pool and—

"For Evil's sake get your mind off that woman!" Raspnex rumbled. "Can't you at least wait until her husband's gone? Your skull sounds like elk pasture in rutting time. Now think about that deed or I'll make you think about it."

Gods preserve us! Wasn't this the sort of misuse of sorcery the new protocol was going to stamp out?

"I expect it is." Raspnex sighed roughly. "But we don't have it in place yet. You've got a mind like a butterfly, know that? No control, no discipline. I'll give you one more chance. How does it begin?"

Ylo closed his eyes and thought. *We, Emshandar the Fourth, by* . . . He opened his eyes. Yes! Very faintly, he could see the big historiated capitals and the black text following like smoke. He began to read the words aloud, and even as he did so, they flowed and solidified on a sheet of vellum congealing underneath. Incredible! He would never have believed he had remembered so much of something he had merely glanced at months before. He stumbled a few times when he came to the finer print, but that was mostly a description of Mosrace itself, which would not be important to the warlock, who only wanted the general pattern and would obviously change the details to suit his own . . .

"You're daydreaming again," Raspnex growled. "But it's good enough. I can tidy it up." He snatched the parchment and began rolling it.

"That's quite a trick," Ylo said admiringly. "You could deed me title to any estate in the Impire!"

"Can't think why I'd want to."

"Of course, you'd have to put a matching copy in the Imperial records."

The little man looked up at him sourly. "I won't risk it at the moment, because of the Covin, but it's been done often enough."

"What! You're serious?"

"You ever heard of a dwarf joking?" Raspnex stamped off to join the male discussion party, leaving Ylo with his mouth open, wondering how many of the papers in the state archives were occult fakes.

At that moment, Eshiala rose and headed for the door. She glanced at him as she went by. He thought she was going to speak, then she changed her mind and swept by him as if he did not exist, being the Ice Impress. She seemed unaffected by the sudden stress of becoming an outlaw, but then she was probably under much less strain now than she had been the day before, playing for an audience in the Rotunda.

Gorgeous creature! Maybe even worth a dukedom. He knew if he were offered a clear choice now, he might yet take the woman. Even if he could enjoy only one long, lingering session of lovemaking he might. The very thought of her made his flesh burn. And Shandie was going to go off and fight his impossible campaign and leave his signifer to guard the royal family in his absence. From now until the daffodils bloomed—there was a challenge to speed a man's heart!

Now the countess was alone, minding Maya and quietly munching candies. Well! She must have asked one of the sorcerers to produce those for her. Trust Eigaze! His mouth watered. He went across to the shabby armchair Eshiala had just left.

"May I join you, Aunt?"

Her plump face creased in a smile. "Of course! Have a chocolate?"

He accepted eagerly. "You are bearing up very well, if I may say so."

"Oh, but this is exciting! I have never seen history being made before. I'm old enough, of course, but I've never been involved."

"Not that old," he countered automatically. He hoped that it was history that was being written in this grubby saloon, and not farce. "The historic Conference of the *White Impress*?"

"Winterfest, 2998!" She chuckled. " 'Who was present at the conference? Why was it held on a ferryboat? Discuss how Emshandar's Protocol differed from Emine's.' Generations of school children will curse us for adding to their labors!"

"Can you tell me where we're going?" he asked.

She looked surprised and automatically reached for another candy. "I suppose so—now Lord Umpily's gone. Rap said it was better if he did not know . . . just in case. It's not that they don't trust him, of course."

"Of course." But Ylo wondered if that was true. Umpily's loyalty was unquestionable, but he was not the most discreet of men. In a war against the Covin, one careless word would bring disaster.

"Have another chocolate. Not his fault, you understand, but no one can keep secrets from sorcerers."

"Yes, I understand."

Eigaze moved back to safer conversational territory. "As to where we're going, you know the place." Her eyes twinkled. "In fact, it probably belongs to you! It's called Yewdark House. Remember it?"

"Vaguely." He recalled sunny childhood days and misty memories of ponies and sailboats.

"That's why Shandie wants you to accompany us, I think. You can be our host."

"One of my aunts lived there?"

Eigaze nodded wistfully. "Lady Onnly. She and I were at school together. I visited her a few times at Yewdark. I remember you and your mother there once, when you were very small. But she didn't live there very long, Onnly didn't. It has rather a bad reputation, you know."

Aha! More memories surged to the surface. "What sort of reputation?"

"Er . . . It's supposed to be haunted." Eigaze chuckled and quickly ate two chocolates.

No, not haunted. Ylo recalled his oldest brother telling him certain stories about Yewdark, but Yyan had not been spinning a ghost yarn. He had spoken of omens, magic, prophecy, and Ylo himself. Yyan would have been about fifteen then, perhaps, and Ylo about nine, a good age for baiting. Naturally, Ylo had rushed off to complain to his father, and the consul had reluctantly confirmed the tales, while insisting that they had no importance. He had then forbidden all his sons to discuss them and given Yyan the thrashing of a lifetime to emphasize the point. It was that thrashing that had fixed the episode so firmly in Ylo's memory.

"Haunted by whom? Or what?"

"Oh, I have no idea. It's been empty for years, because of some fantastic lawsuit. Such a shame, because it used to be such a beautiful place."

Dear old Lady Eigaze was trying to change the subject, and normally she was far too skilled at conversation to get herself trapped like that—curious! What had she remembered?

Chairs scraped over in the corner. The conference was breaking up. The light was too poor for writing. Beyond the windows, the shore was drawing closer.

"Ion and I called in there a couple of weeks ago," Eigaze said, in suspiciously vague tones. "On our way back to Hub, you know. One of the horses went lame practically at the gate. The weather was bad, and it was late. We called in to see if anyone we knew lived there now and might offer us a bed for the night."

"And who does live there now?"

"No one. Well, remember Ukka?"

"No."

"Onnly's housekeeper. She's still there. Old as the Protocol." Eigaze took another candy so that she could chew and not say more.

"Living there alone?"

"Apparently. Mad as a cornered badger. Ah, Ion!"

The old count sank onto the sofa, carefully not disturbing the sleeping princess. "Yes, my dear?"

"Tell Ylo about that lawsuit. Yewdark must already belong to him, mustn't it?"

The gaunt old man's stoop showed even when he was sitting—he leaned forward, always. He seemed to peer at whomever he was speaking to, which gave his conversation a sense of urgency. He smiled wearily at Ylo under his snowy eyebrows. "Well, it certainly belonged to the Yllipos, and Shandie told us he was going to restore their properties to you. So I suppose it is yours, lad. Or it will be, when this mess is cleared up."

Some mess! That bloodthirsty old scoundrel Emshandar was barely a whole day dead, and how things had changed since then!

"But the lawsuit?" Eigaze said quickly.

"Oh, that? Well, even the closest-knit families have their squabbles, you know. Apparently there was disagreement over who owned Yewdark, and it went to court."

"So?" Ylo recalled vaguely that the estate had been in the family for a very long time, which meant several centuries by Yllipo standards. Records could become very confused in such cases. There were no family quarrels now, with only one Yllipo left alive.

"Well, when the Yllipo Conspiracy . . . I mean, three or four years ago, when . . ." The old man floundered.

"When Emshandar murdered Ylo's family," Eigaze said firmly.

"Well, yes. Most of the property was attaindered, you know. Consequently, the crown succeeded to all existing legal actions. Which meant that the imperor was suing himself in this case."

"That's absurd!" Ylo said.

Ionfeu smiled sadly. "But lawyers love such absurdities! The defendant claimed that the imperor could not be sued without his permission, and the plaintiff insisted that the imperor could sue anyone he liked—stalemate! I'm sure the barristers expected to build careers out of it. Anyway, the estate sank into a legal swamp, and it's just sitting there, deserted. When Shandie asked if anyone knew of a good bolthole for us, Eigaze thought of Yewdark. It's perfect! Shandie agrees."

A country mansion on the shores of Cenmere, about a day's ride from the capital? Ylo nodded thoughtfully. "Isn't it a little too close to Hub?"

"That was discussed," the proconsul said, "but King Rap

thinks it's a good idea to stay fairly close, and the warlock agreed. They should know how Zinixo's mind works, if anyone does. Nowhere is really safe, you know.''

"But . . ." Ylo felt oddly uneasy at the idea of holing up in Yewdark, and he was not sure why. "This Mistress, er . . .''

"Ukka," Eigaze said, beaming bravely. "She was your aunt's housekeeper, and she was left in charge, and she's still there.''

"Mad, you said?"

"Well . . . odd. She's lived alone a long time. But she was quite delighted when we told her there was one Yllipo left alive. She'll be overjoyed to see you.''

"Did she mention the Sisters?"

Eigaze shot a brief glance at her husband. "She . . . she may have done. Who were they, do you know?''

"They were sorcerers," Ylo said. "At least, I think they were. Sorceresses, I mean. They lived at Yewdark—before Aunt Onnly." He wished he could remember more of Yyan's stories. "They prophesied.''

"Prophesied what?" the count demanded.

"Disasters." Ylo racked his brains. "Disasters that I might or might not be going to survive.''

"What sort of disasters?"

"The destruction of the family."

"Oh! Well, that did sort of happen, didn't it?"

"And the overthrow of the Impire."

Eigaze and Ionfeu turned to each other in shock.

That seemed to have happened, too, didn't it?

2

White Impress was gliding toward a jetty, under cover of a fortunate flurry of snow. There were no other vessels in sight, and the shore itself was heavily wooded. A few gables and tall chimneypots had shown above the trees before the snow started. That, apparently, was Yewdark.

Eshiala stood within the deckhouse, steadying Maya, who had climbed upon a chair to see. Maya was ignoring the scenery, being much more interested in watching the men running around the deck while the sailor woman shouted directions. Blocks squeaked as the sail was furled. Apart from Jarga herself, the faun seemed to be the only person aboard who knew anything about ships.

"Obviously the place is still deserted," Countess Eigaze remarked with a cheerfulness that sounded forced. "No one's walked on the pier since the snow started."

"It doesn't look as if it's been used for years," Eshiala agreed, feeling real joy.

"Candy?" Maya demanded hopefully, having learned that the countess was an unfailing supply of chocolate.

"Ask nicely, dear." Eshiala thought her child would soon be as fat as the old lady herself.

"Here you are, darling. No, it hasn't, I expect—been used, that is. You'll find Ukka amusing. A little strange, but that's to be expected, living alone for so long. Life will be rather dull here after the court." She made the statement a question.

"It can't be too dull for me!" Mother and daughter alone, far from the odious court! Eshiala felt guilty at the prospect, as if the Gods had answered prayers she had not dared to ask. There was going to be one problem, though. No—two problems. She wished that Shandie could stay with them, also.

She really did.

Given time together beyond the reach of pomp and duty, she thought she could learn to know her husband properly, and learn to love him. And he, perhaps . . .

The other problem went past the window at that moment and flashed her a toothy smile. Even unshaven and in nondescript civilian clothes, Ylo was still astonishingly eye-catching.

She hoped she had not returned the smile, but she must have reacted, for she sensed the countess stiffen, as much as anyone of her baggy build could stiffen. The old lady was shrewd, and she knew Ylo. Even if she had not heard of his reputation, she must suspect, surely?

"It will be very dull for all of us," she murmured thoughtfully.

"Better to be bored than enslaved by sorcery."

"Yes, of course. Er . . . Ionfeu and I will have to use our own names, of course, because Mistress Ukka knows us. The warlock made out the conferral in the name of Lord Eshern, so Ylo will be Lord Eshern and we shall have to think up another name for you."

Mistress Nobody, Eshiala thought. They would insist on giving her a spurious title, of course. They all thought of her as impress now, but in her own mind she was still only a grocer's daughter.

The ship nudged gently against the ramshackle jetty. The king of Krasnegar jumped over the rail, holding a rope.

"The warlock said he would go ashore and scout," Eigaze remarked. "We shall have rather a difficult walk up to the house, I'm afraid. As I recall, it is quite a steep path. It will be snowy. Overgrown, too, probably."

Stealing someone's house seemed very wrong behavior, somehow. It was not the way grocers' daughters were brought up. Perhaps aristocrats had other standards. Even if Yewdark legally belonged to Shandie, as imperor, his grandfather had stolen it when he persecuted the Yllipos. Grocers' daughters did not comprehend that sort of action, either.

Behind her the door opened and closed; boots sounded on the threadbare rugs.

"His majesty," Eigaze murmured. She took Maya's hand. "Jump down, dear, and we'll go and look for some more chocolate."

"You got some in that bag!" Maya protested, but she went off with her new honorary aunt.

Shandie moved close. Eshiala smiled, and he embraced her awkwardly. He was not accustomed to displaying affection in public—or at almost any other time, for that matter.

"There it is, my dear. Safe haven for you and our daughter. What you wanted." His face was giving away nothing. It never did.

She had hurt him that morning. She had not meant to. She hurt him far too often, always without meaning to. She did not know how not to hurt, somehow. Nor did he. They were both well meaning, and both clumsy.

"It would be a happier haven if you could stay and share it with us."

"Of course it would, but that is not possible. You know that. Time is not on our side. We must act quickly."

She nodded. The Impire came before the impress, of course. "I understand." She didn't, though—not properly. She never would.

"I don't know how long it will be. Months, I am sure."

"Will you tell me where you are going?"

"I haven't even decided yet. And even if . . . But we have not discussed it yet. We need to get you settled first. That has priority."

He wouldn't have told her, anyway. Perhaps that made good sense, because if the Covin discovered her, then it would force her to tell. But the refusal still hurt.

"I understand."

"And the sooner we can split up, the better, too. The Covin will be hunting for a group of a dozen or so. We must separate."

Again she repeated her mantra. "I understand."

"We all serve the Impire as we can. And yours is the most important job of all—to preserve the line of succession."

When she looked at her child she saw a little girl, not a line of succession.

"If I am caught," Shandie said harshly, "then of course I shall be perverted to serving the dwarf. I expect I shall send for you then. I just hope it never comes to that."

And the dwarf would enslave Eshiala, also. Perhaps she would be happier then, playing her role under sorcerous compulsion. Her loyalty to the sorcerer would override all her other loyalties—to Maya, to her husband, to the Impire. Then she might be free of her doubts and sense of failure. Did a puppet feel stage fright? "We must pray," she muttered.

"Of course. The old couple will be good company for you. We couldn't have found better. The warlock has supplied money—I wish the Imperial Treasury could turn out gold the way he can! You can hire a few servants, live quietly. Discourage visitors, of course, but the houses around here are usually deserted in winter. And Ylo will be a good defender."

Eshiala drew a deep breath and steeled herself to make a protest. Shandie must have felt her move, and misunderstood. Naturally.

"Not that I anticipate danger!" he said hurriedly. "But you need a strong young man to keep order among the servants and so on. So that they know there can be no nonsense. He will have to walk into Faintown tomorrow and buy horses and food and hire people . . ."

It had all been carefully planned. The trouble was that no one had asked her to share in the planning. That was part of what was bothering her. The realization made her feel petty for being annoyed, but perhaps it also steeled her to voice a complaint about the bigger problem.

"Ylo?" she said.

"It has to be him or Hardgraa," Shandie said with a trace of impatience. "The old fellow would be heartbroken if I left him behind now, after all these years."

"Of course. Your safety is the most important thing, of course. You will be in far greater danger than we will."

Shandie himself had warned her of Ylo's reputation. She must not confess her own self-doubts, her terror that she would not be able to resist his glib tongue and roguish smile, even when she knew that he was only philandering. She must not inflate her own misgivings into a major quarrel between the two men.

"Actually Ylo's by far the better horseman," Shandie said. "In that way I suppose it would make more sense . . ." Suddenly he realized. His face did not change, except for his eyes, but he knew. *"What has he said?"*

Danger! There was death in that imperial glare. "Nothing!"

"One word! If he has spoken one word of disrespect, I will have his head!"

"No! Nothing! He has said nothing!" Now she had started lying to her husband.

Fury seeped into his expression then, as if he had been holding it back by an effort of will and was relaxing. "Then what! What is bothering you? You will have the count and countess to support you!"

He did not understand! How could she possibly explain? Had Shandie ever been afraid of anything? Did he know what fear was? "Darling, listen! A man like Ylo doesn't need to *say* anything! Not a word. He can convey everything he wants just by raising an eyebrow. Oh . . . a woman knows, always. It's like the caliph."

"The caliph?" Shandie echoed, bewildered. "What's he got to do with it?"

"He's a threat, isn't he? Even if he does nothing, just because he's there the Impire has to keep its defenses up, doesn't it?"

"Er. Yes."

"Well, when men like Ylo are around, a woman has to keep her defenses up. That's all. He doesn't *say* anything or *do* anything. All he needs to do is smile!" She smiled, then, and put her arms around him. "Don't worry! I can handle Ylo." Liar, liar!

"Where in the world did you learn that about the caliph?"

"From Marshal Ithy, at dinner the other night."

"Amazing. Yes, I see what you mean, then. Ylo won't take 'no' for an answer?"

"Not for long. But don't worry about it. It will always be 'no.' I promise!" Ylo at mealtimes. Ylo escorting her wherever she went. Ylo smiling, joking, flirting. He was always so convincing, so sure of himself. She was always so uncertain.

Shandie nodded a few times. "I should have asked you, of course. Fool that I am! Why didn't I think to ask you? Well, if you would rather have Hardgraa, then so you shall. Excuse me."

He turned and stamped to the door.

Heart pounding, Eshiala stared out the window. She had made Shandie change his mind! She knew how rarely that happened. She had won! How many times did that make? In the last two days, she had asserted herself more often than she had done in all the years since he had first walked into her father's store, back in Thumble. How she wished she had asserted herself then, instead of letting her parents bully her into accepting him! She would have been much happier had she married a plowman or the miller's apprentice.

Still, now she felt a surge of triumph, mixed with a huge relief. Shandie trusted her—it had probably never occurred to him not to. She did not trust herself, that was the real trouble! She did not believe she could have resisted Ylo. He would have smiled and talked, flattered and joked, teased and sworn oaths—and eventually he would have won. Sooner or later he would have found a way around her defenses.

Probably sooner.

3

Shandie emerged from the deckhouse and announced loudly that he had changed his mind—Signifer Ylo would accompany him, and Hardgraa would remain to guard the impress. Scrambling back over the rail, Rap watched the reactions with some amusement. Although he made a point of never prying into other people's thoughts, in this case he could read them quite clearly on the two faces.

Hardgraa was driven by a fierce personal loyalty, and Shandie was heading off into danger without his bodyguard—that was folly! The old warrior's urge to protest struggled with lifelong obedience, but before either gained a clear advantage, he felt a stab of alarm that he was being discarded because of his age; then came insight into the probable reasons for the change, which brought a surge of satisfaction and pride, and finally a quick rationalization that the baby princess was even more valuable now than Shandie, and not least to Shandie himself. Therefore the new posting was the greater honor. It was all over before he completed his salute.

Young Ylo's emotions traveled a different road, but just as quickly. His first reaction was disbelief: *It is prophesied!* Then came anger and chagrin—the promiscuous rascal was totally besotted with Eshiala at the moment. They were followed by cold calculation: If he believed the prophecy, he must now assume that he was destined to return to her before daffodil time and would therefore survive any dangers he might encounter in the next few months. Finally he, too, resorted to rationalization—an adventurous journey with the emperor would be much more interesting than baby-sitting a group of civilians in a lonely country house. So Ylo also smiled. The young rake took life very much as it came, Rap concluded, but self-interest was always uppermost. He never considered other people.

Raspnex's stocky image flickered into view in the ambience, smirking. *"He's not as stupid as I thought, that imp."* He meant Shandie, of course.

"He's in love," Rap replied. *"That explains everything. You going to go and take a look around?"*

"Might as well do it from here. Nobody'll notice with all that din going on."

There was no mundane din. Water slapped sleepily at the pilings of the jetty, and ropes squeaked. Far away a temple bell tolled, audible only when the wind veered a little, muffled by the drifting snow. Big fluffy flakes were flying and the short winter day was already drawing to a close, the sun a white disk above the trees.

Nor did the warlock refer to occult noise. All day the ambience had been creepily silent, as Rap had noticed every time he had emerged from the shielded deckhouse. Probably Zinixo had ordered the Covin to do nothing except listen and keep watch.

There was still no sorcery active, but a quick scan showed Rap what the warlock had already detected—a strong outpouring of grief off to the east. Proconsul Ionfeu had said that the village of Moggly lay about half a league away in that direction. Probably the entire population was attending a memorial service for Emshandar, because the emotion rose and fell in unison. That would explain the bell, too, and it would serve to muddy the Covin's vigil.

"If you think you can risk it."

"Certainly." Raspnex's image brightened—or became louder, for there were no exact words to describe the ambience. Either way, he was much less conspicuous than Rap would have been in surveying the big house in the trees.

In the slow-moving world of mundanes, Shandie was still discussing his change of plan with his subordinates. Sailor Jarga headed for the deckhouse, her work done for the moment.

"You will have to be Lord Eshern," the imperor told Hardgraa.

The centurion pulled a face. "I'm not a very convincing lord, sire."

Shandie smiled. "Perhaps not—although you will be before I'm done with you! I'm planning to make you at least an earl. The housekeeper knows Proconsul Ionfeu, though. I'd better ask his Omnipotence to change the name on the title deed."

"They don't need to produce Lord Eshern himself," Ylo said. "Why not let her Majesty be Lord Eshern's wife, and keep his fictitious lordship out of it?"

Astute young fellow, Rap thought.

Shandie nodded. "That's very good! They probably won't ever need to produce the document anyway, and that way if they get any awkward questions, they can always refer them to the imaginary Lord Eshern. Excellent! I'll go and tell them."

"What can you make out?" Rap asked.

"One old woman cooking supper," the dwarf said. *"Huge, fancy place. More rooms than the crystal mines of Traz. Sort of comfy, though."* To a dwarf, "comfy" meant "well worn."

"No tracks in the snow. It was shielded, once upon a time."

"That could be useful!"

"Naw. It's threadbare. It'll muddy things a little, I suppose, if they start a house-by-house search."

"Even Zinixo can't try that unless he already has a rough idea of where they are," Rap protested, and hoped he was right.

Lord Umpily had been led to believe that *White Impress* was heading north, to the far shore. When, inevitably, he was apprehended by the Covin and his loyalty turned, he might divert attention away from the vicinity of Hub. On the other hand, he might not.

For the thousandth time that day, Rap pondered the impossibility of fighting a whole army of sorcerers. He could not imagine a more hopeless task. On the other hand, he could not imagine any way to avoid it under the present circumstances. If duty and remorse did not impel him to make the effort, then the need to defend Inos would. She also would be on the dwarf's list of foes, just because long ago she had foiled his attempt to murder Rap. There could be no truce with such a madman. There was no defense except attack.

On the ineffable plane of the ambience, Raspnex twitched, or flickered, or flared—he registered surprise.

"Something wrong?" Rap demanded.

"Something odd. Looks like the old woman's expecting visitors."

"Impossible!"

"She's lit a fire in the great hall, and candles, too. Ah!"

"Ah what?" Rap said crossly. The temptation to use his own farsight was almost irresistible.

The dwarf chuckled. *"Maybe the place is haunted, at that! There's something . . . Two somethings!"*

"Ghosts? Wraiths? Can sorcerers see ghosts?"

"Never have before, but there's sure something there. They're hiding from me . . . Nothing serious. Can't corner them without using real power. Forget them. They're harmless."

"You're sure?"

"Quite sure."

Rap hesitated. If anyone mentioned wraiths to Shandie, he would balk at leaving his wife and child here, and the fugitives' hunt for safe refuge would have to start again from scratch. Every hour they spent on Cenmere increased the risk, for Zinixo must know by now how they had escaped, and his minions would be scanning the lake for suspicious ships. A vessel that showed to vision and not farsight would definitely class as suspicious.

Wraiths were old wives' tales, weren't they? Rap had never seen one or even heard any convincing stories of them. On the other hand, nobody was more hard-headed than Raspnex, and if he said there were ghosts at Yewdark, there probably were. How would the impress and her companions feel if they discovered they had been tossed into a sanctuary that contained ghosts?

"We'd better warn them," he thought uneasily.

"Naw! There's no danger. Here—look." The warlock opened his mind, so that Rap could see through his vastly greater powers.

It was an astonishingly trusting thing to do, especially for a dwarf. It was also an eerie and unpleasant experience. The soul of a dwarf was alien, cryptic, and cold. It was chilled by lurking threats and connotations of stone—ramparts and bastions and dim-lit tunnels. The world seemed much darker and less friendly to Raspnex than it ever had to Rap; it was filled with hard edges and stern duty; it lacked cheer or comradeship. Its values were grim, practical, and unimaginative.

Trying to ignore this uncanny discernment, Rap inspected the ramshackle old mansion. As the warlock had said, it was a sprawling edifice, much of it in poor repair, dusty and deserted, although still furnished. Faint residues of ancient shielding blurred his view here and there, but nowhere was it strong enough to defeat the warlock's farsight. Once this rambling chateau would have been a glittering palace, but wind and weather had gnawed it ragged, and the erstwhile jeweled gardens had rioted into tangled wilderness. A couple of very cluttered rooms in the basement were obviously in use, and there an old woman was boiling a pot on a stove.

Upstairs in the main hall, a fire crackling in the great hearth had not yet consumed all its kindling. Dust covers had been dragged off chairs and piled behind a sofa; candles had been set out and recently lit, although the sun had not set yet. Obviously the housekeeper expected visitors. As Raspnex had already remarked, the long driveway was cloaked in untrodden snow, so she could have received no mundane warning.

And somewhere, something else . . . The sense of awareness was faint, barely detectable. Amusement? Expectancy? In the rafters? Then, as Rap tried to draw near, eagerness became alarm, and the presences vanished. A moment later he realized that they had moved somewhere else. He could chase them all night and never discover their true nature. He detected no evil intent—in fact, almost no intent at all, almost no intelligence. Just disembodied emotion, lost memories, dead hopes.

He pulled back to his own mind with relief, and the chilly winter evening became warmer and friendlier again. Hardgraa, with professional caution, was unpacking the baggage and inspecting everything the warlock had prepared: food and gold and spare garments. The women were emerging from the deckhouse.

"Weird!" Rap said. He wondered if Yewdark was a Zinixo trap, and discarded the idea at once. The man's mind contained no humor whatsoever. If he knew where the fugitives were, he would strike at them instantly, and with all his power. Practical jokes and simulated ghosts were not dwarvish, and certainly not Zinixo.

"But harmless." Raspnex had already dismissed the wraiths as being of no practical importance.

"I think so. There isn't enough power there to do anything. Just a sort of yearning. Is that how you see it?"

"See them, you mean. I think there's two. But nothing to worry about."

"The sisters that Ylo mentioned? Can sorcerers survive death?" Once Rap had been a superlative sorcerer; indeed he had been more than a sorcerer, a demigod. In those days he would have known the answers to such questions.

"Dunno. I don't intend to try."

"You will go and inspect this place, your Omnipotence?" Shandie asked.

"We already did," the dwarf said, gesturing up at Rap with a horny thumb. "One old woman, no visitors, and enough space to lose that kid of yours a hundred times a day."

Shandie turned to Rap.

Choking back a few lingering misgivings, Rap said, "It looks ideal. The only problem might be if the neighbors get nosy."

"Country gentry?" Shandie shook his head. "Snub one of them once and they'll all stay away forever." He spun around to Hardgraa. "Ready to go, then?"

"Yessir."

"I think I'll come with you and see you all settled."

"No, you won't!" the warlock snapped, with typical dwarvish tact. "The more footprints you put in that snow, the more suspicious this place will seem. They're grown-ups, imp. They don't need you to wipe their noses for them.''

The imperor's expression did not change, and only a sorcerer could have know what that self-control cost him. He turned to Ionfeu.

''Proconsul, no family had served our house more loyally than yours these many generations, yet none of our forbears ever placed greater onus upon yours than that we now place upon you and your dear wife. We charge you both to guard and cherish your impress and the princess imperial, bidding you protect them in this hour of danger as if they were of your own blood.''

The bent old aristocrat straightened as well as he was able. ''Sire, your trust honors us beyond words. I swear that the well-being of your wife and child is as safe in our hands as it could be in any.''

Apparently moved beyond words, Eigaze attempted a curtsey on the slippery, snowy deck.

''And you, Centurion,'' Shandie said, ''for many years have guarded our person well. Now we give into your charge those whom we value dearer yet, and we do not doubt your dedication to their welfare.''

Hardgraa saluted, his eyes filling with tears. Rap was impressed. He would never fully understand the strange bond between imps and their imperor, but he could see that Shandie did. He knew how to use it, too.

But then the imperor turned to his wife, and was suddenly at a loss for words. He opened and closed his mouth several times before he blurted out, ''My dearest! It may be a long time before we meet again. May the Gods be with you.''

''And with you, sire,'' she muttered. ''I fear you travel a hard road, and a long one. Maya, say bye-bye to Daddy.''

''Bye-bye,'' the child echoed, not understanding or caring much.

As Shandie stooped to hug his daughter, Ylo stepped forward into the midst of the silence. Bowing, he took Eshiala's hand and raised it to his lips.

''Crocuses in springtime,'' he said softly. ''Light without shade.''

Apparently the imperor did not hear the words, nor notice the sudden flush on his wife's cheeks.

But Rap did, and he broke his personal code of ethics by

reaching into the woman's mind to find the reason. It was a poem, probably elvish, and Ylo had misquoted it.

> *Daffodils in springtime,*
> *dancing, eager,*
> *light without shade,*
> *like lovers.*

4

Why could she never be happy? Why did she feel so guilty? Had the myriad Gods Themselves in all Their glory knelt before her, each granting her a wish, she could not have dreamed of an arrangement better than this.

True, she was soaked to the knees by the snow and Maya was a dead weight in her arms, fretful and difficult. But she was free of the court, free of pomp and ceremony, free of playing at being impress. The old count and countess—wallowing gamely through the drifts ahead of her—were dears. She had found sanctuary. No one could be more reliable than Hardgraa. She would not have to fight off Ylo by day, or submit to her husband's attentions by night. As far ahead as she could see, she had no worry except Maya, and her daughter was her joy and most welcome duty.

White Impress had sailed away into the cottony snow. The path was, as Eigaze had said, steep. In places the trees had shielded it, but mostly it was thickly drifted and very hard going. Even Hardgraa was having trouble under his load. All four adults were sweating and gasping out puffs of steam in the bitter air.

But obviously Yewdark was big, and isolated, and private. Eshiala could not have invented so wonderful a refuge, a personal paradise.

Eventually the path emerged from the woods and vanished into a tangle of thorny bushes that had once, perhaps, been a rose garden. Straight ahead was the great sprawl of the house itself, inscrutably gray in the drab winter evening, crouched under its burden of snow. Its innumerable windows were dark, the walls furred with ivy. The only touches of color were the tall orange chimney pots, one of which trailed a welcome banner of smoke.

"There!" The countess had paused to catch her breath. "It's delightful, isn't it?"

"Lovely," Eshiala agreed, wondering what her parents would think of such a mansion being left to decay while lawyers argued over its corpse. "See the pretty house, Maya?"

"These thorns will be tricky, ma'am," Hardgraa growled. His craggy face was flushed and shiny from his exertions, for he was bowed under an enormous pack.

"I think we can go around them," the proconsul said, head thrust out like a turtle's, as usual. "Let's try that way. Front door's round there."

He was right. A few minutes' easy walk brought them to wide steps, leading up to the main door. It was open.

Hardgraa grunted. He slipped out of the straps and dropped his burden to the ground. He was dressed in civilian clothes, but he bore a legionary's short sword, and now he drew it.

"Centurion!" Ionfeu exclaimed.

"Don't like this, my lord! Smoke? Door open?"

"Obviously no one has trampled this snow." The old man gestured at the untrodden white.

"But it looks like we're expected!"

"Nonsense!" the count snapped. "There's no danger here! Come, my dear."

Nevertheless, Hardgraa went by him and strode ahead, leaving his bundle where it lay. Eshiala followed the unsteady old couple. By the time they had reached the entrance, the centurion had vanished inside. The others paused for a moment in front of that ominous dark opening. Before any of them moved, a figure emerged from the shadows within, advancing to meet them.

She was short, and round, and her wizened face peered out from a strange collection of clothes. In one tiny, gnarled hand, she brandished a five-branch candelabra, flames dancing faintly in the daylight. Filmed old eyes blinked blindly at the sun. "Where is he?" she shrilled.

The newcomers stopped in astonishment. Maya screamed and buried her face in her mother's collar. Eshiala herself could not hide her twinge of alarm. Eigaze had mentioned an elderly housekeeper, but had given no warning of this apparition. She was swathed in innumerable misassorted garments. Ball-gown lace trailed around her boots, overlain by gowns of wool and taffeta of many colors, the inner layers revealed at neckline and cuffs; there must have been at least six of them, and three or four cloaks over them, at least two with fur collars. Her head was draped in several shawls, capped by an incongruous antique hat, a man's hat topped by an ostrich plume. A wide sash tied around her in an enormous bow made her look like a badly wrapped parcel.

"Wrong!" she exclaimed, waving the candelabra. "Wrong, wrong, wrong!"

"Mistress Ukka!" Eigaze exclaimed. "You remember us, of course? And—"

"Where is he? They said he was coming!"

The countess fell back a step, colliding with her husband. "Who was coming? I mean, who said?"

"The voices said!" The crone peered around suspiciously. "The duke! Duke Yllipo? Where is he?"

The newcomers exchanged uneasy glances. How could this ancient hag in her hermitage have possibly known about Ylo? It must be coincidence, surely? Ravings? Eshiala wondered what had happened to the centurion, although he was likely just exploring the warren.

"Oh, he is probably still in Hub," Ionfeu said. "The property has changed hands, weren't you informed? The imperor deeded it to—"

"The imperor is dead!" Ukka exclaimed, and cackled. "Good riddance! Bloody-handed old bastard!" She fell silent for a moment, her wrinkles writhing in amusement. Then the urgency returned. "But they said he would be here, said he was coming at last."

"You are mistaken . . ."

Then the old woman's uncertain gaze seemed to light on Eshiala for the first time. She opened her mouth, displaying a few rotted pegs of teeth. "Ah! It is you!"

"Who? I mean, me?"

"His love!" cried the housekeeper. "The Promised One!" She flung the candlestick away and fell to her knees in the snow before the impress.

5

"It's my turn to be cook," the king of Krasnegar announced.
"But I should warn you that there is only one dish I ever manage
successfully. Anyone object to my trying?"

"If you refer to your celebrated chicken dumplings," Sagorn
said quickly, "then I testify to your expertise."

Shandie made some tactful, noncommittal comment. Ylo
noted traces of amusement on the faces of Sir Acopulo and the
Jarga woman. The alternative would be another meal conjured
up by the warlock, and dwarvish cuisine was notably lacking in
both flavor and quantity. At noon Raspnex had produced meager
portions of watery gruel and hard black bread.

If the little man detected the implications, he gave no sign.
He was slumped back in the shabbiest armchair, which was so
much too large for him that his oversize boots barely hung out
over the edge. He seemed to be lost in thought, making raspy
noises as he scratched at his curly gray beard.

The six men were grouped in an irregular circle in the deckhouse. The sailor sat back by herself in a corner, showing no
evidence that she had stood watch for almost a whole day and
night. She was a sorceress, of course. Ylo wondered what sort
of meal a jotunn would favor. He decided that the portions would
be generous, but her taste would likely run to some sort of
disgusting boiled fish or seal flipper soup.

Darkness had brought a change in the weather. The ship
rocked at anchor, and sleet pattered on the deckhouse roof.
Mundane sailors could not travel in such weather, and the sorcerers had decided not to risk drawing attention to themselves
by doing so.

King Rap had observed the reaction to his offer. Smiling wryly,
he rose and walked over to a table, balancing easily against the
roll of the floor. "How about a little wine first?" He picked up
a dusty flagon that had not been there a moment before, and
pried off the seal. Then he began to pour, and each time he tilted
the flagon, a crystal goblet appeared to catch the flow.

He began handing the drinks around. Only the dwarf declined, being suddenly in possession of a foaming tankard of
beer, which would be more to his taste.

Ylo decided that sorcery was handy stuff. The saloon was
sleepily warm, and bright with an occult light that had no de-

tectable source. When he had gone out on deck a few moments earlier, he had discovered that the light did not show out there at all. Now he accepted a goblet of wine, reflecting that he had never before been served by a king.

"Excellent, sire. Valdolaine?"

"Valdopol, the seventy-two," the faun solemnly said. He tried a sip from his own goblet and pulled a face. "No, it tastes more like the ninety-four."

"I would have sworn it was Valdoquoon sixty-seven," Doctor Sagorn stated firmly.

The sorcerer picked up the bottle again and peered at it. "By the Power of Evil, you are absolutely correct! Now, how could I have made such a mistake?" Shaking his head sadly, he headed back to his chair.

Ylo had already registered that the king of Krasnegar had a sense of humor. He wondered why the ancient scholar would join in the foolery. He could hardly be such a complete ignoramus about wine, for the excellent vintage the faun had produced tasted nothing at all like sickly sweet Valdoquoon. But then the old man was a mystery all around. Why was he still here? Why had he not gone ashore with Eshiala and her companions? He was much too frail for the kind of wild adventuring that must lie ahead.

"Too much wine means too little sense," Acopulo remarked in his usual sanctimonious tones. "I assume we are about to hold another council of war?"

"I assume the same," King Rap said, stretching out his long legs—jotunn legs, not faun legs. "If anyone knows the answer, will he please speak up clearly?" He raised expectant eyebrows at the little man.

Acopulo declined the honor with a pout. He had been very subdued ever since he learned that Sagorn was an occult genius. He was outclassed and would not be enjoying the situation.

Ylo himself had no illusions of being a tactician. He looked around the rest of the group. This expedition was beginning to feel like one of those elimination games children played. Thirteen had escaped from the Covin. Lord Umpily had gone first. Now another five. *And then there were seven.*

King Rap's question remained unanswered. He quirked a sad smile and asked another. "The problem is to recruit sorcerers to our cause. How do we spread the word of our new protocol? No suggestions?'' •

The dwarf scowled at him under his bushy gray brows. "You could issue a proclamation."

"Thank you, not today!" the king said hastily. "And if you plan to, please give me warning."

The warlock bared quartz-pebble teeth in refusal and took a long draft of ale.

The two scholars perked up.

"Proclamation?" Sagorn asked, ice-blue eyes gleaming.

The faun chuckled and seemed to sink back deeper in his chair. "When one of the Four dies, how do you suppose the others find a replacement?"

Even Shandie roused from his reverie to look interested. Acopulo and Sagorn exchanged glances.

"Promote a votary?" the jotunn suggested, but his craggy face showed that he expected to be corrected.

"Sometimes," the king admitted. "But it's not a popular solution, as you can guess—wardens tend to look down on sorcerers who get trapped that way. And sometimes there is no vacancy to fill, as when Zinixo overthrew Ag-an. Usually the remaining three issue a proclamation; they call for volunteers. Then the in-fighting starts! It's quite simple. In mundane terms, if you want to spread news you slip a groat to the town crier, right? And he shouts the word all around. Same principle."

He frowned, rubbed his forehead, and took a drink.

"You mean you could just, er, shout?" Shandie said disbelievingly. "And all the sorcerers in the world would hear you?"

"I'm not strong enough. Three wardens together can cover all of Pandemia. Raspnex alone might do most of it, at least as far as the stronger listeners were concerned."

Everyone looked to the dwarf, who pulled a truly gruesome dwarvish scowl. "And the Covin would be on me like a cat on a rat."

"Ah!" Shandie nodded sadly. Of course there had to be a catch.

The sailor wench spoke up from her corner. "If he had some other sorcerers to protect him, he could probably survive long enough to pass the message."

Raspnex turned his big head to glower at her. "If you can't

make sense, stay silent. Suicide is an offense to the Gods! I don't plan to try it and I certainly wouldn't ask you to.''

The big woman flinched at the reprimand and looked away.

The warlock was not being very consistent. The previous night he had sacrificed several votaries in making his escape. No one seemed inclined to comment, though, least of all Ylo.

Then the faun said, "It would solve all our problems, but I can't see that a proclamation would work. You might get out a word or two, but the Covin would blast you before you got farther than that. It would need an army to protect you, and an army is what we don't have. Pity.''

When the big man spoke like that, there seemed nothing more to say.

The wind must be rising. The ship was pitching harder, and the creaking noises were growing louder. A vessel with three sorcerers aboard should be safe enough, shouldn't it? The king of Krasnegar caught Ylo's eye and raised an empty glass meaningfully. Ylo rose and fetched the bottle. To his surprise, it was full. He went unsteadily around the group, refilling goblets, and it was still full when he laid it down. He wondered if he could ask for it, to keep as a souvenir.

Shandie stirred, preparing for business. "I like your new protocol, Rap. I like it a lot.''

"Yours, sire.''

"No, yours. Even if we did not have Zinixo to worry about, it would be an improvement on the old one. If I could ascend my throne tonight, I should summon the wardens and urge them to adopt it. It would make a better world!''

The faun smiled bashfully. "Yes, I think it would. As the countess pointed out, sorcery could become a force for good.''

"The key to it is the ban on votarism, of course,'' Shandie said. "Do you suppose such a reform has been suggested in the past?''

"And rejected?''

"Yes.''

"Probably.'' Rap chuckled. "Then if we can pull this off, Zinixo will have done us all a favor!''

Everyone was carefully ignoring Raspnex.

"Good frequently comes from evil,'' Acopulo remarked primly.

"I know Olybino fairly well,'' Shandie said, "as much as a

mundane can ever know a warlock. He would not willingly give up his occult minions, I am sure. Under your new order, he would soon be demoted by a stronger sorcerer.''

"That's better than what Zinixo might do to him.''

The imperor murmured agreement. ''But the new protocol will do no good unless the sorcerous can learn of it, and I know of no sorcerers except yourself and the wardens.''

The faun sipped his wine thoughtfully. ''The wardens are important. They have votaries to form the basis of an army, but we also need their authority and support. We have your signature on the new protocol, and Raspnex's. We must try to collect the other three also. They will give us authority, and credibility. Lord Umpily will get word to Lith'rian if anyone can. Your Omnipotence, have you any idea at all where Olybino has gone?''

The dwarf grunted and shook his head. ''Not a clue. He may well be dead.''

"Why do you say that?'' Sagorn demanded. The old scholar had chosen a high, hard chair, which stressed his height. He had been following the conversation intently. With beak nose and scraggy neck, he resembled a hungry vulture looking down on a battle far below.

"Because he's a very old man,'' Raspnex said. ''It's sorcery lets sorcerers live so long.''

"Ah! And now he does not dare use his power lest he give himself away?'' The jotunn beamed fiercely and turned to the faun. ''There is an advantage you overlooked, lad! The Covin is a threat to free sorcerers in a way we had not thought of!''

The faun nodded, but with a quiet smile that hinted he had already seen the possibility. ''And what of Witch Grunth?''

The warlock shrugged his big shoulders. ''She probably went back to the Mosweeps.''

King Rap sighed. ''So one of us will have to go there.''

No one made any encouraging noises. Ylo drained his goblet. If anyone tried to volunteer him for such a mission, he would desert at once—defection beyond the call of duty! Of course a troll would go to the Mosweeps to hide. Trolls were not exactly inconspicuous people. But to find anyone in that soggy, impenetrable jungle would be impossible, and trolls were the most solitary of races, with no social organization at all.

"There is another reason to look for sorcery in South Pith-

mot,'' Acopulo said, smirking as he did when he thought he
was being clever. "Someone has been freeing slaves there."

"Slaves?" The faun raised an eyebrow. "In the Impire?"

Shandie grimaced. "Not officially. My great-grandmother
abolished slavery a hundred years ago, but the army has been
flouting the law. It's common knowledge that the army trades in
trolls. That was going to be one of the first things I looked into
. . . will look into. But for the last year or two, these so-called
penal workers have been escaping with surprising frequency.
Legionaries trying to track them down have been blocked.
Someone has been using illicit sorcery in the Mosweeps."

"Grunth?" The king looked to the dwarf.

"Naw." The little man pulled the gruesome expression he
used as a smile, and scratched at his beard again noisily. "She
denied it. Said it was nothing to do with her, but it was in her
quadrant and she wouldn't let Olybino interfere."

"Why didn't he complain to the Four?" Shandie demanded.

"He did."

"Grandsire told me he hadn't heard from the Four in a couple
of years . . . How did the vote go?"

"Well, Grunth voted against him, of course, and so did Yel-
lowlegs. So he lost." The dwarf's pebbly eyes twinkled.

There was a pause. Shandie smiled. Then Sagorn. The others
were catching on, one after the other . . .

The only politics Ylo knew was what he had picked up as a
child from listening to his father, plus some tips he had gained
from Shandie. Everyone else in the room was grinning by the
time he worked it out. A dwarf would never willingly side with
an elf, so when Lith'rian supported Grunth, Raspnex had just
abstained. If he'd voted against them, the Four would have been
evenly divided and the decision would have gone to the imperor.
Had Emshandar still been capable of understanding, he would
inevitably have supported the army. So Raspnex had let Grunth
have her victory without actually backing the same side as the
elf—typical occult politics.

"Well, that settles it," King Rap said. "One of us must go
to the Mosweeps. And probably go on to the Nogid Archipel-
ago, too."

Shandie looked disbelieving. "Why there?"

"Because the source of—" The faun winced and shook his
head. "Can't say. Because the Impire has never managed to

subdue the anthropophagi. It hurts sorcerers to talk about sorcery, did you know that? Just take my word for it, the Nogids are a very likely place to find sorcerers."

"You'll get yourself eaten."

"I'll try not to. Which reminds me . . . is anyone ready for dinner, or shall we have some more of that rotgut wine?"

Ylo took the hint, and went to fetch the ever-lasting flagon and refill the goblets. He was a little more unsteady than the ship's rolling justified. It was potent stuff.

"So we try to track down Grunth," Shandie said. "You must have some more ideas than that?"

"The answer lies outside the Impire, I think," Rap said. "It will be very hard for us to do much here without giving ourselves away. We shall have to start with the mundane authorities, you see, and ask them to spread the news. I can't think of any alternative. That means the outlying races."

Shandie laughed. "Nordland, for example?"

"Very much Nordland! Remember Kalkor?"

"Not well. I was only a kid, and in bad shape the day you killed him. You know that. But you mean you're serious—"

"Kalkor liked to make out that he was only a humble raider, but he was a sorcerer. Yes, I'm serious! Words are assets and can be looted like other valuables—one at a time, of course. I'd bet there's barrels of sorcery rolling around Nordland."

"You think the thanes know of it?"

The half-jotunn king smiled his faunish smile. "They will deny it vehemently! Sorcery is sissy stuff! Sailors hate it. Nonetheless, I 'spect your average thane has a fair idea who within his domain has occult powers. That's not important, though. All we need ask is that they spread the news. We're not secret slave-hunters like the Covin. We're publicly calling for volunteers, and there we have a huge advantage over Zinixo."

"We'll need it." Obviously Shandie was not enthusiastic about Nordland. "I'd sooner argue with a pack of polar bears than a group of thanes."

"Certainly. Anyone would. But for centuries the jotnar have enjoyed immunity to magic because of the Protocol. They won't like the idea that Zinixo may now decide to enthrall them."

"Could be an improvement. Will he?"

"If they annoy him, yes. He won't feel safe until he rules the world. Not even then, of course, but that won't stop him. Certainly we must get word to the thanes.''

Shandie frowned. ''Jotnar? How about goblins?''

''Goblins. Djinns. Trolls.''

The frown became icy. ''You make me feel like I'm rallying the outlanders against my own Impire!''

As if abashed, the faun ran fingers through his shaggy hair. ''Sorry, but in a sense you have to. Zinixo holds the Impire now.''

Acopulo coughed. He was wearing his most priestly expression, Ylo noted. If Sagorn was a vulture reading the menu, the little man was a sparrow hopping around a stable yard in total disregard of the great hooves all around.

''Krasnegar, sire? The preflecting pool told you to go to Krasnegar. Wherever the rest of us go, that must be your destination.''

Shandie looked to the faun, who had not moved from his sprawled position, but who suddenly seemed larger, and very threatening. For the first time Ylo saw the jotunn in him.

''The harbor will be frozen for half a year yet,'' the imperor said. ''I can't hope to sneak across the whole width of the taiga without the goblins seeing me. Correct, Rap?''

''Correct!''

''So, Acopulo, how do I get to Krasnegar in midwinter?''

The scholar shrugged his narrow shoulders. ''Perhaps you don't, but you should strive to think on a larger time scale. This struggle may well go on for years! The War of the Five Warlocks lasted a generation.'' He shot a sly glance at the faun. ''The king got out. Can't an imperor get in?''

King Rap thumped a fist on the arm of his chair. ''The pool did not direct you to Krasnegar. It didn't show you being there. It showed you my son. He's your only, single reason for wanting to go to Krasnegar.''

The imperor nodded. ''That's how I understand it.''

''*Name of Evil!* He's only just turned fourteen! Today's his birthday.''

''My daughter has only just turned two.''

The two monarchs glared at each other. Perhaps they both knew that tragedy was inevitable. As soon as the preflecting pool had shown the boy's face to the future imperor, the king's son had been branded a participant.

"He won't stay fourteen for long," Shandie said harshly. "The Impire takes the big ones at sixteen. I've sent beardless boys into battle often enough and watched them become heroes, at least in their own eyes."

"And seen them die?"

"Die like men, kill like men. Physically, Rap, there's very little you can do that that son of yours can't. Judgment and experience, yes, you're his master there and always will be. In some things he's yours already."

Fauns were notoriously stubborn. This one was no longer the bantering humorist who had played jokes with magic wine bottles. He looked implacable and dangerous. "You stay away from my son!"

Shandie tried again. "This is Gath's world we're fighting for. Wars *eat* young men and die of starvation when they've eaten up *all* the young men. Gods save me, Rap, I didn't choose your son! I didn't choose this war! I didn't even choose you. Now, do I have your consent to go to Krasnegar and talk with him?"

"*Talk?* What in the Name of Evil would the two of you have to talk about?"

"What else would I do? Do you think I can take him by force? Will Inos sell him to me? I can't imagine why he is important—"

"Perhaps he isn't!" Acopulo said. "Never jump to unwarranted conclusions! The pool showed me Doctor Sagorn but the result was that we met King Rap and the warlock. Sagorn was a sort of signpost. The boy may just be another."

Mm! Sometimes the old relic came up with intriguing ideas. Ylo's improbable vision of Eshiala might have also been a diversion—except that the only real change it had produced in his life was to keep him away from Rivermead. Surely nothing that might have occurred there could be worse than what he had landed in now.

The imperor had never taken his eyes off Rap. "I promise that I will not lie to him, nor to your wife. What else can I swear? That I will abide by her wishes, not his? I can guess what a fourteen-year-old's will be."

The king sat up straight, as if about to launch a physical attack. His face held all the menace of a naked blade. "*You will not go to Krasnegar!* Don't you see the risk? I told Tiffy my name. Zinixo must know by now that I was in Hub that night.

Warlock—does he know my power is not what it was when I thrashed him?''

Raspnex uttered a low, rumbling laugh. "He didn't before, or he'd have settled with you long since, I think. He may know now, but he won't ever rely on it. He sees tricks in blue sky. I'm sure he died a million times from sheer terror when he found you'd emerged from your lair at last, and on the very night he made his move.''

"So the Covin must be hunting me just as hard as it's hunting Shandie?''

"Likely.''

"And if Zinixo ever gets a hint of my whereabouts, he'll blast me with everything he's got, just to be on the safe side?'' The king scowled all around, to see if anyone disagreed with the logic. "And he will have set a watch on Krasnegar!''

Remembering the legends of the Dark Times and the Dragon Wars, Ylo realized the cause of the faun's anger—he dared not go home now, lest the whole town be blasted to cinders, as had happened to cities in those days. At Lutant the harbor had boiled.

"Surely the watchers will be looking for yourself, not his Majesty?'' Acopulo muttered with none of his usual smug confidence.

"How do you know he hasn't smashed Krasnegar already?'' Sagorn inquired waspishly. "Spite would be in character.''

"I don't, of course,'' Rap said.

"Naw.'' Raspnex scratched his wiry beard audibly. "He wouldn't take the risk—just in case Rap's still a demigod, just in case it's a trap. He'll make sure of Rap first. Then he'll go after his family.''

"Then I should go and warn them of their danger,'' Shandie said quietly.

The king opened his mouth, but the warlock spoke first. "Say, that's a good idea! And you going to Krasnegar is so evilishly improbable that it could well foul up whatever sorcery my nephew's setting up.''

Now it was the dwarf's turn to endure the faun's deadly glare. Eventually the king climbed to his feet. "Let's eat,'' he said.

6

All through the meal, Sagorn and Acopulo discussed elvish philosophy. Possibly they were being tactful. Perhaps they were baiting the dwarf. More likely they were just showing off, unwinding logic as snarled as kittens in a string bag.

Ylo did not listen to a word of it. Instead, he thought about Krasnegar. From the look of the place in Jalon's painting, it would never be worth the trouble to visit it. The journey would be hard and dangerous. It would take months—time that could be much better spent in other pursuits. If Shandie dragged his signifer off on such a fruitless expedition, he was going to finish it alone. Ylo would double back to Yewdark.

He might, he decided, go along as far as Rivermead, just out of curiosity. There could be no harm in that. He had not seen the ancestral home since he was a child, but after one quick look he would desert and head back to Eshiala. And then . . . rich widow?

The chicken dumplings were superb. So was the blueberry pie that followed, and the wine flagon dispensed an exquisite elvish liqueur to wind up the meal. The deckhouse rolled remorselessly from side to side, yet his meal stayed where it was supposed to. Marvelous stuff, sorcery.

Warm, sleepy, and replete, Ylo returned to his comfortable chair to watch the council of war resume. *The Krasnegar Question, Round Two*: Fauns and dwarves were the two most stubborn races in Pandemia. Which would yield?

It was Acopulo who set the discussion going again. "Does your son possess any occult powers, sire?"

The king of Krasnegar shot him a glance as deadly as a poisoned arrow. "He is slightly prescient at times."

"Ah!" The little man smirked.

The faun's expression implied that strangling would be too good for him, but evidently he had accepted the inevitable. He sighed.

"You can get to Krasnegar in winter, Shandie. There is a back door, a magic portal. Any sorcery is a risk now, as you know, but devices such as portals are not easily detected if they are in good repair, and I can vouch for the workmanship in this one." He forced a grim smile. "You may find Zinixo waiting for you on the other side, of course."

"Where is this magic portal? Close to us?"

"No. It's at Kinvale, a ducal estate in northwest Julgistro. The duchess is a distant relative of Inos'. If I give you a letter, I think she will at least inform Inos, even if she will not reveal the portal itself to you."

"I know Aquiala," Shandie said quietly.

"You do?"

The imperor smiled at Rap's evident astonishment. "Two years ago I toured the Pondague front. I always call on the senior nobility when I visit a new district. She's a very impressive person."

"She never told us you'd been to Kinvale."

"I should hope not!"

Ylo grinned to himself. The duchess owed her allegiance to her imperor, not to any foreign friends.

Acopulo rubbed his wizened hands. "His Majesty's devotion to duty has frequently paid handsome dividends. The Gods reward diligence."

For a moment the faun seemed to contemplate the prospect of immersing him in boiling oil. "Then the matter should be simple. Except that the journey took me six weeks."

"And we can't use the horse posts," Shandie agreed. "The enemy will watch them. This is no brief campaign we are facing."

The faun began talking about writing a letter to his wife . . .

Rivermead was somewhere in the middle of Julgistro. It should just be possible to ride there and back before daffodil time. Ylo stifled a yawn—this had been a long day.

The king was addressing the warlock.

"The imperor goes to Krasnegar, then. I have a horrible feeling I get nominated to hunt down Grunth in the Mosweeps and do lunch for the anthropophagi in the Nogids. How about you?"

The dwarf shook his big head. "Jarga and I have some matters to attend to. Never mind us."

The others frowned, but dwarves gave away nothing, ever, not even information.

"You'll put us ashore somewhere?" King Rap asked.

"I think it would be safer to drop you off on fishing boats as we did with your fat friend."

Shandie nodded, and then stretched. "Ylo goes with me. Have we a mission for Sir Acopulo?"

"Azak."

Ylo started, wondering if he had heard correctly. Evidently so, for most of the others looked as surprised as he was. Old Sagorn was smirking. Acopulo wore an expression of horror.

"The caliph?" he said. "Zark?"

"I know Azak." Rap smiled meanly at him. "He had a very nasty experience with sorcery in his youth. He detests it with a passion. But I dropped in to see him once—I went to collect my dog, as a matter of fact—and I detected power in use within his palace. How do you think he made himself overlord of a continent?"

Shandie swore under his breath. "He enlisted sorcerers? How?"

"Perhaps he appealed to their patriotism."

"Olybino never told me. He never even hinted at that!"

Acopulo *humph*ed. "But he certainly helped you against the djinn army at Bone Pass. Perhaps that was why!"

"And that was Azak's only real defeat! Yes, I can see that the caliph should be informed. We agreed to seek out the mundane rulers, and the caliph is the most powerful ruler." Shandie scowled bitterly. "Except the imperor, of course! I'll write a letter for you to take."

"So will I," Rap said. "He doesn't like me, but he's a smart man. And if he's planning an invasion of the Impire, as everyone seems to be assuming he is, then he will be interested to know that the rules have changed."

Obviously Shandie and Acopulo felt uneasy at that. So did Ylo, although he had never considered himself a rabid patriot. This program was sounding more and more like an attempt to rally the outlanders against the Impire. Was this what was required of outlaws?

"I have never visited Zark," the scholar said, pouting. "The weather should be pleasant at this time of year."

"You may find it overly warm," King Rap said innocently. "The djinns roast spies over slow fires. So we are decided? Shandie and Ylo to Krasnegar and then perhaps Nordland? Me to the Mosweeps and Nogids. Sir Acopulo to Zark. Warlock Raspnex to wherever the Evil he wants. After that, we sing what the Gods hum." He paused and scratched his unruly mop of hair. "Ilrane . . . Zark . . . The preflecting pool? You know, I have the strangest feeling I've forgotten something!"

"Old age catching up with you?" Sagorn remarked acidly.

"Perhaps. Well, I expect I'll remember as soon as it's too late. If I survive the anthropophagi, then I may head to Ilrane and try to visit with Lith'rian." He regarded the imperor thoughtfully. "And you? You might think about the Nintor Moot."

"In Nordland?"

"Why not? Every summer the thanes go to the Nintor Moot and chop each other up for sport. I don't suppose they'll mind a few imps to use for practice. The moot would be your only chance to spread the word in Nordland."

For a moment the listeners fell silent. The distances involved were enormous. This campaign had begun to look like the rest of their lives. Ylo shivered. He had not realized that the pool might have been showing him not the next crop of daffodils, but the one after.

"We shall need to set up a rendezvous," Acopulo said prissily.

The faun shook his head. "If any one of us is taken, he will reveal it. The same would be true of anyone else we had told. A rendezvous would certainly be betrayed somehow."

"A date, then?" Shandie said, frowning. "A date for the uprising? A call to arms?"

"Not even that, and for the same reason." The king looked to the warlock; the dwarf nodded his big head, sneering in agreement.

"You must understand," the faun said, "that this is not a mundane war. This is not Guwush and we are not gnomish rebels opposing the Imperial might. No sneak attacks and hideouts in the forest and secret passwords. It won't work that way!"

The imperor stared at him incredulously for a long time and no one else spoke.

Rap shrugged. "If you want a picture, it's more like a houseful of mice planning to mob the cat."

Shandie pulled a face. "You are saying we try to rally the mice but we don't tell them when or where to rally? That's crazy! What are we trying to accomplish? What do we tell these sorcerers we seek to enlist? What message do we send when we speak to mundane leaders?"

"Just that there is hope, and a cause worth fighting for." Rap sighed. "One day there will be a battle! We don't know when, or where, or who will provoke it. When it comes, we shall have to gamble everything we've got—at once, to the death. But every sorcerer in Pandemia will know of it as soon as it starts. We want them to come and help, that's all. Until then, they can only do what we are doing—pass the word and keep the faith."

"As I recall," Sagorn said, his tone implying that his recall was normally perfect, "all the Dragon Wars were like that. Enormous battles followed by long periods of uneasy quiet."

Shandie sat in silence, his face blank, which was his thinking expression. Then he nodded. "I suppose it makes sense. As you say, it's a different sort of fighting." He smiled faintly. "I wish you luck in the Mosweeps—and with the elf. Ylo, we head north, it would appear."

"Sounds like fun," Ylo said blandly. But not much.

The imperor rose and stretched. "It's been a long day, and I'd like to sleep on this. We all have our parts to play, it would seem. You realize that we may scatter tomorrow and never all meet again? May the Gods be with us!"

"Amen," Acopulo said.

"You have left one out," the dwarf growled.

Everyone looked to Doctor Sagorn. He glanced around at the attention, twisting his long jotunn face in an arrogant sneer that raised Ylo's hackles.

The faun chuckled. "Old age, Doctor? How do you feel about scrambling in and out of fishing boats tomorrow?"

"I abhor the prospect. If you have concluded your deliberations, then the time has come for me to leave."

"And go where?" the imperor barked.

"Nowhere."

Such an absurdity demanded explanation. Obviously the faun sorcerer knew the answer but was not about to disclose it. Smirking, he yawned and snuggled down more comfortably in his chair. The silence dragged on.

Glaring, the old jotunn said, "You will not warn your companions what to expect?"

"But you can tell the tale so much better than I, Doctor! And one of us certainly must."

"Very well!" Sagorn turned to the imperor. "Your Majesty . . . this is a strange tale, and one I have rarely told anyone. It may sound improbable, but I shall demonstrate its truth in a moment.''

Shandie sat down again. "Carry on."

"If I asked you to estimate my age, I expect you would guess me to be in my seventies, perhaps early eighties."

Acopulo released a long hiss of breath.

The jotunn shot him a killer glare out of the corner of his eye. "Yes, there is sorcery involved, as you suspected and I denied."

"When were you born?" the little man demanded.

"You will not . . . 2859."

"Even better preserved than I thought!" Acopulo said jubilantly.

Now, thought Ylo, some mysteries were about to be cleared up.

Scowling, Sagorn turned back to the imperor. "I age at a normal rate, sire, but I have not lived through all the intervening years. When I was ten, I irked a sorcerer. I was the youngest of a group of five boys whose presence in his house in the middle of the night he found distasteful, as he had not instigated it. In retribution, he laid a sequential spell on us.''

Shandie's eyes narrowed. "Explain 'sequential spell.' ''

"It means that only one of us can exist at a time."

"The artist!" Ylo had shouted without meaning to; he had made everyone jump.

Sagorn pouted—his long upper lip was well shaped for pouting. "As you say, the artist. Master Jalon is one of the five. At one time he was older than I, in fact I think he was the oldest. How old does he seem now—late twenties? When you forced your way into our house last night, Jalon was present. You demanded to see me, but I did not exist! That was why he refused to let the centurion accompany him when he went to fetch me. He invoked the spell, and I replaced him. Now he does not exist. I propose to depart by the same method, which should wipe the skeptical expression off your pretty young face."

"So sometimes you are you and sometimes you are Jalon?"

Sagorn grimaced impatiently. "You do not listen, boy. I am not Jalon, and never have been. I do share his memories, but we are two separate people."

"So now you disappear," Shandie asked, "and Master Jalon appears?"

"No."

The king of Krasnegar seemed to be struggling with a need to laugh.

Sagorn glared at him briefly. "There are constraints, sire. I can neither call the man who called me, nor the man I called the last time."

"Perhaps you should also explain the time limits," King Rap said, turning pink with his suppressed mirth.

"Why?" snarled the jotunn. "Oh, well . . . There are other restrictions. They are complicated, but in short I could not remain here for more than a few days."

"Rap!" the imperor barked. "Share the joke!"

The faun flushed even redder as he struggled to catch his breath. "It may not seem as funny to you as it does to me. For many years, Doctor Sagorn and his . . . associates, I suppose is the word. They are never a group and yet they are not exactly separate, either. But for over a century they kept on trying to find some way to break the spell that bound them—tried one at a time, of course. When I was a much more powerful sorcerer than I am now, I removed it for them. They were reunited! Then they discovered that they disliked the experience and changed their minds. At their request, I put it back again. But Sagorn had been hogging more than his share of the years, and another of them, Thinal, had been shirking. They agreed that they ought to cooperate more, so I rearranged the original sorcery a little. Now they have to be more considerate of one another. That's all. The doctor can't stay around as long as the others can, so they will eventually catch up with him in age. Thinal can't just vanish right away every time and stay forever young. And if Sagorn says that now he can't remain with us very long, that means that lately he's been hogging again."

The old man bared his teeth in a snarl. "I was engaged in a very complex piece of research!"

The faun smothered another snigger. "Oh, quite!"

The audience looked at one another. It sounded like some sort of elaborate hoax, and yet neither man was the type to indulge in such foolery.

"I want a demonstration!" Shandie said coldly.

"As you wish, sire."

The king chuckled. "You can't call Jalon, because he called you. So who will be the new recruit to our cause? Whom will his Majesty have the honor of meeting?"

"I shall let you choose." The old man was enraged by the mockery. "Last time I called Andor. You have a choice of Darad or Thinal."

"Darad?" Ylo said. "The gladiator?"

"That's the one," Rap said. "But we have no work for him at the moment, so we should save him for later. I look forward to meeting Thinal again—an invaluable recruit, who can play a noble role in our mission."

"Highly improbable!" Sagorn snapped, and another man was sitting in his clothes.

He was youthful, and an imp—a slim, dark youngster with poxy features. He glanced all around cautiously, then slid down on one knee and bowed his head to the imperor.

Acopulo had turned pale. Even Shandie was displaying shock. The dwarf was leering, seemingly as amused as the faun.

"This," the king of Krasnegar said, "is Master Thinal."

"A businessman," Thinal muttered without looking up.

"Oh, *Gods*! A businessman, sire."

"What sort of business?" Shandie demanded.

"Monkey business!" King Rap threw his head back and roared with laughter.

Parts to play:
> A place in the ranks awaits you,
>> Each man has some part to play;
> The Past and the Future are nothing,
>> In the face of the stern Today.
>
> Adelaide Anne Proctor, *Now*

❬ FOUR ❭

True avouch

1

In a gray foggy dawn, the fishermen put Lord Umpily safely ashore on an icy jetty somewhere on the east side of Hub. He did not know whether it lay within the bounds of the capital proper or in some best-forgotten suburb—he was just glad to have land under his feet again. He had expected to be relieved of his bag of sorcerous gold and dropped overboard in the night.

Muttering prayers of gratitude to the appropriate Gods, he struggled off through snow-packed alleys in search of an inn. Emotionally he was sure he would be coshed and robbed before he found one, even though intellectually he knew that his apprehension was excessive—that no one else could know what caused that bulge in his cloak. His cloak bulged in many places. The lump that bothered him had a harder center than the others, but its mere appearance should not attract undue suspicion. Yet every time he passed a dark doorway, he thought he heard it jingle.

Umpily was no stranger to wild adventuring. He had visited almost every corner of the Impire in the past few hectic years, but then he had always been accompanied by well-armed youngsters prepared to bleed in his defense if necessary. Being alone did make a difference.

Unmolested, cold, wet, hungry, and stinking of fish, he stamped into the Sailors' Haven. He had patronized worse, although not often. He demanded a room with a fire, hot water, and breakfast. He sent the potboy off to the nearest tailor with orders to attend him at once, bringing a selection of raiment suitable for a gentleman of stalwart physique.

As Umpily was stripping off his wet clothes, he came upon the magic scroll in his pocket. It unrolled into an oblong strip of vellum no larger than his hand, completely blank. With it was the silverpoint the warlock had given him, although he had been told that any writing instrument would suffice. He wrote, *Am ashore. Streets impassable. Bells still ringing.* He let the leather roll up again and laid it on the dresser. The bells were important because they meant that the old man was not buried yet. The life of the city must be almost at a halt, with travel blocked by snow and the population driven half insane by the incessant tolling.

When a warmer, cleaner Umpily rang to summon breakfast, it was brought up by the landlord himself. The tray was copiously heaped with plain winter fare—broiled beef and dumplings and a bread pudding, all washed down with a passable porter. Umpily ate until he could éat no more, as was his custom, but he encouraged the fellow to remain and talk. The man seethed with complaint—business had come to a stop, the bar was almost deserted, roofs were leaking, fuel was short, fish spoiled on the quays, and so on. He lamented all through Umpily's meal, except when he had to run downstairs to fetch seconds.

Satisfied at last, Umpily sent the man off with the dishes, demanding ink, paper, and quills. Then he sat back to digest and consider.

His mission was to discover what was happening in the capital and then report it all to Shandie. Right now he could not do so. The bells had informed everyone that the old imperor was dead, but the smothering snowstorm had stopped all other news from reaching even this far. Here, just five leagues from the Opal Palace, no one yet knew that the wardens' thrones in the Rotunda had been destroyed, or that the new imperor had promptly vanished from the palace, or that several buildings in the southern precincts had exploded in fire and ruin. Even Umpily himself did not know if the Red Palace had survived the siege. He was not certain that the old Imperor's funeral could proceed without the new imperor's participation. If it couldn't, he decided, the entire population would soon be driven mad by those Evil-begotten bells, himself included.

He took a look at the magic scroll. The words he had written were gone. In their place he found *Gods be with you* in Shandie's neat hand.

Amen to that!

Unlike most male nobles in the Impire, Umpily had never served in the army. His father had died in battle when he was very young. His mother had been a bitter widow and a jealous parent, keeping her son very close to her. He had grown up more familiar with gossiping dowagers at tea parties than with companions of his own age.

His family was small and unimportant, but his title alone had gained him entry to court, even without a sponsor. By the end of his teens, he had wormed his way into court life well enough to be a popular member of the nobility, a skilled collector of gossip, and already plump.

At forty he was obese, married to a permanently miserable invalid wife, and bored to madness by the pointless, sterile existence of an aristocratic parasite.

One evening a chance remark informed him of a petty plot to entrap a certain youth, a motherless, fatherless adolescent who could easily be enmeshed in an apparently compromising situation. The threat would be scandal, the price of silence at least a lifetime pension, possibly land. Such things happened all the time and the victims always paid. Usually a hint would escape and then the court would purse lips and snigger and mutter that boys would be boys although not usually *that* way . . . and then forget the whole incident in a month.

In this case, though, the victim was to be the heir apparent. That solemn, solitary fifteen-year-old would not forget such a humiliation in a month, or even in years. Umpily dropped a word of warning and the prince avoided the snare. He was grateful, and also sharp enough to realize that next time he might not be so lucky. Within days, that intense, stick-limbed boy took over Umpily in a strange and almost undefinable partnership. He acquired a mentor and advisor with a subtle grasp of palace politics; Umpily obtained a patron twenty-five years his junior, and also a purpose. For the first time in his life, he learned about loyalty, given and taken. He became as much a confidant as that lonely boy possessed, and thereafter he guarded the lad's trust as he had never cherished anything before.

He had watched that shy, awkward youth turn himself into a leader of men by sheer strength of will. He had given what help he could, although he knew it had been small. They had never been close, though—no one was ever close to Shandie, not even his cousins. Umpily himself had an enormous galaxy of acquaintances, and no friends.

When Shandie arrived at manhood and embarked on a military career, Umpily expected an end to their collaboration, but the prince would not hear of it. He needed eyes and ears within the palace, he said. Later, when he rose to legate, he summoned his chief spy to join the government-in-waiting that was growing up around him.

Thus military life caught up with Umpily in middle age. For five years he lived in the field. He heard the animal screams of men disemboweled, saw earth turned to mud by boys' blood. The aging fat civilian came to know more of high-rank military thinking and the true working of an army than most soldiers ever did. He especially understood the value of reliable intelligence. He knew that shrewd commanders would sooner be blessed with first-rate information than first-rate troops. He appreciated that scouting was the most dangerous job in the army and a scout's career the shortest.

He could see, therefore, that the odious task he had been given in this present crisis was vital, and yet he could not quite shake a memory of the time Shandie had sacrificed a thousand men to entrap a horde of gnomes. Highscarp had been a brilliant victory, but would those two lost cohorts have thought so?

Still, today Umpily had no choices to make. The roads were impassable and he was a long way from the palace. Scouting must wait for the thaw. He could concentrate on the other half of his duties.

If there was any way out of this sorcerous disaster that had befallen the Impire, it lay with the revolutionary proposals made by the king of Krasnegar. A most interesting man! Umpily smacked mental lips at the impact the past two days' events would have on his memoirs. That future posthumous publication would hold even more importance for scholars than he had ever dreamed—the forging of the second protocol, an epic chapter in the history of the Impire! He might even see it published in his lifetime.

But the new protocol would remain a dream unless it could be implemented. Somehow the proposals must be advertised, so that all the sorcerers still at liberty could rally to the cause. Logically the first people who should be informed were the missing three wardens—Grunth, Olybino, Lith'rian.

Grunth seemed unachievable. Trolls were a race of solitary barbarians. She might very well have reverted to isolated savagery, heaving rocks around in sodden jungle. Umpily had not the faintest notion how to establish contact with the former witch of the west.

Lith'rian would be easiest. He must be down in Ilrane, elf country. He might be avoiding his ancestral enclave of Valdorian, but surely he could be reached somehow. Umpily was on first-name terms with many distinguished elves, and no elf would ever completely sever the ties that bound him to his sky tree. Ancient Lord Phiel'nilth, for example, Poet Laureate of the Impire—he would do for a start.

Umpily's planned letter to Valdonilth proved surprisingly hard to compose. The first few drafts read like the ravings of a maniac. By the time he had achieved a satisfactory text, he was ready to ring for a waiter and order a light lunch of turnip soup, roast pheasant and lentil mash, accompanied by a dry white wine and followed by some surprisingly savory cheese.

Refreshed by that and guided by his first letter, he dashed off three more letters, to other prominent elves.

He took a brief break, then, to ease his aching back and the cramp in his fingers. He rang for candles, for the brief winter day was failing. He noticed that a warm wind was turning the street below his window into a morass of slush. A few carts were creaking by—and the bells had stopped at last.

That was worth reporting. He unrolled the magic parchment. It was blank, as he had expected it to be, for Shandie's message would have faded as soon as it had been read. He wrote out an account of the new developments, remembering this time to add the day and hour.

Then he turned his mind to the Olybino problem. The warden of the east was an imp. He might be hiding somewhere in Hub itself, or he might be anywhere in the Impire. He had been a warlock since before Umpily was born, and Umpily had no knowledge at all of the man's family or background.

Women, though . . . Olybino had always had an eye for the ladies, and several of them had flaunted the notoriety. The warlock had often been generous to them when he had tired of their company—generosity came easy when one could make gold with a snap of the fingers. Was it not possible that he might have taken refuge with one of his recent lady friends?

Mistress Olalpa was a logical first choice. She had appeared from nowhere in Hub only a few months since. She was young, vivacious, voluptuous, and dripping in wealth. She had never concealed the source of her good fortune. Umpily wrote a carefully phrased letter to Mistress Olalpa. Of course Zinixo might have tracked her down, also, and might even have tracked down Olybino himself, but that was a risk that could not be avoided—the warlocks Umpily sought might be dead men already. Against that danger was the possibility that some of their votaries might have survived at liberty and might hereby learn of the new protocol. He certainly had nothing better to do with his time.

The day was ended. Water dripped steadily from the eaves. And the bells had stopped! Why had he not realized the significance of that blessed release sooner? The state funeral must be over. People were getting around the city now, obviously. He should seek out some news, and where better to start than in the taproom downstairs?

He donned his cloak and headed for the stairs, clutching his packet of letters. He ran into the landlord in the hallway. The surly fellow was in a much better humor now that his customers were returning. Besides, he had learned that this guest was a willing source of bullion. He took the letters and promised to send a boy to the post without delay. With less enthusiasm, he agreed that Umpily could withhold full payment until he had seen the receipts.

Clutching a foaming tankard of beer, Umpily began edging his way around the saloon, eavesdropping on the conversations of fish merchants, porters, and storekeepers. He learned nothing new, although he heard some mention of the sorcerous battles he had witnessed. Rumor fell short of truth, for the damage was being attributed to freak lightning caused by the storm. He was too early.

He adjourned to the public dining room for a hearty repast of

Cenmere sturgeon, pork cutlets with sage stuffing, roasted spareribs in yam sauce, two bottles of wine, and three different types of cake. There was a fourth cake available, but he didn't like the look of it.

Then he returned to the bar to try again, and found what he wanted at once—indeed, he could hardly have missed it. A large audience had gathered around a single speaker. Artisans and tradesmen parted respectfully to let the gentleman move in.

Emitting strong odors of horse and wet garments, a poxy-faced youngster was propped against the bar, earning his tipple with an eyewitness account of the imperial funeral. It sounded genuine. He was a skilled raconteur, spinning out his tale and generously allowing many of his listeners a chance to buy the next installment. The glittering procession seemed to be leagues long—bands, ambassadorial delegations, representatives of half the legions in the army, senators and assemblymen and aristocrats. Umpily began to wonder whether the old man would be safely underground before the teller fell down himself.

"A great sight they was," the boy said blearily, and drained his tankard yet again. He leaned back and peered hopefully at the listeners. His capacity was remarkable.

Umpily had finished his own beer. "Waiter!" he said.

The raconteur beamed as another stein was laid at his elbow. "Your health, my lord!" He was not so drunk that he could not recognize a gentleman. "Where was I?"

"The imperor himself?" Umpily said sharply. He knew the sensational climax the storyteller was holding back, and he wanted to get it out of him to see how the audience would take it.

The lad frowned uncertainly. "Battle honors? Or the Praetorians was next?"

"No, the imperor! I mean, the imperor *was* there, wasn't he?"

Hiccup! "Oh, yesh! His majeshty was there, Gods bless him, on a pure white horse. I saw the tears in his—"

"You're certain?"

"Certain I'm certain! Think I don't know Shandie, me who drove the first mule train into the camp at Fain?"

Umpily's tankard slid from his fingers and crashed to the floor. An illusory imperor? A Shandie mirage?

Of course! What could be easier for Zinixo and his evil Covin to arrange? Rap, Raspnex, Ionfeu, Acopulo—none of them had thought of that obvious ploy!

2

The enthronement of the new imperor was to be held at noon on the following day. Umpily must be there. He knew he was crazy, but he could not force himself to stay away. If the sorcerers were going to produce a Shandie mirage convincing enough to fool the entire court and government, then he must see it for himself.

As soon as he heard of the imperor illusion, he rushed up to his room and wrote about it on the magic scroll. The message he had written earlier was still visible, meaning that Shandie had not unrolled his copy yet, but there was room on the vellum for more.

The enthronement was not the coronation. That would not happen for a long time, after the official mourning. A new imperor must be confirmed by the wardens, though, so mourning was traditionally suspended for a couple of hours to allow that unique consecration. The enthronement would be the last state ceremony for months, the last time the new imperor would appear in public. Umpily must attend!

He went back downstairs and tried to arrange transportation. That proved to be impossible. The city was in chaos. Some horses and carts were getting through, but not a coach could be found for hire, nor yet a horse. He even contemplated commissioning a boat, then remembered the wind and changed his mind. He decided to walk. Five leagues was not so far—legionaries marched that much day in and day out, every one of them loaded like a mule. Shandie had often led his men twice that far in emergencies, and on forced marches he did so in person, on foot.

Of course Umpily carried more weight all the time than a legionary ever did, and he had never walked a league in his life, but this was certainly an emergency. He would betray Shandie's trust if all he reported was hearsay.

He could hire some locals as guards, but they would guess why they were wanted and therefore be more dangerous than stray footpads. He was an outlaw now; like a true conspirator, he must rely on stealth. With his magic scroll in his pocket and his bag of gold slung at his waist, he hugged his cloak tight about him and strode out the back door.

He realized eventually that the distance on the ground was much more than five leagues. The roads were thick with drifts and freezing slush, and they were mostly very dark. He set his teeth and prepared to face the worst night of his life.

Dawn found him close to the Gold Palace, already within the five hills that defined the ancient center of Hub. His toes were frozen, his feet chafed raw by wet boots, his ankles aflame. He wished he could cut off his legs at the knee.

Rain had started to fall, turning snow to slush and mud.

The time had come to choose a destination. When he had returned to the capital the previous summer as a widower, he had sold his home and moved into Oak House, residence of the prince imperial. To return there would be to capitulate to Zinixo. He had many acquaintances who would take him in, but none he would trust not to mention his presence. If Legate Ugoatho had been bespelled by the Covin, then the Praetorian Guard was hunting for Lord Umpily, and the Guard had many excellent informers within the aristocracy. It was aristocracy.

Inevitably, Umpily decided to find himself a rooming house. There were many of those around the palace, patronized by provincial officials when their duties brought them to the capital. Many of them were comfortable, even luxurious. As soon as the sun was up, he chose one with a VACANCY sign in a window, and invented a vague story about luggage delayed by the snow. He had gold, and gold solved all problems.

He ate a large breakfast of roast venison and brussels sprouts followed by rolls and honey, and felt better.

Common sense said that he should now catch up on his sleep. By evening, the events in the Rotunda would be general knowledge, and he would be able to find out everything he wanted in the nearest saloon. Common sense said that to enter the Rotunda would be disaster.

The magic scroll remained unchanged. Shandie had not yet read the message. That was unfortunate, for he might guess what his agent in Hub was planning and forbid him to take such an absurd risk. Umpily would welcome those orders!

Yet he was an imp—left to himself, he could not bear to stay away.

His first requirement was a toga, and that was not hard to find. A couple of bedsheets might have sufficed, but his new landlady was impressed to learn that her boarder was invited to the enthronement, and she had a nephew in the drapery business. Fortunately, Umpily had practiced with his valet only a few days before. He was confident he could wrap himself adequately.

With the capital in its present turmoil, transportation proved harder to arrange. Again his landlady proved resourceful, although the fee quoted would have purchased the vehicle and its horses outright in normal times, and probably the coachman as well, at least for a night or two. Another nephew, probably.

And then it was late arriving. Having had no chance to rest at all, Umpily found himself swathed in fine white flannel, sitting on the edge of his bed, eating a few precautionary ham and cheese sandwiches with a dry mouth. He was shaking, but how much from fatigue and how much from terror he could not tell. He was a listener, a talker—not a man of action! He had never considered himself a coward, merely cautious, but he had few illusions about being a hero. No matter how often he reassured himself that all eyes would be on the performers and none on the audience, he did not believe a word of it. Some of those Praetorians had eyes in the back of their helmets. Sorcerers could see around corners.

But he was too much an imp to stay away.

Then his jumpy gaze lighted on the magic scroll, lying where he had put it on the mantel. He rose and shuffled across the room in his ill-fitting ornamental sandals. The vellum bore a note in Shandie's writing: *Am advised that imposture more probable than illusion. Your information invaluable. Take no unnecessary risks. E.*

Hooves splashed in the street outside the window, wheels rumbled. The rain was growing heavier.

Should he take the scroll with him or not? If he was apprehended, he might still have time to dash off a warning note. On the other hand, Raspnex had warned him that a sorcerer would see the spell on it. Discretion prevailed. In a shaky hand, Umpily wrote, *Going to attend enthronement. Will leave this behind.* He tucked the scroll under his pillow and went out to the coach.

The landlady and her household had assembled to applaud their distinguished guest. With one arm and both shins bare, he felt completely ridiculous. Shandie, he remembered, hated togas with a passion, and now he saw why.

Ten minutes later, his undistinguished common cab came to a halt at the end of a long line of splendid carriages waiting to enter the palace gates. The coachman tapped on the hatch. "What name, my lord?"

Only then did Umpily realize that he would not be admitted to the Rotunda without an invitation. He was completely unqualified for such deceitful business. A real spy would have foreseen this! Panic stabbed in his bowels like a sword.

"Praetor Umphagalo." That was the name he had given at the rooming house, the name of a minor official he had met once in Pithmot. It satisfied the driver, who closed the hatch again, but it would not convince the guards without some credentials to back it up.

Sweating, Umpily peered out the window. Already his cab was solidly locked in by others, and to order the driver to break out of line and head home for a forgotten invitation would attract attention and probably investigation—there were scores of guards standing around with nothing much to do.

Right ahead of him, though, was a splendid eight-horse equipage with outriders, ducal insignia, and a senatorial pennant. He knew every duke in Hub, more or less. With the speed of desperation, Umpily opened the door and stumbled down into ankle-deep slush, almost falling in his haste. Pausing only to thrust a gold imperial at his astonished driver, he splashed forward to the grand carriage, dodged past a surprised outrider, and rapped on the door.

"Lady Humilio!" he cried to the astonished face at the window. "Now my day is made! You don't mind if I join you?"

The occupants of the carriage certainly must mind, for they were already packed in like eels in a jug, but they were too polite to say so. There were six of them in there already, including the ancient Senator Oupshiny, whose equipage it was.

Muttering greetings and confusing explanations, Umpily squeezed his bulk inside.

No guard would question a senatorial carriage.

"My lady!" Umpily chirruped, leaning against the door and trying not to sweat. "You look bewitching in that chiton. My lord! And your Eminence, you are well?" Old Oupshiny, of course, although he was older than the Impire, was married to the impress's sexy sister. "Your dear wife? She will be one of the participants, of course?" It was odd that Ashia was not present, though, or that the old relic wasn't with her . . .

"Eh?" the old man shouted, reddening. "Wife?"

Ripples of shock seemed to shake the carriage. After a lifetime in society, Umpily knew a major blunder when he saw one—or made one, although that was extremely rare. Not having a clue what was wrong, he changed the subject at once, squeezing a corner of his bulk onto the tiny space that had been reluctantly cleared for him. "I should be quite happy to stand, my lord, thank you, except that I have contracted a swelling of the ankles, as you may notice. The doctors suspect inadequate nutrition due to—"

"Wife?" a couple of voices muttered. The carriage lurched forward and stopped again.

"Thought you'd been posted to Guwush, eh?" the old senator bellowed.

"Guwush, your Eminence?"

"That's what we heard, wasn't it, Utha?"

"It was indeed. Secret mission for Sh— for his majesty."

"Just a blind," Umpily said cheerfully. His head was starting to spin. He had only been gone two days . . .

"And what can you tell us about the prince?" Lady Humilio whispered conspiratorially.

"Prince?"

"His cousin! They quarreled? I mean, why else would Emthoro have rushed off to Leesoft even before the funeral?"

Umpily flapped his mouth like a landed fish. "I really mustn't betray confidences, my lady . . ."

"What were you yattering about my wife?" demanded the senator. "Can't believe you'd even remember her."

"You misheard me, Eminence!" *God of Liars assist me!* "Not your wife . . ." He began to babble.

The carriage lurched forward and stopped again.

* * *

When the distinguished party reached the door of the Rotunda, Umpily descended first and handed down the ladies. He helpfully collected all the invitations and passed them over in a wad. He gave Lady Humilio his arm as they paraded along the corridor. When they reached the crowded clamor of the Rotunda itself, he excused himself with vague explanations that of course he must find his proper place in the ceremony. He squirmed away through the throng. The hall was already packed, and yet still cold as a root cellar. No one else there was sweating as he was.

The huge round hall was mercifully dim, most of the great dome still cloaked with snow. He tried not to remember that sorcerers could see in the dark as well as in sunlight. A few of the crystal panes were clear, and icicles hung perilously from the fretted stone ribs, dripping water onto the seated throng. Once in a while one would fall and shatter on the floor. Nearby onlookers would laugh nervously.

Umpily bustled around to the southeast quadrant where he would have a good view of the throne. He picked out a couple of ancient earls, persuading them that his allotted seat was right between them. They both knew him by sight, and they were both too deaf to attempt much conversation. Soon he was so packed in by the crowd that he did not think even Zinixo himself could extract him. Safety in numbers . . . His terror began to subside a little.

The Opal Throne was turned to the south, facing the Blue Throne, so this was—

Five thrones?

Five thrones!

Umpily had witnessed four of those thrones being blasted to rubble by the warden of the north. Now they were restored completely, exactly as before. He shivered so hard that one of his neighbors demanded to know what was wrong.

Nothing was wrong. That was the problem.

The guests crammed in until there was no room to breathe, and still they kept coming. Gradually their body heat began to warm the Rotunda, and icicles crashed down more frequently. Some provoked ominous cries of pain, but the press was too great for the casualties to be removed. Only the circular space in the center stayed clear.

An hour or more drifted by. Umpily felt sick and faint with apprehension. Then a trumpet blared a fanfare, and the congregation struggled to its feet. The participants came marching in from the north door, dividing into two lines as they paraded around.

Shandie!

Yes, it was Shandie, in a purple toga. For the coronation he would arrive in plain white and don the purple as part of the ritual, but today he wore purple. It was Shandie to the life, a nondescript imp with a spotty complexion.

Eshiala! Gorgeous in her purple chiton, leading the far line . . .

Shandie hated togas, Umpily remembered. He had sworn he would wear uniform instead. And had Eshiala ever smiled with such confidence?

Umpily sat down slightly ahead of the elderly earls, gaining a little more of the bench than he had held before. His brain was gyrating wildly. It couldn't be Shandie. It certainly was Shandie. Every mannerism. After all these years, he could not be mistaken.

It couldn't be. Shandie was somewhere on a ferryboat, or perhaps already in his chosen bolthole on the far side of Cenmere. Or was this the real imperor, and that whole, horrible adventure had been a hallucination? That was much more likely.

Worse—when the new imperor stood by the throne and raised Emine's ancient sword to strike the buckler, Warlock Lith'rian materialized on the Blue Throne to acknowledge him with a cryptic elvish smile. Then the troll, witch of the west. Then north—*Raspnex!* There was the dwarf himself, squat and bearded in a white toga, his bare arm thick as something hanging in a butcher's.

Nothing was wrong.

Umpily wrestled with physical nausea. Had he been deceived? Had those mad adventures with dwarves and fauns all been illusion? Surely it was easier to believe that than to assume that all this was faked?

There was nothing wrong. Everything was going just as it had been described in the briefings and rehearsals . . . except that Prince Emthoro was missing. And Duchess Ashia, the impress's sister, was missing also.

And so was he. Peering carefully through the gloom, he established beyond doubt that the group to which he had been assigned in the rehearsals did not contain a bogus Lord Umpily.

He couldn't be there, of course.

He was in Guwush.

True avouch:

BARNARDO

How now, Horatio! you tremble and look pale.
Is not this something more than fantasy?
What think you on't?

HORATIO

Before my God, I might not this believe
Without the sensible and true avouch
Of mine own eyes.

Shakespeare, *Hamlet*, I, I

❰ FIVE ❱

Stormy clouds

1

"Uomaya?" Shandie said. "I don't think my mother would have appreciated having her name put on this old tub."

She certainly would not have approved of her imperial son being an outlaw within his own impire, either, but the situation presented opportunities—

"Very appropriate, I'd have thought," Ylo said airily.

The imperor shot him a disbelieving glare, then nodded reluctantly. "That's good! Keep it up. And I'll try to respond. I haven't ever had much experience at banter, though." He sounded almost wistful.

It would do no harm to learn, maybe. Baiting Shandie would be an unfamiliar amusement—how far dare Ylo take it?

"I have an imperial edict on that? An unlimited, open-ended pardon for all sedition, misprision, and lese majesty?"

Shandie's smile was ominous. "Revocable retroactively."

"That's not bad for starters," Ylo admitted.

They huddled together on the upwind side of a very smelly fishing boat. The lout at the rudder would not be able to hear, and did not look intelligent enough to understand anything anyway. The rest of the crew—both of them—were inside the tiny cabin and out of sight. Probably they were disputing how they would divvy up the largesse brought by these unexpected passengers.

Emshandar's death had almost shut down the fishing business, although the storm had probably helped. *White Impress* had fared far to the west and used up a whole day in search of smaller craft to carry the outlaws on the next leg of their insane quest. Acopulo had gone first; then the king of Krasnegar and the inexplicable Master Thinal. Now she had released the last of her fledglings and vanished into the mist, bearing warlock and sorceress away to whatever mysterious business they had planned but would not discuss.

Yesterday's rain showed no signs of diminishing; indeed the weather was going from horrible to ghastly. The clothes King Rap had provided included warm cloaks, but they would not keep out the bone-chilling damp. Ylo was trying not to shiver.

Shandie was visibly edgy, which was very unusual for him. Now he was obviously trying to make cheerful conversation. Last night's message from Umpily had depressed everyone, even the sorcerers, and the news that an imposter had been chief mourner at his grandfather's funeral must have been an especial blow to the rightful imperor.

Ylo, by contrast, was starting to feel quite cheerful—or he had been until he noticed the motion of the boat and the stink of the fish barrels. For the first time in months, even years, he need not worry about paper piling up on his desk every time he went outside to breathe fresh air. A couple of carefree weeks in the saddle might be a very pleasant vacation, he had decided. The sooner the better.

Cheerful conversation, then . . . "To be honest," he said, "I find I am looking back on *White Impress* with nostalgia, sire."

"Me, too. But you must stop giving me titles. We need new identities. Who am I?"

Ylo had foreseen this. "You're certainly not a farmer or a weaver. Your haircut's military and your talk aristocrat. You're tribune of the first cohort, XIVth Legion."

"Why aren't I in Qoble, then?"

"Dispensational leave. Your father was created marquis of Mosrace last summer. You're going there for a family Winterfest."

"Good. And you?"

"I'd better be your brother, so we can use the same excuse."

"Why aren't we traveling on the highway?"

"Well, if anyone dares ask us, we're detouring to visit old friends."

"That's not bad at all! Outlawry has not spoiled your ability to be a resourceful aide."

Ylo ignored that obvious flattery. "I'm your signifer. We're both bachelors."

"Yes, that's very good! Our names?"

"Er . . . Yyan and Yshan."

Shandie adjusted his hood and peered hard at Ylo through the drizzle. No one had ever accused him of being stupid, except possibly where women were concerned. "Your brothers?"

"Yes, your . . . Yes, Yshan."

For a moment the imperor studied Ylo's face as if he had not done so for a while, and wanted to renew his memories of it. Then he nodded sadly. "Yshan, then! I'll take that name as an honor."

"He would have been very proud to lend it to you." Then Ylo wondered if that was true—Yshan had been one of the last of the family to die, and even his patriotic fervor must have flagged a little near the end. There were reliable reports that he had been racked.

Shandie said nothing more for a while. Perhaps he knew the truth behind the gruesome stories.

Ylo had not been joking when he said that the warlock's old ferry had been better than *Uomaya*. He pulled his cloak tighter around him, feeling the rain driving against the exposed corners of his face. *Uomaya* seemed to roll in all directions at once, and certainly with no pattern. The little cabin would be drier and possibly warmer, but he could guess how it would stink. Even here on deck and on the upwind side, the air grew unbreathable every now and again. Up. Down. Up . . . Every board was mottled silver with decades of fish scales.

He decided he would never eat fish again, never! He must not think about eating ever again, either, but his eyes kept wandering back to all those staring eyes in the barrels, shiny dead horrors.

His queasy brooding was interrupted by an exclamation from the imperor, who had pulled one of the little magic scrolls from his pocket and opened it.

"Idiot!" Shandie muttered. "Look! Umpily is going to the enthronement."

Ylo's insides quivered. "He's lost a wheel!"

"No. In spite of his looks and his prying, Umpily's a very determined man, and a brave one!"

A very crazy one. Ylo could not imagine what would drag him there. The Rotunda would be a hive of sorcerers.

Scowling, the imperor produced a silverpoint. "It's probably too late to stop him!" He scribbled a note, then stuffed vellum and stylus back inside his cloak. He sat up and adjusted his hood so he could see Ylo better. "I know you said you wanted to be part of the team, but I will not hold you to that, now we know what lies ahead of us. You have no personal stake in this battle, unlike the rest of us. As soon as we reach land, you should go. I shall think more of your brains."

It was a tempting thought, but of course a cautious warrior like Shandie always tested his weapons before the battle. Ylo shook his head. "What, and desert my brother Yshan?"

"Be sure! I would much rather shake hands and part as friends than have a companion climb out a window on me."

The window gambit had already occurred to Ylo. First, though, he must lure Shandie along the Krasnegar road far enough that he would not just head back to Yewdark to collect Hardgraa as replacement bodyguard. A week ought to do it. Then Ylo could defenestrate, backtrack, and arrive at Yewdark long before the daffodils did. He was going to be very surprised indeed if he could not talk his way into Eshiala's bed within three days. Probably two. Four at the outside. And then—ah!

But it might not be wise to mention that program to her husband. He would not enjoy his trip to Krasnegar so much if he knew what Ylo was doing with his wife.

"I'm still your man, sire."

The imperor sighed again. "You've lost as many wheels as Umpily. But I'm grateful, very grateful. Ylo, it's true I offered you the honor of Rivermead to redress the wrong my grandfather committed against your family, but there was more to it than that. Your service over the last two years has been impeccable. I value your honesty and loyalty and capability enormously. I'm not exaggerating when I say that there is no one I trust more."

This conversation was quite embarrassing. Furthermore, Ylo could no longer ignore that other problem creeping up on him. *White Impress* had taken her sorcery with her, and its absence was becoming more evident every . . .

"Whom did you see in the pool?" the imperor asked quietly.

Danger! Ylo felt a pulse start to hammer in his throat. "The loveliest woman in the world."

"Yes, but you told us you'd identified her."

"Tribune Uthursho's wife."

Shandie considered his fellow outlaw for a moment. "And have you? . . ."

"Not yet. She wants a divorce and marriage."

"And you don't?"

"Divorce yes, the other no. Not yet, anyway."

"The army disapproves of divorce, you know." Clearly the commander in chief did so, too. "The theory is that an officer who can't discipline his wife can't possibly handle troops."

"I know. I was going to ask you to arrange it as a special favor, your—er—Yshan." Ylo was spinning as he went, spinning like a spider. But the web seemed to be sticky enough.

Shandie shook his head disbelievingly. "You young demon! That's the first favor you've ever asked me for, and what you want is another man's wife! If I ever, I mean *when*, I recover my throne, then you can have as many wives as . . . No, I mean of course I'll arrange it for you."

Saved! Ylo's heart slid back to a more normal rate. And the Other Problem came back with a rush.

" 'Scuse me—"

He made a dive under the boom and only just reached the leeward side in time. He doubled himself over and a moment later he heard Shandie having the same problem. The fishermen came out of the cabin to watch how gentry puked.

2

A few leagues to the southwest, a very different conversation was taking place in a very similar fishing boat. Knowing how imps reacted to sailing, Rap had taken the precaution of adjusting Thinal's seaworthiness before leaving the shielded deckhouse on *White Impress*. It was a small magic, which would wear off before they reached land. He wanted a serious talk with his young companion. The two of them had the tiny, fetid cabin to themselves and no one would overhear them. He soon saw, however, that he should have adjusted a few more things, like backbone. As a proficient cat burglar, Thinal was completely unafraid of heights. Anything else terrified him. He was sitting on a bunk, clutching the sides of it with white-knuckled hands, and his eyes were rolling far more than the boat. He had never been a shining beacon of heroism in adversity.

After two days of relative relaxation, Rap was again having to discipline himself not to use his sorcerous senses. Off to the east, the overweening evil of the Covin hung over Hub like a foul cloud of darkness, although it conveyed no great urgency. Now it was resting, waiting, considering where to strike next, and he could dare to peer ahead a little into the shadows. He felt like a blind man in a lion's den. To use premonition too boldly might betray him to the listeners or bury his will under an avalanche of despair, for the future was very black. Cautiously, therefore, he had sniffed out a day or so ahead, and he was virtually certain that he was in no immediate danger.

He longed with all his heart to go speeding back to Krasnegar—to be with Inos, to warn Inos, to save Inos. To hug his children. That would be the worst possible thing he could do. He had written letters for Shandie to deliver.

With a sigh he brought his attention back to the terror-stricken imp on the other bunk. He found Thinal fascinating. When they had first met, he had seemed about the same age as Rap himself—a whiny, weedy guttersnipe with the fastest fingers in Pandemia and enough agility to scramble up a plate-glass window. Rap, Thinal, and the goblin—three youths lost in the jungles of Faerie, all boys together. They had not thought of themselves as boys, of course, and had not understood then that they were enjoying the good old days.

Thinal had never been a trustworthy friend, but they had shared misfortune together, and youth. Now they had nothing in common at all.

Rap was in his mid-thirties and Thinal in his early twenties, even if he was mathematically older than Sagorn. He was still short and slight, but he had displayed some manners around the imperor. Those, together with clean hands and well-styled hair, suggested that his talent had trended away from the cruder forms of robbery and flowered into something more sophisticated. He had refused to discuss exactly how he passed his days now, except to say he was in business. He would never come close to his brother, Andor, in either looks or charm, but he had developed a sort of appealing naïveté. Surely anyone who bought anything from that innocent-looking young imp would find that it leaked or collapsed or suffered from fatal disease.

"Enjoying yourself, are you?" Rap inquired.

Thinal curled a lip at him in a soundless snarl.

"Well, we'll be ashore in an hour or two. As you know, I'm heading for South Pithmot and the Mosweeps. I would appreciate your company if you care to come along."

The ratty face twisted into a smile. "Love to. Adventuring on the road with my friend Rap? Just like old times."

He was lying, of course. He would vanish up the first available alley and when he was gone, so were Sagorn and Darad and Jalon and Andor, some of whom might have been willing to help. That was Thinal's right, though. To compel loyalty with power was Zinixo's evil game; the good guys must not use magic for immoral purposes, however great the temptation. This impossible idealism was the heart of the new protocol. Having invented it, Rap must not violate it on its first outing.

Thinal licked his lips. "Horses? Months and months of horses? Bug-infested taverns and bad food? Wind and snow and no skin on my ass? Ain't my hinny. Save the world by yourself, King."

"I'll get lonely. Why don't you call one of the others, then?"

The little thief sneered maliciously. "I can't! And it's your blame. You're the one who twisted the spell."

"Been shirking again, have you?"

"Naw. They've been ganging up on me."

It was possible, of course. Rap wondered what Thinal might have been up to that his companions disapproved of. Some major malfeasance, perhaps. "Why?"

"Mind your own potage. Just know I'm overdue for some time, and I can't cop out until I've done it."

Rap snorted angrily to himself. He had not anticipated that problem. The rules he had imposed on the sequential gang compelled Thinal to exist about a third of the time. The limits were flexible, but if Thinal had fallen seriously short of his quota, then he truly could not call any of the others in his stead until he did some catching up.

"Actually I wasn't thinking of horses. The Covin will be looking for a faun."

Thinal sniggered. "A jotunn-size faun!"

"Yes. So I'm planning to buy a coach. I won't be so conspicuous driving a coach. You can ride inside and read poetry."

"Your father loved livestock."

"I ought to change you into a frog and drop you overboard."

"You don't dare use sorcery!" Thinal looked alarmed, though, and that was hopeful.

"No. And neither do you."

"Whatcher mean with that?"

"Come on! You're not so stupid. You know what Sagorn concluded—your word's worth more than your life."

The thief thought about it, eyes narrowing. He seemed to have forgotten the peril of his position in a small boat. Now he had realized that he was a potential danger to Rap and that therefore Rap was a danger to him. He was calculating his chances of deceiving Rap, and trying unsuccessfully not to show what he was thinking. Double-dealing was second nature to him; he did not know how to be honest in anything.

"What choices I got?"

"If you want we can say good-bye in the first town we come to. You can head back to Hub."

"What then, I rat on you?" Thinal asked cagily.

"You won't. It would be suicide. Or you can come along with me and put a healthy distance between you and Zinixo."

"Been nice knowing you."

Rap shrugged. "You think you can resume your business career? Trouble is, your house is gone and you rattle the ambience."

"I what?"

"Remember Oothiana, in Faerie? She could hear you stealing even before we got to Milflor. You make more noise than the others, Thinal. When you exercise your talent you shoot sparks, and the Covin will catch you soon, I'm sure."

The poxy impish face paled again. "Truth?"

"I swear it."

"Mean I gotta go straight from now on?"

"Jobbery will be very risky for you in Hub. Out in the boondocks you'd be safer."

"Then I got no choice, do I?"

"Not much of one. I know this sort of jaunt isn't your style, but I'd like you along. I'm thinking of myself, I admit. Darad could be very useful if I get in trouble. So could Sagorn. I'd love to go adventuring with Jalon again. I promise I'll warn you if we start getting into danger."

Thinal smiled weakly. "Then I suppose I'll come. Y'know me, Rap. Honest work would kill me."

Rap laughed and held out a hand to shake—not that such a gesture meant anything to Thinal. But he had come as close to being honest as he knew how. For the time being, that would have to do.

3

No one had presumed to instruct Lord Acopulo how he should proceed to Zark—he would have responded to such presumption with appropriate sarcasm. Nevertheless, the problem was meaty. He bore magic scrolls, a supply of gold, and missives addressed to the caliph, so he must avoid the attention of sorcerers, thieves, and soldiers respectively. He had farther to go than either Shandie or King Rap, and he was as old as the two of them added together. Half a year on horseback held no appeal for a man of his age. Nor did a long sea voyage, but it was the lesser evil.

The direct approach was often the wisest, as he had frequently advised the imperor. As soon as he was set ashore in Faintown, therefore, he sought out a secondhand clothing store. Then he headed for the nearest temple and said a brief prayer to the God of Truth to remind Them that major good must sometimes be served by minor evil.

The local priest was only too happy to send word to a member of his congregation, one of the wealthier merchants. That worthy citizen, in turn, was willing to demonstrate his fealty to the Gods by putting his chaise and chief gardener at the disposal of the stranded visitor. He had no use for them, anyway, that day, so they might as well make themselves useful by earning merit for their owner.

Thus, near to sunset that first day, Acopulo was driven in style to Wylpon, on the Great South Way. Anonymous in his new apparel, he caught the night stage south, heading for Malfin, on Home Water. Zinixo's minions would probably be watching the traffic on the main roads, but they would not be looking for a priest.

He was ashamed to discover that he was enjoying himself. He had often wondered if he had missed his calling when he decided his brains would be wasted in the priesthood. This would be a unique opportunity to find out.

Clerics traveled at a reduced fare, too.

4

"I have the strangest sensation that the ground is going up and down," Ylo said. That, and the pack on his back, were making him roll as he walked.

Shandie grunted. "Me, too."

"Of course we're not really on dry land yet, are we?" The grubby little fishing village was ankle-deep in mud, and blurred by a steady downpour. There were no stores or inns or even streets, only wattle shacks cowering in random disorder along the waterfront. Whatever the place was called—if it even had a name—it would not be on any map. The few locals slopping around in the mud were eyeing the two strangers with undisguised impish nosiness, but even the dogs were too wet to do anything about them. The only brightness Ylo could detect in the gloom was that his current civilian dress included boots in place of military sandals.

He shot a worried glance at his companion. Shandie had never been a chatterbox, but at the moment he seemed unusually taciturn and depressed. Was this merely an aftereffect of seasickness?

"Something wrong, Sire?"

"No. Well, yes, of course. Everything is wrong." The imperor straightened and smiled with a complete lack of conviction. "I suppose I'm upset about Emthoro. Worried, I mean. Just because he and my wife's sister weren't at the enthronement doesn't mean that they're *necessarily* the two impostors. If they're not, then they must be in real danger."

"I'm sure they didn't volunteer." Ylo could think of nothing more encouraging to say than that.

"No, I suppose not."

Umpily's latest devastating message had appeared on the scroll just before the fishing boat docked. It made sense that the fake imperor and impress were the missing Emthoro and Ashia. Even with unlimited sorcery available, some family background knowledge would make such a pretense easier.

Shandie must certainly be upset by the news, but perhaps not quite in the way he had said. Imps put great stock in family loyalty, and Emthoro had not been overly trustworthy to start with. There was no evidence that he had cooperated willingly with Zinixo or was enjoying his new status, but the suspicion was inevitable.

For a few minutes the two men trudged in silence through the weedy soup. Soon they had left the miserable hamlet behind and were shivering their way along a track that was barely distinguishable from the surrounding marshes. Clouds and rain merged with mists and puddles so that heaven and earth seemed to have turned to gray water together.

Then Shandie said, "Ylo—Yyan, I mean . . . This looks worse all the time! Creating an imposter imperor was a master stroke. Now the Covin can take all the time it wants to hunt me down. Zinixo doesn't even need me anymore! He can have me killed, or just forget about me, even."

Pessimism was not Shandie. If he ever had doubts, he always kept them to himself.

Startled, Ylo said, "But look on the good side! The Covin won't be hunting you nearly as hard as it was, or at least as hard as we thought it was."

"But how can I ever claim my throne? How can I ever prove who I am, even? Anyone I ask for help will dismiss me as a madman!"

"You need Sir Acopulo," Ylo said sternly. "He would remind you that there's good in every evil. If the imperor were missing, then everyone would be out looking for him, and you've been seen by half Pandemia in your time. With a fake Emshandar dancing at balls in Hub, anyone who recognizes you will just congratulate you on your resemblance to the great man."

Shandie grunted and said nothing. The next time Ylo spoke to him, he did not answer.

Eventually a stand of firs solidified out of the rainy mist, marking the end of the dismal swamps. Ylo headed for them, braving a ditch and some scratchy shrubs so he could take shelter, crouching under the branches. He was soaked to the inside of his skin, but it was relief to be out of the downpour, even if only for a few minutes. He unslung the pack and balanced it on a tangle of roots. Then he took a hard look at his companion, and did not like what he saw.

Blue-lipped and shivering, Shandie glared back at him. "Are you planning for us to walk to Krasnegar in this, Signifer?"

Ylo flinched. The weather was not his fault, and what had happened to their agreed false identities? "Should be able to get mounts just along this road—*Sire*."

"Then go and fetch them! On the double. I'll wait here." The imperor turned his back.

In two years, he had never spoken to Ylo like that, even when delivering a deserved rebuke. Neither hardship nor seasickness nor the bad news from Umpily could explain such un-Shandyish behavior. Possibly he was coming down with a fever. More likely he was just testing Ylo's loyalty again.

"I'll be as quick as I can, sir." Ylo ducked out into the rain. He headed back to the trail, striding fast. He would not let a little rudeness discourage him from his purpose. Nevertheless, he had an uneasy feeling that something unexpected was going wrong.

The fugitives dared not use the posting inns, because they would surely be watched. There were no hostelries close, anyway, or so the fishermen had said, nor a horsetrader either. But this was the Impire, so there would certainly be a constabulary within reach, and they had said that it was only a league or so away, along this wretched apology for a road.

The guard would be a retired centurion, most like, or perhaps merely an optio in a desolate nothing place like this. Whatever his former rank had been, he would certainly be a veteran, and the army always looked after its own. Ylo would spin some tale of shipwreck and a legate in distress. The guard would have at least one horse. He would willingly commandeer another from a neighbor—probably two, with a boy to bring all three of them back. They would be cart horses, likely, but better than walking. Ylo and Shandie could ride to the nearest decent-size village and there buy some mounts. It was a fairly obvious plan, but not so obvious that Shandie should not have asked about it.

The fishermen's league was an unusually long one. The guard turned out to be ancient and surly and very uncooperative, but his horse was worse; it had not been ridden in years and had become almost feral. As he floundered through mud and undergrowth after the brute, Ylo could not help reflect how much less trouble two men would have catching it. Three would do even better.

Still, the horse Ylo could not bridle had never been foaled, and he eventually persuaded the decrepit, spavined, ill-tempered hack of that simple truth and rode it in bareback just to emphasize the point. The guard's smelly little shed contained a surprising quantity of tack. It was rusty and filthy, but there was plenty of it. By then Ylo was beyond observing niceties of law. He saddled his mount and headed for the nearest farm.

Rounding up was much easier on horseback than on foot. Riding the guard's horse and leading a stolen one, he set off in search of the imperor.

Somehow, he was not surprised to find him gone. Any sensible man would have headed to the hamlet by now to find warmth and shelter. But the pack was still there, under the trees. That was worrisome.

The marshes were flooding. Shandie was almost at the little village, wading through thigh-deep water. He staggered at the waves set up by the horses' great feet, then turned to Ylo with a sour expression.

"I thought you'd deserted!"

Ylo slid from the saddle, wincing at the icy bite of the water. He began tightening girths on the spare mount.

"I was delayed by some beautiful girls and a hot meal. Which hack do you fancy? That one's Brute and this is Loot. We'll trade them both in at—"

"Return them." Shandie began wading again.

"And where the Evil are you going?" Ylo bellowed.

The imperor swung around to glare at him. "I have decided to return to Hub. You may follow if you wish. If you prefer not to, then go with the Good." He hesitated. "Er—thank you for past services."

"*What?* I think I deserve an explanation!"

Shandie's teeth were chattering. "I mean what we planned was crazy! How could we possibly prevail against the Covin? Pandemia hasn't seen its like in a thousand years! My duty is to go back to Hub and give myself up." He was avoiding Ylo's eye now.

"You? *Give up?*"

"What else? I know I can do a better job of running the

government than anyone else can. I don't suppose the dwarf will interfere much, as long as he is not threatened in any way. He'll just stay out of sight and leave me alone, to rule as a figurehead. That's what the sorcerers predicted. Thank you again, Signifer, and—"

"And what about King Rap? And Acopulo? And the warlock who risked his own life to save you?"

Shandie shrugged in silence.

"You've sent them off to the ends of the world to fight a battle for your sake, and a few hours later you desert the cause? What of your daughter and descendants? What of your cousin, and your wife's sister, impressed into a vile crime for your sake?"

"I can rescue those two, anyway."

Ylo took a deep breath. "You're crazy!"

That should have provoked an earthquake. Shandie did try another glare, but it held none of the old fire that had once burned in those dark eyes, the imperious flame that had been the only notable feature in an otherwise unremarkable appearance. Now his face showed mostly a sick hopelessness. "Sometimes it takes more courage to admit that you've been wrong than to continue making a fool of yourself."

"This is sorcery," Ylo said crossly. "The Covin's putting ideas in your mind! This is not the Shandie I know."

That impertinence produced a flicker of doubt.

"Reason it out!" Ylo insisted. "You have never made a major decision in your life and then changed it so quickly, and without any real cause! It's a sending from the Covin! For two days you've been shielded from magic, but now you're out in the open and they can get at you."

Shandie's shoulders slumped. He rubbed his hands together— he was half frozen, of course, but the gesture made him seem curiously vulnerable and indecisive. Perhaps that was because he so seldom gestured. "You could be right, I suppose."

"Of course I'm right!"

"But suppose it's the other way? Suppose I was deluded by Raspnex and the faun on the boat, and now I'm away from them I'm starting to think straight again? How can I know which is right?" His voice was a despicable whine, like a spoiled child's.

For a moment Ylo was tempted. This was not his war, as Shandie had told him earlier. He was an insignificant pawn in the political game. He could abandon the cause, vanish into the teeming population of the Impire, and the Covin would never bother him. But if Shandie gave up without a fight and went back to court, then he would take Eshiala with him, and Ylo would never have a chance to enjoy the gorgeous body he had seen in the preflecting pool. That would not do.

"I'll tell you how," he said. "There is a way to test that! Let's be on our way as we planned. In a week or so, we'll have put some ground between us and Hub. We should be out of range of the Covin, and out of range of the faun and the warlock. Believe me, then you'll be back to feeling as you did this morning."

The imperor considered that, shivering convulsively. "I suppose you're right. A big decision like that shouldn't be taken hastily."

Ylo breathed a sigh of relief. "Good. Up you get." He cupped hands for the imperor's muddy boot. "The first thing we need is a comfortable inn—a hot meal, a room, and a couple of warm girls!"

Shandie pulled a face as he took the reins. "One girl and two rooms."

Wiping his hands on his cloak, Ylo turned away to mount the other horse. "You're crazy and you always were crazy," he muttered, but he made sure that Shandie did not hear him.

5

It was on a brisk winter morning, three days later, that King Rap caught himself whistling. Somewhat shaken by this discovery, he eventually decided that he was feeling almost maniacally cheerful. The faun in him took to a coach and four as his jotunn half took to ships, and a Krasnegarian could ignore the cold. He was far enough from Hub now to have escaped from the sprawl of satellite towns and rich-folk country mansions. The surrounding plains were lush with orchards and farms. He gloried in the scenery and fine weather—wind in his hair, sun on his back, ice crackling under the wheels, the stark beauty of branches against the frosty fields.

There was more to it than that, though. He was caught up in a sort of wicked juvenile glee at this mad adventure. Even a king could crave a change once in a while, and now he was a hunted outlaw. There could be no greater change than that. And his cause was just. If, by the grace of the Gods, Shandie and his tiny band of supporters could pull off the miracle they planned, they would have made a better world. If they failed—well, they would have tried. A man could take heart from that prospect, no matter how unlikely success might seem at the moment. With a little effort, Rap could probably recall some suitable proverb of his mother's on the subject.

Thinking of his mother, though, brought on thoughts of pre-science and young Gath, back in Krasnegar. That was not a cheerful topic. And he missed Inos as he would have missed both legs and an arm.

He had done well in his choice of horses, although the roan was weaker than the other three and might need to be traded off soon. They had a long way to go, so he was setting an easy pace for them. Who would question a faun driving a coach? He had thought to make himself some passable livery before leaving *White Impress*, so he looked the part.

At his back, the hatch clicked open. He twisted around to see Thinal's gaunt face peering out like a ferret in a burrow. His nose was red with cold and the tip of it sparkled wetly.

"I'm hungry!" he complained.

Whined.

Thinal was bored to distraction, that was the trouble with Thinal. Scenery and adventure held no interest for him. Nothing did, except extracting wealth from its rightful owners.

"Then you should have gotten up earlier and eaten break-fast," Rap said crossly. He recognized the tone he used on Kadie at her worst, and stopped himself before he broke into a lecture on what happened to people who sat up until all hours gambling in bars. Admittedly Thinal had rattled the ambience very little, and he had won more than enough to pay for their joint board and lodgings. Gods knew how much he could have collected had he really tried.

"Wait an hour, and we'll give the horses a rest."

"You care more for them than you do for me!" Thinal snarled—which was perfectly true—and slammed the hatch shut on an obscenity.

Rap continued to drive on along the road, but his cheerful mood had dimmed. Obviously he was going to lose his traveling companion very soon, for Thinal would not endure much more bouncing around. A faun driving an empty carriage might be asked questions. Thinal himself Rap could do without, but he was potentially four other men, also, and they were handy accomplices in dangerous escapades, as experience had demonstrated, long ago. Pity!

At noon, Rap felt he had barely caught his second wind, but the horses needed a rest. He pulled into a stable yard in some anonymous little farming town. Only the great trunk roads of the Impire provided posting stations, and the inn he had chosen was a humble establishment. Thinal, the thief, stalked off in search of lunch, playing gentleman. The king of Krasnegar rubbed down the horses and saw to their needs. Fortunately his sense of humor was capable of appreciating the irony.

He joined the servants in the inn kitchen for a quick slab of cheese and rye bread, deflecting questions with vague tales of taking the master home for Winterfest. The only fauns who ever roamed the Impire were hostlers; despite his size, he was inconspicuous in that role. Nobody spoke of sorcery or politics or the new imperor, only the unusually cold weather and the price of grain. He was much more at home with these humble, honest folk than he was with royalty like Shandie. When the time came to dash out and rig up again, it seemed much too soon.

Thinal sauntered out, accompanied by a well-dressed middle-aged couple—a portly, florid-face man and a lady even more so. Rap lowered the steps for them and held the door, keeping his face straight with extreme effort.

Thinal paused before following his guests into the coach.

"Master Orbilo and his lady have kindly offered me hospitality for the night," he explained airily. "Carry on along the river road and we'll direct you where to turn off."

"Yessir." Rap touched his cap in salute.

"We shan't be going far out of our way," Thinal added, his eyes glittering with mischief. "And, boy . . ."

"Yessir?"

"Remember what I said about tiring the horses, or it will go hard with you."

"I'll be very careful, sir." The king of Krasnegar bowed respectfully. As he closed the carriage door, he said a prayer that Thinal would be able to restrain his larcenous instincts. A little finger work would do no harm, but he might attract occult attention if he started romancing these worthy citizens about his grandfather's lost gold mine.

An hour or so later, the road came to a bridge. Rap reined in at the toll gate. At once a half-dozen legionaries appeared from nowhere to surround the carriage, and his heart began to thump with rare enthusiasm. They were looking at him, not the door, so their interest was in the driver, not the passengers. That was very bad news. He needed no occult talent to see the suspicion in their gaze. Zinixo controlled the Imperial army, and could have issued warrants for the arrest of all oversize fauns. Normally mundanes could be no threat to Rap, but the Covin would still be listening for any use of power near the capital.

The centurion drew his sword as his men took hold of the reins. "You, boy! Down!"

"Master?" Rap exclaimed, trying to look stupid, and thinking that it would be altogether appropriate under the circumstances. He began tying the reins, although legionaries were holding the lead pair's cheek straps. He moved clumsily along the bench, taking his time so he could analyze the situation. The closer he could come to the centurion himself, the less power he would need to use to influence him. And then, amid the sparkle of sunlight on chain mail, he saw a faint shimmer of sorcery on the man.

It might be a loyalty spell, in which case he was one of the dwarf's votaries. That seemed unlikely, for this was a very minor road, one of hundreds in the Capital District. Zinixo could not possibly have enough manpower to post sorcerers on them all. The centurion did not show in the ambience, not at the moment, so probably he was just a bespelled mundane. Rap dared not pry deeper, to discover what the magic did. It might make the wearer immune to mastery, or sound alarms if it was used near him, or . . . or . . . Holy Balance! Now what?

Then the side window of the carriage clicked open, revealing the rubicund face of Master Orbilo.

"What's happening? Oh, it's you, Uggleepe!"

Startled, the centurion saluted. "Uncle!"

"Well? What's going on?"

"Just a routine check, sir."

"Well, you've checked. You know me, I hope?"

"Of course, Uncle!"

"Good. Then clear the road." Orbilo disappeared. Uggleepe backed up quickly, sheathing his sword and shouting at his men to stand clear.

Saved! Rap climbed back on the box and took up the reins again. "Have a nice day, Centurion," he murmured quietly.

Thinal was going to be unbearable over this incident when he got Rap alone—bless him!

6

Shandie roused himself as if he had been riding in his sleep. He stared at the gates of the city ahead and then turned in the saddle to fix an angry gaze on Ylo.

"Newbridge?"

"That's right."

Apparently he was only now registering the bustle of traffic on the highway—coaches and wagons and groups of riders—and yet it had been all around him for the last half hour. "I thought we were going to stay on side roads and avoid crowds?"

"Where else can we cross the Ambly?" Ylo said patiently. "I don't fancy swimming it in this weather."

"There are ferries!" Shandie's eyes were dark slits of suspicion.

Ylo sighed. "We discussed this."

"Discuss it again!"

"We agreed we'd be more noticeable on a ferry than crossing a bridge in a crowd, and more easily remembered."

"I don't remember discussing that at all!"

"Well, we did. You don't listen."

Shandie grunted and fell silent, absently chewing a fingernail. Soon he seemed to sink back into the black brooding that occupied so much of his time now. Every day was worse than the one before. Distance had brought no lessening in the Covin's hold over him; if anything, his doubts and depression were increasing. He rarely spoke, except when he had found yet another reason to turn back and surrender to the usurper. Hub was calling him, and either the call was growing stronger or his resistance was fading.

Ylo also was rapidly sinking into despair. He was exhausted by Shandie's arguments, depressed by his lethargy, and worried sick by his unpredictable fits of temper. He hardly dared let the

imperor out of his sight for fear the madman would disappear.
Emshandar had died after a fifty-year reign, the wardens had
been overthrown after three thousand—fine! Ylo could accept
those changes as being no more unexpected than weather. But
to find Shandie, of all people, behaving like a sulky child was
enough to unseat the heavens. As well expect trees to walk or
fish to sing.

Now came a new worry, for Newbridge was an obvious trap.
Here the Great West Way crossed the mighty Ambly and here,
surely, Zinixo would have sorcerers watching the traffic. As Ylo
and his ward rode in through the gates, he offered a prayer that
there would be safety in numbers.

Winterfest was coming and the Impire was on the move. Imps
went home at Winterfest as bees sought their hives at sunset.
Highways were solid with horses and carriages as half the population headed to family reunions with the other half. In the
rainy gloom of a winter evening, Newbridge was packed. Im-
mobilized traffic jammed the narrow streets. Angry coachmen
shouted and argued, demanding right of way, proclaiming the
importance of their passengers. Women and children wailed in
fear as they were crushed tight by the press of the crowd. At the
best of times this road would be shadowed, and now it was
almost dark. Ylo struggled to keep his horse close to Shandie's,
aware that his legs were going to be black and blue from the
battering they were taking.

"Yshan?"

The imperor grunted. "Humph?"

"If we get separated, wait for me at the North Gate."

"Humph."

"Crushed a couple of dozen yesterday," a cheerful voice at
Ylo's elbow remarked.

He glanced around and decided he had never met the young
man whose horse was crowding into his. Danger was making
normally taciturn strangers talkative. "Should be able to do better than that if we try."

The youngster sniggered nervously. "You're not wearing
spurs, are you? Saw a yokel back there with spurs on."

"Ought to be a law," Ylo agreed. One horse pricked unexpectedly could create a disaster. "What's the delay?"

"The army tries to limit the numbers getting on the bridge.
They don't have much luck at this time of year."

"They close down at sunset?"

"Uh-huh. Well, usually allow an hour or so longer. Frightened of a riot if they're too early, my dad says."

The crowd edged forward. Ylo urged his horse after Shandie's. His new friend followed. He was obviously a local, probably an apprentice.

"Going far?"

"Mosrace."

"You sure won't make that by Winterfest."

"At this rate I won't make it by Harvesthome," Ylo agreed, with a mental note to revise his cover story. Mosrace must be farther west than he'd thought.

Shandie glanced around. "Ylo?"

"Yes, *Yshan*?"

"The bridge here is too narrow. It needs widening. Remind me when we get back to Hub."

Ylo sighed. "Yes, Yshan."

Shandie set to work chewing another fingernail.

"Who's he?" asked the youngster. "Looks familiar."

"Sh! He's very sensitive about it."

"Oh."

Shandie might have passed through Newbridge a dozen times or so in the last few years. Once or twice he might have been conspicuous at the head of troops, but usually he would have been fast and anonymous, and his was not a memorable face. Almost certainly the boy was mistaking him for someone else altogether. The crowd surged forward a few paces and the talkative youth was detached. In a few moments Ylo found himself trading chaff with a buxom housewife looking out of a carriage window. She had a nice line in innuendos.

Nothing lasts forever, and eventually the crowd oozed out of the alleyway and onto the approach to the great Emthar II Bridge. There it slowed down. The bridge itself snaked away as a ribbon of darkness across the silvery brightness of water, and the far bank was invisible in the misty winter evening. Ylo was horrified when he saw how many guards there were. Perhaps they were only regulating traffic, but he suspected they were inspecting the travelers, as well. Nothing he could do about it now, though—with Shandie at his side, he was being borne forward by the crowd as irresistibly as a boulder on a glacier.

"Yyan!" Shandie exclaimed, jerking alert again. "I've got it!"

"Got what?"

"The real story! Listen to this. It was all the faun's doing! Why didn't we see how unlikely it was—that he would turn up on the very evening Grandsire died? That's got to be more than coincidence!"

"I don't see why. You suggesting he assassinated your grand-father?" Personally, Ylo could imagine no less likely murderer than King Rap.

"Possibly!" Shandie's eyes were gleaming with excitement. "He used sorcery on Grandsire once before, remember! And got away with it! Then he faked that scene in the Rotunda. That wasn't Raspnex we saw at all, it was the faun!"

Ylo groaned at this insanity. "Was he Grunth, as well?"

"Yes. No. She never spoke, remember? Just bowed. So she was merely a delusion. And so was the destruction of the four thrones. We were made to imagine that!"

Ylo could recall being hit by a flying rock, but he said nothing as the nonsense poured out—

"So the wardens knew nothing of what was going on! Rap's an enormously powerful sorcerer, remember. He lured us away to Sagorn's house . . ." Shandie paused, frowning. Then he beamed. "Lured us away with fake memories of a preflecting pool, of course. Obviously that whole business never happened! We were given false memories of it, that's all. I mean, is it likely? Magic pools just lying around? For half a year we do nothing about those supposed prophecies, and then we manage to track down Sagorn in a couple of hours?"

"We saw Rap and Raspnex there together," Ylo said wearily. "You suggesting that the dwarf was a sort of ventriloquist's dummy?"

He should have known that logic wouldn't work.

"Certainly!" Shandie shouted. "I hadn't thought of that. Brilliant!" He went on to explain how the faun was trying to lure him away to Krasnegar—for reasons he had not worked out yet—and how the wardens were trying to cover for him, hiding his disappearance with the help of Cousin Emthoro and Duchess Ashia, of course, and there was no Usurper Zinixo, it was all just a story the faun had made up . . .

When he ran down at last like a dried-out water clock and

said, "Well, what do you think?" Ylo realized that they were in the middle of the river, halfway across the bridge, and had safely passed the guards.

In a spasm of relief, he threw caution to the crows. "I've seen lots more attractive stuff on barn floors," he sneered, and took the rest of the crossing to tear the imperor's absurd fantasy to fragments.

Shandie went into a sulk after that. For an hour he said nothing at all, just trailed after Ylo as he scoured the northern half of Newbridge for a vacant bed. When the search at last turned up a grubby little inn, he did not comment on it. The stable was already crowded, and no grooms were available to attend to the horses. Still Shandie said nothing. He dismounted in silence, handed his reins to Ylo, and began pacing up and down, brooding.

Normally Ylo enjoyed horses, but he was weary and hungry, and would have appreciated some help. The change in his companion frightened him, but it also annoyed him. He detested being thrust into leadership over a man he had followed so faithfully. He had not expected this responsibility, or asked for it, and he resented it strongly. He placed himself in Shandie's path.

"Here!" he said, waving the key. "You'd better take possession of the room, or we may find half a cohort asleep in our bed when we get there. Take the packs. Number seven."

He stopped in horror, realizing he had just given orders to the imperor. Yet Shandie did not protest. He wandered off, trailing the saddlebags. Snorting with either relief or disgust—he was not sure which—Ylo grabbed up some straw and went back to polishing sweaty horsehide.

The sun set. When he finally plodded up the creaky stairs, he discovered the key in the door, and the room empty. To be exact, he found no imperors in it. The one bed nearly filled the tiny space, the only other furniture being a very spotty mirror bolted to the wall and a large china chamber pot, equally unprepossessing.

For a moment he almost panicked. Shandie could not have gone anywhere without the horses, and he had not come out to the yard to use the privy. Could he have been kidnapped?

The saddlebags had been stuffed down between the bed

and the far wall. Underneath them was Shandie's satchel, containing the king's letters to Krasnegar and the supply of gold. Obviously Shandie had taken leave of his senses altogether if he had left the gold unguarded. If that was ever lost, everything would be lost.

After locking the door and looping the satchel over his shoulder, Ylo went clattering back downstairs. The saloon was crammed, noisy, and dim. There were no spare seats, and so many men standing that there was barely room to move. He hunted around, with no success. He went outside and searched the stables, the privies, the yard, even the street. With any other man, he would have suspected a girl and a bed, but not Shandie.

Now what was he supposed to do? Rouse the city guard to hunt for a missing *imperor*?

Fatigue forgotten and fear a bitter taste in his mouth, Ylo went back to the bedroom and began all over again. When he reached the saloon, he set out to quarter it methodically, squeezing around crowded tables and between loud huddles of men locked in argument. Eventually he found his quarry slumped on a solitary stool in a corner, gazing solidly at the wall. He clutched a tankard of bad-smelling beer with both hands. It had to be bad-smelling beer if it was the same stuff that made the room stink as it did.

Ylo managed to ease in beside him and kneel down, almost leaning on him.

"What's wrong?" he demanded. "You sick?"

The imperor looked around slowly and stared at him with an expression of distaste. He muttered, "Uomaya!" and took a leisurely draft from his tankard.

"What about her?"

"What about her?" Shandie mumbled. "What sort of man deserts his child and runs away just because a dwarf says to, huh?"

"Whileboth's faster," said a harsh military voice at Ylo's back.

"Poor little Maya!" Shandie moaned. "I left my baby!"

"Whileboth and the Ister valley and then Mosrace."

Mosrace? That was where Ylo had been telling people he was heading. He choked off what he had been about to say so he could listen. In the clamor of voices all around, he did not make out an answer, but then the nearest man spoke again.

"Naw, too hilly. And not Lipash township neither. Roads'll be waist-deep in mud this time of year."

Ylo relaxed. Nothing to do with him, just a party of legionaries heading home on Winterfest leave, obviously. Mosrace was a largish place, so its mention was merely coincidence. He returned his attention to Shandie and the wild, bitter look in the coal-black eyes.

"You left the baggage unattended!"

"Should have stayed in Qoble, stayed with the legion. Deserted my post. Not fit to be an imperor."

"Tell me what I can do to help."

Shandie raised his stein to drink. Ylo thought he was not going to get a reply, then it came. "Tell me what you've done so far."

"Huh?"

The dark eyes narrowed. "What's in this for you, Signifer? You've never been an idealist before. You only care about the itch in your crotch. Why should you suddenly start acting hero?"

For a moment Ylo wanted to make a stupid retort about being the only man in the army entitled to wear a white wolfskin. Then he remembered that he had earned that honor by accident, and Shandie knew that. All right, so he wasn't a hero. He'd never said he was.

And Shandie went on. "Who bought you, Signifer? What were you promised?"

"I don't have a clue what you're talking about!"

"Don't you? You expect me to believe all this puke about covins and almighty sorcerers?"

"You don't?"

Shandie smiled slyly into his tankard. "No, I don't! Not now. Oh, they fooled me to start with, that dwarf, that faun. Now I see it was all a plot! They've stolen me away from my throne with their feathery tales of millennia and votaries! And I don't think you believe it, either—I think you're one of them!"

God of Madness! The Covin was winning, distance had not helped.

"Er, your wife believed in it."

"Ha! What do women know of politics, huh?"

Plenty, in Ylo's extensive experience of pillow talk, and they were usually a great deal more astute at judging men. For him to bring Eshiala into the conversation with Shandie in his present mood might provoke all sorts of unfounded suspicions. So—

"Maybe you're right! What do you think we ought to do?"

Shandie blinked at this sudden capitulation. Odd twitches of expression flickered uncertainly over his face. Then he drained his tankard and lowered it with a gasp. He wiped his lips on his sleeve. "Go home, of course! Go back to Hub and do my duty. Catch all the liars and hang 'em from the flagpole."

Ylo needed a sorcerer, quickly. He needed help and he certainly needed advice. If Shandie persisted in these delusions, he might take off back along the Hub road like a madman. He might do worse—he might just give himself up to the local authorities. Why had the faun or the warlock not foreseen that this might happen? Just as it had in inventing the imposter imperor now reigning in Hub, the Covin had pulled a trick the godly had not anticipated. What evilish horror might it play next?

If Shandie could be taken into a shielded refuge like *White Impress*, then he might recover. Maybe. But a mundane like Ylo had no means to locate such shielding. If he could lay his hands on the magic scrolls he could ask the sorcerers for advice, but the scrolls were in Shandie's pocket. To ask for them would only fan the madman's suspicions—perhaps he could try to steal them in the night. A reply might not come for days, though.

"Can't go anywhere tonight," Ylo said, smitten with sudden inspiration. "They close the bridge at sunset."

Shandie grunted. He was still staring at his companion with undisguised suspicion. The legionaries' geographical dispute was growing louder in the background.

"I don't think we'll get any food here," Ylo continued. "And it would be old and ill-treated if we could. We've still got some apples and stuff in the packs. Why don't we go and have a snack and then make an early night of it?" He was talking too fast, almost babbling.

"What, no wench tonight?"

"Same argument as the food."

"It's never stopped you before." Shandie was not so far out of his mind that he had lost his shrewdness. If anything, his crazy suspicions would make him even harder to deceive than usual, and marble was malleable compared to Shandie.

"I'll have two tomorrow to make up," Ylo said, wishing he

could wipe the sweat off his face without drawing attention to it. "Come on. This place makes me ill."

Shandie reluctantly put his tankard down among the boots around him and rose to his feet. He swayed, steadying himself with a hand on the wall. "You're right," he muttered. "Hard day."

It had not been a hard day at all. They had covered less than fifteen leagues, which was as much as they dare ask of the horses on these roads. Shandie had been known to ride three times that far in a day, often.

Then he sat down again, heavily. "Get me 'nother beer."

This unshaven, unkempt wastrel was a far cry from the dapper prince Ylo had served so long. He was either a very sick man or he was drunk. The idea of Shandie drunk was unthinkable, but then this whole experience was unthinkable.

"You've had enough beer, Yshan."

"Am not Yshan!" Shandie roared, coloring. "I'm done with your stupid games! From now on I'm not hiding who I am, and I'm going back to my palace, and I'm not going to Mosrace, and I'll not believe all that evilish nonsense about threats to the Impire!"

God of Mercy! What was Ylo to do? The fate of the world had suddenly been dumped in his unwilling hands. He didn't want it. He didn't know what to do with it. He could still think of no solution except to get Shandie as far away from Hub as quickly as possible, in the hope that the sorcery might yet weaken with distance and let him recover his wits.

For a moment he considered taking the imperor along by force, but that was obviously impossible. Tie him to the saddle? Shandie was probably as strong as he was, and could shout for help. Get him up to the room and stun him with the chamber pot? Stun the imperor? Keep him stunned for weeks? Ylo had seen too many men crippled by head wounds to consider that fantastic solution.

Then he realized that a local cloud of silence had settled over the table at his back. He looked around, and up, into the inquisitive stare of the man he had heard earlier. Beyond him, behind a forest of tankards, his three companions were watching.

They had heard Shandie shouting about Mosrace, and other things, dangerous things.

They wore civilian clothes. They were all about the same age, old to be soldiers, and yet their steady gaze held the unmistakable look of legionaries—tough, hardened, self-reliant. The nearest one bore a jagged old scar across his nose. Four men in their middle forties . . . Without a doubt, these were veterans, legionaries who had completed their twenty-five-year stint and were heading home with their requital in their pockets to find themselves wives and farms. They might be honest, or they might not. They might cherish a virulent dislike for aristocrats like the officers who had ordered them around for a generation, or they might hold to the instinctive respect and obedience that had been hammered into them so painfully in their youth and reinforced every day of their manhood.

Ylo was still staring up at the scarred man staring down at him, and he seemed to be the leader. He was not unlike Hardgraa in appearance. In fact, he had *centurion* written all over him.

A sudden germ of an idea . . .

"Perhaps you can tell us," Ylo said, "how many days' ride to Mosrace?"

"Too Evilish many. What of it?"

Shandie registered the conversation and twisted around on his stool to see. He scowled. "I told you we're not going to Mosrace. We're going back to the palace!"

Four pairs of eyes blinked.

Ylo rose to the occasion. "My name's Yyan—cohort signifer with the XIVth." He indicated Shandie. "Tribune Yshan. We're on our way to Mosrace—"

"I am not a tribune! I'm the imperor."

The four faces inspected one another and then came back to their previous direction.

"Had a little too much, has he?" the centurion inquired.

"It's worse than that, I'm afraid," Ylo said sadly. "He's been prone to these attacks ever since Nefer Moor. I'm his brother. I'm trying to get him home, you see. He was all right when we started out, but—"

Shandie barked, "Ylo!"

"Ylo?" another man said. "Nefer Moor? He was at Nefer Moor?"

"We both were," Ylo said with becoming modesty. "The stories don't really do it justice, though. Ever since then, he's had these odd notions. Not all the time, just—"

Shandie bellowed, *"Ylo!"* He lurched to his feet, but he was penned in the corner by the crowd.

Ylo twitched eyebrows meaningfully, and the other men nodded in silent sympathy. Veterans knew what battle could do to a man.

"At times he thinks he's the imperor and I'm—"

"Ylo!"

"Ylo," Ylo said touchingly. "I am his signifer, you see. He sometimes thinks I'm that other one."

The whole army knew of Shandie's defeat by dragons at Nefer Moor, and how his heroic Signifer Ylo had saved the legionary standard in the rout. The situation definitely showed promise.

"Here, your Majesty," the centurion growled, like a bear trying to make friends. "Pull over your seat and quaff some ale with us."

Bodies squirmed. Shandie's stool was drawn up to the table, and heavy hands pulled him down on it. Two of the other men were sharing a bench and somehow made room for Ylo.

In the dim light, the imperor's face was dark with fury and frustration. Whatever vile plot had been suggested to his mind by Zinixo's sorcery and whatever part he thought Ylo was playing in it, he had enough wit left to see that anything he said now was only going to sink him deeper into the morass. As imperor or as tribune, in every way, he was pinned.

"We're hoping a few peaceful months at home with the family will do the trick," Ylo said, wiping foam from his lips. He felt much better already. "He finds the road tiring. I was thinking of hiring an escort to help, er, protect, er . . . you follow me?"

Again the men exchanged glances.

Shandie paled suddenly and made a choking noise.

"Well, now," Scarface said, "it so happens my friends and me's heading up Mosrace way."

"How about a crown per day?" Ylo contrived to jingle his satchel.

Four pairs of eyes gleamed in the shadows. *"Each?"*

"Yes. It must be done discreetly, you understand."

"You just hired yourself a legion, Signifer Yyan!" The centurion pushed away his beer. "Name's Eemfume. Iggi and me'll take first watch. Bull, Squint, you go eat and get some sack time. Now, your Majesty, tell us about Nefer Moor."

When in doubt, delegate, Ylo thought happily. He would be able to go wenching tonight after all.

Stormy clouds:

O doubting heart!
The stormy clouds on high
Veil the same sunny sky,
That soon, for spring is nigh,
Shall wake the summer into golden mirth.

Adelaide Anne Proctor, *A Doubting Heart*

❦ INTERLUDE ❧

At the dying of the year came Winterfest.

Within the Impire it was a bittersweet celebration, a time for telling tales of the beloved old imperor now gone, and for hopeful prayers for the new one. Without all the traditional merrymaking, a surprising number of people discovered the festival dragging on rather longer than usual; many found themselves becoming unimpishly sick of their relatives before it was over.

Hub itself seemed strangely subdued without the great balls and banquets. Small gatherings of friends and family took their place. The rotund form of Lord Umpily appeared unannounced and uninvited at an astonishing number of those—gossiping, inquiring, listening, and soon disappearing as mysteriously as he had come.

In remote Krasnegar the customary revelry was as boisterous as ever. Yet even there the usual sparkle was oddly dimmed by a sense of someone missing. The royal ball was less riotous than usual, with very few serious injuries. Of course only a small fraction of the population could ever attend court functions, but the humble folk were not neglected. Traditionally, anyone planning an affair of any size notified the palace in advance, and either king or queen would drop in for a few minutes. Rap held the current record of eighteen parties in one day, although Inos' great-great-grandfather was reputed to have managed twenty-nine once and almost died in consequence. This year the queen had to manage on her own, despite her elder daughter's earnest offers of assistance.

In the little speech she repeated over and over, her majesty made her first public reference to the king's absence. "My husband and I," she said, "have always taken great joy in these Winterfest celebrations, and regarded them as an occasion to reaffirm the bonds of loyalty and service which bind us to you, and you to our family. He will be truly regretful that he cannot be here with you this morning/ afternoon/evening. As you know, he has been gone for some time now on a mission of great secrecy, a mission vital to all our well-beings. I am sure that you look forward to his return with almost as much anticipation as do his children and I . . ." And so on. She did not explain where he was or what he was doing, though.

To the south, on the far side of the taiga, the impish garrison at Pondague stood to arms all through the festive season, for a goblin attack at that time had become traditional. That year nothing happened. The forests remained quiet—eerily so.

So began the year 2999, and the peoples of Pandemia hunkered down to endure the long dark in expectation of better days to come. Even the rich, who could afford candles, found winter tedious.

In Malfin, Sir Acopulo fretted and fumed, hunting in vain for any ship willing to set sail in the continuing stormy weather.

In the southern provinces of Pithmot, a somewhat road-worn coach meandered on its way, frequently detouring from one country house to another as Thinal befriended local worthies. Whenever his cheating, embezzling, or filching became dangerously occult, Rap would quietly intervene to stop it. As the weeks went by, though, the little scoundrel perfected his technique to the point where he could elicit sizable gains without rippling the ambience hardly at all. He no longer talked of abandoning ship, even when Rap made him replace his loot where he had found it. He was using the journey as a training course.

Ylo's abduction of the imperor proceeded without a hitch, aided by Centurion Eemfume (Retired) and his three friends. On the road, in bed, at board—even when he went to the latrines—Shandie was never out of sight of at least two of them. He sulked, ranted, argued, and ordered, and was treated with the polite sympathy due a deranged aristocrat. Ylo was able to relax and enjoy the journey, wenching his way across Julgistro.

Gradually the days grew longer.

In Thume it was the rainy season.

⊄ SIX ⊅

Life's young day

1

Snowflakes big as feathers danced in the air, tickling eyelids and turning the sun to a brilliant blur. The air was warmer than it had been for days. Hooves clopped on the smooth stone of the Great West Way, and winter scenery drifted by in a monochrome of white and gray. Even the grasses of the ditches were colorless.

"The turnoff's just ahead, as I recall," Centurion Eemfume said.

"All great friendships must end eventually," Ylo responded. He had been lost in a reverie about waitresses, trying to decide whether he preferred the slim, energetic ones or the plump, comfortable ones. It was a difficult choice, although not a very important one. He enjoyed both very much.

He realized that Eemfume had arranged this discussion, edging his horse aside and thus Ylo's also. The others were several paces back, out of earshot.

"You'll be all right now, Signifer, I think," the centurion said cautiously.

Ylo laughed. "Perfectly! Did you ever see such a change in a man?"

It had happened only three days since. Shandie had gone to bed still a wild-eyed, bearded maniac threatening terrible torments on all those who kidnapped their rightful imperor. He had awakened sane, icily furious, demanding a razor and hot water.

Even his guards, who had never known him before, had recognized his authority from that moment on. Indeed, if he and Ylo were to give contradictory orders now, it was more than likely that Eemfume and his friends would obey the imperor.

The Covin, in short, had given up.

"Course we can come all the way to the door if you feel it's needful, Signifer," the centurion said wistfully. Never in his life had he earned money as he had these last few weeks.

"No, I'm sure we'll be all right now—thanks to you and your friends." For the mythical Yyan and Yshan to turn up at the lordly estate of the rightful marquis would provoke embarrassment, to say the least, as no one there would have ever heard of them. "Yshan was talking about giving you all a bonus, if that would not hurt your feelings?"

The old warrior pursed his lips. "Twenty-five years in the ranks, and you think we have *feelings*?"

Ylo laughed again. "Well, it was just a thought. We are very grateful, both of us!"

He meant that. Shandie was cured and could take charge of his quest again. Now, at last, Ylo was free to implement his own plans—return to Yewdark and Eshiala, defection and seduction.

The turnoff appeared on schedule, a track winding off through the leafless black trees and over the iron-gray hills of winter. Somewhere along that trail Eemfume and his three friends would find their childhood homes, half-forgotten relatives, perhaps wives and future children, plus shelter for their old age. A milestone reported Mosrace itself close ahead on the highway. Somewhere thereabouts was the estate to which Ylo and Shandie were supposedly heading.

The parting was gruff and manly. Gold clinked. Shandie thanked each man in turn, shaking his hand and making sure of his correct name. Ylo could guess that there would be further rewards in future if the imperor won back his throne. With a few final jocular remarks, the two parties separated.

Shandie kicked his horse to a canter, and Ylo rode at his side. The fluffy snow whirled by playfully.

"Good men!" Shandie said. "Fine men! It's men like those that made the impire, not us fancy rulers."

"Believe me, those four were much better than most." Ylo spoke from experience, having served in the ranks.

They rode on for a while without speaking, both aware that there were things that would have to be said, now the two of them were alone together for the first time since Newbridge.

"There's supposed to be a fair inn at Mosrace," Ylo remarked.

"There is. I know it well."

"Food good?"

"Superb, last time I was there. Feeling like a celebration?" Shandie shot a sideways smile at his companion.

"Why not?" Ylo said innocently, thinking it might well be their last evening together. He must start back to Yewdark soon, or he would miss the daffodils—not that he was about to mention those, of course.

The horses thundered by a creaking wagon loaded with firewood.

"Ylo," Shandie said, speaking loudly over the beat of hooves, "I am not one for sentimental speeches . . ."

"I'm not much of one for listening to them."

"Well, you're going to listen to one now! At the moment I can offer you only my heartfelt thanks and my eternal gratitude. When I regain my throne, then whatever reward you want will be yours. Political office? You can be consul, proconsul, senator—name it. Lands? I offered you a dukedom once and you turned it down. I shall not be refused again, I promise you! I thought you deserved it then because of what Grandsire did, but by the Gods, Brother Yyan, now you've earned anything I have in my power to give!"

Ylo found that idea funny, somehow. *How about your wife?* "What did I do? Kidnapping the imperor, you mean? You'll set a dangerous precedent if you give me a dukedom for it."

Shandie turned a steady dark gaze on him. His face was windburned by the long winter journey, and he was even leaner than he had been before. His hair was longer, so he seemed more like a civilian than a soldier, but there was no hint of madness there now, only a dangerous, implacable purpose.

"You saved me from the Covin. I was dead set on going back to Hub, absolutely determined. I was convinced the whole thing was a fraud. I thought you'd lied to me, Rap had, Raspnex had—everyone! At times I thought Emthoro had set up the whole thing to steal the throne. And, I'm profoundly ashamed to say this, but I even suspected you of having designs on my wife!''

"Well, you were correct there, sire! Any man who has ever seen her majesty starts having designs.''

Shandie laughed, pleased. ''I expect so. But I wonder if those were real Zinixo thoughts? I wonder if that's how he sees the world, with everyone plotting against him and no one to trust?''

"Could be,'' Ylo said with a yawn.

"And you defeated him! That is a noble accomplishment.''

"It was pure luck that Eemfume was handy.''

"Or the Gods sent him. And you were man enough to see the opportunity and take it!''

Shandie sounded disgustingly sincere. Ylo felt rather ashamed of how he had treated his imperor and would prefer not to discuss it. After all, he was still planning to desert and head back to Eshiala, wasn't he? Maybe he had better wait a day or two yet, in case the Covin tried its siren call again.

Shandie flickered another smile at him, a bashful one. ''Fortunately I now know that I was wrong. I now know that there are men I can trust, and luckily one of them was with me in my hour of need. You had no need to endure what you did. You did not do it for personal gain, for I am penniless, nor for the Impire as an institution, for I am without authority. You did it for friendship alone. Ylo, from now on I am proud to regard you as my friend.''

Ghosts of a hundred ancestors whistled warnings in Ylo's ear. Historically, the post of Imperor's Friend was the most dangerous job in the Impire. Everyone went after *him*! The one thing court factions could always agree on was the urgent need to sabotage the imperor's best friend, whoever he was.

This appointment must be resisted. Ylo stole a thoughtful look at Shandie and was annoyed by the appeal in his face. Imperors did not have real friends. Imperors were different— they learned that as children. What did the man know of friendship? Friends were for fun, and Shandie did not know what fun was.

Furthermore, Ylo himself was an imp, and imps served their imperor. Friendship would impose a different sort of loyalty. It would raise the sort of questions King Rap had asked him once, questions involving daffodils and moral responsibility. If there was one thing Ylo detested it was moral responsibility.

"I'm honored to be your friend, of course. Tonight you'll let me pick out a wench for you, also?"

Shandie flushed scarlet. He turned his face away as if something very interesting had developed in the hedges. His ears were red.

The horses had covered a furlong before he forced his eyes back to Ylo's mocking gaze—and nodded. He smiled nervously. "Just make sure she's pretty."

God of *Lust*! This was more serious than Ylo had thought.

2

Gluttonous as cattle looting a grain field, the close-packed winter clouds drifted over the Sea of Sorrows. Black and bloated, they moved on into Thume and no hedge or fence impeded them; but then their way was blocked by the thorns of the Progiste Mountains. The leaders balked, but the followers pressed in behind, driving the front ranks to destruction. Day after day the slaughter continued. The turgid herd was butchered on the peaks, and none escaped to reach the desert of Zark beyond. Muddy torrents coursed the slopes.

It was the rainy season.

Thaïle awoke at the first contraction, but for a few minutes could not think what had roused her. Even then, when enlightenment arrived with a little shiver of joy and excitement and fear—even then, she could not be sure. She moved her awkward shape on the ferns, seeking a long-forgotten comfort, and waited to see if there was going to be another. Beside her, Leéb stirred briefly and then sank back into deeper sleep.

From the smell of the night, dawn was near. Rain pattered doggedly on the leafy thatch of the roof as it had done with hardly a break for weeks. Leéb's handiwork was sound, though, and water had found no chinks. Even beetles fleeing a flooded world had trouble penetrating the tight weaving of his walls, and he had completed four whole rooms before the rains began. He was planning another room also, although Thaïle could think of no reason why she should need a house so huge. He made rooms much faster than she could make babies to fill them.

But maybe she had almost completed this one.

Kaif if he is a boy, Frial if she is a girl. That was what they had decided before going to sleep. Yesterday it had been Shaib and . . . someone. No matter. Hurry, Kaif, or Frial, or you may be somebody else when you arrive!

She jerked in needless shock as Leéb twitched, then realized she had been drifting back to sleep again. Leéb was dreaming. She could Feel the muddly emotions of his dreams, punctuated with wrenches of pulsing lust. Oh, my poor love! The last few weeks had been hard on him, since the baby had come between them. He needed her and wanted her so much! Leéb was such a happy, peaceful man, so gentle a lover, that she was always astonished to Feel the heat of his desire. At first it had frightened her, but now she knew him and understood that he would never loose the beast she Felt in there. She had learned to love the beast, also, and tease it a little . . .

Soon, soon, my love! She adjusted the cover over him and again tried to ease her aching back into an easier position. Alas, there was no easier position for a pixie shaped like a mango.

Kaif, she thought, not Frial. Lately she had been able to Feel some of that new little person inside her, and he had a boy's temper. Sometimes when he kicked her, he was utterly furious. She was quite sure it was a boy, and Leéb wanted a boy very much. He wanted a boy to take fishing with him, as he had gone fishing with his father. Thaïle knew she was too fidgety to be a good fishing companion, although he had never told her so.

Nine moons had come and gone since Leéb had shown her the place he had found by the river. She had never doubted his descriptions of it, though, and the journey from her parents' house had been a torment for both of them. Even when they arrived, exhausted by the long walk, there had been a worse delay while they both ran frantically around in search of the one ideal spot to be their Place. Too far to carry water . . . too close to the river, it will flood . . . not enough shade . . .

As darkness fell, they had found their Place, among the cottonwoods, and had made it theirs forever. True, that cataclysmic moment had not been quite as joyous or soul-inspiring as she had hoped. Leéb had been too impatient and anxious, she too nervous, and the twigs on the ground very unromantically prickly, but with a little practice they had been doing it much better in a couple of days—doing it well enough to bring Kaif into the world.

Nine moons. She thought she could Feel his impatience. Definitely a boy.

Nine moons, and the recorders had never found her. It would be very sad if Kaif never met his grandparents and even sadder for Gaib and Frial never to know their grandchildren. Coming from a Gifted family, she might bear more than two babies. Leéb didn't know it yet, but Thaïle had decided that in a few years, when they had produced two—or more—children, then she would take them on a visit to the Gaib Place. Surely by then it would no longer matter if the recorders found her, no matter how strong her Faculty? Surely even they could not be so cruel as to drag a mother away from her family, off to the College?

So even if Kaif had Faculty, as she did, he would never have to keep Death Watch, as she had been required to do—never have to learn a word, as she had.

Oooo!

She had been asleep again. The window was showing gray. And that had definitely been her tummy doing something she had not told it to do, something it had never done before. Kaif was on the way.

She wanted to jump up and clean out the whole room and put in all new ferns and get out the new bed cover she had woven . . . And that was silly, because she spread all new ferns just yesterday, and the cover was in the basket in the corner. She had cleaned the whole house with her broom yesterday, twice. There was lots of time yet. Leéb would have to go and fetch Boosh from the Neeth Place, and he could not paddle a boat in the dark. The river was in spate, but that was good, because he could take a shortcut across the flooded grassland and then have a fast run home. It wouldn't take very long, and Kaif was going to be hours yet.

As she twisted again to find a more comfortable position, her hair fell all over her face. Amazing how much her hair had grown in nine moons! She wasn't sure that long hair was worth the bother, but it was a sign of womanhood, and she wore it proudly. Leéb liked it. She tickled him with it, sometimes, and that roused him almost faster than anything. Perhaps that was why mothers wore their hair long and kept their daughters' short.

Oooo!

Kaif, you are too impatient! Or maybe not. Thaïle had been

dozing again. The window was quite bright now. And the rain had stopped. Good.

Oooo-ooo! Getting serious, are you?

Thaïle rolled over with a grunt and munched on her goodman's ear. Leéb did not have nice, flat, pointy ears like pixies should have. He had big, round, stick-out ears, very suitable for munching.

"Mmmph?" Leéb said, brushing her hair off his face.

"Darling?"

"Mmmph."

"Baby."

"Mm? *What?*" Leaping up from the bed, Leéb missed the doorway and ran straight into the wall. Disregarding his goodwife's shouts, he regained his balance, found the exit, rocked the house again as he tore open the front door, plunged out into the dawn, rounded the chicken coop too closely, lost his balance, and sprawled headlong into the mud, narrowly missing the woodpile.

She Felt his emotions—confusion, panic, shame . . .

A few moments later he followed the sound of laughter back to the window.

"How long have I got?" he asked sheepishly.

"At least enough time to put some clothes on. Boosh is quite a prim old dear, you know, and may not want to get in a boat with a naked man—beautiful though you are."

"You are very cruel to mock me!"

His eyes were twinkling, though. No matter how clumsy or inept he might be on occasion, Leéb never took himself too seriously. That was one of his better qualities—not that any of his qualities were inferior.

"Mock you? I am completely serious, my darling man. If I did not think you beautiful, would I ever have consented to let you sire this baby that I am about to, er, produce?"

Thaïle passed out his breeches and a kiss, and he accepted both. "Go and wash off the mud before you put them on," she said, preparing to close the shutter. "And you don't want your shoes, do you? They're not dry yet from yesterday. You don't need hat and cloak yet. And don't forget . . ."

"Yes?" he said urgently.

She smiled. "To milk the goat and let out the chickens and

then come back and have something to eat. After that, we'll decide whether you have to leave yet.''

Then she said, ''Oh!'' and sat down hurriedly as Kaif rattled the latch again.

There was a watcher in the woods.

There were two watchers in the woods.

''No complications?'' asked the newcomer.

''Perfectly normal,'' the first said. ''Good-size boy. I'm tempted to do something about its ears before anyone sees them.''

''I was reminded that the child is also precious.''

The other sighed. ''So was I—several times.''

''Her Faculty is as strong as they said?''

''It must be. She can Feel those families up on the ridge. Keep your guard up.''

''Go and have your break, then, and I'll stay here. Bring the body back with you.''

There was only one watcher in the woods.

Rain began falling again as Leéb departed in the boat. It did not wet the watcher, though.

3

Leéb was poling the boat across the wetlands in the drizzle. Thaïle could Feel his nervous urgency—poor Leéb was much more worried about what was happening than she was. Women had been having babies since the world began. She was healthy, barely sixteen. The younger the better, the old women always said. Lying contentedly on the bed, she could even Feel old Boosh herself, rousing to her morning chores, grumbling amiably at Neeth as she always did. Thaïle could Feel his tolerant amusement.

If she tried hard, she could Feel other neighbors in the remote distance, several families—on the hill, and downriver. Boosh must have told them about the newcomers, but none of them had ever come to pry. When the dry season arrived, she would go visiting to show off her baby.

Oooo! That was a bad one. Patience, my darling! Wait until Daddy returns.

A beautiful home, she had. Near her feet was a hamper with

her spare dress and some other clothes. Along one wall was a shelf Leéb had made for her, loaded with her precious things, the few she had been able to bring—colored shells, bright stones, the stuffed dragon that had been her plaything when she was tiny, a man's elbow carved in stone. In the next room was a wickerwork cradle, with fluffy cotton blankets she had made herself, all ready for Kaif. Or possibly Frial.

How wonderful to have a real baby of her own, to suckle and cuddle . . .

Ah! Leéb had reached the Neeth Place, or else he was within shouting distance. She Felt excitement and impatience from him, surprise and joy from the two oldsters . . . The river was running very swiftly, she knew. That boat would be back in no time.

Oooo . . . Ouch! Despite herself, she whimpered. *Already?* she thought shamefully. She had promised herself she was not going to make a scene over this. Poor Leéb would be terrified if she yelled and screamed, the way some women did. Two years ago, when Hoan was having her first, Thaïle and some of the other girls had crept close to the Jurg Place to listen. Such a fuss about a perfectly normal business! It couldn't possibly be as bad as Hoan had pretended.

Leéb would be back soon with Boosh. Maybe even Neeth, also, to keep Leéb company. Soon. The rain was really pelting down. They would be cold.

The outer door creaked.

For one instant, Thaïle felt a wild surge of panic. Who could be there? Who could approach without her Feeling them? Jain of the College, of course! He was a mage, and she could not Feel him if he did not want her to.

Then a strange calm fell over her, washing away her rising anger, and she remembered that Jain could do that to her.

She stared up without a blink as two women came into the room—one tall and elderly but not really old, the other shorter, younger, but not really young. They wore frilled pure-white blouses and long skirts of smooth cloth, brightly striped in greens and yellows, all very grand. Their hair was neat and shiny, and their faces seemed smooth and unweathered, their expressions stern. They were not wet.

They stood at her feet, towering over her.

"Recorders?" Thaïle whispered.

The younger woman frowned. "Certainly not!"

"She doesn't understand," said the elder. "Thaïle, my name is Shole; I am an analyst. Mearn, here, is an archivist. We are more important than recorders, but we are from the College, which is what you meant, wasn't it?"

Thaïle nodded. And they were both sorceresses. Black horror howled somewhere in the depths of her mind, kept at bay by that sinister calm.

"Go away!" she said. "It is very rude to enter a Place when you are not asked in."

"Rude?" the younger visitor snorted. She had very ugly eyes, sort of muddy brown color. "Child, you have no idea how important this is! The whole world is in danger of—"

Shole snapped, "Mearn!"

"I am having a baby!" Thaïle shouted.

"That's why we came, of course. We shall help you have it."

"I don't want your help. Go *away*!"

The younger woman made an impatient noise and knelt down beside her. "Don't be foolish, child. The other way is messy, and exhausting, and we need you healthy and fresh. This will be very easy, quite painless. It's a boy, you know, a little early, but fine and healthy. Pull up your gown."

"No!" Thaïle protested. She tried to rise. Her arms went limp and she sagged back. She stared up at the roof, wondering if she had gone mad.

Her cover and clothes vanished, leaving her naked. She whimpered.

"Not too far along," said the younger. "Good."

Thaïle was ashamed to feel tears in her eyes. "My goodman is on his way. I don't need your help. Leave our Place!"

"Foolish child!" the older woman snapped. "Do as you are told, for once! This unpleasantness is entirely your own fault. Had you obeyed the law, all this sorrow and pain would never have happened."

"Just relax," the younger woman said. "Close your eyes. Take a deep breath."

"But I must clear the ferns and squat on the earth!" That was the way it was done, the way a pixie must be born.

"Stupid superstition! Just relax."

Then a very odd sensation . . . *Ooops!*

"Fine baby," the woman said.

Slap.

Wail!

Tiny Feelings of terror . . .

Something hot and wet squirming on Thaïle's belly . . . Wailing.

"My son!" Again she tried to lift herself, and again her arms failed her. Even her neck had gone limp, so she could not lift her head.

"Not your son, Thaïle," the older woman said. She seemed to grow, larger and menacing, and her eyes were terrible. "He can never be yours. Do not try to look. It will only hurt worse if you see him."

Leéb, Leéb! Hurry! He was coming—she could Feel him coming.

The burden was lifted from Thaïle's abdomen. The Mearn woman rose and turned away quickly, carrying something. The little yowls faded as she left the room, but she could still Feel his terror and bewilderment.

"My baby!" Thaïle scrambled up on her knees and then to her feet. Her great bulging tummy had gone. She felt cloth reappear on her, covering her nakedness. She registered vaguely that it was her best smock, so her breasts must have shrunk back to almost their normal size also. Her insides felt very strange, but not sore. She swayed. The tall Shole reached out a hand to steady her.

Oh, those eyes!

"You were warned, Thaïle! Jain warned you, didn't he?"

"My baby!" She tried to struggle, and that weak-looking grasp on her arm held her helpless. The eyes held her, burning gold eyes.

"He warned you that you must come to the College." The little, wrinkled mouth pursed, showing teeth as spiteful as a rodent's. "But you didn't! You disobeyed a recorder. You broke the Blood Law. Your folly has brought tragedy into three lives, Thaïle! And do you think we enjoy this either, you foolish, headstrong child?"

"Leéb is coming!"

The old woman nodded, seeming to restrain a smile. "Yes, he's coming. He will be here very soon. He will find the baby, alive and well. But he will find you dead beside it."

"No! No! No!"

"Yes. Oh, not you. But the body he will find will seem to be yours."

"Monster! How can you be so cruel?"

"Cruel? We, cruel? You do not know what you are saying." The woman shook Thaïle one-handed, raising her voice shrilly and shouting in her face. Her tiny teeth were very white and even. "Evil is abroad in the world, and you have duties so far beyond that peasant and his spawn that I cannot even attempt to explain them to you. Your folly has delayed your preparation and perhaps weakened our defenses. The Keeper was furious when we discovered what you had done."

"Leéb! Oh, Leéb!" Thaïle thought of him rushing up from the river and finding—

"Forget him, foolish girl! He will bury the false body. He will raise the brat on goat's milk, with the old crone's help. Soon he will find another Place and mate again. Stop your weeping! Do you think Mearn and I enjoy this squalid deception?"

Thaïle tried to break free of the bony grip and was helpless as a fly in a web.

The sorceress smiled thinly. "Now we go to the College. *You must forget the child, Thaïle. You must forget its father.*"

"Never! I will not leave my man!" Thaïle felt a strange shimmer. "If you take me away I will come back!" she screamed. All around her the Leéb Place disappeared and there was sunshine . . .

4

A swan slid close to the verge, snowy white on dark water, sailing so smoothly it did not stir its own reflection. Then it waded out of the pond and was suddenly awkward, trudging black flippers on the mud. Drops and ripples broke the empty mirror left behind. Divine beauty became unsightly effort as it rolled forward with in-toed gait, snaky neck stretched out before it. Ugly.

"I love these mixed-up days," Jain remarked cheerfully, amber eyes twinkling as if the remark held some hidden meaning. "White clouds and gray clouds and patches of blue—unsettled, full of surprises. Makes you appreciate the sunshine instead of taking it for granted. And it isn't really cold, is it? You're warm enough?"

"Yes," Thaïle said. There was something she wanted to say, and she could not remember it, something lingering at the back of her mind.

They sat side by side on a bench. From their toes, the turf ran down to the pond, which had swans on it, and ducks. All around them green hillocks were ablaze with flowers—white and gold creeping through the grass, festoons of purple and scarlet draped over bushes like washing hung to dry, blue and white and crimson standing up to dance in the breeze. Even some of the trees had exploded into blossom. The world was twinkly and sparkly after the rain, but the sun was shining now. High forest enclosed the glade with a comforting wall.

A pair of bare-chested young men went trotting along the path by the shore. She Felt a momentary flash of man-interest, cut off sharply. One of them waved. Jain waved back and watched them go, but Thaïle knew the wave had been directed at her. She was puzzled—what were they running from, or after, at that pace?

Jain said, "Exercising."

"Exercising?"

"I expect they have to sit a lot. People don't work on their feet all day long in the College."

Thaïle thought of her mother. Frial mostly sat while she worked—sewing, weaving, plucking chickens. Her father? No. Scraping a pigskin, maybe. Everything else Gaib did required standing: weeding, digging, pruning . . . Odd she'd never realized that before.

What was that other thing she wanted to think about?

"This is the Meeting Place," Jain said. "Anytime you want company or feel like talking with someone, you come here. It's a good place to sit and think, too. Just to lie on the grass and count the birds."

She could Feel nothing of his emotions, of course—he was a mage. But there were other benches in among the rainbow-draped shrubbery; there were little open cabins, too, to keep rain off, maybe. She could see about a dozen people, sitting or walking, in twos or threes, all too far off to obtrude. The nearest were a boy and girl standing together, holding hands and gazing spellbound into each other's eyes. She could Feel very clearly what was in the girl's heart, but the boy and all the others . . . she could Feel none of them.

"Sorcerers?" she muttered. "Or mages—like you?"

"I was a mage," Jain said tersely. "Now I've been told a fourth word, so I'm a sorcerer. I didn't rank quite as high as I'd . . . but not too bad. And I'm not a recorder anymore. I'm an archivist now."

An archivist was more important than a recorder.

How did she know that?

"Congratulations."

"Have you any idea what I'm talking about?"

"Not the muddiest!" she admitted.

He laughed. "You'll learn all that soon enough."

Most of the people in the glade wore long cloaks and wide hats like his. And she . . . she was wearing a thin, brown thing that was oddly familiar, and yet she couldn't quite remember . . .

"I'm sure you'll love it here at the College," Jain said. "Just remember how important it is. Did you have a good journey?"

"Journey? Oh, fine," Thaïle said vaguely.

"We have a Place ready for you, of course. I think you'll like it. Mist'll be here soon."

"Mist?"

"Another novice. He'll show you around. Give him something to do."

If what the College did was so important, then why did this Mist person need something to do? She supposed the answer must be obvious, so she didn't ask.

"Normally you would be welcomed—and shown around—by the mistress of novices, Archivist Mearn. She's tied up today on a matter of some importance. She sends her apologies."

Thaïle muttered a polite-sounding nothing. A novice would be better company, likely. She rubbed the back of her neck, which felt oddly cool as if there were a draft blowing on it. She ran fingers through her hair.

"If you're not too tired," Jain continued, "Mist'll help you pick out some new clothes."

He meant that she was wearing a rag. He was contemptuous of her poverty, although he'd told her once that his family had been poor, too. That should have made him sympathetic, she would have thought. Probably he was trying to be kind, as best he could, and make her welcome, and she shouldn't be just sitting there like a pillow, paying more attention to the swans than to him. He had frightened her when he came to the Gaib Place back . . . how long ago? He did not frighten her now, and if he still spoke to her as if she were an ignorant, willful child . . . well, compared to him she probably was an ignorant child. She still did not trust him, although she could not imagine why. He had a quiet voice and a nice smile. He was tall, and good-looking, with very pointy ears. He was wearing a green, fur-trimmed cloak that she remembered. Together they had eaten a picnic off that cloak.

Clothes?

Thaïle shook herself. "That would be wonderful, but I have nothing to trade."

He chuckled softly. "No need to trade. You're a novice now, and the College will look after you . . . Why so solemn, Thaïle? Where's the bubbly, happy girl I met at the Gaib Place? Missing your parents, are you?"

She did not need occult Feeling to hear the sneer in his voice. Jain of the College thought very little of Gaib and Frial. It seemed like a long time since she had said good-bye to them. "Not missing them much."

"Well, this is your first day at the College, and you should be thrilled. I promised you all sorts of wonderful things, and now you're going to see them, or some of them. You ought to be excited."

"I'm sorry," she said. Why sorry, though? He knew she had never wanted to come, so why should he expect her to be excited now?

"I told you how important our work is here. You haven't forgotten your catechism, surely?"

"Of course not."

"Then you know how the Keeper and the College defend Thume from all the demons. You're part of that now, Thaïle. Mearn will explain more tomorrow, but it's very important. You're important!"

"I understand." Now she was here, she must make the best of it and do what was required of her. All her childish dreams of finding a young man with a nice smile and bulgy arms were just that—childish dreams. She must forget those now. The College was important. She had Faculty, so the Keeper wanted her, for some unimaginable reason. There was an escaped thought at the back of her mind . . . Her head was stuffed with feathers.

"It's just . . . Do you know that funny feeling when you wake up and you've had a nightmare and you can't remember what it was, but it still bothers you? I feel like that."

Jain grunted, not looking at her. "Well, it'll pass. Here comes Mist, I think."

But Thaïle had already Felt someone new. Now she saw a tall young man striding along the path, emitting boredom and pique, with hints of nervousness pushed down underneath. He was swathed from neck to ankles in a cloak of gold and blue and scarlet, very dazzling. Its fur-trimmed hem swirled around his boots as he marched, a long, fur-trimmed hood swung at his back. He held his bare head high, scanning the glade, as if searching.

Jain waved. Mist changed direction, heading for their bench, his boredom abruptly replaced by surprise, pleasure, man-interest . . .

"Novice Mist seems to have been expecting a person of some other gender," Jain murmured, amused. "Could Mistress Mearn have misled him, do you think?"

A twinge of worry penetrated Thaïle's strange lassitude. "Can I trust him?"

Jain snorted. "If I had your looks, I would trust nothing that spoke below a high soprano. But you're in no danger here in the College. Any real fright would bring a torrent of sorcerers to your rescue. Anything less—slap as hard as you can." He paused, studying the approaching youth. "No, this one's all talk. Fancies himself a lot."

Mist arrived, and he was even taller than she had expected. He swirled his splendid cloak as he bowed to the pair of them.

"Archivist Jain?" he said, but his eyes were inspecting Thaïle. He had nicely slanted eyes—big and innocent and pale as butter. The man-interest became stronger, mingled with approval as he registered from her short hair that she was still single.

Jain introduced novice to novice. Thaïle had an odd sensation of waking up . . . Bright sun and wind on her face . . .

"You must be frozen!" Mist exclaimed. He unclasped his cloak and swung it off. "Here, you need this!"

"No, I'm fine," she said, disconcerted by a huge rush of amusement from Archivist Jain. He must have lowered his defenses to let her Feel that amusement, inviting her to share it with him. What was so unspeakably funny? Ah, Mist's clothes, of course. *Fancies himself a lot . . .*

The tall young man was almost as colorful as the flower-infested glade itself. Gold buckles adorned his half-boots. Above them came tight white stockings, full pantaloons of green and blue, and a sleeveless shirt of silver cloth patterned with red sequins. The stockings displayed nothing special, but he did have unusually wide shoulders, and he had obviously chosen the skimpy shirt for that reason.

"You're too tall to be an elf, Novice," Jain said, rising. His face revealed none of the laughter inside him.

"Archivist?" Mist said blankly.

"Nothing. You'll show our new hatchling around, then?"

"It will be a pleasure and an honor," Mist agreed. Thaïle Felt sincerity and an alarming eagerness in that statement.

"I shall leave you to it," said the sorcerer. "Welcome again, Thaïle. We'll meet often in future, I'm sure. Soon you must come to my Place and meet my wife and our, er, . . . and try her cooking. Well, I'll see you around." With a flourish of green cloak, Jain turned and headed down the slope to the path.

Novice Mist slid into the place the sorcerer had vacated, but he twisted around to look at Thaïle, leaning a bulgy arm on the back of the bench for her to notice. He gazed at her solemnly with his butter-yellow eyes. He had a very plain face, and his ears neither especially pointy nor especially round. He reminded her a little of her father—solid. It would take a strong wind to ruffle Mist, she thought.

"Been here long?" he demanded.

"Er . . . no. You?"

"Ten days. Very dull, mostly. It'll be better from now on, though."

"Oh?"

He grinned. "You're here. You're Novice Number Five at the moment. The other three are pimple-faced brats. One more and we start lessons. Need at least six for a class, the old bag says. Have a good journey?"

Thaïle did not want to talk about her journey. "Fine," she said quickly. "You?"

"I was this much taller when I arrived," Mist said solemnly, gesturing with his fingers.

"Taller?"

"Blisters!"

She was startled, then laughed as she realized that his blank expression was intended as humor. She Felt his satisfaction. Mist was not quite as simple as he looked.

"Which Gate'd you come to?" he asked.

Gate? Why did everyone keep asking her about her journey? She did not want even to think of it. She was here, wasn't that good enough? "Oh, let's not talk about that! Tell me what happens next, and what did you say about lessons, and what you're going to show me."

"Where do you want to start?" he asked. *Man-interest* . . .

"I don't know. What am I supposed to see?"

He shrugged those big bare shoulders, making the sequined shirt twinkle in the sunlight. "I can only show you the bits I've seen, and that's only a small part of the College, I'm sure. Your Place, of course. And this is the Meeting Place. The Market, the Commons, the School. I can show you my Place, or where the three spotted warblers nest, but I am absolutely positive you don't want to meet them."

"You decide."

"Market first, then your Place. You like canoeing?"

"Er . . . I've never been in a boat." Why did that feel wrong? "At least, I don't think I have."

"I love canoeing," Mist said, closing his eyes dreamily. Then he opened them and regarded her appraisingly. "There's a lake at my Place—a little lake, but a lake. I'll take you canoeing."

"Market first," Thaïle said firmly, and jumped to her feet. She staggered, almost falling to the grass. Mist sprang up and caught her, and held.

"What's wrong?" *Alarm*.

"I—I don't know! I feel sort of off-balance."

"Blisters?"

"No, no blisters." She pushed away his hands, feeling very annoyed at being so stupid. She tried a step, then another, and decided she had a mysterious compulsion to lean over backward.

Mist's arm hovered nearby. "Let me help?" *Hope*.

"No, I'm fine." Placing bare feet carefully on the grass, she marched down the gentle slope to the path. Mist strolled at her side, still eager to provide support.

He stopped at the path. "This is the Way," he said, waving

a hand. He had big hands—useful for wielding paddles, no doubt. "You'll see it everywhere in the College."

The Way was wide enough for two people to walk abreast, paved in very fine, sparkly white gravel, smooth and level. Thaïle didn't like the look of it. Why so wide? She mourned for all the grass that could have grown there, or flowers. Paths should be one narrow strip of moss or pine needles, just wide enough for feet, squeezing in and out between trees and bushes. A few deadfalls and gullies always made a walk more interesting. The Way went racing off over the grass, up and down the hillocks, so smooth you could roll a melon along it. Oh, it had some curves and slopes, but it seemed nastily artificial to her.

"Left or right?"

"Doesn't matter," Mist said, watching her as if waiting for her to see a joke. "You choose."

The Way seemed to circle the pond, all around the clearing. To the left were the mooning lovers, who had adjourned their mutual adoration to a bench. Thaïle turned right, looking up at Mist's smile distrustfully as he fell into step alongside her. The sun slid behind a cloud, shadowing the world.

"The way out is exactly at the far side? I mean, the path goes all the way around?"

He smirked. "You'll see. Sure you don't want my cloak?"

Clearly there was something about this mysterious Way that he expected to surprise her. She did not want to be surprised by this overlarge, fancies-himself canoeist. His obvious man-interest was flattering, and not entirely unwelcome, but somehow it felt like trespass, usurpation . . . like *wrong* man. Tugging at her hair in confusion, she refused the offer of his cloak and just strode along in silence. Puzzled and a little hurt, Mist paced at her side, taking two steps to her three.

Apparently the Way did not go all around the Meeting Place as she had thought. Soon it abandoned the parkland, and led them off into the forest. Mist continued to carry his cloak over one shoulder, although the air was much cooler here in the woods. Obviously if Thaïle was warm enough, then he must show that he was. He had enough tact to remain silent, and the half-tasted memory at the back of her mind began to niggle at her again. So it was she who spoke first.

"Three other novices, you said?"

"Grub, Maggot, and Worm."

She laughed. Just when Mist's placidity was most reminding her of her father, he would make a genuinely funny remark. Had Gaib possessed a sense of humor at Mist's age? "What's wrong with them?"

Mist shrugged. "They may be bearable in four or five years. Two of them, anyway."

"How old are you, Mist?"

He glanced down at her thoughtfully. "Nineteen. You?"

"Er—Sixteen." She meant she would be sixteen at the beginning of the rainy season, but obviously this was late in the rainy season, because the leaves were green and all those flowers . . . Yet she was sure she was sixteen already. Birthday? Winterfest? God of Madness, why was she so confused today? She shook her head, half expecting to feel hair swinging against her neck.

"I'm old for a novice, of course," Mist said, and she Felt his embarrassment. "I was late getting my word, because there weren't many Gifted families around Dad's Place. I was scouting out Places of my own already. Then a recorder came by and said I mustn't, not yet. Sent me on a three-day trip up the Fastwater Valley. I had to hang around for *months* before the old relic finally got around to dying. After all that, he decided I didn't have Faculty—the recorder did, I mean. So I started exploring again. Took my time, though. Don't rush into things, usually."

Thaïle thought Novice Mist would never rush into anything. He had a large sense of inertia about him.

"Why are you here, if you haven't got Faculty?"

"Another recorder came by. Decided maybe I did." He shrugged again—more embarrassment. "So now I suppose I get told another word, and then they decide for certain."

"Do you want to stay here or go home?"

The pale yellow eyes looked down at her again. "Might be nice to be a sorcerer. Easier than picking cotton."

She agreed doubtfully. She wanted to know what his talent was, but he would ask her the same question. Talents were dangerous topics for conversation.

"I can't decide," he said. "I thought I'd found my Place, see? Was trying to choose between three girls. One of them was very like you." He fell silent, lost in reverie. In a few moments his lust became deafening. She wondered why it did not disturb her more than it did. But she knew it was just young man's dreaming; in a way, she could almost feel sorry for him. The curse of Faculty had disrupted his life just as much as hers.

The forest was deep and dim, smelling woodsy, full of trees that were strange to her, towering like giants. Here and there were more flowers, also strange. Shafts of light struck down from the high roof to throw swathes of brilliance on ferns and bushes. A curious nostalgia chilled her spirits.

Mist, to his credit, noticed her shiver. "Here, take my cloak!" He tried to drape it over her and contrive a mild hug at the same time.

She refused. It would trail on the ground, she pointed out.

"Well, it's not far now," he said. He sniffed loudly. "I love the smell of the air here! There's all sorts of forest in the College, but this is my favorite. It's like home."

"Not my home."

"No, I know. You're a hill-country girl."

"How do you know that?"

Mist smirked. "Because I was shown the Place I have to take you to, and the woods there aren't like this!" He began naming trees for her—monkeypod and ebony and hydrangea and bread-fruit. Some of them seemed vaguely familiar, although she was sure that they had not grown near the Gaib Place. Maybe she'd seen them on that journey she didn't want to think about?

The Way continued ahead, white and smooth, winding out of sight. It felt gritty below her feet, but not unpleasant. She walked in silence for a while, trying very hard to shake off the aftertaste-of-nightmare feeling.

The Way tipped down a hill. She heard voices, low at first, soon becoming louder. Cheerful, laughing voices. Brightness showed ahead, the trees thinned out and then stepped aside altogether to reveal a small valley. And people! Thaïle stopped. "I don't like crowds," she said.

There were many, many people ahead—twenty or more, perhaps—as many as she had ever met all at once, at a wedding or a funeral. Men and women both, they milled like starlings among the colorful stalls and tables. She could Feel none of them.

"No pixie likes crowds!" Mist said cheerfully, an expression of certainty on his so-ordinary face.

"Does anyone?"

"Imps do, I'm told. That's one of the things we get taught, apparently—all about other peoples, Outside. Can't see why they matter, since they're not allowed in Thume. But this is the Market. You get clothes here, and food if you want it. I mean, we can cook for ourselves at home if we prefer. I'm not much of a cook, so I eat the ready-made meals at the Commons. Much easier."

Screwing up her courage, she went on at his side, letting the crowd swallow her up. She discovered that it was not like a funeral. Nobody spoke to her, she did not have to meet people's eyes, and soon she was caught up in the wonder of all the things displayed on the stalls: fruits and vegetables, mysterious tools, and clothing—explosions of colors and fabrics like she had never seen.

"Sorcery?" she whispered.

Mist nodded, displaying much more confidence on the outside than she knew he was feeling inside. "Yes, it's sorcery. Take whatever you want. You could work all day and never empty one of those tables. They fill up as fast as you clear them. Now, what color do you fancy?"

For the first time, Thaïle began to feel properly excited. Here were riches such as her parents had never known in their lives. The women wore long skirts of amber or green or brown, and frilly blouses of lighter shades. They were picking over the wares and helping themselves, trading nothing in return that she could see. There was no one in attendance to trade to. She caught a few surprised, appraising glances in her direction and suddenly felt awkward in her dreary rough-spun frock.

"Try that one!" Mist suggested, pointing to a rich auburn fabric.

She held it up to admire it. It was a full-length dress.

"That's nice," he said.

"It's too big for me."

"No, it isn't. You chose it, so it'll fit perfectly. Look!" He tossed his cloak on the table and pulled off another, in royal blue and silver. He held it against himself. "See? It's the right length, and there can't be many men here tall as me."

She must be plumper than she had thought, then. She must have filled out lately . . . on the journey, perhaps? The journey was very vague in her mind. Glancing over the other women, she saw no one wearing anything as bright as that auburn. And none of the men was as dazzling as Mist. She replaced the dress.

"Start with shoes," Mist said, "over here."

She rarely wore shoes, but everyone else was wearing shoes. He made a few suggestions and soon she was clutching three pairs, shiny leather beauties. One pair had shiny metal buckles that must be worth a fortune.

He took them from her and led her back to the garments. Once started, she couldn't stop; he encouraged her. In a few minutes her arms were loaded with skirts and blouses and a couple of heavy capes—after all, this was the rainy season, Mist remarked.

"And a hat," he said firmly. "You never know what sort of weather you're going to run into here. There! That's enough to carry, isn't it?"

"Oh!" she said, with sudden dismay. "Is it far?"

He shook his head, grinning. "No, but you can come right back again if you want, now you know the Way. Let's go."

Reluctantly she tore herself away from all the wonderful things. Mist led her back along the path, retracing their steps up the hill. The silence of the forest returned, and the sandy surface was cool under her feet. He continued to carry her shoes for her, while she labored under the weighty burden of skirts and cloaks and blouses. She thought he might offer those bulgy arms to assist her, but evidently such thoughts did not occur to Novice Mist.

Still, the Market had made her feel better. She was going to enjoy trying on all these wonderful things.

"Sorcerers?" she said cautiously. "Some of those people were sorcerers?"

He smiled down at her with his pale yellow eyes. There was something almost appealing in the sleepy way he did that. "I expect so. 'Most everyone here seems to be either a mage or a sorcerer. There's novices and recorders and archivists and analysts and archons—and the Keeper, of course. And a few oddball specialists, like Mistress Mearn. We'll get all that explained to us when lessons start. Something to do with the moon and needing a sixth novice. Right now, we just wait, and enjoy ourselves."

The sky must have clouded over very quickly, for rain had begun to fall. She could hear it on the leaves, high above. Very little was getting through, so it wasn't heavy. In the distance she heard wind, as if a storm were coming. The air had more of a piney smell to it now.

The path was steeper than she had remembered, winding up a hillside. Strange that she did not recall noticing the great mossy rocks scattered around the forest floor. Big as cottages, some of them. And now she was seeing trees more familiar to her—cedars and cottonwoods. And even conifers.

"This isn't the way we came!" she said, with sudden alarm. She had seen no branchings, or side roads.

Mist chuckled. "Yes, it is. It's the *Way* we came, but the Way is not a usual sort of path, Thaïle. We're going to your Place."

Inexplicably, her heart leaped. "My Place? The . . . the . . ." Her confusion flustered her. "The Gaib Place?" That sounded wrong, somehow.

"No. The Thaïle Place. Of course you're Thaïle of the College now, to anyone outside, but here you can talk of the Thaïle Place if you want. Almost there."

Thaïle Place sounded horribly wrong, somehow. Thaïle of the . . . Gaib Place? What Place? That thought at the back of her mind . . .

Then the Way swung around a massive cedar and came to an end at the edge of a rain-soaked clearing, carpeted with grass of brilliant green, speckled with tiny white flowers. At the far side stood a cottage.

"Oh! Oh, my!" She stared. She looked up disbelievingly at Mist's triumphant smile.

"Mine? Really for me?"

"Yours. All yours. Unless you want to invite some young man to come and share it with you, of course. That's entirely up to you."

She did not need Feeling to know what thought lay behind that smirk. Her happiness faltered. Young man? Live with her? The elusive shadow at the back of her mind . . .

"I'll show you the Mist Place," he said. "Quite different! It's on a lake, and I have a canoe. Take you canoeing."

"One Place at a time!" she said. "Let's run."

They ran over the grass, although the rain was not too heavy. The cottage became ever more wonderful as she approached—a porch for sitting on in warm evenings and windows with some sort of shiny stuff in them and a tall chimney so the fire wouldn't smoke. Gaib had tried to make one of those several times, but it had always fallen down in the next storm.

When she drew near, she saw that the walls were made of flat

wood with tight, straight edges. Disloyal as it seemed even to
think so, the Gaib Place had been very drafty, because the
chinking between the logs kept falling out. This sorcerous place
did not seem to have any chinking, it fit so well.

Probably Mist's cottage would be woven basketwork, as
that was how houses were made down in the warm lowlands.
How did she know that? Could she have learned it on the
journey? She really did not have any clear memories at all of
a journey . . .

There was no chicken coop, not that she could see, and no
vegetable patch. No goats or pigs, either, but Mist had said she
could help herself to food at the Market, and that would certainly
be easier than growing and digging and weeding. What on earth
was she going to do with herself all day? Apart from fighting off
Mist in a canoe, of course.

5

Even had Thaïle believed all the marvels Jain had promised
her, she could still never have imagined the glory of the cottage.
She would not have believed that one person would be expected
to need so much space: a room for sitting, a room for sleeping,
a room for cooking, a room for washing. Floors and walls and
furniture were all made of the flat, shiny wood, smooth and
gleaming, and she had never seen a *smooth* wall in her life
before. There were thick cloths to walk on, and soft chairs to
sit on, all prettily patterned. More cloths hung by the windows,
instead of shutters, and magical stuff like clear ice kept out the
rain. Even the lanterns were sorcerous, needing no oil or candles.

Perhaps the greatest wonder of all was the mirror. Thaïle
knew about mirrors. Her great-grandmother had owned one,
and when Thaïle had kept Death Watch over her, she had passed
the time by playing with it. The family had almost come to blows
afterward, determining who would inherit the mirror and who
must continue admiring themselves in water. Phain's mirror had
been foggy, an irregular shape, and about the size of a cowpat.
The mirror on Thaïle's new bedroom wall was straight-edged,
taller than Mist, big as a door, clear as air.

She was definitely plumper than she had thought.

Something about the Place roused her to assert herself. She

was a pixie, this was her Place, and Mist was only a visitor. She resented his supercilious air as he showed how familiar he was with magic bathtubs and magic cookpots and beds made of feathers—less than two weeks ago, he must have been just as ignorant as she. She especially disliked his emotions when he demonstrated how to submerge in the featherbed. Let him fantasize about the girls he had left behind, she would rather be left out. She wanted to explore every tiniest corner of this wonderful cottage and experiment with all the magical gadgets, especially the hotwater bathtub. She wanted to try on all the sumptuous clothes now heaped so carelessly on a chair, and see what she looked like with no clothes at all. She most certainly did not want this brash canoeist with his oversize hands and buttery eyes rolling around when she did so, not even if he sat outside on the porch. Maybe there were no chinks in the walls, but there might be knotholes.

"Are you hungry?" she inquired.

"Yes!"

"Well, you may not be much of a cook, but I am. So you go back to the Market and get some food."

A big smile lit up his very ordinary face. "Right. What?"

"Anything you like. And, Mist?"

"Yes?"

"Don't hurry back."

For a moment she Felt hurt, then resignation. "An hour?"

"Make it two."

She watched through the glass pane of the window as Novice Mist went striding off along the Way in the rain, magnificent in his gleaming new blue and silver cloak.

6

By the time he returned, the strange day was almost over; shadows were lengthening. She Felt him as he approached along the Way, but the urgent desires that now troubled Novice Mist originated more in his belly than in his groin. She was hungry, too, now.

She had managed to stop her weeping some time before, and had washed her face in cold water. A last glance in the mirror persuaded her that the remaining tinge of red around her eyes was faint enough to escape Mist's attention. She would certainly not start weeping again with him present.

She stepped out on the porch, prepared to force a smile of welcome, but it came easier than she had expected. Jain and the recorders were the evildoers. Mist was innocent, she was sure. Well, not quite *innocent*. He had some illicit longings that must be discouraged, but he was not part of the conspiracy, only a fellow victim.

Clutching a basket, he came hurrying along the path with giant steps. The rain had ended shortly after he left, but Thaïle had worked out the sorcery of the Way now and was not at all surprised to see that his cloak and hood were soaked. Then he noticed her standing there in her frilly white blouse and dark gold skirt, and for a moment food dropped back to second place on his wish list.

"What did you bring?" she asked, grabbing the basket almost before he stepped up onto the porch.

"Fish! You know how to cook fish?"

"I can try."

As he stripped off his wet cloak, she went inside, rummaging in the basket already. By the time she had spread out the contents on the kitchen table, he had followed her and was looming in the doorway. He had changed his clothes again, to a frilly white shirt—open all the way down to his silver belt buckle—and very snug green velvet tights. Oh, he really did fancy himself! The cottage was growing dim, and somehow he seemed even larger than before.

Thaïle stared at the four enormous fat perch, the crusty loaves, onions, yams, eggs, lemons, butter, three bottles with labels she could not read . . . "We're entertaining the whole College?"

"I can eat every bit of that," Mist said firmly. "But I'll spare you some. Do you like wine?"

"Never tried it," she said, and Felt a surge of satisfaction that raised her hackles.

She took out one of the gorgeous metal knives and set to work. Her father owned one metal knife, and she had a dozen! Mist busied himself with opening a wine bottle. He filled two beakers, then brought a chair in from the sitting room and made himself comfortable to watch. She had a fairly good idea now what his talent was.

Her hands moved deftly, needing little direction from her. "Funny," she remarked airily. "I've completely lost track of time."

She Felt no reaction—no alarm, no guilt. Unless Mist was a sorcerer who could convey false emotions, he was innocent.

"Not quite first quarter. This wine is delicious."

She lifted her goblet with care—he had filled it to the brim. "Which moon, though?"

"Second!" He was surprised by the question, of course.

"I don't think I care for wine."

"It grows on you!" he said hopefully.

I'll bet it does. She could guess its effects just from his anticipation.

Second moon of the year . . . that confirmed what she had worked out while he was gone. She began peeling the onions so she would have an excuse if her eyes misbehaved again.

The cottage had been wonderful, and heartbreaking. As she had uncovered all its marvels—working out how drawers worked, and door handles, and the chimney flue—she had become more and more distraught. Eventually she had realized that she was frantic with the need to *share* all these marvels with somebody. Gaib? Frial? Or Sheel, her sister? None of those. Nor her brother Feen. Nobody she knew.

Knew now?

She had soaked blissfully in the bathtub with its magical hot water—after scalding her foot on a first attempt—and at the same time discovered that she was utterly miserable. Eventually she had begun to wonder if she could just be lonely. Lonely? A pixie? Many times she had spent days on end wandering the hills by herself and been almost sorry to go home and reassure her parents she was still alive. Pixies never got lonely!

In the end, the mirror had convinced her.

A thousand times in her childhood Thaïle had helped her mother and sister wash their hair, as they had aided her. She could easily call up their image in her mind, kneeling by the spring. The back of Frial's neck had always been paler than the back of Sheen's neck, because a goodwife wore her hair long and a maid did not.

Today, in the mirror, Thaïle had seen that paleness on the back of her own neck. Then she had noticed the edges of her hair. She had never seen hair cut so neat and even—until today,

here at the College. All the people she had observed at the
Market had been well trimmed like that, although the detail had
not registered with her at the time.

The second moon of the year . . .

She could not even remember Winterfest!

At fourteen she had kept Death Watch for old Phain in the
first moon. Almost exactly a year later, Jain had come to the
Gaib Place and told her she had Faculty. She had hung around
there, moping, for a couple of moons. Then she had gone to
visit Sheen at the Wide Place. And then . . . And then what?

She could not remember. She could not recall coming to the
College, even this morning. She had just been here. Trying to
think about the journey made her feel sick.

She must have run away!

So Jain and the other recorders had followed her and found
her. She remembered how strangely sleepy she had felt at the
Meeting Place, and his curious probing questions, testing what
she could recall and what had been deleted from her mind.

"Smells terrific!" Mist remarked.

Thaïle stared down at the sizzling fish in the pan.

When had she learned to cook fish?

She was a hill-country girl. She had never eaten fish at the
Gaib Place, but now her hands had known what to do, how to
gut them and scale them, how to smear them with egg and roll
them in breadcrumbs. Who had taught her?

Part of her life had been stolen away. Months were missing,
the better part of a year.

And *someone* was missing, the person she had wanted to
share the wonders of this cottage with. Who? The boy she had
always dreamed of ? The one with the smile and the pointy ears?

She looked up at Mist with eyes that nipped, and onions had
nothing to do with it . . . This was not the one, certainly! Not
him, with his empty glass and his open shirt and his fancy boots
up on a stool and the trail of mud wherever he walked. Never
him. She would not have run away with Mist.

She must have run away with someone, though, or why had
she let her hair grow long?

Jain and his foul friends had done this awful thing to her.

She gulped away the ache in her throat. "You say you can't
cook, but you knew exactly what supplies to bring."

"I've seen it done often enough," he remarked blandly. "You haven't touched your wine."

"You take it. I'll stick with water. And I think this is ready to eat."

He swung his feet down to the floor. "I know I am."

She would not have run away with Mist. Oh, he was likable enough, but she knew now what his talent was.

Mist pushed his chair away from the table, stretched out his long green legs, and wiped his mouth with the back of his hand. "That was delicious! You are a terrific cook."

Thaïle had finished her meal some time back. She had never seen anyone put away quite so much at a sitting as Mist just had. "Thank you, my lord."

He smiled tolerantly, missing the sarcasm. His emotions were oddly fuzzy, because of the wine. "It's very nearly dark out there!" He stared at the window for a moment and then began to emit worry. "There's a lot of places I was supposed to show you and haven't."

"There's a moon."

"There is here . . ."

"But it may be raining elsewhere? Mist, how big is the College?"

He shrugged blankly. "No idea."

"There's only the one path, isn't there, the Way?"

" 'Sright." He grinned. "That's quite a trick, isn't it? No branchings, no side roads. It starts where you are and ends where you want to go."

"Provided you've been there already."

He nodded, and stretched. "You have to be shown the Way. Just means you have to know what your destination looks like, I think—it's only a Way back! But I ought to show you a few more places before it gets too dark. Course we can take a lantern."

"Can you show me the Gate?"

He shook his head as he stood up. "No, I was blindfolded when . . . You mean you weren't?" If butter could look suspicious, then it would look like his eyes now. "Why do you want to know the Way to the Gate?"

Thaïle was not worried by Novice Mist, or what he was thinking. "Maggot and Worm and whoever the other one is—they were blindfolded also?"

"Yes."

"So you've talked about it with them?" She Felt his uneasiness and did not wait for an answer. "I was just wondering if you and I came in by the same Gate. There must be several, mustn't there?"

He bent over to lean his elbows on the chair back; he regarded her warily. "So I'm told."

"How big is the College, Mist?"

"You think it's all over the place?"

"I think it's all over Thume—hill country for me, river bottom for you. Hot lands, cool lands . . . That's why the weather changes along the Way."

"Evil take it!" He smiled sheepishly. "It took me a week to work that out! Something Maggot said about the seashore to the south tipped me off. I just thought you were gorgeous, I didn't know you were clever, as well."

Compliments were nice, but an offer to wash up would have been nicer. Sensing trouble ahead, Thaïle decided it was time to move Novice Mist out into the cool night air.

Stars were appearing in the darkening sky, the waxing moon was bright enough to cast shadows. As they set off along the Way together, Mist reached for her hand and she moved it to safety.

"It's a beautiful evening," he grumbled. "Romantic!"

It was. He wasn't.

"But we have all our lives ahead of us here in the College," she said. "Don't we?"

The implications silenced him. Mist, she suspected, did not think very far ahead. About twenty minutes would be his limit.

The forest grew deeper, and dark, but the Way glimmered pale before them. Leaves whispered busily all around. Soon she smelled rain and heard a faint patter on the canopy high above. An owl hooted in the distance.

"Where are we going?" she asked.

"The Commons. That's where you eat if you don't want to cook. Great food! I don't mean better than yours, of course. After that, maybe the Library?"

"Fine." What was a library?

A few minutes went by. Thaïle sniffed suspiciously. The air was warmer, muggier, bearing a strangely familiar scent. River? Yes, it might be a river. Not one of the mountain torrents she knew from her childhood, but one of the slow, sinuous floods of the lowlands, muddy and weedy. And that chirruping sound?

"Is the Commons near a river, Mist?"

"River? No. Why?"

"Just wondered. What's that noise?"

"Frogs."

Of course frogs—she knew that now. Not a river, but a swamp, perhaps? Or a lake.

She Felt no guile in her companion—he was genuinely puzzled by her questions, still foggy from the wine. But then he must have detected the change in the air, also, for his puzzlement rose to worry, and confusion.

The trees thinned out to reveal a moonlit glade and wide water beyond. And a cottage, with a canoe inverted on trestles beside it. She winced at the explosion of embarrassment from Mist.

"This is your Place!" she said wryly. "On a lake, you said, right?"

"Thaïle! I'm sorry! I truly didn't mean . . . I didn't mean to bring you here. Not now. I was hoping maybe later. I don't understand!"

No one could lie to her, and he wasn't trying. She laughed uneasily. "I think you weren't thinking hard enough about where we were going, Mist. You took the wrong Way by accident!"

"That must be it." He was genuinely upset at seeming foolish and worried that she would think evil of him. All talk, Jain had called him.

"Well, we're here now. You want to show me?" The surest road to a pixie's heart was to praise his Place, her mother had taught her. It was only good manners to ask to be shown around.

Eagerly Mist led her over to the little house. He pushed open the door and called light from magic lanterns, then bowed in mock formality. "I am Mist and welcome you to the Mist Place."

Before she could invoke the Gods' blessings in response, he rushed on: "It isn't very tidy, I'm afraid."

As an understatement, that remark would be hard to equal. The floor was muddy and every scrap of furniture was littered with clothes. She saw dirty dishes, banana skins, orange peels, leftover scraps that would be certain to bring vermin—already a legion of bugs whirled around the lantern. An open door showed a rumpled, unmade bed. He had managed all this in only ten days?

"It isn't, is it?" she said sadly. It would be a pleasant cottage otherwise. She could hardly scold a man so much older and larger than herself—indeed, his woebegone expression made her more inclined to demand a broom and start a cleanup. She resisted that temptation, for she recognized his talent at work. She had guessed what the second recorder had recognized in Mist— an occult ability to make other people want to tend him. Cook his meals, for example, wash his dishes. For all his size and muscle, he just stood there looking likable and helpless as an oversize puppy.

Then her eyes wandered to the cottage itself: walls of tight-woven basketwork, roof thatched with banana leaves, rafters of bamboo. A pulse in her throat began beating uncontrollably. A terrible sense of familiarity engulfed her. Somewhere she had known a house like this, impossibly like this. She backed away, taut with a growing horror, feeling unknown wraiths rise to gibber in the dark corners of her mind.

Even the unperceptive Mist had registered her alarm. "What's wrong?" he demanded.

"Nothing. Just very tired . . . It's lovely, I'll see it better in daylight, excuse me."

She turned and fled out the door—ignoring his shouts, ignoring the rain, racing off across the clearing and along the Way, awkward in her unfamiliar shoes, with her cloak streaming behind her. As she rounded the second bend, his fear and distress cut off abruptly and she was alone again. A few more panting steps, and the warm mugginess of the lowland air faded also. Moonlight began to filter down through the trees. The spectral path glittered pale before her.

Bamboo and wicker. Somewhere she had known a house like that. Somewhere, sometime, it must have mattered greatly to her.

The Thaïle Place, she thought. She must concentrate on her destination. If she worried too much about Mist's cottage, the Way might take her back there. The Thaïle Place, home . . . Except that the shiny dream cottage she had been given did not feel like home. Thaïle of the Thaïle Place—it sounded wrong!

Thaïle of *Who's* Place?

She slowed to a walk, conscious of the painful pounding of her heart. She forced herself to breathe more slowly and un-clench her fists. Fool! What was there to be afraid of? Jain had said she could be in no danger in the College. Forest never troubled her, even at night. Open grassland would be much more scary.

Soon she smelled the air of the high country, the familiar tree scents. The moonlight grew brighter. She came around a bend and saw the Thaïle Place ahead . . . dark, deserted. Not home, true, but a familiar refuge. She stumbled up the porch steps and went in, closing the door on the terrors of the world.

—

Life's young day:
    I've wandered east, I've wandered west,
        Through mony a weary way;
    But never, never can forget
        The luve of life's young day!
                William Motherwell, *Jeanie Morrison*

⟮ SEVEN ⟯

Come by moonlight

1

Thaïle was still tidying away the dirty dishes and the remains of supper when she Felt anxiety approaching. Mist's distinctive emotions were familiar to her by now, and so was the sudden starting and ending of Feeling caused by the sorcery of the Way—had he been coming by any mundane road, she would have detected him hours ago. Peeking around a corner of a drape, she saw a lantern flicker in the trees.

Then came hesitation. He had followed her to make sure she was all right, that she had reached home safely. Now he could see the light in her window. She did not want to talk with Mist any more that night; she needed time to think before she talked with anyone. She marched across the room, letting her shadow traverse the curtain. She Felt his relief . . . regret . . . resignation. A few minutes' indecision, and then he turned for home. His emotions were abruptly cut off by the Way. When she looked again, his light had gone. Poor Mist! He meant well, even if a hailstorm was more considerate.

But the day would not end. She washed the dishes; she washed herself. She turned out the lights, shed the last of her garments. She sank into that cloud-soft featherbed. And the day would not end.

Yesterday? She had no yesterday. She had no memory of her journey, or her arrival at the College. She could remember going to the Wide Place, to visit Sheel. She could not recall returning home. Had she just run away? By herself? That seemed very unlikely.

Almost a year had been stolen from her life—of that she was certain. She was plumper than she remembered herself, and *fat* took *time. Hair* took time, too—she climbed out of bed, turned on the light, and inspected her neck in the mirror again. Maybe . . . she could not be sure. Everyone tended to grow a little paler in the rainy season and darker in the dry season. The neck evidence, she admitted, was weak. It might be only imagination, or the rainy season. She could hardly accost Sorcerer Jain, point at her neck, and demand an explanation.

She turned out the light and floated down into the bed again. It was much too soft, but she knew she would not sleep, even if she lay on the floor. She had never felt more awake in her life. Too soft . . . and empty.

Why did an empty bed feel so wrong when she had always had a bed to herself? Ferns or feathers—a bed was a bed.

She thought about praying, but almost all the prayers she had ever learned were addressed to the Keeper, and here she was in the Keeper's lair. Even the Gods might not heed a prayer from within the College itself.

Almost a year of her life. She might be able to live with that loss. *Whom do we serve?* asked the catechism. *The Keeper and the College*, of course. She had been taught those words by her parents, as all pixies always were and always had been. If she had truly run away, disobeying the recorder's edict that she present herself at the College, then she had sinned. Crime deserved punishment. Perhaps that dark void was her punishment.

But who had lived within that void? A boy with a kind smile whom she had loved? A man, perhaps, who had built a Place of bamboo and wicker? Who had taught her to cook fish? A lover? A man of her own?

Loss of life she might accept, but loss of love was unforgivable. She must know! She must find more evidence and be sure. She trembled as she followed her logic to its conclusions.

If she had learned to cook fish, then she might have learned other things as well.

Thaïle arose and pulled a dress at random from the closet. She wrapped herself in a cloak. She did not need shoes to walk in the forest, nor any other garment for what she planned. She stepped out into the moonlight and set off along the Way, shivering a little—partly from the cold, but mostly from shame.

There was still light showing in the Mist Place. For a moment she hovered nervously on the stoop, sensing the boredom and worry and loneliness within. A pixie, lonely? Poor Mist! She could not imagine Mist as a sorcerer. *Easier than picking cotton*, he had said. Easier still to see the devious, sinister Jain as a sorcerer and the placid, easygoing Mist pulling weeds or just dipping a paddle into sunlit water . . .

The frogs were louder than they had been earlier, yet why could he not hear the beating of her heart? Her Feeling gave little sense of direction, but she was fairly sure that he was in bed, or at least in his bedroom. A faint undertone of disgust suggested that he might even be trying to tidy up the Place so that Novice Thaïle would not be upset when she saw it again tomorrow.

Are you sure this is what you want to do? whispered a tiny voice within her.

I must know, she replied, and rapped knuckles on the planks.

Wild alarm within . . . The floor creaked.

"Who's there?" Mist demanded from the other side of the door, deep and threatening.

"Thaïle. Let me in."

Relief and delight . . . "Wait a minute, then. I haven't any— I mean, I'm not respectable."

"Doesn't matter."

Incredulity . . . excitement . . .

The door opened a crack, and two eyes peered out below a tangle of hair, all silver pale in the moonlight.

She said, "Are you going to keep me here shivering all night?"

Excitement became tinged with embarrassment—and shame. "But I . . . I haven't any clothes on."

She pushed the door, and Felt his disbelief and wildly mounting joy as it creaked slowly open. He retreated behind it, peering around the edge incredulously. She entered, blinking in the lamplight. She could still see nothing of him except his eyes, yellow again now and stretched impossibly wide.

Her mouth was dry. "Promise me you'll be gentle?" she whispered.

"I promise! Oh, I promise!" He pushed the door closed and wrapped her quickly in his arms. "I do love you!"

2

Faint lichens of moonlight clung to darkness on the cottage walls. Frogs croaked far away. Mist snored softly at Thaïle's side, facedown, one heavy arm across her. The performance was over: the heaving, the sweating, the gasps and cries and—yes, admit it!—the heart-stopping surges of rapture.

Over. She felt soiled and guilty, as if she had done something sinful. She also felt *used*, although it had been she who had tried to use Mist for some insane, nonsensical purpose. What in the world had she hoped to achieve? And what had she in fact achieved, apart from a sort of all-over pummeled feeling, as if she had been rolled down a long hill?

More sorrow, that was what. She knew now that she had not come to this man's bed as a trembling virgin. There had been no surprises there. Her body had known what to do, how to respond to his and encourage it. It was probably a lot more experienced than Mist's was.

She shivered as her sweaty skin cooled. He stirred. She Felt his sleep fade into a drowsy smugness.

"I did good, didn't I?" he muttered.

She countered, "You mean that's all?" and at once scolded herself for being catty. Ungrateful, even. A girl ought to appreciate a man willing to exert himself so hard and long.

Mist's satisfaction was proof against teasing. He chuckled silently. "Sure is all! Try me again in the morning."

She was not going to be here in the morning, that was certain. Her pulse rate had returned to a bearable level. A long cold walk lay between her and that wonderful bathtub waiting at her own Place. As she was about to remove Mist's sticky hand, though, he seemed to rouse a little more. "Who's Leéb?"

Her heart began to hammer again.

"Who?"

Mist yawned, and stretched sensuously. "That last time. You got kinda wild. Kept calling me Leéb."

Leéb? It sounded like someone's name, but she knew nobody called Leéb. "You heard wrong."

"Nawp! It was Leéb, Leéb, Leéb . . . Leéb this, Leéb that.

Well, I did everything you wanted, honey, and then some. One last kiss . . . Hey! Where'yu going?''

"Bathtub." She slid her feet to the garment-strewn floor. Mist grunted and rolled over, sinking down into sleep even as he did so. She pulled a cover over him and went out into the front room. She managed to locate her cloak near the outer door. Curiously reluctant to call for lights, she decided to leave her dress wherever Mist had thrown it; doubtless he would keep it as a souvenir. She left the cottage, closing the door quietly.

The moon was low in the sky, the forest cooler and dark. There was no rain. *Thaïle Place* she thought firmly as she reached the shimmering paleness of the Way, and its grittiness was pleasantly familiar under her feet.

Leéb? The word meant nothing. A man? A place? A river, perhaps. But she had called it out at the ultimate moment of ecstasy, the moment—so an old song said—when the God of Love caressed the soul.

Most of a year missing from her life, nine or ten months at least. Almost long enough to . . . No, that was absurd. She wouldn't think about that. But now she was sure. Certainly that had not been the first time a man had made love to her. Leéb? Who else?

Gods, but she was tired! Kneaded! Mist was heavy.

Leéb! She had a name for him now, at least, if not a face yet.

Now what? All her life she had been taught to revere the Gods, the Keeper, the College.

Who defends us from the demons?

The Keeper and the College.

Whom do we serve?

The Keeper and the College.

Who never sleeps?

The Keeper.

But now the Keeper and the College had stolen away a year of her life and the love of her life. They had brought her here against her will. They expected her cooperation, yet they had coerced her, and tricked her. Could anything demons might do be worse than that?

Leéb? Who was Leéb?

To serve the Keeper and the College—to serve the Gods . . . But the Gods Themselves must seek to aid the Good. The Gods, the College, the Keeper, and humble little Thaïle—they all should follow that highest loyalty. She could see little evidence that any of them had been doing so.

The wind was rising, stirring the trees, and she hugged her cloak tight against the chill. Her feet were frozen. The moon was low behind her, throwing her shadow far ahead along the Way, amid the many writhing shadows of branches.

Was there any escape from the College? If she and Mist were correct, then the College was no single place at all. There were bits of it scattered all over Thume. Her own cottage stood in woods familiar to her, among trees like the trees that grew near her birthplace. The Mist Place was familiar to Mist. It made sense. It was very convenient. Nice magic.

What would happen, then, if she just left her cottage in the morning and headed west, say, or south—or any direction except along the Way? Would she emerge from the sorcery of the College and find herself in the foothills of the Progiste Mountains, close to her parents' Place? That seemed very unlikely. There must be sorcery to stop strangers blundering in. There would be sorcery to keep the inmates from blundering out.

It might be worth a try, though.

But even if she could escape from the College, it was certain that Jain and his friends could find her again before she ever discovered Leéb. She did not know where to look.

She did not even know what he looked like.

His memories of her might have been destroyed as utterly as her memories of him. And perhaps he did not exist at all. Leéb. Leéb? The name meant nothing except her own romantic delusion.

The trees were wrong! She stopped, feeling a jolt of childish alarm before she could remind herself that she was safe in the care of the Keeper. The College would certainly not go to all the trouble of bringing her here and then let her be hurt.

The Way ran on ahead along a hillside, a faint glimmer in the dark. The ground sloped down to her right and in that direction she could see dark branches waving against dark sky and a few silvery shreds of cloud. A distant ridge marked the far side of the valley, dark, also, and anonymous. To her left the forest rose steeply, scrubby grass and trunks cutting off her view. Moonlight danced through waving pines behind her. The air smelled of pine, not of the familiar woods around her cabin.

She listened, hearing only the wind in the trees and a hint of water far below. And the beating of her heart.

Gods preserve me!

She had been walking far too long anyway, she realized, and this was certainly not the Way she wanted to go. It was new to her. It was not the Way to anywhere she had been taken in the College. Shivering, she tried to work it out. Could this be the Way to the Gate? Perhaps her desire to escape from the College had unconsciously led her the wrong Way, just as Mist's romantic hopes had caused him to take her to his Place when he had not deliberately planned to. Sometimes, obviously, the Way heard the heart and not the head.

But Mist had said you could only follow the Way to somewhere you knew already, so her chances of arriving at the Gate must be slim. Yet if she did not keep moving, she would freeze. She was wearing nothing under her cloak except a triple layer of goose bumps. Sternly repeating to herself Jain's statement that she could be in no danger within the College, she decided to carry on and see where this Way led.

As she limped along, weary muscles stiffening in the cold, some other, nastier, possibilities came to mind. She had gone to Mist's Place and accepted his seed. In the ways of the pixies, she had bound herself to him for life. True, neither of them had made any promises. She had intended none and was quite certain he had not, either, but it was the acceptance that counted. By strict reckoning she was now Thaïle of the Mist Place, forever. So perhaps this Way led nowhere at all, and the Thaïle Place no longer existed. She would have to turn back and go home to that big parasitic canoeist.

Which might be what the foul scheming Jain had intended. He had deliberately thrown her into Mist's company. How strong was Mist's talent? If her suspicions were correct, friend Mist inspired other people to care for him. She had cooked his supper and very nearly volunteered to clean out his filthy den. She had gone to his bed of her own free will, she had thought. Believing that she was using him for her own purposes, she might have been serving his. God of Mercy!

Thaïle of the Mist Place? Now there was a revolting prospect!

The valley was narrowing, and the trees thinning out. She could hear a mountain torrent below quite clearly now and discern the bare ridge across the valley—silver grass in the moonlight, with only a few stunted trees casting long shadows. The moon was near to setting and dawn was hours away.

She must be very high, up near the timberline. She would not be at all surprised to see snow soon, and the wind felt fresh from mountain crags. Wandering unknown hills in the middle of a winter's night? This was madness!

She spun around and headed back, with the moon in her eyes.

"The Thaïle Place!" she said aloud. "Take me to the Thaïle Place!" She called up a clear mental picture, and hurried.

She would accept the Mist Place, of course, if that was to be her only choice. To climb into bed beside that big lunk and lay her icy feet against his back would be purest bliss.

Don't think about the Mist Place!

Thaïle Place!

The Way was curving more than she expected. She did not remember so many bends. She was not back into the forest yet—in fact, trees seemed to be even scarcer.

With the valley on her left now, and the moon temporarily slid around to her right, she came to deep shadow, where the Way's pale trace skirted a high buttress of rock. She had not seen this before!

Nor had she crossed a bridge, and yet the Way ahead quite clearly swung away from the vertical face and crossed to the far side by a narrow stone bridge. It was old, its parapets half fallen away, and it glimmered with the same spooky pallor as the Way itself. She had most certainly not seen it, or crossed it, earlier.

Whimpering with cold and fear, she sat down on the path and chafed her feet while she considered the prospect.

Obviously the sorcerous Way changed all the time; it just had not changed quite so blatantly before. Also obviously, if she crossed that bridge, she would again have the valley on her right and the hill on her left. And the valley itself bent out of sight—to the left, of course—so she would then have the moon behind her again. Obviously.

The Way was taking her somewhere, whether she wanted to go there or not. Her retreat had been cut off, and both directions led to the same place. She had two choices—go where the Way led, or stay where she was and freeze.

She could not even be sure of the second alternative. If she shut her eyes for a minute, the landscape might start changing on its own.

Evil take it! "Can't fight the weather," Gaib would say—usually under his breath when her mother was laying down the law. Here was an excellent example of weather not to be fought. Groaning with stiffness and weariness, Thaïle clambered to her feet and hobbled across the bridge.

As she had expected, she soon found herself going the same Way as before, trudging along a hillside with the gorge to her right and the moon behind her. The wind was really whistling along the valley now, the noise of the stream much louder. She must just hope that wherever she was being taken had a roaring fire and something steaming hot to drink. And a bed. With no men in it.

She had sinned, of course. Virtuous women did not go to strange men's Places and seduce them; but the Gods rarely dispensed punishment so candidly. Her brother-in-law, Wide, was a libertine, but his philandering did not attract divine retribution, so far as she knew. A couple of her childhood friends had told her stories they would never have told their parents.

Perhaps . . .

Just maybe . . .

Could the Gods have taken pity on her? Could it be that this so-willful Way was taking her to Leéb, whoever he was?

She did not dare to hope for that, but she decided she had better do some praying. Not to the Keeper, though, just to the Gods. She began muttering prayers, making them up as she went along.

The valley became a gorge, the wind buffeting at her with icy fists, trying to hurl her from the narrow path, down into the shadowed chasm on her right. On her left, the rock rose almost sheer. Moonlight glowed on racing clouds overhead, but did not penetrate this sinister cleft in the hills. She had only the spectral gleam of the Way itself to guide her.

And then a final bend brought her to what had to be her destination. A single shaft of moonlight fell on white masonry ahead, closing off the ravine. Ragged and undoubtedly ancient, a single arch spanned both the Way and the chasm, the stonework springing out from the steep rock on either side. Once the arch had supported a gatehouse, for she could see remains of windows in the ruins above, and trees growing there. Water roared in the unseen depths, sending up a faint odor of spray.

Old—and evil. It was gloating at her in the moonlight.

"No!" she cried aloud. "I am not going in there!"

She turned and fled, floundering down the path on hurting feet, repeatedly stumbling against the rock in her efforts not to tumble over the precipice on her left. The wind blustered at her, pushing and tugging without pattern or reason. She rounded a corner, and saw a bridge ahead, and the same gateway beyond. She staggered to a halt, whimpering. Both Ways led to the same end.

Suddenly her perception changed and in place of a moonlit ruin she saw an idiot, leering face—the irregular, tree-covered top as hair, empty windows staring at her like eyes, and the arch itself as a gaping mouth, with the silvery Way lolling out one side like a tongue. Whatever it was, she was convinced that it was evil.

Her limbs began shaking harder than she could ever remember. Frightened of falling from the ledge, she leaned back against the cliff.

"No!" she screamed into the wind. "I will come no farther! I will stay here!" She heard only the roar of the falls below and the whisper of branches above.

Stay there and freeze? If necessary, yes! What other tricks could the Way use? She glanced nervously behind her— suppose a bear appeared on the path, to drive her toward that gloating aperture? When she looked back to the bridge and the gateway beyond, she fancied they had already crept closer. Could that demonic mouth draw in the Way like a tongue, with her on it?

Any real fright would bring sorcerers to her aid, Jain had promised. She had never felt so fearful in her life, and yet no one had come. Perhaps the sorcerers were all abed and asleep.

The final words of the catechism: *Who never sleeps?*

The Keeper.

This was the Keeper's doing.

"No!" she cried again. "If you try any more tricks, I shall leap from the path!"

She hoped she was bluffing.

She cowered down small, hugging the cloak tight around herself, keeping her gaze firmly on that leering archway lest it creep closer while she was not watching. She would stay there and freeze! Except that the moon was setting and when dark came the gate would draw in its tongue with her on it like a crumb. In her fear, she recalled the humble prayers of her childhood, the pleas every pixie was taught: *Keeper keep me in the right, Keeper keep me through the night . . .*

Something moved in the corner of her eye. She looked around sharply. A patch of moonlight and shadow? She peered harder, striving to make out the dark shape in the darker. It wore a cloak that hung motionless to the ground, as if the wind did not know it was there. It seemed to peer at her, but the face was hidden in the utter blackness of its hood.

Thaïle sprang to her feet. The apparition drifted closer like smoke. It was taller than she was.

"Child?" The rustly whisper was dry as wind on dead grass. "What are you doing here?"

"Nothing, er—my lady." She thought it was female. Her Feeling could detect no one there, though. Her teeth chattered frantically and her whole inside had turned to ice. What had she summoned? The Keeper Herself ? Or·a wraith?

"Thaïle?"

"Yes, ma'am."

"Ah!" The apparition sounded surprised. "Why did you come here?"

"I didn't want to! The Way brought me! I was trying to go home."

Thaïle heard a faint sniff, as if of surprise.

"But why here? Had you been shown this place?"

"No, ma'am."

" 'Tis strange." The cowl moved as if the apparition shook its head, but still the wind did not ruffle it. "The time is not right. The Defile is dangerous enough when the moon is full, especially to those whose Faculty is strong. At the quarter it would . . . Who told you of it?"

"N-n-no one, ma'am."

"Strange indeed. But we must save you from freezing, mustn't we? Or you will never meet your destiny. The mistress of novices will be most upset to hear that one of her charges has been wandering the night." A hint of a chuckle seemed to confirm that the invisible presence inside the cloak was at least partly human. "To which bed shall I send you?"

Thaïle shouted *'Leéb's!'* before she had time to think.

The apparition did not reply for a dozen heartbeats. Then she sighed, and the dead-leaves voice became fainter than ever. "Child, child! How did you . . . ? Oh, I see. Incredible strength! I could not have, at your age . . . But you must bear the sorrow. I would not let them use a greater oblivion on you, and it would have done no good anyway. If I apply all the power your mind could endure, I fear you will still shake it off in time. Best to suffer the loss now, while you are young. Close your eyes, child, and I—''

''Where is Leéb? Who is Leéb?''

The cowled dark surged closer and Thaïle shrank back hard against the rock. The voice came more quietly yet, crackling like thin ice on a winter puddle. ''He is a young man, of course. You fell in love, Thaïle, tragic error! For you, there can be no love, not ever. It would destroy you, and it would destroy him. Will you believe that?''

''No I won't!''

''It is true, nonetheless. In time you will understand. Romp in men's beds if you want. If a man attracts you, enjoy him, as you did that boy tonight—you will not lose your heart to him. But do not love. Never love. Do you want Mist's comfort again now?''

''No!''

''Then close your eyes and I will return you to the Thaïle Place.''

Come by moonlight:
>   Look for me by moonlight;
>   Watch for me by moonlight;
>   I'll come to thee by moonlight, though hell
>   should bar the way!

Alfred Noyes, The Highwayman

⊄ EIGHT ⊅

A new face

1

The sun had not yet arrived in Krasnegar, and when it did, it would not linger long.

Nevertheless, in a cozy little kitchen in a modest dwelling near the docks, Captain Efflio had just completed breakfast. His landlady, Mistress Sparro, was plying him with innumerable "last" cups of tea, plus even more numerous questions about the queen's council and the business of today's meeting. Efflio declined the tea, being already awash in it. He was answering the queries as well as he could without betraying confidences, and he knew she would just invent the rest anyway. Having a member of the queen's council as lodger had given Mistress Sparro an enormous boost in status on the gossip circuit. She would be off to visit with her friends as soon as he was out the door.

Half a year had passed since he had settled in Krasnegar. His first choice of lodgings had not been a success, but he had since found a worthy anchorage with Mistress Sparro. She was a widow in her forties, a typical imp, dark and dumpy, although she had two huge jotunnish daughters, both married. Such mismatches were not uncommon in Krasnegar. Her cooking was excellent. There was nothing significantly wrong with her figure. She had already dropped hints that a proposal to make their cohabitation permanent and intimate would not be declined. He was thinking about that quite seriously.

If Efflio had regrets about *Sea Beauty*, it was only that he had not sold the old hulk years earlier. Life on the beach had turned out to be much more tolerable than he had expected. Krasnegar was a quiet and friendly haven, and secure. After a lifetime at sea, he did not find it small. He had made friends, found interests, and was loaning out his surplus savings at very attractive rates. Any time he needed a little excitement, he could always drop in on one of the jotunn saloons and watch the fights. True, the climate was unspeakable, but a sailor found nothing untoward at wearing fur boots while eating breakfast, as now. He had learned to do without the sun, and already it had started its return, anyway.

And he was a member of the queen's council. That was both an honor and an interest—imps and jotnar together could never be dull, as he knew from his life afloat. Only once had he watched the king chair a meeting. The queen did very well in his absence. Before Efflio came to Krasnegar he would not have believed for an instant that any collection of male jotnar would ever allow a woman to call it to order.

He was quite looking forward to today's meeting, therefore, but he was not looking forward to getting there. With his weak lungs, he could not walk up the hill. In the summer he had traveled by coach. When winter plugged the road with snow, he had resigned himself to missing the meetings. The queen had not. The queen of Krasnegar was not easily balked.

Mistress Sparro lifted the kettle from the hob and topped up her best pink china teapot without dropping a stitch in her cross-examination. Abandoning the subject of the recent rise in prices, she tacked back to the matter of the king's disappearance and what the council knew of it. All the imps in the kingdom were going crazy with curiosity on that subject. So was Efflio, and he knew no more than Mistress Sparro did, but of course he could not admit that.

"Matter of state, ma'am," he said for the hundredth time. "Can't discuss it."

There was a knock on the door.

To be precise, something drummed deafeningly on the door, slamming it to and fro on its hinges, almost ripping the latch from the wall, and creating enough noise to be heard in Nordland. Before either Efflio or Mistress Sparro could rise, the door surrendered and flew open. Two youths burst in, making the kitchen seem very crowded. There was something about young male jotnar that could make *anywhere* seem crowded.

Efflio stayed in his chair. He would still have to crane his neck if he rose, for they were both an arm's length taller than he was. They looked very broad and bulky in their winter fur and wool. They both sported uncertain mustaches, one silver and one almost reddish. Red professed to have a beard also, but it was the sort of beard that needed a good light.

"This the baggage for the palace?" Silver boomed, jabbing Efflio with a finger like a belaying pin.

"Come on, Granpop!" the other said, equally loudly. "Can you walk as far as the door?"

Mistress Sparro slammed down her kettle. "Captain Efflio is a member of the queen's council!" she snapped.

"He's baggage to us," Red said. "Salted herring or fat old men, it's all the same."

"Listen!" Silver cupped a large horny hand to his ear. "Can you hear a pussy cat somewhere? Charge extra for livestock."

Efflio could do nothing about his wheezing, but he did not intend to tolerate the ill manners of a pair of common porters. He had been taken unaware the first time the queen had sent a carrying chair for him; he had thus had to endure the effects of what jotnar regarded as a sense of humor all the way to the castle. He had been jeered at and insulted; he had been rocked and bounced to establish whether he was prone to seasickness; he had been stranded at a saloon halfway up a steep staircase until he agreed to buy a round of beer.

That had been the first time. Since then he had traveled with more dignity. He had a lifetime of experience in handling jotunn louts. Young ones were easy, no matter how big they were.

"There's been a mistake," he said, and held out his cup to Mistress Sparro for a refill.

"Huh?" Silver said.

"I am expected at the palace shortly. Major Domo Ylinyli was supposed to send a sedan chair and two men. There has been an error, obviously."

"What'djer mean?" Red demanded.

"Men. Not boys."

With no visible effort, Silver took the front of Efflio's doublet in one hand and lifted him to his feet. "Don't get smart, Fatso!"

"Somebody should." Efflio sat down again. "We agreed we

needed men and he sends boys. We agreed we needed imps and he sends jotnar. Oh well, the queen can manage without me, I'm sure."

"Another muffin, Captain?" Mistress Sparro said calmly, offering the plate.

"Imps?" Silver said, looking bewildered. "What'ju want *imps* for?"

Efflio paused with his hand poised over the muffins. "So I can get there before midsummer." He looked up in exasperation. "Off with you both! Tell Ylinyli to be more careful next time, and close the door quietly."

"We was told to carry you to the palace!" Red said stubbornly. "Silver penny apiece."

"You couldn't." Efflio sighed. He leaned back and stared up at the two giants—Silver's woolen cap was actually touching the ceiling. "Listen, sonny! In the Impire there are lots of sedan chairs, see? They're all over the place in the cities, and *they are always carried by imps*! Imps can run, you see. Jotnar don't have the wind for it."

Silver said, "Wotchermean, *wind*?"

Red said "Run?" with a hint of caution—that one might discover he had a spark of intelligence if he wasn't careful.

Efflio took a sip of tea. "I mean that a couple of impish bearers from Hub, say, or Shaldokan, would run that chair back up to the castle in a few minutes. You northerners make good sailors, and I agree you've got muscles to spare, but you don't have the wind that imps have. Not for running with a burden. It's a knack. I don't plan to spend all day in a carrying chair while you two lumbering hulks stagger around. Tell Ylinyli I stayed home." Wheezing contentedly, he took another muffin.

Red was suspicious. "Vark and Zug never said nothing about running!"

Efflio had no idea which pair they had been. He laughed. "Of course not! They wouldn't!" He smirked at Mistress Sparro. "Remember me telling you? The jotnar who tried to run?"

"Oh, yes!!" Mistress Sparro sniggered. "Was that one of the ones who fainted on Whalers' Steps?"

"And the one who kept throwing up. I did warn them that jotnar shouldn't try to run with a load like that, but no, they thought they could do as well as imps . . ."

Silver's wispy mustache bristled with fury; pale-blue eyes

burned. Again he lifted the captain bodily to his feet, and this time he stooped, so that they were nose to nose. "Get your coat on, Imp! We'll show you running!"

"Oh, don't give me that!" Efflio protested. "You young jotnar think you're tough, but I've seen what happens, and you'll never—"

Silver raised him off the floor, still one-handed. Tea slopped. The kid's face was scarlet with anger. "Get your coat on or you go without it!"

Red and Silver did very well, the best pair yet. They made a fast trip, and neither had breath to mar it with jokes about the captain's asthma. Had it been physically possible for two men to run all the way up Krasnegar carrying a sedan chair with a fat old sailor in it, then they might have been the first to do so. Alas, they collapsed simultaneously at the top of Royal Wynd. Efflio left them crumpled on the ground and embarked on an easy stroll to the palace gate. At that point, their breathing was a great deal louder than his.

2

"Rank profiteering, that's what it is!" Foronod screeched, thumping a fist on the table. His decrepit old jotunn face was flaming red, his skimpy silver hair awry, as if it were trying to stand on end. He was drooling in his fury.

The old man was past it, Inos thought sadly. He contributed nothing to meetings now, but he was a Krasnegarian monument, the nearest thing the kingdom had to an elder statesman; to dismiss him from her council would be unthinkably unkind.

"And what you propose is outright robbery!" Across the table, Mistress Oglebone was becoming even redder, swelling ever larger and more pompous as the discussion grew more heated. She was blustering, but for any imp to face up to the old factor was an unusual display of courage and conviction. "One quarter the stock at the usual price means one quarter the income, and the merchants will starve!"

"Starve?" Foronod sprayed the word. "Live off your fat, you oversize pigs!"

"Councillors!" Inos hammered with the whale's tooth that

served as gavel at meetings of the state council. Candlesticks shuddered, dribbling hot wax.

The resulting silence presented an unfortunate opportunity for Havermore to intervene. "Indeed, your Majesty, honorable ladies and gentlemen, I think our first moral duty here is to consider the poor, who certainly may starve, or freeze, or being faced with the choice may, in the way of our less fortunate brethren . . ." The old bishop could be counted on to blether for at least ten minutes, but perhaps that would give everyone else a chance to calm down.

The council was discussing the price of peat.

Looking along the length of the long table, Inos reflected that her advisors were growing old and predictable. She needed some new faces, with some youthful spark and fresh ideas. She had made few appointments since she first came to the throne, and even the youngsters she had added at that time were showing their years now—Kratharkran, for example. Then he had been a gangly, muscular young giant, vigorous and restless. Now he was a stolid human walrus, who made chairs creak when he squeezed into them. She could not wait for the oldest to die off; she must expand the council again. It could use at least another six members. Young ones. She would ask Rap . . .

Another idea that must wait for Rap's return.

"And who's to pay for that?" yelled Oglebone, her substantial bosom heaving with outrage. The bishop had just suggested a distribution of free peat to the poor.

The council had split along the usual lines, imps versus jotnar. Although he was an imp the bishop was an outsider, from the Impire, and should have been able to conciliate the two factions. His blundering efforts usually just antagonized everyone.

And this time there was good reason for the division. The imps were largely drawn from the tradesmen and merchants, with Oglebone their leader. The jotnar represented artisans and fisher-folk, all of whom—being jotnar—were hopelessly short of money so late in the winter, and especially this winter, with the cost of fuel rising faster than smoke. Farther down the agenda the price of credit lurked like a hungry bear. It would certainly provoke allegations of usury and demands for royal decrees.

Rap had warned months ago that fuel would run short, and the weather had been harder than usual, if that was possible. The cold at Winterfest had been the worst in memory. Some children and old folk had frozen in their beds. Foronod and Oglebone were both shouting now, and others joining in.

Inos gritted her teeth. This was when Rap would have intervened with some quiet, sensible suggestion. She hammered again. Nothing happened. "Councillors!" She was ignored. She rose to her feet and hurled the whale's tooth clattering along the length of the table, scoring a strike on the fourth gold candlestick. Lin caught it just before it fell over.

"Quiet!"

Shamefaced silence. Inos sat down again, seething. "The next person who speaks out of turn will be evicted from this meeting!" She glared around, meeting every eye in turn and watching their owners cower before her royal fury. That was Rap's old sorcery at work, she supposed, but she was almost mad enough to throw a few subjects into dungeons.

A hand rose at the far end. Peering around the flames, she recognized the junior member of the council.

"Captain Efflio?"

"I have a couple of questions, ma'am, if I may?"

The old seaman had not spoken a word so far. The few times she had noticed him, he had been watching the fracas with amused tolerance. He was an outsider, and a newcomer, and he usually made sense on the rare occasions when he chose to intervene. She hoped he was going to do so now. "Certainly."

"We have been given figures on the reserves of peat remaining and average monthly consumption. Obviously that will change as the weather warms up. If we had some more detailed numbers, we could assess the situation better. And how about previous years? Are there records? Do we have any idea of the normal requirements between now and springtime?" He paused, wheezing. "And, finally, are there no alternatives? I seem to recall seeing quantities of driftwood along the mainland shore, outside the bay."

"Driftwood?" Foronod bellowed scornfully.

The logistics of winnowing driftwood from pack ice and dragging it back through a subpolar night would be nightmarish. The present situation might be serious enough to justify the effort, but at the moment driftwood was a monstrous irrelevancy. If the council took off after that, it would never be seen again.

But Efflio continued serenely, "And I note that the next item on the agenda is the Timber Moot. I realize that the purpose is to acquire building lumber, but trees do burn, ma'am. Surely we can negotiate supplies of firewood from the goblins?''

The Council's sudden silence spoke volumes. Why had no one else thought of that? It had been Rap's idea to appoint the crafty old sailor to the council, and Inos breathed a silent word of thanks to him, wherever he was.

"We are grateful for your observations, Captain! The goblins will trade the shirts off our backs, I am sure, but we may have to pay the price. I appoint you a committee to investigate the reserves of fuel—peat and all possible substitutes—and estimate the town's needs. Co-opt whoever you want to help you."

Efflio wheezed louder. "I'm not as mobile as I should like, ma'am."

"Send the guard. They have nothing better to do." Inos heard a sniff of protest from Sergeant Oopari on her left, and ignored it. "Lin will find you a room in the palace if you want. You have my authority in the matter, Captain. Report to our next meeting."

She pressed on quickly. "Let us discuss the Timber Moot, then. We're a month past Winterfest already. A week or so from now the goblins will arrive. In the king's absence, whom do we send to trade?"

The room went very still.

"Well?" she said. "Can anyone here speak goblin?"

Even stiller. Foronod could, she knew, but probably not well and not for a long time. In any case, he was far too frail to struggle across the ice-packed causeway. He obviously knew that, or he would have volunteered by now.

The continuing silence surprised her, though. Goblin was not truly a different language, just a dialect, more a matter of primitive grammar and barbarous pronunciation than of vocabulary. As a child, she had played at speaking pidgin goblin with her friends, probably not very accurately. She would have expected someone in the room to know it.

"Then we shall have to appoint an agent. Nominations?"

The door creaked behind her. She felt a cold draft on her spine—and yet that was impossible. Everyone else was looking to see who had the unprecedented temerity to interrupt a meeting of the royal council.

She peered around the back of her chair. Kadie stood in the doorway, her face as pale as a jotunn's.

Oh, Gods!

Inos jumped up and scanned the table. Who? Who could she trust with the imp and jotunn still breathing fire at each other? Technically her deputy was probably Bishop Havermore . . .

"Captain Efflio? Take the chair, please, until I return."

The old sea captain blinked at her in astonishment. "Me, ma'am?"

"And see that all the blood is mopped up afterward!"

That raised a laugh. She swept out to discover what the disaster was.

3

It was Gath, of course.

He was being borne in on a stretcher, a footman at his head and the head groom at his feet. Two cooks and a chambermaid flustered around uselessly. The procession was apparently bound for his bedroom, but that would be icy at this time of day.

"To the parlor!" Inos snapped. Her heart was beating in her throat; she wanted to scream at the top of her lungs.

Gath was limp, apparently unconscious. Walking alongside, she took one of his hands. "Gath?"

Nothing happened. His knuckles were bloody and swollen, but his face was unmarked except for a red swelling on his chin. He had apparently suffered no more damage to his teeth. Then she saw a dribble of red creeping out from the golden cockscomb of his hair. She always had nightmares about head injuries.

From the look of his hands, his assailant or assailants would be well marked.

Excellent!

God of Mercy, stand aside! This had gone on too long. This time she was going to wreak vengeance. This time someone was going to pay, and if the culprits were too young to be punished she would flog their fathers instead.

She looked at Kadie's pale terror and forced a motherly, queenly, reassuring smile.

"Looks like he lost this one, doesn't it?"

Kadie sniveled. "He's hurt bad!"

"Can't be sure. It may be no worse than a headache. Someone's sent for a doctor?"

"Yes. I'm sorry I broke into your meeting, Mom."

Inos could not recall the last time she had not been "Mama" or even "ma'am" to Kadie. She put an arm around her daughter's shoulders as they walked—and those shoulders were not far below her own now.

"A year ago—maybe even six months ago—I'd have bitten your head off and burned you at the stake afterward. Now I knew right away you must have a very good reason. You did exactly right."

Kadie swelled a little. She deserved the praise. She had probably been the only one around brave enough to interrupt the queen in her council meeting. All the usual authorities had been in the meeting themselves, people like Lin to whom Kadie would normally defer in an emergency. Inos made a note to find out exactly what had happened. There ought to be an alternative chain of command, and she had never thought to create one—and now she didn't need to, of course. From now on everyone would rely on Kadie.

"Go back there, please. Knock, enter, and ask Captain Efflio if Sergeant Oopari can come here."

Kadie swelled even more. "Of course, Mama!" She marched off, too dignified to run.

And here was the parlor. Inos hurried ahead, threw the door wide and went to the sofa. Pret the footman took the other end and they pushed it close to the hearth. This was Gath's fourth beating, they were well practiced.

Fourth and perhaps the worst. Poor, gentle Gath, who never used to get in trouble, who'd never had an enemy . . . His prescience should have warned him. Perhaps the insight had come too late, perhaps he'd been too proud to run away. Not all bad things were avoidable, he'd told her.

The bearers laid the stretcher on the floor. Before Inos could intervene, they took Gath by legs and shoulders and swung him up onto the couch. He uttered a groan, then choked and said something that sounded like "No more stairs, Mom!"

"Clumsy dolts!" Inos raged. "More peat! Blankets. Hot water. Towels!" Servants fled.

She stared at the youthful form draped on the sofa. He looked longer every time. He was growing incredibly fast, at least a fingerlength since Rap left, his clothes bill bankrupting the king-dom.

She pulled a sleeve over her hand and wiped his forehead. He opened his eyes slightly. "Not stairs, Mom!" he muttered. He grimaced and seemed to fade away. She would have expected more bruises if he had been thrown down stairs.

Then Kadie was back, accompanied by a scowling Sergeant Oopari—a tallish imp, graying now, and permanently worried by his responsibilities.

"Do you know who did it?" Inos demanded.

Kadie shook her head. "I wasn't there. Jotnar, not imps, I'd say."

"Why?"

" 'Cause he doesn't look like he's been stomped." Kadie showed her teeth.

True. Inos shuddered as she thought of a pack of impish brats cornering their victim, starving wolves pulling down a caribou. That would be the next stage, and she was not going to allow it to happen. Meanwhile, this had already gone too far. "Sergeant! Find the culprits and put them in the cells."

Oopari was a cautious soul. "If it was a fair fight, ma'am?"

"I don't care if it was one five-year-old gnome and Gath started it! Lock 'em up! And tell me about it tomorrow."

"Yes, ma'am!" The sergeant's eyes gleamed. He'd wanted those orders the last time and Inos had held him back. He spun around and strode off without another word.

She knelt down. "Gath! Wake up!"

Nothing happened. *Oh, Gods!* Her anger chilled before a win-ter blast of fear. Head injuries! She peered at his ears and saw no trace of bleeding there. She tried to inspect his eyes. The lids flickered at her touch and his lips moved.

"Can't hear you," Inos said. "Speak up!"

He clutched at her. "No!" he mumbled. "Fire! Smell fire." He began to struggle. "Fire, Mom!"

She pushed him down. "No, that's only the peat on the hearth. Just relax. The doctor'll be here in a minute."

Much good that would do him. Krasnegar was more re-nowned for its banana crop than the quality of its medicine. She'd tried for years to coax some decent Imperial medics to come and settle in the kingdom, but with no success. She'd sent promising youngsters south to study, and they had never returned. Looking at the wreck of her son, she knew she could not tolerate the local incompetency in this case. Gath might be in real danger. He might be crippled; he might be dying. Fortunately she had a little sorcery available, but just how she should use it she didn't know yet—did she take the bucket to the well, or bring the well to the bucket?

Where was that sawbones?

Then everyone arrived at once—the peat and the blankets and Doctor Gundarkan and Eva and Holi, who was walking now and into everything. Pret began stoking the hearth. Eva erupted in screams and Holi began to cry, also, not understanding. Inos sent them off with Kadie. She realized that she had started to depend on her daughter a lot just lately.

Gundarkan was a tall, rawboned jotunn. He was pompous and ignorant, but he happened to be the jotnar population's favorite physician, so he had extensive experience with fight injuries. The impish doctors were better at treating illnesses.

"I'll have to do a complete examination, ma'am." He looked at her expectantly.

"Everybody out, please!" Inos said. The servants headed for the door. Then she realized that Gundarkan meant her, also. Gath was no longer a child.

She stalked out into the corridor, closing the door just as her daughter came hurrying back.

"Kadie, I want you to do something secret, all right?"

Kadie's eyes widened at this hint of intrigue. Her romantic soul would be thrilled. "Of course, Mama!"

"Get outdoor clothes for you and me—boots, cloaks, everything—and wrap them up in a couple of thick blankets. Put them in the room above the Throne Room. Try not to let anyone see."

"But . . . ?"

"No questions! And bring a set of clean clothes here for Gath."

Kadie gave her a very odd look as she left. The Throne Room was off the Great Hall, and a long way from outdoors.

Inos went back into the parlor and stood just inside the door. Gundarkan was bending over Gath, on the couch. Gath was whimpering and mumbling protests as he was prodded and flexed. The doctor looked up with a frown, then spread a rug over his victim and straightened.

He wiped bloody fingers on a dirty rag as Inos went over.

"There's a bad bang on the back of his head."

"I saw that, thank you."

He pulled a face. "He has concussion, certainly. Did you see his hands? And these?" He pulled one of Gath's skinny arms out from below the blanket. From wrist to elbow, it was already turning yellow. "I'd say he fought a good fight, ma'am."

"I don't give a whistle whether he did or not! How badly is he hurt?"

Gundarkan sniffed, disapproving of her attitude. "Against a very powerful opponent, or maybe two. They may have only laid that one blow on him." He pointed to Gath's chin. "Then he hit his head in falling. Nothing to be ashamed of, I'd say."

Idiot! "How badly is he hurt?"

The doctor shrugged. "Too early to say. He may just have a fractured skull." To a jotunn, of course, scrambled brains were unimportant. "I find no other bones broken, except possibly in his hands. They're too swollen to tell. He won't be able to fight again for a week or two."

It would be ironic if Gath had broken bones in his hands. After his last beating, Inos had bullied Gundarkan into diagnosing a cracked wrist and encasing Gath's arm in a plaster cast. That, she had assumed, would stop the fighting—jotnar would attack smaller opponents without scruple, but not injured ones. The deception hadn't worked for long. Gath had endured the cast for three days and then removed it, explaining cheerfully that his prescience had told him his hand would be all right without it.

Gundarkan picked up his black bag. "There may be internal trauma. It could be serious."

She did not need a doctor to tell her that. "So what do we do?"

"Keep him resting and warm. Try to waken him once an hour or so. He may fade in and out quite a bit after he starts coming around. Give him plenty to drink if he wants it. I'll look back this evening and probably bleed him to relieve the swellings."

Inos restrained a sharp retort. Krasnegarian doctors loved to bleed their patients. Bloodletting seemed to be the only treatment they knew, and it probably kept the victims bedridden a lot longer than they would have been otherwise. She made a polite response and escorted the pompous dolt to the door.

As the latch clicked shut, a groan from the couch made her rush back.

Gath stared up at her, as if in terror, trying to rise. He mumbled, "Goblins, Mom! There's goblins here!" Obviously he was delirious.

"Yes, dear. Don't worry." She pushed him down and laid gentle fingertips on his lips. "Shh! Try to rest."

Gath sank back; his staring eyes wobbled and then closed. Soon his twitching slowed, and he seemed to go to sleep, breathing heavily.

Well, at least he had started to come around. She hoped Kadie would return soon. She wanted to make her move before everyone collected in the great hall for lunch. The council would have to complete its business without her.

Doubtless a man of fourteen years and two months would be very embarrassed to be dressed by his mother, but Gath merely mumbled vaguely, not knowing what was going on. Inos made Kadie turn her back on the performance, though.

The bucket to the well, or the well to the bucket . . . If she fetched a competent doctor through the magic portal from Kinvale, then the great state secret would be hopelessly compromised. Even if the doctor himself was discreet, the palace staff would wonder where he had come from. Moving Gath in his condition was a real risk, but a necessary one. Moreover, he could then be kept away from Krasnegar until Rap returned and the problem was solved.

Fortunately it was almost noon, and there was daylight.

She would have to let someone else in on the secret, and Kadie was the obvious choice, as she would have to know eventually. She was old enough to respect a confidence now, and almost as tall as her mother. Surely Gath wasn't all that heavy . . . If the two of them couldn't manage, then they would have to enlist Krath or someone; but she thought they could.

"Mama?" Kadie said, without looking around.

"Yes, dear?" Inos tugged Gath's underwear into position, restoring decency.

"If you don't tell me what you are doing, I shall probably scream piercingly very soon now."

"I'm dressing your brother."

"I know that," her daughter said sweetly to the fireplace. "I want to know why. Is there a history of insanity in the family?"

"Probably. You can look now. I'll need you to hold him up while I put his shirt on. Gently!"

"Mama!" Kadie's green eyes flashed.

"I'm going to show you a secret, a big secret."

"That's nice." Kadie steadied Gath.

His head lolled drunkenly. "Goblins," he muttered.

Inos pulled a sleeve over a limp arm. "You know your father went away by sorcery. If you didn't know, you must have guessed. Well, we're going the same way."

"Going *where*?"

"To Kinvale, dear. Hold his head, if you can . . ."

4

By the time Gath was dressed, Inos had had another bright idea. She marched out into the corridor in search of an accomplice, and found Pret waiting patiently outside—in case he was needed, perhaps, or so no one else would give him something to do. Sounds of many voices came drifting along from the hall, meaning that lunch had begun.

"Is the council still in session?" she demanded.

"Er . . . yes, ma'am." The little footman seemed sober enough, although one could never be sure with him.

"Good. Go and sound the fire alarm."

His pale jotunn eyes widened like two snowballs. "Ma'am?"

"A practice. You heard me. Go!" She had not held a fire drill all winter and this would be a very good time, with Lin and the other leaders tied up in the council, but she was not going to explain all that to Pret. "I'll look after Gath," she shouted as he hurried off.

She went back into the parlor and closed the door. "Let's see if we can lift him."

Kadie looked just as disbelieving as Pret had done. "Is this wise, Mom?"

So Inos was back to being *Mom* again. "No, it isn't, but we have to do it. He hasn't any broken bones, the doctor said."

Gath was taller than either of them and heavier than his willowy shape would have suggested—or perhaps he just seemed so because he was so limp. He hardly seemed to notice as he was maneuvered back onto the stretcher, although his gray eyes opened. He was more delirious than unconscious, muttering anxiously about imaginary goblins. As soon as he was tucked in, he went back to sleep.

Inos raised one end of the litter, and Kadie the other, and they exchanged worried glances.

"Can you manage?"

"I think so," Kadie said doubtfully.

The corridor was empty. In the distance Pret was beating a carillon on the fire gong and there was shouting farther away yet. "Come on!" Inos said, and they headed for the hall.

The room above the Throne Room had once been called the Presence Chamber. Now it was just a storage for unneeded furniture, and it was *cold*. Inos wrapped Gath up in the extra blankets. He roused again, slightly, seeming to use his eyes alternately, as if they were pointing in different directions. He mumbled, but all she could make out was "Mustn't! . . . screaming? Torturing people!"

"Yes, dear. Terrible." Shivering, she pulled on her winter furs. "Come on, Kadie. Your father used to call you a little mule. Now you're going to have to live up to it."

The stairs winding up inside the walls of Inisso's Tower were steep and narrow. Inos made her daughter go first, which left her struggling to hold the stretcher high enough to keep Gath from sliding down on top of her. She recalled tales of lionesses defending their young and the maniacal strength attributed to desperate women rescuing their children—right now she could use some of that. She reminded herself that Rap had carried her up this tower once, and she had certainly weighed more than Gath. Rap had a lot more muscle than she and Kadie did, though.

They paused for a rest in the next room, their breath coming in huge clouds of smoke, as if the castle truly were on fire.

Kadie looked very worried. Perhaps she really believed her mother had gone mad. Inos did not wait until the questions could start again.

"Next level!" she said, and bent to lift the burden once more. In the stairwell, she banged her knuckles on the wall, but she did not have enough breath to say any bad words. Dim daylight filtered through tiny snow-covered windows.

Level followed level. The rests grew longer, but if they could do one stair, they could do them all. The air seemed to become ever colder.

Once in a while Gath would stir and mutter urgently about goblins. She wondered why his delirium had fixed on them. Was it possible that he had been attacked by a gang who had painted their faces green as a disguise? If so, Oopari would only have to look behind the ears of every young imp in the kingdom.

She did not die of heart strain. Nor did Kadie. They did not drop Gath, or let him slide off the stretcher, and eventually they staggered into the room that had once been the royal bedchamber. The furniture was still there, shrouded in cobwebs.

"One more to go," Inos gasped, as soon as she could speak. "Open the door."

Kadie gave her mother a sick glance, looked carefully around the room, and said, "What door, Mama?"

The door was in plain view, but of course there was an aversion spell on it.

"That one."

Kadie tried again. "Oh! I didn't notice." She took a step, and stopped. Another. No more. "I can't, Mom! I just can't!"

Inos said, "Holindarn!" but she was still too short of breath to speak above a whisper, and that whisper wasn't loud enough, apparently. She could feel the occult revulsion stopping her also.

"Holindarn?" Kadie shouted angrily. "What's Holi got to do with it?"

That worked. Kadie rushed over to open the secret door.

5

The final stair brought them at last to Inisso's arcane chamber and there they again laid down the stretcher to catch their breath. Gath mumbled in his stupor.

The big room was bare, with nothing marring its circular emptiness except the angular shape of the royal treasure chest—Inos certainly did not intend to tell Kadie the secret word for that yet! Faint marks in the dust on the floor showed a path crossing from the stairs to the magic portal, but the traffic had been slight this winter. Occupied with being both a mother and a full-time queen, Inos had come up here only twice since Rap left, each time in answer to a summons from Aquiala. Whenever there was need, the duchess would come through from Kinvale and leave a piece of parchment against the eastern casement, which Inos could see from her bedroom. The first time the marker had been a note from Rap, two days after he left, and the second paper had been an invitation to the Kinvale ball, which Inos had declined. She had done so in person, and thereby enjoyed a pleasant afternoon tea party.

As she stood and puffed, recalling dramatic memories of things that had happened in this chamber, her daughter was excitedly moving from casement to casement, peering down at the Winter Ocean. The sun was vanishing into the ice fog already, the brief arctic day almost over. Krasnegar did not sport as much smoke as it usually did in cold weather, which was a reminder of the peat shortage. The fire drill was probably over by now. The council would be back in session and Inos ought to return and take charge again before it voted in a republic or something . . .

Kadie said, *"Eeeek!"* She had discovered the magic portal itself, and was peering through one of the two windows that flanked it. Straight below her, a very long way down, was the castle courtyard.

"You go first," Inos said, still puffing.

"After you, Mama!" Kadie said politely.

"Let's move Gath over there, and then I'll explain."

Kadie came to lift her end of the stretcher. Within the circle of her fur hood, her face was flushed with excitement. Inos thought of the day she first learned of this chamber—her father, and Sagorn, and Kade's tea party . . . She had not been so very much older then than her daughter was now, a couple of years maybe. How time passed!

They rested their burden again right beside the door. "The secret word is the same as before," Inos said, still puffing. "It was my father's name, of course. But watch out for the wind."

"I think I'll watch for the step, mostly." Sometimes Kadie showed signs of Rap's dry humor.

"You'll be in Kinvale, don't worry."

"Darling Mama, please don't think I don't trust you—"

Inos laughed. "I know it looks scary, but remember this is sorcery! When you step through that door, you'll find yourself in a very charming little parlor, in Kinvale. It belonged to my Aunt Kade, and no one uses it now. It's been left just as it was, as a sort of memorial to her. It's a wonderfully cozy room, you'll love it. Go ahead.''

Kadie nodded uncertainly.

''Watch out for the wind, though,'' Inos added. ''There's always a wind. Sometimes the door will hardly move, sometimes it flies open in your face. You want me to do it?''

''Er, no.''

''Then go ahead—try it.''

Squaring her shoulders, Kadie turned to the magic portal and twisted the handle. Nothing happened, because of course there was no door there yet.

''Magic word!''

''Oh! Holindarn!'' Kadie proclaimed. The door rattled and she jumped.

''Well, open it!''

Kadie heaved. With a great struggle, she managed to haul it wide, while the cold air of Krasnegar wailed through the sorcerous opening, filling the little parlor beyond with billowing clouds of fog. Propping the heavy door with a foot, she stooped to lift her end of the stretcher again. Stumbling, Inos followed her as she lurched through. The journey ended with a rush as the door closed on Inos's back, propelling her forward. Then it slammed shut with a shuddering *boom!* The whole episode was over so quickly that the matching slam of the parlor door itself came a moment later.

Now that was odd! Why should the door of this unused little room have been open? The fog swirled, misting the windows, slowly clearing to reveal the comfy old chairs, the elegant little tables . . . Kadie screamed and dropped her end of the stretcher.

Taken off balance, Inos tripped over a footstool and sprawled to the floor. Gath rolled on top of her with a cry of protest.

''Mom!'' Kadie shrilled. *''A body!''*

Body? Inos lifted her face off the rug and stared in horror. It was a body. It was Aquiala, duchess of Kinvale. There was blood all over her gown and the carpet around her.

Smoke! She could smell smoke. And all that noise in the distance . . . Obviously Aquiala had been trying to reach the magic portal . . .

Gath was trying to rise. ''Mom!'' he wailed. ''I told you!''

The door to the corridor flew wide and the goblins came in to see who was slamming doors and screaming.

There was blood on their swords.

A new face:
> There's a new foot on the floor, my friend,
> And a new face at the door, my friend,
> A new face at the door.
>
> Tennyson, *The Death of the Old Year*

❰ NINE ❱

Questionable shapes

1

"Funny," Ylo said. "I hadn't realized it was so far from Hub."

He was sitting on a hillside, eating lunch. Shandie sprawled beside him, doing the same. Their horses grazed the dreary winter grass nearby. For once, the sun was shining almost warmly, dappling the landscape with cloud shadows. The wind had a nasty edge, but there was a vague odor of spring in it. The vast ducal palace of Rivermead sprawled below them, its paddocks, outbuildings, and ornamental gardens filling the valley floor from side to side.

"I never imagined anywhere so big, either," he added.

"You've never been there?"

"Once, when I was very small. We weren't on the main line, you know." Great-uncle Yllipo had been a distant, awesome figure in his childhood.

"Well, you are now," Shandie said, gnawing on a hunk of sausage. "The first thing I do when I regain my throne will be to make you duke of Rivermead. That's a promise!"

"It looks like an awful lot of work. All that grass to cut!"

Shandie flickered a grin. "It's virtually a small kingdom within the Impire. Most of the great dukedoms originated as warlord fiefs during the last interregnum. But if you'd rather have something closer to the capital, then you'll only have to ask. I mean that, Ylo. I will grant you any honor within my power!"

Ylo chewed for a moment in silence. So that was River-mead. Now he had seen it, and there went the last of his excuses.

He had never meant to come so far with Shandie on this journey, but one thing had led to another. First there had been the Covin's siren call, and the need to save the imperor from that, with the aid of Eemfume and his three friends. When the Covin had given up, he had decided to hang around for a few days to make sure that was not just a trick. And then there had been the opportunity to pervert Shandie's too-rigid code of ethics by introducing him to the arts of wenching and debauchery.

That had been a lot of fun, but the need for further education seemed to be over. The imperor was still a reluctant lecher, but he was a great deal more competent than he had been. He could roister with the best of them now, and Ylo never heard complaints from the next bed anymore. Shandie was a lot more human than he had been. In fact, he was excellent company, and that was the root of Ylo's problem—he was enjoying this excursion. Somehow he always seemed to put off his departure for one more day. Recently he had justified his procrastination with the never-to-be-repeated opportunity to take a look at Rivermead.

There it was. Now what? If he did not depart soon, he was not going to make it back to Yewdark in time for the daffodils. Who was he to negate the prophecy of the preflecting pool?

"Wonder what that is?" he muttered, pointing westward. A faint haze of dust on the skyline looked eerily familiar—looked, in fact, like the dust raised by a marching army.

"What what is?" Shandie asked. He rose to his knees and stared.

2

At the bottom of the hill, Rap eased back on the reins and let the team come to a halt. He set the brake and jumped down to the dirt. As he stretched to ease his stiffness, Thinal peered out the coach window. For the last hour, Thinal had been expertly shaving dice.

"Something wrong?"

"Just letting the horses have a breather."

The sun shone low in a cloudless blue sky. Here in the dry

lands it gave real warmth even so early in the year—Rap wiped his brow. All around him, the land was rumpled and brown, bereft of signs of human habitation except for a few crumbling cattle pens in the distance. In another month the grass and scrub would turn to a brief green lushness before summer burned them dry again. An ominous line of cloud to the south concealed the icy summits of the Mosweep Range, the highest mountains in Pandemia. This side was almost a desert; the far side held the great rain forests that were his destination.

He strolled forward to comfort his weary stock. Thanks to some skillful trading, they were a far better collection of horses than he had set out with, but they had had a long day already.

Thinal climbed down and looked around with disgust.

"Desert does not appeal," he remarked sourly.

"Quite." Rap walked back to confront him—that being the main reason for the halt. "By evening we should be in Ysarth."

"So?" The thief's ratty face became even more cagey than usual.

"So tomorrow I'm going to sell off the coach. It's served its purpose." Here, in the south, fauns would be less exceptional, and there would be few observers anyway in a land so thinly inhabited.

"Horseback?" Thinal muttered, pouting.

"Horseback. Quicker."

"Not my style."

" 'Fraid of that. Besides, I promised to tell you if I smelled danger. I don't, yet. But I feel I'm going to, soon, if you follow me. Can you call a replacement now?"

Thinal hesitated, as if making some internal test. "Yup. It'll be an effort, but yup. Who do you want?"

Rap smiled. "What's my choice?" Obviously Thinal could not call Sagorn, who had called him.

"Andor or Jalon." The thief grinned back. "I can't call Darad for you this time. You might be safer with someone who can, if things are going to get dicey."

Jalon would be good company. Andor would not, but Rap would have to deal with Andor sooner or later. "Let's have your brother, then."

Thinal nodded. "How's your war coming, King?"

He had never shown the slightest interest before. Was he mel-

lowing, or was he only concerned with his own chances of sur-
viving in a world ruled by the Covin?

"Not much happening," Rap said. He pulled out the magic
scrolls and skimmed through them. They were all blank. "The
warlock's disappeared completely. I've had nothing from him.
Umpily seems to be still at large, which is incredible. Acopulo
was last heard from dying of seasickness. Shandie had some
problems at first, but young Ylo pulled him through."

"Ylo's still with him? Ain't that a purple chicken, then?"

Rap raised eyebrows. Thinal was a very shrewd judge of people. "Meaning?"

The thief grinned. "Thought he had other ideas. Every time
he looked at the impress, his pants just about strangled him.
Oh, well, we can't all get what we want out of life, can we?"
His eyes twinkled mischievously as he held out a hand. "Good
luck, Rap."

"Thanks, Thinal."

Rap found himself shaking hands with Andor. The changes
were always like that—instantaneous. They released each other's
grip quickly.

Andor scowled. His face might be a trifle plumper, but ba-
sically he had not changed. He was still much too handsome,
much too devious. He was freshly shaved, his dark curls neatly
combed.

"Welcome to the great cause," Rap said.

Andor snorted. He glanced down at his garments, which were
obviously tight on him. "My brother's taste in clothing has not
improved, has it?"

"He has, though. He helped a lot. I was impressed."

The dark eyes flickered contemptuously. "And you want to
know if I will?"

"Please."

Andor surveyed the empty hills. "Think you'll be safe here
to impose a little compulsion on me if I get awkward?"

Rap shook his head. "No. There's still no sorcery being used,
not even here in Pithmot. The Covin's being quiet, but it's still
there, and it could hear me here if I did anything very much."
He reached out with his premonition, cautiously. The great evil
lay far to the northeast, now, over distant Hub, but it still dom-
inated the ambience like a black mountain. "I don't detect any
excitement in the immediate future."

Andor shrugged. "My primary aim has always been to keep my blood inside my skin, your Majesty. You know that. But I'll stick around."

His reservations showed to a sorcerer. He was no more trustworthy than his larcenous brother, and he would undoubtedly seduce any pretty girl who came within reach. Fortunately Andor's talent rattled the ambience much less than Thinal's did. Rap was not about to admit that to Andor, though. In fact, he ought to give him a warning lecture . . .

Tremor!

Rap jumped, and turned to stare at the north. For a moment he reached out, querying—and then hastily restrained his power before he gave himself away. At least, he hoped he had not given himself away.

Andor had noticed. "What's wrong?"

"I'm not sure. Felt something."

He had felt *Inos*, a faint glimmer of Inos. Now it had gone. Impossible! His feeble sorcery was not nearly strong enough to scrutinize Krasnegar. It must have been imagination.

"Don't know." He shrugged. "Nerves, maybe. Those clouds are the Mosweeps. How do you feel about lady trolls?"

Andor shuddered. "Don't even joke about it."

Rap had little desire to joke. He wished he had not felt that sinister little premonition of Inos in danger. Still, she would soon be warned about Zinixo and the Covin, because Shandie must be almost at Kinvale now.

3

Goblins! There were a dozen or more of them packing into the little room—thick, short men in buckskin breeches, some in tunics, others bare-chested, with khaki skin shining greasily. They all bore swords, and some had bows and quivers on their shoulders also. Their ugly, angular eyes were bright and angry within ugly arabesques of tattoo.

Absurdly, as she struggled to her feet, Inos could think only *Thank the Gods that Kade did not live to see this!*

Then one of the men grabbed Kadie in a one-armed hug. He pushed his mouth on hers, bending her over backward in a forcible kiss, choking off her scream. His companions laughed, or jabbered in guttural amusement.

"Stop that!" Gath shouted. He tried to stand, and a goblin banged him with a knee, knocking him flying—more laughter. Then Inos was on her feet and the nearest goblin reached for her also, grinning white tusks through the bristly fringe on his lips. The reek of rancid bear grease made her stomach churn. She backed away, and felt a chair blocking her.

"Stop!" she yelled.

He blinked, and stopped, looking puzzled and then angry. Released, Kadie staggered away, retching. For a moment no one spoke. There was noise outside—screaming, and much coughing, and a muffled roar. Smoke billowed in through the open doorway. Someone shouted urgently in the corridor.

Somehow Inos had to get back through the portal, and take her children with her. She couldn't speak goblin. She mustn't let the raiders discover that secret way into Krasnegar. Where was all that smoke coming from?

A goblin lifted a table and smashed the nearest window, and that broke the spell. The leader shouted orders. Inos was seized and dragged, her shouts ignored. In a pack of stinking, half-naked goblins she was hauled out into a smoke-filled corridor. Coughing and weeping, she tried to struggle free. A leathery palm slammed into her face, dazing her.

The outside air was cold, but enormously welcome. The pale sun of a winter afternoon was blinding, sparkling in the tears that streamed from her eyes. She was hauled along by a single stocky goblin, whose hand seemed nailed to her arm. He ignored her efforts to break free or resist, until she thumped at him. Then he slugged her across the face again. She stumbled; he held her upright without effort and kept on going. She called out, "Gath! Kadie?" and thought she heard an answer . . . She was tossed forward in one easy gesture as she might throw away an apple core. She sprawled, rolling into a group of people sitting on the ground, provoking cries and shouts of protest.

Hands were helping her sit up . . .

"Mom!" That was Kadie, kneeling beside her, her face a white blur.

"I'm all right, dear." Inos clutched her daughter's hand. "You all right?" Ignoring pain, wiping the torrents from her eyes, she looked around. She was within a group of thirty or forty people, all sitting on the flagstones of the south terrace, penned against the stone balustrade. The ground was dry, but icy cold. There was no snow anywhere. Half a dozen goblins stood guard with swords and bows. Others were still streaming from the burning mansion. She saw Gath approaching, being dragged by the scruff of the neck. She began to rise and the nearest guard came forward, swinging the flat of his sword at her head. She sat down again quickly. At best, it would have stunned her. He leered big goblin fangs and said something mocking.

Gath was tossed into the heap. His mop of golden hair disappeared, then popped up again, so he was conscious. He looked around wildly, saw Inos, and registered relief on chalk-white features.

The west wing was an inferno, flames roaring into the sky. Nearer windows were streaming black smoke, so the whole place was going up. *Oh, that beautiful mansion!* What would Kade have said? And what was all that terrible screaming? There were goblins everywhere Inos looked. This was no small raiding party; there were hundreds of them in sight. Most of them were bare to the waist, oblivious of the cold. She was shivering convulsively inside her heavy Krasnegar furs, but perhaps that was mainly from shock.

The other captives were mostly women in servant dress. She recognized some of the faces vaguely, but there was no one she knew by name. If any of them recognized her, they were too terrorized to speak. From time to time others were dragged or driven from the house and added to the group huddled along the balustrade. A body draped over the rail wore a feathered arrow protruding obscenely from its back, so there was no escape that way.

Part of the roof collapsed with an ear-splitting roar. Fire leaped to the skies. Even the nearer windows were starting to explode as the flames spread. Oh, Gods! The magic portal was in there! There was no way back to Krasnegar now.

Gath came wriggling through the crowd on hands and knees. His lips were blue and quivering, but he seemed quite conscious and somehow he had hung on to one of the blankets. Inos peeled off her own fur robe and insisted he wrap himself in it. She took the blanket and bundled all three of them together snugly. She started to say "We shall have to—" and sudden enlightenment changed it to "What happens now?"

"W-we w-wait awhile," Gath said through chattering teeth. "There's one you can t-t-talk to."

"Good stuff!" Kadie whispered.

Good stuff indeed! His prescience would be a Gods-send in this mess—except that, if any of them were going to be killed or raped, then he would know ahead of time. He admitted that bad things couldn't always be avoided. Really bad things were better left unexpected, and some goblin customs were about as bad as mortals could conceive. The shrieks of agony coming from the sunken rose garden beyond the balustrade were mingled at times with bursts of applause. Inos twisted around to try to see between the uprights, but there were too many people in the way.

"Torture," Gath said. "They're raping the women and they have the men tied—"

She had never seen anyone look so pale. "Never mind, dear. How are you feeling now?" She knew the question was absurd under the circumstances.

"Head aches," he muttered, leaning against her. Nevertheless, he was making a very fast recovery.

"Who did it to you?" Kadie demanded.

"Yes, tell us." Inos knew the question was utterly irrelevant now, with the culprit five hundred leagues away in Krasnegar, but she welcomed the distraction, and she must try to keep him conscious.

Gath sighed. "Brak again."

Not surprising—Brak was a head taller and twice the weight, but Gath had knocked him out last time. No adolescent jotunn could live with such a memory.

Kadie snorted scornfully. "He's been after you for months. How come you let him catch you this time?"

"Because it was worth it. I knew. I knew I had to let him have the last punch, too." Gath sniggered faintly against Inos' neck. "But you gotta see his face! Oh, you gotta see it! It's a *guts bucket!*" He smiled, showing the tooth Brak had broken the last time.

Kadie made enthusiastic noises.

Inos reflected that none of them might ever see Brak's face again. While Gath described the massacre in detail for Kadie, she glanced around. The captives were mostly sitting with their faces on their knees, not looking at anyone or anything, but she managed to catch the eye of a nearby woman, one who was older than most and might have some wits left. "How long has this been going on?" she demanded.

"All day, ma'am . . ."

A guard shouted a warning and waved his sword. They were talking too much, apparently.

More roof collapsed. One good thing—the heat from the fire was perceptible now, and welcome in the chilly afternoon. The guards were closer to it, but they did not seem uncomfortable. Goblins were notoriously indifferent to temperature.

Oh, that beautiful house! Inos wanted to weep for Kinvale. Paintings, sculptures, gold plate, fine china, carpets—a huge fortune was vanishing before her eyes, climbing skyward in a pillar of smoke. That same pillar of smoke must be visible for leagues, perhaps even as far as Shaldokan. The IXth Legion was quartered at Shaldokan now. The goblins might have fought their way over Pondague Pass—they had been trying to do so for twenty years—but they were not going to remain very long in possession of Kinvale. She felt a little better when she realized that. Unfortunately, murder and rape could be completed long before a legion could march in to the rescue.

Gath had laid his head on his knees and seemed almost asleep. On her other side, Kadie was cuddling close. Oh, poor children! And Inos could not bear to think about her kingdom. The palace must be a madhouse now, with everyone hunting for the royal family. Nor did she want to think about Rap, returning to Kinvale to find his magic portal destroyed. It would be months before any of them could go home by sea.

Three weeping, naked girls came hobbling along the terrace, clutching their clothing bundled in front of them. Two of them had blood on their legs. They burrowed in among the rest of the captives and were given help in dressing. A squad of six goblins trotted up eagerly and began to argue with the chief guard. Grumbling, the newcomers selected two of the younger women and took them away. Obviously they had wanted more than two. Obviously they were going to rape them. Now Inos understood why the prisoners were all keeping their faces hidden, not looking up. Kinvale had supported a staff of hundreds—where were all the rest?

The screaming and cheering in the rose garden answered that question.

Then another band of goblins came marching along the terrace. Gath shivered and lifted his head. "Mom? You have to do some shouting."

"What?" Inos said.

The leader strutted, looking important. Beside him walked a goblin youth, perhaps no older than Gath, although much shorter and thicker. He was smooth-faced and bore no tattoos. There was a discussion with the chief guard. Then leader and youngster came forward together—father and son, most likely. They looked over the captives. The boy grinned and pointed at Gath's conspicuous blond head. The leader waved for two of the others to come and take him.

Gath croaked, "Mom!"

Inos reeled to her feet. "No!" she shouted. "Not this one! Choose someone else! You will not take this one!" She glared and stamped her feet and kept on bellowing.

And it worked! They could not understand the words, but her tone was enough. The young goblin paled to a sickly green and backed away. The older man scowled, but he also seemed cowed by Inos' fury. He said something to the boy, who nodded and pointed quickly to another captive, a youth in footman's livery.

Inos sat down again before her wobbling knees gave way under her. The footman was pulled out from the crowd and dragged away, howling in terror.

Everyone knew how goblin boys earned their tattoos. Once they had used other goblins. Now they used prisoners.

Gath mumbled, "Thanks, Mom!" Then he rolled over on his side and threw up.

4

The sun sank down behind the smoke. The main house was a glowing shell now, the welcome heat fading before the cold of a winter evening. Very few of the captives remained. Three times Inos had prevented one or other of her children being removed, and now she knew why her shouting had such a truly sorcerous effect. Years ago, Rap had laid a royal glamour on her. When she gave orders, people were compelled to obey. So far it had worked, but she suspected that it was far from foolproof where goblins were concerned. It obviously provoked fury in them, and one of these times it might well get her killed out of hand.

Then Gath stirred and lifted his head from her shoulder.

"Mom?"

"Yes, dear?"

"Remember about Blood Beak?"

Inos stared at him, wondering if he was hallucinating again. Then she realized that his earlier talk of goblins had not been the hallucination she had thought at the time. He looked somewhat better now, anyway. "No."

"Death Bird's son. Dad told us. You must remember!"

"I'm afraid I don't, dear."

"You do!" Gath said urgently, twisting his mouth as if it tasted bad. "Dad met Death Bird at Timber Moot. Blood Beak killed a bear single-handed! Dad teased me about it."

"Oh, yes, I do remember," Inos said, lying. "What about it?"

"He's here. He's coming. The old man speaks impish."

"Right!" Inos gave her son a hug. "Well done!" At last she could see some action in store.

A few minutes later, yet another small procession of goblins came striding along the darkening terrace to inspect the scanty supply of captives. All the men had been removed, and all the younger women. The women were not coming back anymore. The men never would.

The leader was a powerful-looking goblin, but the greasy rope of hair hanging down his bare chest was streaked with gray. That would qualify him as *old* to Gath. At his side walked an adolescent, beefy even by goblin standards.

They came to a halt and Inos jumped up before they even spoke to the guards.

"Hail to Blood Beak, son of Death Bird!"

The goblins recoiled a pace in unison, but perhaps they were more surprised by her blond hair than her words.

"I am Queen Inosolan of Krasnegar! I demand to speak to Death Bird!"

The gray-haired goblin frowned, moving his lips. If he understood impish, then obviously it was not well.

She tried again, speaking more slowly, keeping it simple. Gesture. "Am Inosolan! Woman of Chief Rap. Rap chief of

Krasnegar, friend of Death Bird. Am his woman." Gesture. "These his son, his daughter. His children."

Young Blood Beak asked a question. The old man repeated what she had said, and some of the words sounded right. Everyone turned to stare hard at Inos.

"Friend of Death Bird!" she insisted. She stalked forward on legs like jelly. "Blood Beak? Great hunter! Hear how you kill bear with sword."

"How know this?" the leader barked.

"Death Bird tell Rap, his friend. Very proud of Blood Beak."

Translation . . . The older man was deferring to the king's son, but the king's son brightened at hearing how his reputation had preceded him. He gabbled something, waving hands.

The leader nodded, then spoke more respectfully to Inos. He tapped his chest. "Am Giant Feller of Beavers. Here Blood Beak of Ravens, Death Bird son, as say. How come this place?"

Relief poured through Inos like a spring freshet. "Am guest. Friend of goblins. Not enemy of goblins. Friend of Death Bird many years ago. Long ago knew Death Bird. Was Little Chicken. Very little!" She gestured to indicate a big man.

She was already mastering the awful pronunciation. Amusement flickered on some of the ugly green faces even before Giant Feller translated.

Then young Blood Beak scowled and jabbered something. Everyone looked at Gath.

"Need captive," Giant Feller explained apologetically. He pointed to Blood Beak. "Is killing soldiers all day. Has not shown worthy, er, manhood marks." Then he nodded at Gath, and shrugged. "Is only man left."

Inos recalled with horror how close Death Bird had come to earning his tattoos by killing Rap. She sensed a horrible irony, as if the Gods were about to play a monstrous joke on her—like father, like son!

"Is son of friend of Death Bird!"

"Die slow. Is great honor."

"Oh, no it's not!" Inos screamed.

5

The rose garden was the worst. After that, nothing could ever seem bad again.

The Kinvale rose garden had been one of the wonders of Julgistro. Every summer gentlefolk came leagues to view the rose garden. In the golden days of youth before her father died, Inos had played skittles there; she had listened to music on warm evenings, and blushed at Andor's polished compliments. Now women were being raped wholesale there. Small fires burned where men and the remains of men lay staked out between the bushes, mingling an acrid smell of burning rose twigs with savory odors of roast meat. Spectators applauded and offered advice as boys continued to dismember the living in ingenious ways. In the background, the great house was a blackened ruin, still dirtying the sky with smoke.

Upright, Gath was so dizzy he could barely walk, but to show weakness before goblins was to invite instant execution. He staggered along, leaning on Kadie. Inos followed, trying to make sense of Giant Feller's guttural jabber.

It had been a very close-run thing. She had protested that Gath was already too weak to make a suitable victim for Blood Beak, but the young lout had decided that a king's son was ideal material for a king's son to work on. Only when the case seemed hopeless had some goblin soldiers arrived with a husky young gardener they had just discovered hiding in a hayloft. Gath had been saved, but Inos was certain she would never sleep again. That other boy's face would haunt her forever, and the certainty that she could not have rescued him would be no comfort, because she had lacked the courage to try.

Now she was being treated as an honored guest, being shown the rose garden. Not being taken to Death Bird. Death Bird was not at Kinvale, which seemed to be a minor training exercise, or perhaps a rest and recreation posting. Death Bird was at the front.

"Imp soldiers will come soon," she said cautiously.

Giant Feller laughed, showing yellow teeth. "No imp soldiers."

She was not fool enough to mention the IXth at Shaldokan. She would let the invaders discover that for themselves! But she soon learned that the situation was much worse than she had realized. Giant Feller had no qualms about telling her the details, he boasted of them. The goblins had not come through the defenses at Pondague, they had outflanked them by an unmapped pass and fallen on the Imperial forces from the rear—massacre! They had ambushed the IXth and XXIst legions somewhere south of Kinvale—more massacre! The entire impish army in northwest Julgistro had been wiped out, or so he insisted. Now Shaldokan itself was invested. It would fall within a day, he assured her, and then the goblins would cross the frozen Paddi River. The road to Hub lay open before them.

Yes, it was bluster, but barbarian flavoring did not hide the taste of cold truth. This was Death Bird's destiny, which had been predicted for twenty years. The Gods' decree was being fulfilled at last and there was nothing any mortal could do about it, except maybe the imperor. The ultimate limits of the disaster had always lain outside even Rap's ken.

Inos thought of the unlamented Proconsul Yggingi who had started this war in trying to acquire a word of power that did not exist. She thought of Rap's misgivings about the coming of the millennium. She thought of the dwarvish evil he had seen brewing in the ambience . . . Anything was better than thinking of the people dying all around her in the rose garden.

That night the royal guests from Krasnegar were entertained by the goblin chiefs in the Kinvale stableyard. Death Bird's deputy in the Kinvale area was his nephew, Quiet Stalker, an unusually tall goblin, and dangerously young. Inos did not like the way he looked at Kadie, but then she did not like the way any goblin looked at—or to—anyone!

Giant Feller explained that Krasnegar had a female chief. This freakish institution presented social difficulties and provoked much garbled discussion. In the end Quiet Stalker issued a decree, which was then translated: Inos and Kadie would eat in the corner, away from the central fire that was the place of honor. Gath would sit with the chiefs as official Krasnegarian delegate.

Gath's ash-pale face broke into a smile at that news.

"Barbarians!" his sister whispered furiously.

"Sorry, Kadie. You just have to accept that you're naturally inferior!"

"Furs off!" Giant Feller said.

"What?" Gath stared in horror at the strip of leather the

goblin was offering him. As the fire blazed up in the middle of the courtyard, the assembled chiefs were pulling off their buckskins. That shoelace was formal wear.

"Now we'll see who's inferior!" Kadie crowed, and flounced off to the designated women's quarters by the water trough.

Shuddering with cold, Gath removed Inos' fur robe and his doublet and his sweater and his shirt and his undershirt. He handed them to his mother with an appalled glance, and she turned to leave while he still had pants on. There was nothing else she could do.

Grunts of surprise from the goblins . . . "Say about arms!" Giant Feller demanded.

"Had a fight," Gath admitted. The chiefs crowded around to admire the raw swellings on his knuckles and the purple-yellow bruises covering his forearms. Suddenly he had some status.

Inos headed for the horse trough. When she looked back, he was clad in the skimpy loincloth, kneeling close to the bonfire. The goblins' skin looked dark green in firelight. Gath's gaunt shape was a shimmering pale wraith in their midst, but already turning pinker. His far side, which she could not see, was probably blue.

"Oh, well, the doctor did say to keep him warm," she said.

But Kadie was past seeing jokes. Kidnapped princesses were fine in romances. Rap had always joked that Kadie, were she ever to be carried off by a handsome imp on a white horse or even a jotunn in a longship, would not merely enjoy every minute of it, but would also instruct her captor in the correct procedures. Reality was different. She was understandably crushed by the goblins' barbarity. Her eyes were dry, but they had a strange, jittery look to them. Pale and shivering, she huddled close to her mother, and barely nibbled the abundant roast cow that was brought across to them. And yet she was coping very well for her age.

Inos kept an eye on Gath. He was managing to sit erect. He had no need to make conversation, of course, only stay conscious.

And Inos herself, who had so royally blundered into calamity? She decided just to keep her mind on the children. Nothing else was as important—not her kingdom, abandoned and perhaps falling into chaos, nor her husband, lost somewhere in an Impire tottering before the onslaught of the millennium, nor the uncountable victims of this war. She could do nothing about any of those. She must concentrate on the twins and herself. They were three penniless refugees among thousands, perhaps millions, and they had no way home. This was the worst disaster of her life.

After the food came the entertainment, which was provided by Death Bird's son and the gardener. Then a couple of captured legionaries were brought in and the chiefs took turns with them. Fortunately, Gath was not invited to share in the fun, although he had to watch. Inos and Kadie were luckier, being required only to listen. For Inos this yard was a scrapbook of happy memories of life and fun among the Kinvale horses. She knew every stall in the stable, and could remember most of the horses that had inhabited them all those years ago. Now it echoed with screams that went on and on and on, for hours. *Die!* she kept thinking. *Die! Die!*

It was still not as bad as the rose garden.

Finally, when the last man choked to death on his own blood, Inos and Kadie were summoned to the center, to stand outside the circle of chiefs. The men sat cross-legged on the dirt, grinning up at her with their angular eyes and fearsome teeth. As warriors, they had much to grin about. She positioned herself as close to her son as she could, trying not to look at the caked blood in his flaxen thatch. Logs crackled and sparked on the fire—chair legs and picture frames, mostly. She was on the downwind, smoky side, of course.

Gath looked up. "I agree to what he wants, Mom."

"You do? Why?"

"I'm not quite sure yet, but I know it must be all right."

"Er, thank you, dear."

Quiet Stalker spoke. Kneeling behind the young leader, gray-haired Giant Feller interpreted.

"Says friend of Death Bird friend of all goblins."

Inos was not a subject of the imperor. She was his ally, but there was nothing in the treaty about making war on his enemies. "Am friend of goblins," she agreed.

"Asks if also friend of imperor?"

"Yes."

She feared that remark would be suicidal, but it wasn't. Goblins admired courage above all and apparently bravado also. Nodding in approval, Quiet Stalker spoke again.

"Asks if know imperor?" Giant Feller explained.

"Met him long ago. Very old man now."

Even before that answer was translated, she saw that it was wrong. Odd-shaped eyes glinted suspiciously in the firelight.

"Is dead! Young imperor now."

That should hardly be a shock—Emshandar had been in his nineties—but now the goblins would wonder why she had not known.

"Forgot! Met young imperor long ago, too. Was only child." She could have said that Gath had seen Shandie in a vision the previous summer, but she was certainly not going to. She didn't understand that episode herself.

Quiet Stalker said something too fast for her to guess at, and there was a brief exchange of remarks around the bonfire. No one seemed to argue with the young leader. Then the older man translated the decision.

"Sun rises, send to Death Bird, send children."

That was a real relief, and the best result she could hope for. Death Bird had a smattering of impish culture, and if there was any shred of hope for her and the twins in this new goblin kingdom, then it was with the goblin king himself, Rap's old friend. But there was more to come.

"This night, lies with Quiet Stalker." Giant Feller's finger pointed at Kadie.

Inos and Kadie said, "No!" in one voice.

The goblins grinned.

Gath whispered, "Mom!" urgently.

"You chief woman Krasnegar," Giant Feller said. "Say want friendship. Order daughter sleep with goblin chief! Make good friendship." He was barely translating now, just repeating Quiet Stalker's words in a clearer pronunciation.

So Inos would have to try her royal occult glamour on the whole goblin high command. She drew a deep breath—

At her feet, Gath raised a skinny pale arm. "Let man speak!"

The chiefs guffawed, but Quiet Stalker nodded with a gleam of anticipation.

"Pink one speak."

"Krasnegar women are very wild," Gath said, staring intently across the fire. "My sister is very, very wild! Can the goblin chief tame this girl?"

Giant Feller had trouble passing this on, and when he did, the chiefs all rolled on the ground with mirth.

Very quietly in the hubbub, and without looking round, Gath said, "You can do it, Kadie. They haven't noticed."

Noticed what? Inos stared angrily at the blood on the back of his head and wondered if the blow had knocked out his wits. A fourteen-year-old boy must know what sort of sleep was intended, surely? He couldn't be that innocent! Then she glanced down at Kadie, but her face was so white and rigid that it conveyed nothing at all, a china doll bundled in a fur cloak. She looked years younger than she had that morning when she interrupted the council meeting.

"Give orders, chief woman!"

Inos felt a whirl of faintness. Once she had expected to be married off to a goblin and the prospect had so repelled her that she had contemplated suicide. She could not abandon her daughter to this abomination without a fight . . .

Suddenly Gath was shouting in true guttural goblin. "Am man, give orders! Hear treaty?" He waved at Kadie. "Lies with Quiet Stalker only. No others. No help! Say if can tame her?"

The chiefs were following his jabber better than Inos could. How had he learned their tongue so fast?

"Can tame!" Quiet Stalker insisted, leering.

"Take girl, then." Wave at Kadie, then Inos—"Old woman sleep alone." Wave at all three with three fingers—"See sun, go to Death Bird. All of us!" Again three fingers. "Are friends? Is treaty?" A whispered aside: "Trust me, Kadie!"

Quiet Stalker nodded vigorously. "Is treaty! Are friends." He sprang to his feet and made a swashbuckling leap over the fire, then hauled Gath to his feet and embraced him to confirm the deal. Inos watched in frozen horror as her son pushed his sister toward the green horror—and Kadie went. How could she possibly trust Gath's prescience this far? He was only a child, he did not know. Kadie seemed to trust him, but she was no older.

"No, Gath!" Inos lurched forward to intervene. Gath turned and grabbed her, but he staggered giddily, and they both almost fell.

"It's all right, Mom," he whispered hoarsely, leaning hard

on her. His eyes were wild and brilliant, close to hysteria. "Remember Ollialo? My birthday gift to Kadie?"

The rapier? What good was that, five hundred leagues away in Krasnegar? The kid's brains had been addled! He was crazy.

With no sign of effort, the young goblin leader had lifted Kadie and headed for the sheds—a child in thick furs being carried off by a muscular savage in almost nothing.

"Idiot!" Inos cried, struggling to free herself from Gath's tight embrace. He clamped a hand over her mouth, and again they both teetered off-balance. He must be hallucinating that Kadie had come wearing her sword, concealed below her robe. But Inos had watched Kadie put that cloak on and knew perfectly well that she was not armed with as much as a nail file. And even if Kadie had sneaked the rapier by her, the goblins would have seen the scabbard protruding below the hem.

Quiet Stalker stopped at a ladder that led up to the hayloft. He set Kadie down. She moved aside, bowing. Apparently she had guessed the correct goblin etiquette, because he went clambering up ahead of her. Inos expected her to run then, but she began to climb submissively after the goblin.

Gath removed his hand from his mother's mouth. " 'Sawright, Mom!"

The rest of the chiefs were scrambling to their feet, the social evening completed.

"Woman sleep there!" Giant Feller commanded, pointing to the shed where the shovels and barrows were stored.

"Kadie!" Inos cried, as her daughter vanished into the darkness behind Quiet Stalker.

"Clothes, Mom!" Gath begged, still clinging to her. "You took my clothes away! Help me, I'm frozen." Shivering, he tried to whisper in her ear and his voice broke, half crying, half laughing. "It's all right, Mom, all right! She has her sword! I know you can't see it, because it's a magic sword, Mom!"

Gods have pity! He was mad.

And he kept on raving in a wild whisper, his voice lurching between boyish treble and a manly tenor she had not heard before. "She's worn it every day since I gave it to her, and nobody ever notices it unless she wants them to and we thought it was great fun that you never noticed she was going around with a real sword on all the time and I set it up so that only one goblin gets her tonight—"

"What? You're crazy. How do you know—"

"Watch! She drives him back with the sword and he breaks his neck and the others all make a big fuss but they accept it and the three of us all sleep safely together and everything's all right and who cares what happens to these murdering brutes?"

Sheer madness, but not surprising. He had cracked under the strain, was all. He was only a child. She shook him, and he was not too big for her to shake. "Stop it, Gath! Control yourself! Now, tell me how you knew how to speak goblin like that."

He blinked, and his eyes filled with tears. "Huh? Oh, if I spoke in impish then Giant Feller repeated it in goblin, right? So I just said what he was going to say. It'll be all right, Mom!"

More insanity. How could he foresee something and then stop it happening?

"There!" Gath said. "Told you!"

Inos whirled to stare again at that black opening that had swallowed her daughter. Suddenly Quiet Stalker came into view—wearing nothing, his back to her, moving backward. It was over in an instant. He kept on retreating until he stepped on air. He back-flipped out the doorway with a shriek and fell clear to the ground. The other goblins were busily dressing themselves again and they only looked up when they heard the scream. A moment later Kadie appeared at the top of the ladder, hands on hips, staring down in triumph. There was no sign of a sword, although she had discarded her cloak.

Quiet Stalker had landed on his head. Inos had seen that. Now all the goblins had rushed over, hiding the body, shouting in fury. She stared at Gath's idiotic grin. Her daughter had just killed a man.

"That's Death Bird's nephew!" she cried.

"Well, he's dead now. Serves him right. Give me something to wear, Mom! I'm freezing!"

Inos began to strip off her cloak. "But what happens when Death Bird finds out?"

Gath smiled weakly. "Dunno! I can't see tomorrows."

Questionable shapes:

Angels and ministers of grace defend us!
Be thou a spirit of health or goblin damned,

Bring with thee airs from heaven or blasts from hell,
Be thy intents wicked or charitable,
Thou com'st in such a questionable shape
That I will speak to thee.

Shakespeare, *Hamlet*, I, IV

⫷ TEN ⫸

Minds innocent

1

"And then the bishop looked under the pillow!" Andor said.

Rap had already been laughing. At that climactic punch line he almost fell off his horse, something he had never done in his life. His guffaws raised a flock of tiny red birds out of the hedges in terrified flight. The horses flicked their ears, but kept up their steady clopping.

When he had wiped away the tears and sucked some air back in his aching lungs, he gasped, "I don't believe a word of it!"

"Absolutely true!" Andor said. "Strawberries everywhere! The Gods are my witness. Would I lie to you, Rap?"

"Well . . . it wouldn't terribly surprise me." But Rap grinned when he said it, because Andor had been grinning when he asked.

Three days with Andor . . . it was impossible to stay mad at Andor. His word of power could have no effect on a sorcerer, for a single word could only magnify an existing talent, but in Andor's case that talent was charm. He had been purposefully wielding that charm on Rap for three days, in an unbroken outpouring of concern and reminiscences and funny stories.

They were riding up the wide valley of the Frelket. A day's ride behind them, the river sank away in despair under palm trees and the sands of the desert. About a day's ride ahead it would be a mountain torrent, but here it nourished a little local paradise, an oasis within the withered hills. Most of the native forest had been stripped from the flatland and replaced by rich farms; the valley walls were terraced as if combed by giants. The land looked alive and fertile even now—two days until second moon, and already there was a smell of spring in the air. The sun was hot, even at this altitude.

Second moon was the time for Timber Moot—Rap put thoughts of Timber Moot aside like an unwanted fish bone. He refused to believe that the Gods ever created indispensable mortals. Inos would find someone to deal with the goblins for her.

The Mosweeps were an icy curtain across the head of the valley, a parade of giants. Usually they were shrouded in cloud. Today they were close enough to touch, every pinnacle and glacier sparkling. They rose almost sheer from the foothills—up and up and up until they seemed to overhang. They had grown a lot since his last sight of them, a week ago. They were awe-inspiring. They were daunting.

Noticing his interest in the scenery, Andor chuckled. "I was thinking, Jalon should see that! He'd go into a trance! Wouldn't be able to speak for days!"

"Then let's keep him ignorant, shall we?" Much as Rap was looking forward to meeting the minstrel again, he knew Jalon was capable of wandering off in a daydream and disappearing for hours at a time. This was no kindergarten. There were no more towns ahead. The Mosweep Ranges were colored Imperial on Imperial maps, but trolls had no maps. This was frontier country, where legionaries might appear at any time to ask travelers where and why they were going . . . which reminded Rap that he was not sure of that himself. "How far do you suppose this road goes?"

"Quite a way, apparently. The villa up ahead is Casfrel, but there's a trail goes on beyond. The army built it a couple of decades ago." Andor flashed white teeth at Rap and adjusted his hat to a slightly more rakish angle. His finery would have looked stolen on Thinal, but Andor had style. He was one of those superb horsemen who could make their mounts seem mere extensions of themselves.

"Been doing a little research?" Rap inquired. He hadn't let Andor out of his farsight, so when could he have? . . . Oh—last night, obviously. Or the night before.

"Just a little. Dear girl was one of those talky ones, so I

guided her into productive channels. You do know about the escaped trolls, of course?''

"Acopulo gave me some names of places. Frelket Valley was one of them.''

"It was Casfrel,'' Andor agreed. "Little more'n a year ago, a half dozen 'agricultural workers' went missing. Presumably they escaped up the river and into the mountains. The army went after them, but found no trace.''

"With dogs?''

"Probably. It's quite a racket, isn't it?''

"Slavery is illegal. I don't know how they manage to keep it secret.'' Rap did know that Shandie disapproved strongly—so strongly that he had not explained very well.

Andor shrugged. "Casfrel is a big plantation, owned by some senator back in Hub. A troll is a sort of semi-intelligent ox, very valuable help around that sort of place. The army rounds them up on one pretext or another and collects the money. Helps pay the garrisoning bills. Political favors count, too.'' He eyed Rap thoughtfully. "Who cares about trolls?''

"Shandie does. I do. Remember Ballast, on *Stormdancer*?''

"Frankly, no. I was traveling first class, you will recall.''

Rap hesitated, then returned the smile. "Yes, I remember.''

"Rap . . .'' For once Andor seemed at a loss for words. "Look, I won't say I'm sorry, because you wouldn't believe me. But I am glad things turned out the way they did. Name of Evil! You were only a stableboy, and you had no idea how valuable that word of yours was, or what it would mean to me. And I didn't just get you in a corner and call Darad to work you over, as I could have—I really did try to help you. Now, didn't I? I helped you with your job and your education, and so on. Sure, I was trying to pry your word of power out of you, but who wouldn't?''

Lots of people, Rap thought, but apparently Andor was trying to apologize. It was ancient history, almost a childhood memory for him, although to Andor it would seem more recent, only four or five years ago.

"It wasn't what you did to me I minded. It was Inos.''

"But I was going to *marry* her! Gods, man! That's the only time in my entire life I've ever offered to *marry* a girl and meant it.''

He'd tried the other way first, though, and he wasn't saying how long he'd planned to stay married. Andor's moral vision was sadly defective. He shot Rap a worried frown, then grinned. "And I appreciate what you did for the five of us, when you could. You kept your word. And right now, I admit, I'm enjoying myself hugely. You know how I like traveling! I never seem to get out of Hub anymore. Anytime I've tried in the past few years, or Darad's tried, Thinal or Sagorn has gone right back home again."

"You're offering to help, you mean?"

"I want to help. I think you're on a noble cause."

He truly believed the words coming out of his own mouth at the moment, which meant nothing, because he would lie to himself as much as anyone. All the same, cooperation was better than opposition.

"Then I'm glad to have your help," Rap said. "Gods know, I need all the help I can get! And, since we're baring souls now, I'd better confess that my premonition is beginning to itch. There may be trouble ahead."

Andor's radiant smile faltered. "What sort of trouble?"

"I don't know. It's vague. Maybe nothing. Maybe death."

"I have just remembered I left a toothpick back in Ysarth."

"I also have a hunch that says the risk is worth taking. It's not much of a guarantee, and it won't apply to you anyway."

"Oh, I just love your attitude! Well, it won't be the first time we've been through danger together, will it *Rappie-boy*?"

God of Villains! Only Andor had ever called him that, but who was the youngster now? "No, it won't."

"So if we're going to be allies, you wouldn't mind telling me what you're up to, would you?"

"Thought you knew." Rap was trying to read a road marker ahead. It looked like a boundary stone, and there was a subtle change in the fields beyond it, a hint of more prosperity, more fertility. This might be the start of the Casfrel estate that Andor had mentioned.

"The Mosweep Mountains are about five hundred leagues long and Gods know how wide," Andor said impatiently, "mostly covered with jungle so thick you can't see your hand behind your back. You expect to find sorcery in that mess? Really, truly? How? That's what I want to know."

Rap had already been over this, but Andor could not recognize the truth when he heard it. He expected every man to be as devious as he was.

"There's no great secret." Rap tried to look as innocent as possible, and thereby provoke the greatest possible suspicion. "I want to talk to trolls. When I've done that, I'll go and appeal to the anthropophagi. I'll try not to seem *too* appealing to the anth—"

"Wild trolls or tame trolls?"

"Both or either."

Andor looked exasperated. "Wild trolls are as solitary as comets and about as hard to catch. You could spend a lifetime rummaging that haystack and never prick your fingers once. So you must be planning to use sorcery, and yet you insist that the Covin will hear you if you do!"

"Hunch, remember?"

"Bah! The Covin's back in Hub, isn't it?"

"The Covin is probably just about everywhere now," Rap admitted. "Zinixo must have caught most of Bright Water's votaries, and she had 'em scattered all over. He won't collect all his forces into Hub, because that would be a risk. He must have agents in place just about everywhere, spying for him. The more he knows, the more he'll suspect he doesn't know, of course."

Andor was not happy to hear that, and still not trusting.

"I think you're holding back on me, Rap! You can't hope to find a wild troll in your lifetime, and the brute wouldn't know its next-door neighbor anyway, let alone the address of the nearest sorcerer."

"Which leaves tame trolls."

"What can they know? Even if there is an escape conspiracy working, and even if it does employ sorcery, why would the present slaves know anything about it? If they did, they'd be gone!"

"Maybe," Rap admitted. "But now's the time to find out. Look there!"

Far off across the fields, a wagon was moving through the spring mud. There were no oxen or horses between the shafts, and no driver. The motive power was a human being.

"A troll?" Andor said, peering against the sun.

"Must be." Rap was confident enough that he did not risk using farsight.

"So what are you planning to do?"

"Go and talk to him. See if he knows anything about the ones who escaped—who helped them, especially."

"Rap, Rap!" Andor shook his head pityingly. "What do you expect to learn?"

"Trolls are a lot smarter than they like to make out!"

"Even if they are, this is an illegal conspiracy you're talking about. You just ride out from town in your fancy clothes, and he tells you all about it?"

"Er, good point," Rap agreed. Of course a sorcerer could apply compulsion to win answers. If the Covin had agents in the district, that use of power might be detected. Worse, though, it would require Rap to apply the sort of people mastery he so despised in Andor. "What are you suggesting?"

Andor's brilliant smile could make the icy Mosweeps look in need of polishing. "Start at the top, of course. Those roofs above the trees there are probably Casfrel itself, right? Let's go and accept their eager offers of hospitality. If the manager doesn't know a lot more than his slaves do, I'll eat my hat—feather and all."

He did want to help, apparently. Rap risked a quick glance of farsight. The troll pulling the wagon was a pubescent girl.

"It's worth a try," he agreed.

"Come on, then!" Andor kicked his horse into a canter.

2

Casfrel was an extensive and prosperous plantation, and its station was as large as a village. Andor rode brashly in through the main gate, with a debonair wave to the astonished legionary standing guard. The road wound uphill between barns and cottages, barracks and storage sheds, until it arrived at the main villa, which was an imposing, sprawling mansion. There he dismounted and flipped the reins to a servant.

"Inform Tribune Uoslope that Prince Rapiboy and Sir Andor have arrived," he said, and strode up the steps with an amused faun at his heels.

The staff needed some time to locate the manager, and when he at last appeared he scowled suspiciously at these unexpected visitors. He was a stocky man with gray hair and a prominent paunch, a typical retired soldier, distrustful of well-dressed civilians from Hub and scornful of royal fauns. His broad physique was combined with narrow views. He glowered at Rap as if assessing his ability to muck out stables. If he expected a Sysanassoan accent, he would be disappointed; Rap could not fake that without using sorcery.

Faint tremors of power rippled the ambience before Andor even opened his mouth. "... truly cannot understand why our letters did not arrive, Tribune ... of course the capital is still in a ferment over the imperor's death—never saw such confusion! Even the High Command itself ... not as well organized as it used to be, I'm afraid ... told you were the man to help us ... The countess sends her warmest regards, naturally ... Had our business not been so urgent ..."

It was a magnificent lesson in virtuoso chicanery. Rap could not tell how much information his accomplice had obtained in advance from his pillow-talk espionage and how much he was ad-libbing on the strength of his host's reactions, like a charlatan fortune-teller. Whatever his secret, it worked. Tantalizing glimpses of gossip from the capital, rumors of scandal looming in the army, hints that the futures markets in agricultural produce were heading for a sharp readjustment ... Andor promoted himself into the minor nobility and Rap to an obscure royal house in Sysanasso—traveling incognito, of course.

Uoslope melted before their eyes. In minutes he was beaming and gruffly making statements that always seemed to turn into questions: "Casfrel's got a reputation for hospitality, right? Better than those fleapit hostelries, mm? Daresay you'll appreciate a hot tub after your journey, what?" He asked for confirmation that the road was in terrible condition, that the evilish speculators were ruining the farming business, and that he did not know what the world was coming to.

On that point, Rap thought, he was certainly correct.

Hot water in a marble tub was undoubtedly welcome.

The guest rooms were airy dreams of silk, polished wood, downy pillows, and arched windows displaying breathtaking vistas.

As the setting sun tinted the mountains peach and salmon, Rap found himself sitting on a terrace, nursing a goblet of chilled elvish wine. The gibbous moon silhouetted spiky cactusy shrubs on the hills. Closer, whitewashed walls still radiated heat from the day, tame pigeons strutted on the flagstones and red-tile roofs, while a small orchestra played out of sight nearby. This farmer lived in much greater luxury than the king of Krasnegar did.

Andor was still demonstrating the quintessence of guile and duplicity. The scoundrel's motives were visible now even to a dumb rustic faun—Tribune Uoslope's two daughters were striking beauties. Their dark hair shone like stars, they had donned their best white dresses in honor of the visitors. They were luscious and virginal, but they wore far too much jewelry. They were overdressed rural innocents, spellbound by this urbane gentleman who had dropped into their sheltered lives from the highest circles of Imperial society. That was the idea.

Neither of them was much older than Kadie. Watching Andor's maneuvering, Rap felt depressingly fatherly and protective. It seemed very unfair that life involved growing old.

The sixth member of the group was Mistress Ainopple, the tribune's wife. She was a withered, mousy creature, who seemed to live in terror of her husband. Apparently the senator who owned Casfrel was her uncle, which explained a few things.

Once in a while Andor would turn his charisma on her, oozing compliments on her household and beautiful daughters. She became flustered, stuttering as she tried to simper. "So hard to bring up Nya and Puo properly in such a remote situation . . . Must try to take them to Hub soon . . ."

"Indeed you must, ma'am," Andor responded. "For if word of such beauties ever reaches the capital, then half the eligible young men of the Impire will be flocking here to call on them."

Blushes all round.

"But if your musicians are up to strumming a dance tune after dinner, ma'am, then I shall certainly insist on the honor of treading a measure with each of them, for I never dreamed that this remote land would hide ladies who outshine anything I have ever seen in the palace itself."

It was sickening. It was as effective as a battle ax to the skull. Andor's mastery worked on men as well as it did on women, and he had extracted Tribune Uoslope's fangs completely. The brusque overseer who had greeted the visitors with surly suspicion was fawning like a kitten over them now. Rap could have done as much himself, easily. Ironically, he would probably have had to use a lot more power to produce the same effect, because his heart would not have been in it. Hypocrisy came naturally to Andor.

The resemblance between him and young Signifer Ylo was striking, but the contrasts were interesting, too. In his spare time, Ylo went in for heroics and hard work. Andor shunned both to the very best of his ability. Both men were unscrupulous libertines, but there was an innocence about Ylo that Andor must have lost years ago, if he had ever had it. However much Ylo enjoyed women, he would always expect them to have fun, also. He believed quite honestly that he was doing them a good turn. With his word of power to aid him, Andor was a much more calculating hunter. He knew the damage his seductions might cause. Not only would he care little about hurting his victims, he probably enjoyed that, also. There was a difference between amorality and immorality—not much of one, but some.

The luxuriant valley was growing dim, stars twinkled in the velvet sky. Listening with half an ear to the conversation, Rap was also scanning the whole great compound. He had noted the silver and crystal laid out on the dining table, awaiting his dining pleasure. He had observed the many cooks scurrying about the hot kitchens, preparing the feast. Satisfied that the villa itself contained no unpleasant surprises, he was now studying the barns where the workers lived, and the grim repast awaiting them. A platoon of legionaries was doing a little better in a small barracks—it would be interesting, but probably depressing, to know how those men's upkeep was recorded in the army's rolls.

He had located many imps, and a few fauns, and even a heap of gnomes, only now starting to waken. Eventually he observed three trolls being herded homeward, a big male and two girls. The quarters they were heading for were obviously new, and built strong enough to hold a dragon. Now that was an interesting—

Ripple!

He started to full alertness. Where had that come from? He could not tell. It had been very brief, and very slight. It had not been Andor—he was emitting a low hiss of sorcery, a faint, barely detectable glow. Somewhere close, someone had used a needle of power, a tiny flash.

Chillingly, Rap decided that someone had just scanned him. It might even have been the tribune himself, or one of his womenfolk. If so, the perpetrator was close enough to have detected

Rap's farsight at work as well as Andor's use of mastery. *God of Fools!* It was too late to caution Andor now, or tell him to stop.

Nevertheless, the next time those beguiling dark eyes turned in his direction, Rap risked a warning frown. Andor read the message instantly. He dropped his narrative in midsentence and slapped at his arm. "Mosquitoes? Early for bugs, isn't it?"

With his power cut off, the spell was broken. The listeners seemed to rouse themselves.

"Oh, we do get a few at any time of the year," Mistress Ainopple murmured apologetically, looking guilty, as if the bugs were her fault. "We, er, should perhaps be thinking about dinner?" She shot her husband a worried glance. He would be the sort of husband who would delay a meal for hours and then complain that it did not meet his standards.

Uoslope himself scratched his lower chin as if puzzled. "Tell me again your purpose in journeying through these parts, Sir Andor?"

Andor had not mentioned the subject at all. "Just a guide for my friend here." He waved languidly in Rap's direction. "I was asked to escort him by . . . by certain influential persons. His homeland is having some problems in certain branches of agriculture, and he is on a fact-finding mission." He beamed at Rap, inviting him to explain.

Caught unaware, Rap made a mental note to get even at the first opportunity. How to proceed? A moment ago he would have been more circumspect, but if there was sorcery around, then he should grab for whatever information he could find in preparation for a very fast retreat.

"We are experiencing a shortage of agricultural laborers, Tribune. Recently the supply of felons seems to have dried up."

The listeners all stiffened in shock, even the two girls.

"What sort of laborers, Highness?" Uoslope demanded angrily, his rubicund face darkening.

"I am talking of my homeland, remember," Rap said brightly. "In Sysanasso we do not have the same milksop scruples as some of the bleeding hearts in your country."

"Er, quite, what?"

If there was an illicit trade in slaves between the Impire and Sysanasso—which there might well be—then Rap had no knowledge of it. But Uoslope would not, either, and it was certainly a plausible theory.

"What sort of laborers, exactly?" the tribune repeated.

"Felons. The Imperial army is our main supplier. Trolls, of course. They are invaluable for certain types of work. I am sure you employ some trolls here in Casfrel?"

"We do *employ* a few, mm? Useful, yes, but not very reliable, what?"

"Oh, well," Ainopple broke in to protest, "you can't expect to rely on them. Can't really rely on anyone except an imp."

"I heard a funny story," young Nya said eagerly, "about a djinn, a dwarf, and a jotunn—"

"Not another dumb-jotunn story?" Puo wailed.

"Have you queried your supplier?" Uoslope demanded of Rap.

"He wasn't very helpful. He spoke vaguely of malcontents, disrupting the system and causing shortages. The price of a healthy male has risen ridiculously. I thought I'd come and see firsthand."

"Oh, yes!" Ainopple muttered, wringing her stringy hands. "Last year we lost our whole stock, and just when we were starting to have some success with the breeding program, too! Such a disappointment—"

"But we have replaced them, right?" her husband boomed. "Surely dinner must be ready now, what?"

Trolls were an indelicate subject.

3

The evening that had started so well deteriorated rapidly. Dinner was a social catastrophe. Rap had never been handy at making meaningless small talk, and he was preoccupied in listening for sorcery. He detected no more, and gradually began to hope that he had overestimated that one brief flicker. Perhaps it had come from much farther away than he had first thought. In that case the culprit might just have picked up some fuzzy trace of Andor's talent in use and been trying to locate it. The obvious precaution was to avoid disturbing the ambience any further— no farsight, no mastery!

Unfortunately, Andor had two beautiful girls to stalk, and the use of power was second nature to him now.

Fortunately, Rap was sitting across the table from him. Every time Andor became charming, his leg got kicked.

After a while he seemed to comprehend what this sudden belligerence meant, but it threw him totally off balance. Stripped of occult support after so many years, he was naked. He did not know how to behave mundanely, how to react. He became awkward, jittery, and stilted, which would have been very funny, had the situation not been so serious.

Worse, the spell he had cast over Uoslope and his family wore off. First the tribune himself became surly and suspicious again, obviously wondering why these strangers had come prowling around his fiefdom, asking impertinent questions about his illicit slaves. Then the stars faded from the eyes of Nya and Puo; they began to respond to Andor's now-clumsy blandishments with understandable disdain. The charmer had become a boor.

As for that faun, his place was down with the hired hands, washing horses or something!

Sensing the awkward overtones, Mistress Ainopple became even more dithery and nervous than ever. How had such a gawkish, ungainly woman ever produced two such gorgeous daughters? Her feeble efforts to keep a conversation going only made matters worse. She peppered Rap with questions about his mythical kingdom, but his one visit to Sysanasso had been extremely brief, and he knew very little about his ancestral homeland. He tried to invent a tropical version of Krasnegar and it sounded improbable even to him. She asked Andor about the Imperial court, and that reminded everyone of the imperor's death. Things went from worse to disastrous.

When the meal ended, there was no further talk of dancing. Everyone was willing to accept that the visitors were weary from their journey and needed to catch a good night's sleep. With a few incoherent apologies, Rap and Andor made a break for the stairs.

"What in the Name of Evil was all that about?" Andor demanded in an angry whisper as they climbed. "My shins are black and blue!"

"Someone's using sorcery. You ripple the ambience."

"I shall ripple your neck, my faunish friend! Who? What sort of sorcery?"

They reached the upper story as Rap finished explaining. He

took his companion's elbow and turned him along a corridor. "We're not going to our rooms. We're leaving!"

"How? Where?"

"Servants' staircase. Got to get out before they loose the dogs."

Andor wailed. "Dogs?"

"Along here."

Down they went.

Using the barest hint of farsight, Rap avoided the domestics now clearing away the remains of the meal. Less than five minutes after bidding their host good night, the fugitives were outside the villa, standing in a patch of inky shadow. The air was cooling rapidly, and a bloated moon floated in a clear sky, illuminating the whole valley. The Mosweeps were especially striking.

"Now wait a minute!" Andor said, strident with fear. "This makes no sense at all! We're caught in a dead end here! The only way we can go is back down the valley, and they'll chase us as soon as they find we've gone."

"I know that, but—"

"They're probably counting the silverware already."

"The stables—"

"I'm going to call Darad. He's much more—"

"No!" Rap grabbed Andor's cravat and squeezed. "Now, listen carefully! If you bring Darad, that's sorcery! You'll give us away. You're far better on a horse than Darad is, anyway."

Andor's teeth chattered briefly.

"What's more," Rap said, just so there would be no misunderstanding, "if they catch Darad, they catch you, too. If Zinixo gets any one of you, then he forces your word out of whichever one of you he's got, and then you all die. *All* of you, is not so? Besides, I need you. Come on."

Releasing Andor's throat, he took a firm grip on his arm and led him off through the night as fast as he dared go.

"Need me how?" Andor muttered sulkily.

"I think you'll have to pick a lock."

"I can't do that! It's Thinal you need for that, and I can't call him because he called me. That's all your fault, too. Know something? You really messed up a beautiful piece of sorcery when you mucked around with Orarinsagu's formula, you dumb faun!"

"Not my idea. I know I need Thinal, but you can't call him directly, and two transformations would be totally insane. Thinal must've picked a million locks. You've got his memories, haven't you? So use them."

"Just because you've heard singing doesn't mean you can sing!" Andor objected, but the light was so tricky and Rap was setting so hard a pace that he soon had very little breath for whining. The settlement was sliding into sleep. Few lights showed in the cottages. The gnomes would be scavenging, of course, but they never interfered with the activities of dayfolk.

"Wait a minute, Rap! The stables are over that way, aren't they?"

"No, they're that way. We've got a call to make first."

"What sort of a call?"

"Trolls . . . Oh, do stop bitching, Andor!"

Fighting his way through some prickly bushes, Rap reproached himself for his ill temper. Andor was not the only frightened man among the two of them. With sorcery ruled out, they were nothing but mundane intruders in a private fortress. There were dogs and armed soldiers around. The legionaries might have been stationed at Casfrel as official border guards or just because the senator had pulled political strings to protect his estate; in either case those men would know exactly what to do about mundane intruders.

And if sorcery was not ruled out, the situation was even worse. Rap kept thinking up darker and darker possibilities. Uoslope himself—and he lived very well, as virtual ruler of a private kingdom—or his withered wife, or the butler, or one of the lute players . . . someone had power, perhaps very great power. The greater the power, the less detectable it was in use. Perhaps that person had been eavesdropping on Rap's thoughts ever since he arrived and that one tiny ripple had been just a momentary carelessness.

God of Fools! Why hadn't he listened to his premonition?

The trolls' prison was directly ahead, gleaming where moonlight shone on massive blocks of whitish stone. It was obviously new, and must have been built after last year's breakout. A cell to hold trolls would have to be constructed like an elephant pen—trolls were usually restrained by brute terror, because anything else could be ripped out or torn apart. This close to the mountains, though, even a brutalized troll might feel that the chance of escape was good enough to risk yet another savage beating.

Panting and streaming sweat in the chill night, Rap arrived at the door. Andor was close behind, still muttering under what breath he had left. Fortunately, the entrance was in shadow. A bat twittered overhead in jerky flight.

Again Rap risked the merest hint of farsight, an occult peek . . . surprise!

"It's not shielded," he gasped. "I thought it would be."

"So?"

"So there's a sorcerer around somewhere. Why not shield the building?"

"Bunk!" Andor said. "Where would a plantation manager find sorcery? Or a senator? What market do you go to to buy sorcery? Sorcerers don't need money!" He muttered "Stupid!" a few times.

That was true, and yet Rap had expected shielding, somehow. He leaned against the wall for a moment, trying to puzzle it out. There was something other than logic involved, though, and he couldn't find the answer.

"Can you pick this lock?" he demanded.

"No," Andor said sulkily.

The lock was a bronze box about the size of a suitcase. The door itself was not much larger, like the entrance to a dog kennel. The trolls would have to crawl through on their hands and knees.

"Right, I'll risk it."

"Rap!"

Tumblers clanged, sounding like a fire gong in the still night.

"Couldn't you have done that a little quieter?" Andor wiped his forehead.

"Not without using more power. Come on."

The door grated open. Rap crouched down and wriggled inside.

The interior was one huge room, still hot as a baker's oven and acrid as a pigpen—what would it be like in summer? High slits admitted beams of moonlight, striped by bars thicker than a jotunn's forearm. Straw rustled. He sharpened his vision a fraction and made out two bodies stirring in a corner. They were the women he had seen earlier; they sat up together with grunts of surprise. The man was lying facedown in another corner, breathing harshly. Sacking hung on pegs along one wall. The only furniture was a bucket.

"Phew!" said Andor. "Let's get out of here!"

"My name is Rap. I am a friend."

The two girls whimpered and huddled back into the corner, hugging each other. Making a wild guess, Rap estimated their ages as thirteen and eighteen respectively. They had no clothes on, and their pale skins glimmered with sweat. Even the child would have outweighed him handily, and she must have been the one he had seen hauling the wagon. He thought of Kadie, home in Krasnegar, with her fancy clothes, her fencing lessons, her books and romantic dreams. And then this? There were times when he despised the Gods.

He had forgotten how big trolls were—almost as tall as jotnar and burly as goblins. Their skins were doughy and tough, yet prone to sunburn; their hair was brown and woolly, their strength legendary. Doubtless a male of their own race would appreciate these two maidens' protruding muzzles and sloping foreheads, but it was hard to think of trolls as human when you looked them in the face. Rap had met trolls in Durthing, many years ago, and he knew them to be gentle, worthy folk, placid and friendly.

"I am Rap," he repeated. "Tell me your names."

The girls scrabbled even farther back into their corner. Then the older seemed to understand. She pushed her younger companion away and began stretching out on the straw, making herself available.

A spasm of revulsion made Rap want to puke. He remembered Mistress Ainopple's remark about a breeding program. He remembered things Ballast had told him, years ago, on *Stormdancer.* Ballast himself had been part jotunn. Half-breeds were prized even more than full-blooded trolls, because they were supposed to be more intelligent.

"No! I want to help you. Tell me your names!"

"Rap, for the Gods' sake let's get out of here!" Andor was gagging.

"Master not . . . come to . . . make baby?" Trolls' heavy jaws made their speech slurred. They spoke little, and slowly, which perhaps explained their reputation for stupidity.

"No. I come to help you. What is your name?"

"Urg, Master."

"And the child?"

"Norp."

The big male groaned. Rap swung around to look, and then used farsight. The man's body was a jelly of bruises and scrapes. There was blood on the straw.

"That is . . . Thrugg," Urg mumbled.

"He's been beaten?"

"Masters say . . . Thrugg was . . . bad."

Gods! He looked as if he'd been stamped on by a legion. Trolls were reputed to be indestructible.

"Rap!" Andor squealed. "As soon as the cooks go home, they'll let the dogs loose. We've got to get out! Now!"

"Oh, shut up! I can't leave them here!" Rap strode over to the pegs and scooped up the sacking; he hurled it at the girls. "Get dressed! You heard me! Dress!"

With urgent motions, they began. Ignoring a torrent of shrill complaint from Andor, Rap went over to kneel beside the co-matose male. He stank of fresh blood and vomit.

"Thrugg! Thrugg, can you walk?"

The answer was a subterranean groan.

Andor's protests grew louder. He was dancing from one foot to the other in his impatience. Rap wiped an arm over his brow. He knew he was being just as crazy as Andor was describing him, but he could not imagine himself going away and leaving these people. They were none of his business. The risk was absurd—but he had to take that risk, because he had to live with himself until he died.

To use his power as sparingly as possible, he laid both hands on Thrugg's bloody back. He closed his eyes, concentrating . . . He saw a couple of cracked ribs, but the rest was just bruising, a massive battering. It must have been done quite recently, too. Could anything have justified this? Perhaps he was a killer. A crazy troll would be a human earthquake.

Rap turned his head to look up at the girls. They were both fully dressed now, swathed from neck to ankles and wrists in the all-encompassing cover they needed for protection from sun-light. Their huge, vague shapes loomed over him in the gloom, only their frightened eyes distinct.

"Urg? What did Thrugg do? Why did they beat him?"

Urg nervously wiped her nostrils with her tongue. "Masters . . . helping me. Thrugg . . . was very . . . bad."

"Helping you? Help you to do what?"

"Help . . . make baby . . . Thrugg got . . . angry."

Evil of evils! Rap turned back to the victim.

Andor whimpered. "Rap! What in the Name of Folly are you doing?"

"Be quiet!" *Heal!* The ambience shivered and flared. There was so much damage! *Heal!* He would have to use more power—there!

Thrugg grunted, and then began to move like a horse rolling over. Rap jumped up and backed away quickly, conscious of those enormous muscles and hands like dinner plates.

"Thrugg? I'm Rap. I'm a friend. Feel better now?"

The big, bestial face stared up at him blankly. Thrugg's woolly beard was caked with blood, black in the moonlight. "Friend? Master? You . . . stop pain?"

"I'm a sorcerer. I want to find Witch Grunth. Have you ever heard of her?"

"For the love of the Good, Rap!" Andor screamed. "He's a savage! A slave! What can he know of a warden?"

Trouble was, Andor was absolutely right. The chances of this unfortunate churl being able to help were as close to zero as chances could be. So . . . So a sorcerer could play hunches, couldn't he?

"Get dressed, Thrugg."

Another huge shape moved in as Urg approached with a coarse-woven shirt as big as a tent. Thrugg took it and pulled it on. It was a snug fit.

Andor grabbed Rap's arm, and Rap shook him off roughly.

"Thrugg," he said, "a year ago, some slaves escaped from here. A sorcerer helped them. I want to find—"

The ambience flared with an eerie light. Rap whirled around to give battle and screamed aloud as he was engulfed in fire.

4

It had been a trap all along, of course. That was why the troll pen had not been shielded.

The sorceress stood there in the same ill-fitting gown she had worn at dinner, gloating. Although triumph brightened her pinched, foxy features, it did not stop her being nondescript. Yet even that unappealing aspect was a glamour. Rap had caught a brief glimpse of her true form in the ambience, and she was far, far older than she seemed. She could never be the mother of Nya and Puo—grandmother's mother, maybe.

The battle had been brief, for her power was immeasurably greater than his. He would have made a better showing wrestling Thrugg. She had crushed him easily, then wrapped him in a shielding spell, just as he had once encapsuled Zinixo. He was as completely mundane now as he had been for most of the last eighteen years. The loss felt a lot different when it was not of his own choosing.

Having taken care of his occult powers—and probably Andor's, also, just to be certain—the sorceress had then nailed them both into the walls. Their arms were behind them and their legs bent at the knees. They hung there like a couple of decorations, shoulders and backs against the stone, their limbs within it. Rap's elbows and feet felt so cold that he assumed they went all the way through to the cool air outside. He could move his toes, but not a single finger. It was very effective restraint, but it threw all his weight on his knees and shoulders. The pain was already making him sweat, and increasing steadily.

"Sit!" the sorceress snapped. "Over there! Sit!" The trolls stampeded over to the corner indicated. They sat down in a close-packed heap, huddling together nervously.

Ainopple turned her attention to Andor. "Just a genius, aren't you? Well, you'll use no charisma now. The rest of your magical baggage I shall leave for my superiors to investigate." She sniffed, cloaking anger in disapproval like a schoolmarm. "I had assumed that you were under a compulsion, but I see no signs of one. A faun I can perhaps understand. We must make allowances for such people. But how an *imp* could behave as you have is quite beyond my comprehension. I hope you enjoy your stay here."

Andor howled. "Ma'am, you do not understand!"

"I understand perfectly well, *troll-lover*!"

"No, no! I was—"

The sorceress was not interested in his denials. His voice stopped abruptly, half of a dirty washrag hanging from his mouth.

She turned to Rap, smirking up at him. "Well, you weren't

nearly the threat we were expecting. A pushover!'' Her scraggly mouth puckered sulkily. "After all this time I wish I had a more worthy catch to report.''

Rap felt a faint surge of hope. She did not know who he was, obviously.

She shrugged. "I shall report the news in the morning. I expect his Omnipotence will drop by in a day or two. Until then, do try to enjoy the company. Just remember you chose it.''

"Your master is Zinixo?''

"Certainly not! If you mean the former West, he died years ago.''

"Olybino, then?''

"Of course!'' She smirked again. "And yours is Bitch Grunth, I expect. His Omnipotence may well decide to keep you here as bait for a while, and see if she attempts to rescue you—or put you out of your misery, perhaps.''

"No!'' Rap said. "Listen! You don't understand! You haven't talked with the warlock yet, have you?''

"That's not your concern.''

"Don't go away, ma'am! There's something very important I must tell you. First, I'm not Witch Grunth's votary! Second, I had nothing to do with any other trolls escaping. Third, I— Arrgh!'' Rap's elbows and shoulders moved closer together, bowing his back out from the wall like a cup handle. His arms and legs strained in their sockets. The pain increased tenfold.

"I have no wish to listen to your imaginative droolings,'' the sorceress remarked. She was testing him, of course, in case he had been faking earlier. He could not ease his agony without using sorcery, which meant first ripping off his layer of shielding—and that was as immovable as the Mosweeps, or his hands.

His head was jammed against the wall, twisting his neck so tightly that he could barely speak. "Not lying!'' he gasped. "You can see that!''

But of course she couldn't. The shielding worked both ways, so she could not read his mind. Without that guidance, why would she believe a captured felon's wild excuses?

Rap could not speak through the pain. Just as he thought he was about to faint, that strangely plastic wall adjusted itself again, easing some of the pressure on his head and spine. The sorceress had apparently decided that he was as feeble as he seemed.

"Ma'am, you are in danger . . ."

"Whatever you have to say can wait for your trial. I expect the Four will give you a hearing eventually, or the warlock may just decide to dispose of your case himself. Meanwhile, I shan't wish you a good night. I disapprove of hypocrisy." The door closed and locked itself. Ainopple vanished.

Gods! She had left him to endure this?

Andor said, "Unnnnnnnnng? Unnnnnnnnnnnnnng!"

"Thrugg," Rap said, forcing the word through clenched teeth. "The other man needs help."

The trolls were bait, of course. Obviously, when the Four had turned down Olybino's complaint, he had taken the law into his own hands. The warlock of the east should not be meddling here in Grunth's sector, but he had set a trap for the culprits, perhaps several other traps also.

"Unnnng! Un-unnnng!"

"Thrugg!"

The male troll scratched dried blood out of his beard and smiled a bushel of ivory across at Rap. "Hot in . . . here, Master," he growled. Apparently he saw nothing unusual in a man being fastened to a wall. Without rising, he began to strip off his shirt. The woman and girl followed his example.

Yes, it was still hot in the cell, but outside the temperature was dropping rapidly. Rap wondered if his feet would freeze before morning.

"Thrugg! The other man needs help. Go to him, Thrugg."

Thrugg clambered to his feet—but only so that he could take off his pants. Andor was becoming more and more urgent.

"Thrugg! Come here!" Rap bellowed. Oh, to have his sorcery back!

How many votaries had Olybino posted around the fringes of the Mosweeps, waiting for the next slave-freeing attempt? Ainopple was no more Uoslope's wife than Rap himself was. She was a substitute. Her glamour was a magnificent piece of sorcery, which had escaped his notice just as easily as it had deceived the tribune and his daughters and all the other inhabitants of Casfrel.

The trolls trudged over to the pegs and hung up their clothes. They must have been trained to do that, because clothes were not part of their culture.

Rap tried again, as loud as he could. "Thrugg!"

This time the monster shambled across to him and stopped with his muzzle almost in Rap's face. "Master . . . hurt? Stuck?"

The huge hands closed on Rap's waist, giving him a vivid image of himself being torn in pieces as the troll pulled him loose.

"No! No! Let go! The other man. Over there."

Thrugg turned. "Other . . . master stuck?" Being native to the dense rain forests, trolls had excellent night sight, of course.

"Just the cloth in his mouth, Thrugg. Bring me the cloth in his mouth."

Thrugg crossed to Andor, removed the dirty rag, shuffled back to Rap, and inserted it in his mouth instead. It tasted unimaginably vile. Andor laughed shrilly.

Without warning, Thrugg cuffed the child. It was apparently a playful blow, although it would have stunned a nontroll. "Go!" he boomed. Norp headed obediently for the nearest pile of bedding and lay down. Thrugg put his arms around Urg. "Mate?" He kissed her.

"Unnnnnnnnnnnnnnnng!" Rap said desperately.

Andor yelled, "Thrugg!"

Thrugg paid no attention. He was not much older than Urg was, and apparently neither of them knew that trolls almost never bred in captivity. From the way the embrace was proceeding, this was going to be one of the rare occasions when they did.

Rap solved one of his problems by vomiting violently, rag and all. He coughed and choked and spat, then puked again.

"Rap!" Andor begged. "Do something! Help!"

"Oh, I'm sure he can manage on his own." The agony in Rap's joints was becoming excruciating. He could hardly see for tears, and he was afraid he would start screaming soon. He did not think Andor was in anything like as much pain as he was, at least not yet.

Thrugg had Urg down on the floor now, right in the middle of the cell. He really should have taken her over to the straw, but probably trolls did not worry much about finesse. She seemed enthusiastic enough.

Andor cursed fluently.

"I can't do anything," Rap said. "She's gelded me. I'm helpless." If he tried to ease his shoulders, his knees burned, and vice versa. *Bitch!* "Can you call Jalon?"

No, that wouldn't work. Jalon was much slighter than Andor, and might be able to work his legs loose, but if Andor's arms were bent as Rap's were, then even Jalon could not wriggle out of the stone bonds. The transformation might tear him apart anyway; he was shorter than the imp.

"The magic isn't there!"

"Nor mine." Rap's attempts not to groan were making his voice as guttural as a dwarf's. If Ainopple could blank out Andor's spell, then she was extraordinarily powerful.

"How long is she going to leave us here?" Andor wailed.

"Not as long as she thinks. The Covin must have sensed her use of power. They'll be here shortly, I think."

That did not seem like much of a rescue.

"We're dead!"

"Let's hope it's quick."

That did not seem much like Zinixo.

Thrugg and Urg were grunting and roaring in their joint frenzy. Rap dared not try to speak—if he opened his mouth now he would scream. Andor was weeping. Minute followed agonizing minute. Down on the dirt, the earth-shaking passion came to an end. The dust began to settle.

How much pain could a man stand before he fainted? Rap tried to think of other things. Such as, how long had the fake Ainopple been living at Casfrel? Months, surely. She had not yet heard of Zinixo's usurpation of the Four. She had been lying in wait for a sorcerer, so she had deliberately refrained from using power, just as Rap had done. He had given himself away when he cured Thrugg's injuries. Only a very puny sorcerer would have rattled the ambience so much for a minor healing.

And because she had been staying out of touch, she did not know that Olybino had disappeared. She would discover that when she tried to report to him in the morning, for Zinixo had control of the Gold Palace. It was astonishing that the Covin was not already investigating the use of power at Casfrel.

The situation seemed completely hopeless.

Thrugg heaved himself to his feet. Puffing and mumbling, he shuffled over to Andor and took hold of him. "Master still . . . stuck."

Andor screamed in terror. *"No! No! You'll tear me apart! Stop!"* His voice choked off as he fainted dead away. Rap opened his mouth to yell at the well-meaning lummox also. Then he realized that—first—his pain had stopped, and—second—that he had his power back. And third, Thrugg's very solid image in the ambience was grinning at him hugely.

He relaxed with a gasp of stunned relief.

"Sorry if we embarrassed you, sir." A troll sorcerer could communicate without interference from equine teeth and shoe-size tongue. *"The mistress is a narrow-minded old bag, and I thought that would be the best way to stop her spying on us. She's gone to bed now. I've put her to sleep, so it's safe."*

Thrugg lifted Andor out of the wall. He set him down gently in an untidy heap of limbs.

"I'm afraid I need help, too," Rap admitted. He could make no impression on the sorceress's spell. Feeling almost light-headed with relief, he stared at the two Thruggs—the potent young sorcerer in the ambience and the lumbering barrel of muscle that came shuffling over to help him like a well-intentioned bullock, making the big room seem crowded. "It was you all the time?"

"Yes, just me. Urg really is my mate." The troll lifted Rap out of the wall, also, with no apparent effort, either physical or occult. *"She got caught when I was off doing a job near Dri-mush. I came to help, and then discovered there was a sorceress on guard. I'm 'fraid I frightened your friend."*

Andor was spread out on the floor like a corpse.

Rap leaned against the wall, easing his aching joints and shivering. "No surprise. He needs the rest." And Andor would try to disappear at the first opportunity, but he was still the cabal's best horseman. "It might be a good idea if you left the shielding on him for the time being."

"If you say so, sir." Thrugg seemed shocked, though.

"Please. And please call me Rap."

"Then that was a sequential spell I saw on him earlier?"

"Yes, it was." Rap wondered how many sorcerers were powerful enough—and hence wise enough—to make a snap diagnosis of something as rare as a sequential spell. Thrugg sensed the thought and grinned bashfully.

A laughing Urg handed her man his shirt for the second time that evening. Norp had stopped pretending to be asleep and was sitting up. "Get . . . clothes . . . on now," Thrugg growled at them. *"You the Rap who turned down the Red Palace?"*

"Er, yes. That wasn't yesterday, though." Thrugg could not have been more than a toddler.

"Mother's told me about you."

Mother? Gods! No wonder Grunth had protected the sorcerer who was rescuing slaves—her own son! And while Rap had been hiding his power from Zinixo, Ainopple had been hiding hers from Rap, and Thrugg had been hiding his from Ainopple!

"How long have you been here at Casfrel?"

Thrugg's wolfish face became oddly sheepish. *"Coupla months."* He climbed into his pants.

"Two months as a slave?"

If a hyena could look embarrassed, it might look like Thrugg did then. He scuffed a great horny foot in the dirt. *"It wasn't that bad. Urg was here. Food's quite good. Lots of fresh air and heavy lifting."*

Trolls were notoriously placid, but that was ridiculous.

"You're obviously far more powerful than that Ainopple woman!" Rap exclaimed, straightening up. He was disgustingly shaky. "Why didn't you just swat her, and leave?"

"Well . . . I dunno. Just don't like doing things like that to people."

For the first time, Rap had met a sorcerer who felt as he did about the evils of sorcery—even more so, for he would not have endured what this gentle colossus had.

"You let them beat you?"

Thrugg chortled, a sound like a tree falling. *"Oh, I turned off the pain if it got too bad."* Dressed now, he stooped and lifted Andor like a baby. *"I kept hoping she'd get tired waiting and go away. I appreciate what you did for me, sir. Now, I suggest we leave her here for the Covin to find."* The door clicked open before him. "Mate . . . girl . . . come! *Sir, I think we ought to get out of here smartish and head for the hills."*

"I'll go for that," Rap said.

Minds innocent:

> Stone walls do not a prison make,
>   Nor iron bars a cage;
> Minds innocent and quiet take
>   That for a hermitage.

Lovelace, To Althea from Prison

❮ ELEVEN ❯

Day will end

1

"Another piece of cake, Lord Umpily?"

"Most kind of you, ma'am."

The cake was delicious. It could hardly be otherwise at the residence of Senator Ishipole, who was celebrated for her exquisite taste. She was reported to have originated the epigram "Only quality is necessary." She was also rumored to be the third richest woman in the Impire, but Umpily rather doubted that—she spent too lavishly to be that rich. It was possible, though. Her family owned a couple of toll gates on the Great South Way, and she had been a marquise before she blackmailed her way into the Senate. So there was never any shortage of anything around Ishipole, and everything was always of the finest quality.

He sat on a quality silk divan and sipped quality tea from a quality china cup. The salon was a sumptuous room. Winter sunshine gleamed through high windows and was warmed by the ivories and yellows of the quality decor and the russet fire of her gown. In summer she would be surrounded by cool blues and greens. He hoped she would soon offer him yet another piece of that mouth-watering almond cake. Or even the chocolate one, which was almost as good.

The lady herself was no longer of the quality she must have been fifty years ago, when she had reportedly valued quantity as well as quality, at least in affairs of the heart—both Emshan-

275

dar and his father had been mentioned in the same whispers. She was rumored to have been the model for the famous masked nude that hung in the Throne Room, although whatever likeness there might have been once would no longer be detectable. Now all the flesh had faded from her bones, except on her face, where it had sagged in soft folds like wax on a candle. Her mouth drooped in a permanent disagreeable pout and the bags under her eyes would hold the Julgistro apple harvest. No quantity of paint and diamonds could hide the ugly truth that Ishipole was truly ugly. Perhaps even the third ugliest woman in the Impire, he wouldn't wonder.

"And who is to be the new mistress of the robes?" he asked, adopting an expression of false innocence that would not deceive the old crone for one second even if he wanted it to, which he didn't.

Ishipole and he were old, er . . . *sparring partners* might be a better term than *friends*. Some of his earliest memories were of eating cakes at Aunt Ishi's. His skill in gossipmongering had been learned at her knee. For years the two of them had sought to outdo each other in the pursuit of scandal, the tearing down of hypocrisy, the savaging of reputation. This private little chat was quite like old times, just the two of them in her private salon, except that now it was extremely dangerous for him.

"She has made a complete about-face, you know!"

Ishipole was commenting on the size of the impress's clothing bill. She pursed eggshell lips in silent stricture. "When she was only a princess, she spent hardly a groat on dressing herself! Her ladies were driven to despair! You must know that! And now? Ha! They say if the numbers were known, she outspends the Imperial navy. Another piece of cake? And she can't wear any of them with the court in mourning."

"Have you heard any word of her sister, ma'am?"

The senator shrugged with distaste. "Why should I want to?"

The reaction was not surprising. Umpily had already established that the impress's sister had vanished from the memory of the court. No one recalled seeing her for months. She was assumed to have returned to rural obscurity. Even household servants' minds had been wiped. Zinixo himself might not be so thorough, but his votaries would further his cause scrupulously.

Official mourning would continue for many months yet. This

season the social scene was bereft of the great functions at which the gentry normally displayed their finery and tattled gossip. In some ways that had been a help to Umpily. The social espionage he had achieved in the last couple of months would not have been possible in normal times. Even under present conditions it was a miracle that he had remained at large so long.

And now he was growing reckless. He had scavenged as much information as he could about the court and its imposter impe- ror, but he had uncovered no trace whatsoever of Olybino. The problem of the missing warlock had become almost an obses- sion with him. If any mundane knew the answer, it would be this old hag. He dared not put the question directly; he must lead up to it with great caution.

Meanwhile, he had confirmed that the fake impress was lav- ishing state funds on clothes. That sounded exactly like Ashia, and she would undoubtedly display Eshiala's gorgeous face and body magnificently. Shandie had already been informed of the clothes rumor via the magic scroll, but it was nice to have Sen- ator Ishipole's testimony, which added mass. It was no trivial matter, for if Ashia had enough freedom of will to indulge her own personality like that, then how much did Emthoro have? Who was running the government—the fake imperor Emthoro, or the sinister dwarf Zinixo? How long a string was the puppet allowed?

For example—and Umpily could well imagine Shandie him- self arguing this point at a council of war as he had done so often in the years of glory—Dwanish was rumored to be pre- paring an attack. Zinixo dealing with the war himself, employ- ing sorcery, would produce a result very different from Emthoro striving to react as the real Shandie might react. Did the dwarf have any loyalty to his own kind, or—

"And yourself, my lord?" Ishipole was supposedly almost blind now. Her eyes were dull orbs of amber, and yet they still saw more than most. They seemed to be sizing Umpily up, conveying a sense of getting down to business.

"Me, your Eminence? A well-earned retirement!"

"You quarreled with his Majesty, or so it is said." The with- ered senatorial hand offered the cake plate again. "You had a disagreement."

"Not at all! One does not disagree with imperors, ma'am! One merely agrees less vehemently."

"You have not been seen at court."

Umpily swallowed a morsel of cake with difficulty, his mouth strangely dry. He had held this same discussion many times of late, but Ishipole would be much harder to deceive than most of his acquaintances.

He sighed. "I never held an official position, you know. I was Shandie's advisor—and also friend, I hope—while he was a prince. When he ascended the throne he automatically inherited the whole Imperial bureaucracy. It seemed a good time for me to make way for the professionals, and younger men. We parted on excellent terms! Not parted, I trust—I was merely relieved of my unofficial duties, at my own request. That would be a better turn of phrase. Quite amicable."

"You see him sometimes, then?"

"Certainly. Just private functions, of course, because of the mourning, but—"

"You're lying," she said. "He denies it. You vanished. At first the word was that you'd been dispatched to Guwush on some fairy-tale secret mission, and he denies starting that story. But you were soon observed skulking around Hub—"

For a mad moment Umpily considered taking Ishipole into the great secret and explaining that the imperor she had met was not the real imperor, the impress was not the real impress, that an invisible sorcerer, who might not be a sorcerer in his own right, had stolen the whole Impire, dethroned the wardens, and usurped the ancient rule of the Protocol—but that road led to shackles and straightjackets. He could never dare reveal the truth except to a sorcerer, who would know it already anyway.

"Skulking, ma'am? Really!"

"Like today," she snapped. "We haven't spoken since before the old imperor died and yet today you just *drop in*. Just passing by, you say. No invitation, no note to warn me. Very unorthodox! So now we just have a nice little chat and you just *drop out* again, is that not so?"

Umpily took a sip of tea to give himself a moment to think.

"It's the pattern of your behavior ever since Emshandar died," she insisted, amber eyes studying him glassily—apparently as lifeless as a statue's, yet seeing much more than they revealed.

"I have been finding the winter weather a little hard on the joints, I confess, and not getting around as much as I could wish." He did not think he could deceive the old witch, and he certainly could not trust her. ''I'm told that bands of eel skin worn around the ankles will draw the poison . . .''

She dismissed that irrelevancy with a flick of the thin hairs along her brow. ''You have been *skulking* around the fringes of the court, asking a great many curious questions, and yet never entering the palace itself. Shandie is quite worried about you. He told me so.''

''Then I must call on him and reassure him!''

''Yes, you must.'' The ugly old harridan reached out her knotted fingers and lifted a silver bell from the tea table. ''I think they will have arrived by now.''

Umpily's ample innards seemed to drop a substantial distance. ''Who should have arrived, ma'am?''

The bell tinkled.

''Mutual friends, my lord.'' The waxy, sagging features contorted themselves into a smile. ''Persons who will be happy to escort you to the palace to impart that reassurance you just mentioned.''

The door opened in perfect silence. The big man who stood in the entrance was coated in gleaming bronze. There were other large men at his back. Umpily laid down his tea cup with a clattering noise.

''Lord Umpily!'' the expected harsh voice said. ''We meet again! At last.''

Umpily must have done well. His prying must have alarmed somebody, or annoyed somebody. It was a very great honor to be arrested by Legate Ugoatho himself.

2

''Here she comes now,'' Mist said.

''About time!'' Thaïle snapped.

Within the Meeting Place clearing, they sat side by side within an airy, open-sided cabana. The outside was smothered in flowers, the inside furnished with hard wooden benches. On a hot summer's day she would have judged the building totally unnecessary except to hold up the vines—why not just lie on the grass in the shade of a tree? On a dank, gray morning with rain falling in ropes, the shelter was miserably inadequate. Water streamed from the eaves in torrents and danced in the puddles on the grass; a faint spray blew through all the time, soaking every-thing.

The three other novices were seated on the upwind side, which was wetter, but a safe distance from Mist. Their names were Woom, Maig, and Doob, although Mist still referred to them as Worm, Maggot, and Grub. While they were not as loathsome as he had described, Thaïle had no great desire to make friends with any of them. That was fortunate, for Mist seemed to believe that she was his property—either because he had found her first or just because he was the oldest and biggest. If any of the three as much as smiled at her, he shed his normal affability, becom-ing harsh and aggressive. Normally such arrogance would have annoyed her greatly, but she had ignored it so far because she had worse things to worry about.

The woman coming striding along the Way in a floppy hat and ankle-length sea-green cloak was Mistress Mearn herself, who had summoned all five novices here to attend their first day of classes. There was no one else in sight in the Meeting Place on this foul morning.

About time!

For six days, Thaïle had endured the College—angry, fright-ened, resentful, and bored. For six days she had endured Mist, too. He had shown her all the places she was supposed to know, and none had been particularly interesting. He had clung to her like lichen, impervious to hints, appeals, and the worst insults she had cared to throw at him. No matter how she tried to dissuade him, he just gazed at her with soulful, butter-yellow eyes full of hurt and disbelief. After that first calamitous night, he absolutely could not be convinced that she did not want him to make love to her every night. He wouldn't mind mornings or afternoons, even. He promised to be gentler, rougher, faster, slower, more considerate, more insistent—any way she wanted, he would oblige.

Yet he was tolerable company when he was not explaining why they should be in bed together. He was easygoing and sometimes witty and usually bone lazy, although he was capable of astonishing bursts of exertion when he was in a canoe with a paddle in his hands. He was all she had. She had not seen Jain since the day she arrived, and no one else paid any attention to her at all. Novices were obviously just a necessary nuisance in the College, like small children underfoot. They might be even less than that, because everyone else seemed to have occult powers.

Thaïle had no idea how many people abode within the College—probably more than she had ever met in her life. More than a dozen of dozens maybe! She had tried speaking with some of them, at the Commons or the Market. They had discouraged her, usually with a tolerant "Things will be explained to you soon." Sometimes she'd met rudeness, and a couple of women had just vanished before her eyes rather than converse with a mere novice. To sorcerers, all mundanes must seem less than children, clumsy and foolish and ignorant.

When she'd remarked to Mist that there seemed to be no old people around, he'd assumed the owlish gaze he used instead of a grin. "Who would trust a sorcerer who grew old?"

Who would trust a sorcerer at all?

Archivist Mearn was a sorceress. She was closer to young than old, more than twenty, less than forty. She stepped into the cabana and removed her hat, then swung it so that wetness flew off in a shower. She tossed it onto a bench and unclipped the neck of her cloak, pouting at the awful weather. Mearn had a small, prissy mouth like a perch's, and she wore her hair in a very large bun on the top of her head, probably to display the pointedness of her ears. Her eyes were an ugly brown, her blouse and striped skirt smart and well chosen.

She threw her cloak down beside her hat and looked over her charges with disapproval: Thaïle and Mist sitting at one side, Woom and Maig and Doob at the other. They stared back with fear or resentment or both.

Woom was about Thaïle's age, and nasty. He picked his nose and ate with his mouth open, and she knew he was deliberately being annoying because she could Feel his emotions. He seemed to have chosen her as a special victim. He became very excited and pleased with himself when he managed to provoke her to any show of anger. She had concluded that Woom's talent was to make people dislike him, and he was so good at it that his Faculty must be very strong.

Doob was much younger, a short, skinny child. Thaïle had rarely heard him speak, and he emitted black terror most of the time. She was sorry for Doob, who should be sent home to grow up for a couple of years. If he had a talent for something, it had so far escaped her notice.

She ought to feel sorry for Maig, too, but he wore the vacant smirk of the half-witted, and his surging, confused emotions made her queasy. His talent was juggling, and juggling seemed to be his only interest. He could keep eight plates in the air, or five knives. At the Commons that morning he had been trying for six knives, until a sorcerer had ordered him to go outside before he maimed someone.

And there was Thaïle herself, who had tried to run away from the recorders, Thaïle who had fallen in love when she was not supposed to. Who was Leéb? Where was Leéb? Was he tall and heavy-shouldered like Mist? Somehow she did not think Leéb could resemble Mist in any way. If she had fallen in love with another Mist, she ought to be ashamed of herself.

Last there was Mist, oldest and largest of the novices, leaning back with his legs stretched out in tight-fitting scarlet pants and royal blue boots. In spite of the chill weather, his ruffled lemon shirt was wide open, hanging loose. He, at least, gave Mistress Mearn a winning smile. He put an arm around Thaïle and looked pleased with himself.

"Is there a war on?" the mistress of novices inquired snidely, looking to and fro. "As it happens, I *can* see out of the back of my head. However, I think the atmosphere would be improved if you all sat together."

The obnoxious Woom lurched to his feet at once, and shambled over to Thaïle. He spared Mist a triumphant sneer in passing. He seated himself on her other side, moving in close and whistling happily, staring at the roof. Doob and Maig joined him, neither comprehending the foolery.

Mearn had noticed, though. "One of the first things you will learn at the College," she proclaimed sharply, "is how to behave in a civilized manner. Close up your shirt, Novice. You are no longer a peasant, wandering around in seminudity."

Mist colored. He straightened up and began buttoning. Woom sighed, shaking his head sadly.

Mistress Mearn settled primly on a bench facing them. "Later I shall outline the standards of behavior expected of you. Promiscuity is strongly discouraged." She glanced at Thaïle with undisguised contempt.

The mealymouthed sorceress was about as likeable as a squashed toad. The Keeper herself had said that there was no harm in a girl romping with a boy if she wanted to . . . but of course the cryptic specter Thaïle had met might not have been the Keeper. It could have been a wraith of Evil sent to tempt her. She had not discussed that encounter with anyone.

"You all have a great deal to learn," the mistress continued, "—the ways of power itself, the history and purpose of the College, its workings and organization, the whole edifice of law and duty that the blessed Keef decreed for us a thousand years ago. You must start by learning to read and write.

"Today we begin your education. Normally we prefer to wait until we have six or eight in a class, but for reasons that I may not disclose, we have decided to proceed immediately, with just the five of you." Her muddy dark eyes flickered momentarily to Thaïle, without expression.

"You were selected because you all come from Gifted families—"

Doob spoke for the first time, in his boyish treble. "My uncle Kulth's a sorcerer! He's an analyst."

"But you are only a novice!" Mearn snapped. "In class you speak only when spoken to!"

Doob turned white, and Thaïle winced at the intensity of his fright.

"If you have a question, raise your hand," Mearn said, and then continued, paying him no more attention. "All of you have learned one word of power, and all of you have displayed Faculty. In case any of you still do not understand the distinction, I shall explain. Listen carefully, because I do not intend to tell you anything more than once. Everyone has some sort of native ability. A good ear for music, for example. When a person learns a word of power, that ability is increased, sometimes very greatly. How much it increases depends on two things. One is *Faculty*. Faculty is a talent for magic itself, and it tends to run in families. We know of many such Gifted families, like yours. Any questions so far?"

Five heads shook in denial.

Woom added, "I knew all that."

Mistress Mearn eyed him coldly, but made no comment. Thaïle decided that she disliked the sorceress almost as much as she disliked Woom. The timorous little Doob might be the best of the entire odious company. At least she could feel sorry for a frightened kid.

"The other factor," Mearn continued, "is the strength of the word itself. The words you learned are all known very widely. Each one is shared by scores of people. We call those 'Background Words.' Do you understand so far?''

The four youths nodded. Thaïle did not. She disliked being treated as a halfwit.

Mearn shot her a calculating glance and went on with her lecture. ''When several people know a word, its power is not divided equally between them. People who have Faculty get more of the power than others. Or else they manage to use their share more effectively. Most people show no results at all when they learn one of the background words, or very little. You all showed an increase in talent, and so we know that you all have Faculty.''

Jain had told Thaïle all this a year ago.

Woom raised a hand as high as he could, as if reaching for the rafters.

''Yes, Novice?''

''Which is it?''

''Which is what?''

''Do they get more of the power, or do they just use it better?''

The sorceress pursed her lips, making her little mouth even tinier. Then she said, ''No one knows. Even the Keeper does not know. It doesn't matter.''

''Thought it didn't,'' Woom said with satisfaction.

Thaïle decided he might have some good points she had previously overlooked—he was obviously annoying the mistress of novices. She sighed. She was not usually so crabby about people.

''Here in the College,'' Mearn continued grimly, ''we keep careful track of the Gifted Families, and which persons know which words. That is the task of the recorders, and also the archivists. I will explain the rankings to you another day. We also know many other words of power, much stronger words. We keep track of those words also, of course. Normally each is known by only two people—no more, and no less. Can any of you explain why we take that precaution?''

Thaïle sighed again and looked out at the streaming rain. Even on a day like this, there must be better ways of passing the time.

''Well? Why two? Why not one, or three?'' Mearn pouted at the lack of response, then picked on the dim-witted Maig, who of course could not answer the question. She ought to let him go off and practice juggling sharp axes, Thaïle thought—he might put himself out of his own misery. Even after the obvious reasons had been explained for him several times and he was nodding and mumbling that he understood, she could Feel his incomprehension. A sorceress must be able to Feel it, also, but eventually Mearn pretended to be satisfied.

"Very shortly, all of you will be told another word of power!" she announced, and peered around for reaction. "Yes, Woom?"

"Does that mean I have to watch some other old bag die?"

The sorceress's guard slipped for a moment, and Thaïle Felt her irritation, like lightning on a dark night. "Not usually. If not, at least one of the two people who know that word will be elderly. Under those circumstances, of course, there will be three people who know that word." Her ugly brown eyes narrowed dangerously. "Go ahead and ask it!"

For once the brash Woom seemed taken aback. In an unusually meek tone he said, "Do you kill them off, then?"

"Of course not! If you prove to have real Faculty, you will probably be promoted to sorcerer one day, but not for many years. By that time, the third person will have died naturally."

"And if I don't have real Faculty?"

"You remain an adept. Two words make an adept. Now, who can tell me the powers of an adept?"

The rain roared on the roof and the grass. Mearn pouted her little mouth again.

"Novice Mist?"

"A superman?" Mist said hopefully. "An adept can do anything?"

"More or less," she agreed reluctantly. "Anything mundane. Sometimes, if an adept had very strong Faculty, he may also display some occult power. A second word allows us to confirm the strength of your Faculty. It also lets you become useful." Her manner implied that she had rarely seen a less useful collection of candidates. "Reading and writing, for example. Teaching those skills to you now would be a long, painful business. As adepts, you will learn very easily—most of you."

Thaïle did not want to know how to read and write. She did not want to be a sorcerer, or even an adept. She wanted Leéb, and the life that had been stolen from her.

Mearn studied her disagreeably with her ugly, mud-brown

eyes. "You are all wondering why these things are expected of you. I assure you that life in the College is very pleasant, once you become used to it. You will never wish to return to the lowly peasant existence of your upbringing. However, you are not required to take my word for this. Tomorrow is the full moon."

She paused, while five young novices puzzled over her last remark.

"At this time of year, of course, the moon is not always visible. Fortunately, the exact full moon is not necessary. Tonight will do, or tomorrow, or the night after. You will meet me here tonight at sundown. If the weather is fair, we shall proceed to a place called the Defile."

A knot of fear tightened around Thaïle's heart. Mearn frowned, as if she had Felt it.

"If you're a sorceress," Woom demanded without bothering to raise his hand, "howcum you can't just make the weather good?"

"I could." Mearn's expression suggested that she could do much worse than that, if provoked far enough. "But we do not use power of that magnitude without the Keeper's permission. In time you will understand why we have that restriction. Your education will begin at the Defile, as I said. Once you have walked through there by moonlight, you will understand why you have been brought to the College. You will understand why the College exists, and why what we do here is necessary."

"Is this some sort of ordeal?" Suddenly Woom sounded much less brash.

The sorceress nodded smugly. "Yes, it is. But all of us here at the College have undergone this ordeal. It is not pleasant, I admit. It is not without risk, but I do not think any of you will be in much danger." Again her eyes flickered briefly over Thaïle, who began to feel a rising trickle of anger.

"Once you have passed through the Defile, therefore," Mearn said, "you will understand much better. Until then, there is no use trying to teach you anything practical. However, I shall now outline some of the behavior expected of you. Then I shall dismiss you, and you may continue to enjoy our facilities insofar as the weather permits—" Another glance at Thaïle. "Within certain moral limits, of course."

The trickle of anger was building to a torrent of fury.

"Now," said the mistress of novices, "are there any questions?"

"What about *girls*?" the insolent Woom asked. "Only one girl between four *men*?"

Thaïle clenched her fists. One *woman* and four *boys*! She Felt Mist's temper flare beside her.

Mearn took offense, also, and glared. "In time you may find a suitable partner, Novice, if you are worthy. We of the College pair off in the same way all respectable men and women do in Thume. We bear children, and of course many of them are Gifted. We expect monogamy and fidelity. Promiscuity is strongly discouraged. I trust you will all remember that in future."

And again her ugly brown eyes rested on Thaïle.

"There is one law that you must never break, however," Mearn continued. "Sorcerers do not marry other sorcerers. You will find partners among the mundane population outside of the College. There is an excellent reason for that, which I shall not explain at this time. At the moment you are unable to leave the grounds, so you are expected to remain celibate. You are *required* to remain celibate, and if you break the rules you will be punished severely. Are there any further questions?"

"Yes," Thaïle said, her heart pounding.

"Novice Thaïle?"

"Where is Leéb?"

Mearn's puny mouth shrank to invisibility. "Who?"

"I think you know *who*."

"Indeed I do not."

"Well, I do!" Thaïle shouted, jumping to her feet. "I want Leéb!"

"Sit down!"

"No! I want Leéb, and I want back the years of my life you stole from me, and I am not going to do anything you say until I get them!"

"*Novice!*"

Thaïle was too furious and too uncertain and too frightened to stay and argue. She could stand no more. She knew that the only alternative to anger was to burst into tears, and that would be disaster. "I want Leéb!" she screamed. "And I will never go near that awful Defile place!" She turned on her heel and ran out of the School, into the downpour.

She floundered across the flooded, slippery meadow, and in seconds she was soaked in icy water. She reached the Way and ran headlong, as fast as she could.

Two or three bends brought her to her cottage. She stumbled up the steps, burst through the door and slammed it. She leaned back against it to keep the rest of the world out.

Then, and only then, she let the tears flow, weeping for a lover she could not remember.

3

In her youth, Queen Inosolan of Krasnegar had made many strange journeys. She had crossed the continent of Zark on a camel. She had traveled from Hub to Kinvale in a single morning in an ensorceled carriage. She had ridden a mule over the Progiste Mountains into Thume, the Accursed Land, and miraculously survived to depart on a magic carpet. But nothing in her experience compared with her pursuit of the goblin king.

Although she had not visited the countryside around Kinvale in twenty years, she would have expected it to remain unchanged. For centuries, northwest Julgistro had been one of the Impire's most prosperous provinces. It was famous for hillside orchards and vineyards, for picturesque little towns dozing under coverlets of elms in the valleys, for rich farmland and quaint old temples. Now it was a wasteland, a charnel land, smoking and dead. Even color had fled, leaving ashes and stones, gray branches against a blank white sky, black fields with white snow in the furrows. The only people to be seen were small patrols of goblins, and even those were rare.

Inos had read of war and the horrors of war. She had never visualized such devastation as this, and she thought the people who wrote the books never had, either. Buildings and haystacks and orchards had been torched, livestock slaughtered. Surely not everyone had perished? Surely there must be thousands of survivors hiding somewhere? Not for long, though—this was midwinter, they would be freezing to death. Moreover, fast as the goblins had come, the God of Famine would be treading on their heels.

The Imperial High Command had learned from bitter experience that it must hold Pondague Pass at all costs. Whenever raiding parties of goblins broke through, it was the Evil's own job to corner them. Goblins traveled light, they traveled on foot, and they could outrun even light cavalry. Now the entire horde was moving over the landscape like a winter storm.

Fortunately, they appreciated that their captives could not run like that. Horses were provided, and for six days Inos hardly set foot to the ground between dawn and dusk. Only once in her life had she ever experienced such a mad whirlwind ride, when she and Azak had raced from Ilrane to Hub to outrun a war. This time she was trying to join a war. She had been a lot younger in those days, too, and green men were worse than red. At least djinns treated horses with some respect. Goblins had no such scruples. They insisted that she and her children ride until their steeds fell beneath them. Then replacements would be produced and the awful chase would continue. Fortunately Kadie was a superb horsewoman. Gath preferred boats, but he managed.

Thus Inos viewed the ruins of Julgistro from within a troop of a dozen murderous savages, sweeping across the new desert like leaves in the wind. Hill followed valley followed hill. Life became a continuum of blowing snow, the thunder of hooves on the iron-hard ground; straining, foaming, dying horses, and acrid, ever-present smoke streaming eastward alongside.

The leader was a nightmarish chief named Eye Eater, whose mission was to return Death Bird's son safely to his father's loving arms. The three Krasnegarians were an insignificant addition. For them Blood Beak's presence at Kinvale had been great good fortune, and Inos preferred not to speculate on what might have happened had circumstances been different.

The goblin horde had rolled over the landscape like a rock slide. Behind it nothing stood, almost nothing moved. Obviously it was meeting no resistance now. It had been only a few hours ahead when she set out with Eye Eater's troop, and yet after six days she had not caught up with it. No army should ever be able to travel at such a speed! Eye Eater had wasted no time, except on three occasions when small bands of survivors were sighted. In each case, the imps were run down and overcome without the loss of one goblin. The fighting was over in minutes; it was the ensuing barbarities that caused delay.

She had known that goblins were as savage as any race in Pandemia, but she had not understood the joy they found in wanton cruelty. Burned and mutilated corpses lined the road,

Men and boys had been rounded up and tortured at leisure, even the wounded, even the youngest. Soon picket fences seemed incomplete if they were not decorated with impaled babies.

At first she worried about the effect these horrors would have on her children, but she soon realized that they were adapting better than she was.

"It's the way they were brought up, Mama," Kadie assured her. "Papa explained it to me once. They don't know any better."

"And they have their own rules," Gath added. "They don't kill women." This was true. Women and girls were mainly spared anything beyond rape, and punching if they resisted. Even when they resorted to weapons, they would be disarmed if at all possible, or else cleanly slain. In their way, goblins had standards.

Inos had suggested that Kadie should find some boys' clothing. Kadie had retorted that she was much safer as a girl.

"There would be no danger," Gath suggested cheerfully. "They would take your clothes off before they did anything to you."

"Maybe *you* should dress as a girl!" Kadie snapped.

"Same problem!" Gath said, but he spoiled his worldly grin with a blush.

They were adapting. Inos was both relieved and proud. Even Kadie had picked up goblin dialect much faster than she had. Gath seemed to use his freak prescience to foresee what understanding would eventually be reached and then just leapfrog over the preliminary confusion. It was paradoxical, but it worked.

The evenings were the worst—bonfires and feasts and the inevitable torture sessions. However blighted the countryside seemed, the goblins always turned up a few male prisoners to brighten their evenings. Cruel and destructive, they were like children, the evil part of children. If the countryside was strange to Inos, it was even more strange to them. Often they would demand explanations from her—what a cobbler's last was for, or a butter churn. When she had explained whatever it was, they would smash it.

Eye Eater was a monster, as was to be expected of a chief. His capacity for rape was incredible, his cruelty unsurpassed. Even his own men seemed to go in fear of him, and Inos certainly did. Once or twice he asked her meaningfully if all Krasnegarian women were as hard to tame as Kadie, but the memory of Quiet Stalker's mysterious death protected mother and daughter both. They were not molested, and Inos did not need to use her occult royal glamour. She assumed that it would be needed again eventually; she hoped that it would always be effective.

Young Blood Beak was disconcertingly unpredictable. At times he swaggered with the worst, relishing his newly won adult status and the resulting right to join in the raping and torturing. At times he tried to assert his royal status as the king's son—Eye Eater would tolerate his antics for a while, and then deflate him with mockery. At other times, the youngster showed another side of himself, a keen intelligence and a desire to learn. He would trot for hours alongside one or other of the Krasnegarians, questioning shrewdly. He wanted to know how and why they had been at Kinvale, where Rap was, why Inos was going to visit his father, and a million other things. At first Inos pretended not to understand much of what he was saying, but as the days went by that excuse began to wear thin. She worried what dangerous information he was worming out of Kadie and Gath. She worried even more about the way he looked at her daughter. Several times he told Inos that in his opinion every chief should include at least one chief's daughter among his wives.

For the first two days Gath sprawled on his horse like a tethered corpse. Then his head injury seemed to heal overnight, and he rapidly became his normal placid, contented self. Of course neither he nor Kadie had ever seen countryside like this. They did not know how it should be. The hills, the woods, the ruins were all equally new to them, and equally fascinating. They marveled that the weather should be so warm, although it was midwinter and the ditches were frozen solid. They were impressed by the comparative absence of snow and the dark furrowed fields. They were young and they were having an adventure. They hardly seemed to comprehend their mother's abhorrence.

Welcome though it was, their lack of concern distressed and puzzled her at first. Eventually she decided that Kadie was armored by her romantic ideals, turning a blind eye to the atrocities just as she had ignored the bland tedium of Krasnegar. But Kadie had killed a man. Tentatively Inos inquired if that worried her.

"He was evil!" Kadie snapped.

"Yes, he was."

"Then he got what he deserved, didn't he?"

End of conversation. Romantic heroines were within their rights in slaying villains. Indeed it was their duty. A discussion of real-world ethics would have to wait for better days.

As for Gath—a seer had no need to worry about the immediate future; by nature he did not worry about tomorrows either.

Inos was grateful for her nestlings' immunity, but she knew that every day was moving them farther from the sea that was their only road homeward. War rode ahead of them and Famine trod behind. She could not believe that any of them would ever see Krasnegar again. She steadfastly refused to think about the dread prophecy a God had given Rap.

Six days' riding . . . five nights huddled with her children under hedges or in stinking burned-out ruins, which did no more than keep the wind off. The goblins were indifferent to the cold. Some of them would sleep on the frozen ground without as much as a shirt. They existed on a diet of scorched meat. Inos was terrified that she might sicken and die, leaving her two fledglings alone in this hell of war.

At the sixth sunset, though, Eye Eater led his troop over a hill and into a valley that twinkled with campfires from side to side like a starry sky. Inos caught a glimpse of a spectacular row of arches against the darkling sky and guessed that it must be the famous Kribur aqueduct. At least she knew where she was, then, although the information was not very helpful. Kribur had always been regarded as being about three weeks' journey east of Kinvale.

As the weary horses stumbled down the slope, a heavy rumble of noise arose to meet them—deep male voices, frightened cattle, and already the screams of victims. Inos was astounded by the size of the army. She knew roughly how much space a legion needed for its camp, and she thought these savages were packed in much more tightly than imps would be. Even so, the valley would have held six or seven legions, and a legion was five thousand men.

Lights flickered on the road ahead; the newcomers were about to be challenged.

"Tents!" Kadie shouted joyfully. "Mom, they have tents!"

"That's certainly a welcome sight!" Inos called back. "I didn't expect goblins to have tents, somehow."

"They don't," said Gath, at her side.

She turned to him with a pang of apprehension—she knew the voice he used when he was about to hurl a lightning bolt. "Then who do?"

"Dwarves, Mom. They've joined up with their allies."

"Gods!" Inos said. Gods save the Impire now.

4

Inos had met Death Bird a couple of times at Timber Moot, but those encounters had been brief, and he had been anonymous inside his winter buckskins, showing little more than two angular, suspicious eyes. She remembered him best from a far-off night at Kinvale, when she had spied on his farewell to Rap. The goblin had gone off from there to meet his destiny, and that same evening she had departed for Krasnegar to claim her throne. Then he had been a youth, callow and unsure of himself. Now she was a refugee, and he was a conqueror.

He was holding court in a burned-out barn. The stone walls remained; the roof had gone. In the darkness outside, a multitude patiently awaited his pleasure. Inside, a bonfire blazed, casting strange shadows on the sooty walls, showering sparks upward to the stars. He sat cross-legged on the ground, wearing only a leather loincloth. His huge chest and massive limbs shone wetly green in the flickering light. He had an unusually dense mustache and beard for a goblin, and tattoos obscured the upper half of his face—even now only the menacing glitter of his eyes was readable. The thick black braid of his hair hung over his left shoulder and down to his crotch.

Flanking him, forming a semicircle beyond the fire, were four goblins and five dwarves. Gray-skinned, glowering, gray-bearded, the dwarves wore chain mail and conical helmets. Dwarves were mostly shorter than goblins, but they seemed taller when sitting. They also tended to be broader, but none of these would match Death Bird in sheer bulk.

Inos stood in the doorway within a huddle of other waiting supplicants, and tried to work up a royal anger. She was a queen! She should be granted precedence over everybody else. This was no Imperial court, though, and she did not think outrage would gain her anything at all. She was exhausted, trembling with weariness, barely able to stand; she was also unbearably filthy and unkempt and very close to her physical limits. The stench of the greased goblins around her was nauseating. Only the presence of Gath and Kadie sustained her. She was needed!

This was the first meeting of the allies in the field, and the joint command had many matters to settle. Two chancellors held the door, one goblin and one dwarf, and they argued continuously in whispers—one harsh and guttural, the other dissonant, a couple of octaves lower. When the leaders heard two dwarvish petitioners in succession, the goblin won agreement that it was Blood Beak's turn.

He stalked forward arrogantly, skirting the fire. He knelt before his father and touched his face to the filth of the floor. He sat back on his heels and waited.

Death Bird studied him for a moment, then turned to the dwarf on his right and said something that Inos did not catch. The dwarf responded in a sepulchral rumble, nodding. Introductions followed, but the words were again lost in barbaric pronunciation, the crackle of the fire, and the sea-swell noise of the great army outside. Inos wished she could just swoon and stay unconscious for a century, like the enchanted princesses in Kadie's romance books.

Why had she forgotten? She looked up at the pinched face beside her. She did not like what she saw—fatigue, and windburn, and a febrile brightness in his smoky gray eyes. He had spent a week in the saddle when he should have been in bed. "Gath? What happens?"

He was frowning, biting his lip. "Mm? Oh, they joke a bit, but they make us welcome."

Relief! "Then why are you looking so worried?"

He blinked. "Am I?" He cracked a wry smile, but it barely touched eyes blurred with exhaustion. He looked very young, and vulnerable. "Because I'm going to be worried."

Weariness made her testy. "What does that mean?"

"Dunno. I'm going to foresee something bad soon."

"What?"

"If I knew that then I'd know why I'm going to be worried, wouldn't I?"

All the leaders' eyes had turned to stare in her direction. Evidently Blood Beak had broken the news. He was scrambling to his feet, departing, and she could see his satisfied smile. Death Bird himself was inscrutable, but the dwarves were muttering to one another in disbelief. This was it.

"Come!" Inos pushed past the two chancellors without waiting for formal summons or announcement. She strode forward, hearing the charcoal on the floor crackle behind her as the children followed. She swung around the fire, positioned herself directly before Death Bird, and curtseyed. In her soiled fur cloak it was not a very dignified curtsey, and she did not make it a very deep one. But she felt better for it. She would not kneel like all the others unless they clubbed her down.

Death Bird's eyes seemed larger and squarer than she remembered, which probably meant he was surprised. In the Name of Evil, he should be! And if he didn't speak, she—

Then he laughed and slapped his bulging belly with both hands. "Queen Inosolan! An unexpected pleasure."

He had spoken in impish, and that was a huge relief. The other goblins were excluded, therefore. The dwarves would likely follow the talk easily enough.

"Indeed, *Cousin*, it is an unexpected pleasure for me also."

He chuckled at the formal address. "The timber shortage must be extreme if you follow me here to trade!"

It was the first real joke she had ever heard from a goblin. Of course he was no ordinary goblin. He was wise, crafty, and utterly deadly. Already he had written his name in history among the bloodiest. She had better find some humor of her own to respond . . .

"Right now I will settle for enough lumber to build a chair."

He shrugged. "Long Tooth!" he bellowed to someone by the door. "Bring seat for chief woman!" He smirked up at Inos again. "This is not Hub, Inosolan. Not yet. *Where is Rap?*" The question came out as a jarring bark.

"I don't know. That's one of the things we must discuss."

He grunted, then gestured with a thumb at his co-leader. "Is General Karax-son-of-Hargrax. Is Queen Inosolan of Krasnegar."

The dwarf scrambled to his feet, scowling. The scowl didn't matter—dwarves always scowled. He bowed, and that simple politeness was a heart-stopping relief.

"Your Majesty."

She curtseyed again. "A pleasure, your Excellency! Cousin,

may I present my son Prince Gathmor, my daughter Princess Kadolan?'' For a moment the absurdity made her head spin. Not Hub, indeed! Death Bird was playing with her, and perhaps the dwarves were, also, but at the moment the play seemed harmless enough, and it was a great deal better than most of the alternatives she could think of.

And it continued. She was sweating in her furs, standing before a roaring fire, but she played the game, greeting near-naked goblins and mailed dwarves. The dwarves copied their general's example, rising to bow to her, then sitting down again quickly. The goblins pouted and nodded, and stayed seated. Even the need to nod probably made them feel insulted, but they took their cue from their king.

As the last of the chiefs was named, a goblin hurried forward with a barrel for her to sit on. It was just in time, too. She sank onto it gratefully, wishing it were a little farther from the fire.

Gath gasped, and whispered, ''Mom!'' in her ear.

''Later.'' One trouble at a time!

Death Bird spoke to Karax, but loud enough for the others to hear, and he spoke in goblin. ''Are good friends in Krasnegar. Much trade for goblins, dwarves.''

''But why is her Majesty here now?'' the dwarf rumbled, staring up at her suspiciously with stony eyes. ''Does she bring her army to aid our just struggle?''

The goblin on Death Bird's left muttered a translation for his companions.

''This is a very confidential matter,'' Inos said.

''Have no secrets from Dwanish friends,'' Death Bird countered quickly.

Gath said *''Mom!''* more urgently.

Still Inos ignored him, looking thoughtfully along the line, meeting the scowls with her best regal indifference. ''I am very tired, your Majesty. Perhaps you and his Excellency and I can have a talk tomorrow, when I have rested. Just the three of us. If you wish then to take the rest of your companions into your confidence, then I shall have no objection at all.''

''March at dawn!'' Death Bird snapped, without waiting for her speech to be translated to the others.

''Before dawn, then.''

He shrugged. ''Tonight, after feasting.'' He showed his tusks in a menacing grin. ''General, can you offer a tent for the lady?

She might even enjoy a bucket of water. I expect she has a decadent impish dislike of grease.''

"We shall be happy to provide quarters for her Majesty." The dwarf did not look happy, but he was probably doing his best.

Before she could thank him, though, Death Bird spoke again.

"Tonight we have a feast, Inosolan. You will be an honored guest." His tusks flashed even more ominously than before. "We shall provide some excellent entertainment, too."

The interpreter smiled; the dwarves all grimaced. Inos suppressed a shudder. *When in Hub, do as the Hubbans tell you* . . . "I shall be happy to attend your feast, your Majesty." She had endured six of those barbarous entertainments; she could endure another without going mad.

"Bring son!" Death Bird's tone implied dismissal.

Inos rose to her feet with all the poise she could muster, grateful for a helping hand from Kadie. "As you wish, your Majesty. Your Excellency, I accept your hospitality until then most gratefully."

She tried not to lean on Kadie as they walked around the fire, but she was staggering with both fatigue and the release of at least some of her tension.

Gath was right beside her. *"Mom!"*

"Yes, dear? What is it?" Whatever it was, she was sure it was bad news.

They reached the knot of supplicants by the door, and a way was cleared for them. They moved out into the chill dark of the night. All around were campfires and tents, goblins and dwarves. Horses whinnied plaintively.

A short man loomed out of the shadows. "Follow me, ma'am." His bass voice identified him as a dwarf. She had never thought of dwarves as lovable before.

"MOM!"

"Yes, dear?"

"They're going to torture more men tonight!"

"I'm afraid so." Inos sighed, stumbling as she followed her guide. She was in danger of losing him amid the teeming crowd. Despite the shortness of his legs, he was setting a dangerous pace—over tent ropes and horse tethers, between baggage. "We can't do anything to stop them, and we can't possibly witness anything worse than we have already. Just try to—"

"But, Mom!" Gath sounded almost incoherent. "But, Mom, tonight I recognize one of them!"

God of Mercy! "Who?"

"The imperor!" Gath wailed.

She whirled around and grabbed him, turning him so that light from the nearest campfire illuminated his face. "You're crazy! How can you possibly know that?"

The boy was close to tears, eyes staring, overcome by too much horror. His voice warbled crazily up and down from treble to tenor. "He's the man I saw on the beach! The imperor! I'm sure he is, Mom! They're going to kill him."

5

Far away to the southeast, a lone young man rode like a maniac along the Great West Way. He reeled in the saddle with exhaustion, but he was a fine horseman, who could coax the utmost from his mount, or even doze in the saddle at times. He had been traveling for days; he had weeks of road ahead of him yet.

Now he had even outridden the panic. Doubtless Imperial couriers were already nearing Hub with the terrible news, but the civilian population knew only vague rumors. The scale of the goblin disaster was too incredible to be believed anyway. Eventually all the mounts would vanish from the posts, as they had farther north, but here the lone rider could still hire horses.

He was no longer worried about the Covin. In himself, he was unimportant. Even if they still kept watch on the highways, the sorcerers would not be looking very hard for *him*, and certainly not be expecting him to be heading homeward.

Ironically, even the sorcerers did not know what he knew. Nobody did! How strange that only he, in all the world, was aware of the terrible truth—Shandie was dead. When the two of them had fled from the goblin ambush, Shandie's horse had been killed under him. Only Ylo had escaped. Even if Shandie had survived to be captured, goblins always slew prisoners.

The true ruler of the Impire now was a two-year-old child.

As Ylo pounded along the highway, angling farther south every day, the weather was warming. Here and there, he saw green shoots beginning to thrust up from the soil in the annual miracle of spring. By the time he arrived at Yewdark, the daffodils would be blooming.

Day will end:
> O, that a man might know
> The end of this day's business, ere it come!
> But it sufficeth that the day will end,
> And then the end is known.

Shakespeare, *Julius Caesar*, V, 1

ABOUT THE AUTHOR

DAVE DUNCAN was born in Scotland in 1933 and educated at Dundee High School and the University of St. Andrews. He moved to Canada in 1955 and has lived in Calgary ever since. He is married and has three grown children.

After a thirty year career as a petroleum geologist, he discovered that it was much easier (and more fun) to invent his own worlds than try to make sense of the real one.

TAKE A VACATION . . .

Travel with Del Rey Books to places you've never been before: places as near as tomorrow, as distant as a dream. Visit perilous planets populated with people you'll never forget. Join a journeyman storyteller for a voyage into the vortex of imagination.

Incomparable worlds of magic await you.

Suit up, sit down, and surrender; the stars await . . .

DISCOVER THE EVER-EXPANDING UNIVERSE OF

DAVE DUNCAN

"Dave Duncan writes rollicking adventure novels . . .
one excellent book after another."
—*Locus*

A ROSE-RED CITY

Mera's citizens were all refugees from death, rescued from the distant past and from futures unforseen. The mysterious Oracle had gathered them from every land, and kept them safe inside the high walls that kept out death and time and hell-spawned demons.

Then one day, the Oracle sent Jerry Howard Outside the city on a rescue mission.

Jerry recruited his friend Killer to accompany him Outside. Killer came from ancient Greece. He was a violent, lecherous braggart and a good friend, and his fighting skills were legendary, even Outside.

Beyond Mera's walls, Jerry and Killer found an empty farmhouse on a high plain, sometime after the invention of the radio, but before the laser pistol. And soon Ariadne, the woman they were to rescue, came seeking shelter for her children.

That was when Jerry's mission fell apart. For children couldn't enter Mera. Ariadne couldn't leave them behind. The mortal danger that pursued the refugees would be upon them soon. And the demon enemies of Mera were converging on that little house on the prairie . . .

The Seventh Sword

Book One: THE RELUCTANT SWORDSMAN

The last thing Wallie Smith remembered was a fog of hospitals, grim-faced doctors, and pain. So when he woke in the body of a barbarian swordsman, attended by a beautiful slave girl and a wizened old priest nattering on about some "Goddess," he assumed he was in a fever dream.

But the World could not be dismissed so lightly.

A naked little demigod called Shorty explained that the Goddess needed a swordsman. If Wallie undertook the job and succeeded, all that the World had to offer would be his. If he refused, the results would be . . . unpleasant.

Wallie was not easily convinced. But Shorty was exquisitely persuasive.

Soon Wallie found himself bearing a magnificent sword, with no idea how to use it. He also discovered a plenitude of mortal enemies, all determined to put an abrupt stop to his career as a swordsman for the Goddess!

Book Two: THE COMING OF WISDOM

The Goddess had rescued Wallie Smith from certain death, endowed him with a magnificent new body, and gifted him with the legendary Sapphire Sword of Chioxin. She asked only one service in return . . .

So Wallie became the Goddess' champion—and promptly found himself on the losing side in a battle against magics far beyond any powers the priests of the Goddess could hope to summon. For, after eons of exile, sorcerers walked the World again, claiming lands and souls for their Fire God.

Wallie quickly found that swords were no match for spells—and how could mere mortals prevail against the powers of magic?

Book Three: THE DESTINY OF THE SWORD

Wallie's mission for the Goddess was clear. All he had to do was to unite the arrogant swordsmen of the World and destroy the sorcerers and their Fire God.

Now Wallie discovered that he had already tried it—or, rather that the swordsman Shonsu, whose life Wallie had "inherited," had tried it. And he had been hopelessly defeated.

Wallie's reputation was in tatters. His best friend and pupil was apparently planning to betray him. And worst of all, if he won, he would doom all hope of progress and learning in this World of the Goddess—doom the Goddess Herself.

It made an interesting kind of riddle. All Wallie had to do was find the solution—and survive, if he could!

WEST OF JANUARY

Move west or perish—that's what the angels said. But who could believe that the sun was actually moving? That high noon was on its way, bringing with it dry water holes and burnt grasslands? And, even more unbelievably, that one day night would fall, and the plains would freeze? Inconceivable!

And so the herdfolk stayed where they were, and Knobil's life continued unchanged—until the usurper came. Suddenly the herdmaster was dead, and Knobil, the eldest son, was forced to flee, vowing revenge. But Knobil's travels took him farther and farther from his home and his goal, even all the way to Heaven—where he learned how to take his revenge and help save his world . . .

Winner of the prestigious Casper Award
for Outstanding Science Fiction or Fantasy!

STRINGS

Alya's hunches were never wrong. So the scientists of 4–I were happy to promise her a place in the next offworld colonization team if she agreed to assess the potential of the latest worlds they had discovered. Then she met Cedric, the grandson of 4–I's brilliant and tyrannical director. And for the first time ever, she began to doubt her uncanny intuition.

Cedric dreamed of becoming a scout and exploring other worlds. When he met the lovely Alya, he was more determined than ever to leave Earth—with her. His grandmother, though, needed him as a pawn in her Machiavellian plot to cover up a murder and protect 4–I itself from being destroyed.

Cedric's grandmother had no intention of letting him go. But the director had seriously underestimated her grandson—and the woman whose destiny seemed linked with his . . .

HERO!

Vaun was born a peasant in the stinking mud flats of the planet Ult, but he rose through its hellhole training academy to become the toughest young officer in the Space Patrol. Then the mysterious group known only as the Brotherhood staged a surprise attack. Vaun led the first ship out against them—and returned to a hero's welcome as flaming debris from the enemy ship rained down across the planet.

But the Brotherhood was implacable. Thwarted on Ult, still it advanced. One by one, neighboring worlds fell silent.

Then the Patrol detected a gigantic spacecraft speeding from one of those now-silent worlds toward Ult on a collision course. Vaun knew in his gut that it meant war. And, knowing full well that this time he was overmatched, he set out to save Ult a second time . . .

THE REAVER ROAD

Well met, traveler!

Since you are going in my direction, why don't we walk on together for a while? If luck is with us, perhaps we shall overtake Omar before nightfall, if that pirate of an innkeeper spoke true . . .

You say you have never heard of Omar? Why, he is the finest storyteller alive! His tale of the God of War is a marvel: heroes, and villains, and gods—what's that you say? Yes, of course there is a beautiful maiden—it would be a poor tale, else. And for all the clash of armies and the great deeds of the mighty, it's a story to make you laugh out loud.

Omar himself swore to me that every word was true—but I own I am puzzled over that . . . No matter. Step lively now, friend. Omar is probably just up the road a piece, with a tale to make the miles take wing . . .

And take heart, travelers:
Omar weaves still another glorious tale,
THE HUNTERS' HAUNT,
coming soon from Del Rey Books!

A Man of His Word
Part One: MAGIC CASEMENT

Princess Inos lived an idyllic life in her father's sleepy, backwater kingdom. Krasnegar was a peaceful realm, and Inos was a friend to all—especially her childhood companion, the stableboy Rap.

Then one day a God appeared with an enigmatic warning that *might* mean that Inos should wed. No one was sure, but who could ignore a divine warning? And, since no eligible noblemen ever visited tiny Krasnegar, Inos found herself exiled to the Impire to learn to be a lady.

So Inos was far away when Rap's strange talents began to emerge. The townsfolk whispered darkly of magic. Then the king fell ill, and Rap set out to warn Inos that she must prepare to claim her birthright. But Rap couldn't know as he struggled through goblin-infested wastes that his was a journey ordained by the Gods since before the world began . . .

Part Two: FAERY LANDS FORLORN

Inos had been kidnapped through the magic casement even as the Impish legions overrunning her tiny kingdom were storming the castle tower. Now she was far from home, a prisoner in a desert land ruled by a dockside whore with a talent for magic and a passion for politics.

She little dreamed that the loyal stableboy Rap had jumped through the casement after her. But no one really knew how the magic worked, and Rap found himself not in a desert, but in the steaming jungles of Faerie—half a world away from Inos!

Rap was determined to rescue his queen. He would let nothing could stop him—not the monsters and headhunters of Faerie, nor the paranoid machinations of an evil sorcerer . . .

Part Three: PERILOUS SEAS

Queen Inos was badly shaken. Rap—loyal, trustworthy Rap—had appeared to her, obviously from beyond the grave. His insubstantial image, the echo of his voice . . . She stiffened her resolve. She would serve her people, whatever the cost. Rap would have wanted her to do so.

But Rap was alive, armed with a magic word and an unwavering resolve to find his beloved Inos and give her whatever help a lowly galley slave could give a queen.

Then Kalkor, most dangerous of the cruel Nordland raiders, sailed into port in his longship *Blood Wave*. And Rap's life took a hellish turn for the worse . . .

Part Four: EMPEROR AND CLOWN

The loyal stableboy Rap had fought through hell and high water to rescue Inos, his queen. But at the end of his quest, all his struggle had been in vain.

Inos had married the accursed sultan Azak. Her beauty had been despoiled, her kingdom stolen away. And for her honeymoon, Azak planned the dangerous journey to Hub, capital of the Impire. There, amid the maelstom of fearsome magic and vicious imperial politics surrounding the ailing Imperor, Azak intended to recoup all his losses and be freed from his curse.

A failed and broken man, Rap awaited his fate at the hands of Azak's torturers. And Inos followed her destiny, and her jealous new lord, on a journey whose outcome even the Gods could not have foretold . . .

On *A Man of His Word*:

> "... I read rather a lot of science fiction and fantasy books: many I like, some I ignore, few I rave about. You I will *rave* about—already have done! So to conclude . . . *"Congratulations!* THANK YOU! . . . *and what have you planned as an encore to this tour de force!"*
> —ANNE McCAFFREY to Dave Duncan

Beautiful Queen Inos had married the loyal stableboy Rap and made him her king. They were very much in love, and they lived happily ever after . . .

A Handful of Men
Part One: THE CUTTING EDGE

Fifteen years went by while Rap and Inos raised their family in Krasnegar, well removed from the hurly-burly of great affairs.

But in far-off Hub, the old Imperor's health—and, some said, his sanity—deteriorated inexorably. The borderlands were seething. Prince Emshandar—or Shandie, as Rap knew him—found himself leading his grandfather's armies into terrible battles where victory and justice hung in gravest doubt.

And now the end of the millennium was at hand, ushered in by the prophecies of cataclysmic upheaval on a scale never before imagined. All across Pandemia, sensible people tried to dismiss a growing sense of unease as superstitious nonsense.

Then a God appeared to Rap and warned him that the prophecies spoke the least of the truth. Devastation was a certainty; total destruction loomed. The very fabric of the world was at risk.

And it was all Rap's fault.

The last thing in the world Rap had wanted was another adventure. And it might be the last thing he would ever get . . .

> "Deftly woven and set forth with a refreshingly unpretentious clarity and directness . . . Grab this one . . ."
>
> —*Kirkus Reviews*

Follow the further exploits of Rap and Inos in the upcoming volumes of *A Handful of Men*, coming soon from Del Rey Books!

UPLAND OUTLAWS
THE STRICKEN FIELD
THE LIVING GOD